A COTTON MILL TOWN Christmas

A COTTON MILL TOWN Christmas

Jerry L. Haynes

Hope you enjoy!

Jerry L. Haynes

*If you have any questions, or would like to
inquire about my other books,
please email me at
handh_services@hotmail.com*

Printed in the United States of America.
Cover print by Ravin Bilbrey

ISBN 10: 1-59571-166-X
ISBN 13: 978-1-59571-166-3
Library of Congress Control Number: 2006937925

Word Association Publishers
205 5th Avenue
Tarentum, PA 15084
www.wordassociation.com

**Dedicated to the memory
of my dear friend
Mike Clemons**

~November 14, 1951—September 7, 2005

His body was as weak and fragile
as an autumn leaf,
struggling to hold onto the branch
of a mighty oak
until the last day of fall,
knowing that a wintry gust
would one day capture him
upon its wings
and he would be swept away
into the Heavens.

But his Wildcat Spirit
will forever be as strong as
the roots of that mighty oak,
and will withstand
any winds that will blow,
because over the years
he had found
strength and nutriment
from the town he loved,

Fries

ACKNOWLEDGEMENTS

I know my wife Judy will poignantly point out to me that I have no experience on which to base my comparison, but I have found writing, and the subsequent publishing of my first novel has closely paralleled the joys, and horrors, of conception and childbirth.

Almost nine months ago, a seed was planted. After almost daily visits to the Fries website with which Temple Burris, et. Al. have done such a wonderful job, the seed began to grow. The postings of friends such as Dogman, Bayne, Mike, Terry, Roger, my cousin Liz and others constantly gave me new "water" to go to when it seemed my literary well had gone dry. This book that was growing within me was nurtured also by my occasional visits back to my hometown where, each time, I would run into an old friend whom I hadn't seen in years, and who would provide me with a renewed memory. Photographs so generously shared by such friends as Don Bond, Temple, and David Arnold continued to offer nourishment to my "baby."

Thanks go to all those above, and others, too numerous to mention. To my wife who never complained when I would get out of bed at four a.m. to run downstairs and write narrative that had crept into my dreams that I was afraid would be lost if I waited until morning, and for those times that she would drive on our trips so I could sit in the passenger seat and have creative time. Yes, Judy, I really was "mental imaging" during those times, and not sleeping.

I think I may have given up on finishing the book if it had not been for some special people encouraging me. I thank you so much for that. Another reason I continued was that I wanted to be able to use this opportunity to honor my dear friend Mike Clemons.

Going to the annual Fries Sports Reunion will never be the same, because he will not be the first standing there to greet me. Mike, I love ya', man.

But the time has finally come for me to deliver my "bundle of joy." Special thanks go to my good friend and proofreader, Betsy Wood for her conscientious contributions. Just like a good delivery nurse, she has cleaned and dressed up my baby, so I can now share it with my friends.

A good novel has characters larger than life. Fries has been blessed with some of these individuals and I have used their actual names as my tribute to them, for the contribution they made in making me a better person. Other names are purely fictitious in what I have "coined" my nostalgic novel, which is equal parts fact, fiction, and fantasy.

Remember: our memory is like New River. It flows along on an ageless journey, sometimes slowing, but never stopping, picking up along its path trash and treasures, sediment and sentiments, carrying it all until it can deposit these onto the rich delta of our nostalgia. Then it is our choice as to what we will remember. I hope you will join me in remembering only the best.

I hope you will enjoy *A Cotton Mill Town Christmas*. To find out more about the town I call home and the recreational and scenic opportunities it offers, for photos of the characters I have used, and to see a projected schedule of my future books, please go to *www.acottonmilltown.com*

1

SPECIAL EDITION

ARMBRISTER WINS MAYOR RACE BY ONE VOTE,
Bourne demands recount

read the headlines in the November 12, 1969, edition of the one-page, front and back, *Fries Wildcat Spirit Weekly* newspaper. Suzie Young, a thirteen-year-old aspiring journalist served as the chief writer, editor and publisher of the weekly gazette that she unabashedly advertised as *the two-page weekly newspaper that gives twice the local coverage of that Galax daily.*

The publication's usual print date was each Friday night with distribution on Saturday morning. This schedule was perfect because it did not interfere with Suzie's school work, and for three months out of each year, it allowed Suzie to report on the Fries Wildcats' football games. Like most southern towns, Fries lived and died according to the success of their high school football team.

After the season ended though, the news became very sporadic. Suzie then struggled to find articles worthy of her readers' dime. Sometimes she just wrote a review of the high school play or a feature article on an outstanding teacher or community leader. Sometimes she got so desperate she even listed missing pets.

Occasionally the news was so big that Suzie, refusing to be scooped by the mercenaries from the Galax paper, rescheduled the publication date. Such was the special edition that was prepared late on Tuesday night, the eleventh of November. The teenage girl never dreamed at the time that she would be printing several "special editions" in the weeks to come. For the rest of this year there would be scant reporting of Birddog's lost retriever, or of Ms.

Ace's forever-straying calico cat.

Suzie had a special agreement with local attorney H. Douglas Turner, Esquire. She carried a key to his law office and had permission to come and go as she pleased. There she had the use of Turner's new state-of-the-art IBM copy machine. In exchange for the free use of the copier and paper, Suzie gave the attorney four free advertisements annually and a free weekly newspaper.

The lawyer was a savvy businessman and owned a large portion of the real estate in the town. Accordingly, he only wanted his advertisements on the best quality paper possible. Therefore, the attorney provided a special stock for Suzie to print her newspaper on that was not only a high bond, but had a rich ecru color with ornate gold trim around the borders. Suzie was up almost all night in Mr. Turner's office running off the 250 copies. This was fifty more copies than was usually printed. She was sure there would be extra demand.

In the newspaper she reported that the final mayoral count of 255-254 constituted both a record for the highest number of cast votes in a Fries mayoral election and also the closest vote in the town's history. What the writer did not realize though was that the election was an indication of more than a race between two individuals. It was a clash between two ideologies, two classes, and even two denominations. This small town in the heart of southwest Virginia was at a crossroads. There, standing in the middle of that intersection, would be young Suzie Young. Would she direct traffic, or be run over?

Since the dawn of the town sixty-seven years before, the governing of the small cotton mill community was traditionally handled by the authorities who also managed the Mill. Sure, this was a monarchy, but as with parents rearing a young child, residents of a young town needed certain discipline and strong leadership in order to grow up to become suitable members of society. The current leadership wasn't quite as autocratic as the first thirty-years under John Thorpe, who regulated everything from how the churches and parsonages should be built to what was appropriate conversation for the youth in the corner drug store.

A new generation had arrived, though. A generation no longer content with the status quo, but instead was demanding a transition. A paradigm shift had begun taking place in the mid-sixties. Free love had been born in the Haight-Ashbury section of San Francisco, consummated by Scott McKenzie in his immortal lyrics:

> *If you're going to San Francisco,*
> *be sure to wear some flowers in your hair.*
> *If you come to San Francisco,*
> *summertime will be a love-in there*

A generation chasm, as wide as the Grand Canyon, had seemingly grown overnight and was eroding the morality of the nation, according to the older generation. According to the younger generation, born upon the return of the fighting men of World War II, they were just trying to cure the world's malevolence.

While the older generation grew up worshipping their beagles, the younger generation was growing up worshipping the Beatles.

While the older generation had bought acid to drop into their car batteries, the younger generation bought acid to drop in their bodies.

While the older generation had gone off to fight a war to protect the ones they loved, the younger generation preferred to make love, not war, and would go to Canada to prevent having to fight.

While the older generation was spending the summer cutting grass and stocking wood for the winter, the younger generation was traveling to Woodstock to smoke grass, in numbers larger than the total football fans who would watch the VA Tech Hokies and the UVA Cavalier teams combined for the entire '69 football season.

Yes, the 60's revolution was about to arrive in the small hamlet of Fries. Suzie was not aware of the role she would be called on to build a bridge between the two sides of the canyon that was being carved.

Jonathan Armbrister was the 50-year-old plant superintendent at the Fries Cotton Mill, a position which placed him somewhere between the United States President and God. He was a good, fair man, but he also had to carry out the demands of the stockholders of the Washington Group, a conglomerate of textile mills throughout the South. At times this was a true paradox. He had run for mayor, as was expected of a man in his position, on the platform of good, sound fiscal responsibility.

He was more than capable of that. Many citizens did not perceive it, but Armbrister had single-handedly fought the powers to be for the last three years to keep the Mill open. He did this by constantly balancing the welfare of the employees with the demands of the company suits down in Winston-Salem. For the first quarter of the century, wages had been set high enough to attract new residents to the innovative Washington Village, as Fries was originally called. Families flocked in from the tobacco fields of North Carolina and the coal mines of West Virginia. But now firmly in the latter part of the century, newer industries, such as the Radford Arsenal and Lynchburg Foundry, were paying significantly higher wages. Even the Galax furniture factories had better compensation.

Now the workers were beginning to vehemently bewail the wages and horrendous working conditions. Management was turning a deaf ear because they were fighting a battle with cheap textile imports coming in from Europe and Asia. Mr. Armbrister had been keeping wages just high enough to prevent unions from getting a toe-hold in the town, but to justify the wages and appease the company; the superintendent had to constantly demand higher production from the workers. For many years workers who had low production, due to age or disability, were moved to positions that did not depend upon their production, but this was no longer true. These low production workers were no longer tolerated. To many, especially the younger workers, this was a sign of greed and arrogance on the part of management.

Mr. Armbrister was very strong in his faith, and served as a deacon, and at times lay speaker, in the Fries Baptist Church. Like most of the tar heels who had moved from the Piedmont up into the mountains, his ancestors were Moravian. The plant superintendent, although now a Baptist, still enjoyed sharing his Moravian heritage. He told how they had been the earliest reformers of the Catholic Church in the fifteenth century, even before the Protestant Reformation. He related how the early church, which was centered in the Bohemia and Moravia area, was so persecuted, they left Europe for America. He recited the history of the church's sending a group to settle in the flatland area of North Carolina to form a town called Salem. He would describe how the settlement ministered and educated the Cherokee Indians. He loved to tell of the deep unyielding faith, the compassion, and the hard work ethic of the Moravians because he was positive that this heritage made him the man he was today.

On the other hand, the other mayoral candidate, forty-year-old Herbie Bourne toiled as a loom fixer in the mill. His family had lived in the area for over a hundred years. The Bournes had been Methodists since the late 1800's when the fiery evangelist, Reverend Robert Sayers Sheffey, had transformed the non-practicing Christians of the Appalachian Mountains into church-going, filled-with-the-Holy-Ghost Methodists. Bourne's platform was simple:

Let's ease the torture of working in a hot, noisy environment by adding to the quality of life in the town.

For the last ten years, Herbie had mentored the youth of the town. As the head of the Methodist Youth Fellowship, he had tripled the MYF membership by organizing camping parties, bus trips for skating and bowling, and teenage dances. He showed that church could be fun, even for young people. Many of the teens he had brought into church through the MYF were now of voting age. One of his proposals was a new town park complete with a boat landing, picnic tables, and playground. He was proposing that any child who could not pay the $25 annual membership to the Thorpe YMCA should be given free membership. His problem was that he had not found the funds for these items, and considering the Cotton Mill provided 90% of the tax base for the town, it might prove difficult to find the money if Bourne did win the recount.

But the people had voted. A little less than half voted for a better way of life, for a better tomorrow. They had never witnessed the pangs of hunger, and their only craving was to enjoy life to its fullest. A little more than half voted for the status quo, with hopes of just having a tomorrow. These had known hunger, when as children or young adults they had gone through the Great Depression.

"I can't believe Herbie lost by one vote. He should have stomped Armbrister." Spunkie Akers, one of the local young people, said as he read from the *Fries Wildcat Spirit Weekly* while he loitered at Charlie's Barber Shop.

Even on a Wednesday evening the shop was full, standing room only. Customers getting a haircut relaxed in one of the two cracked, black leather barber-chairs. All twelve of the wooden straight-back chairs, lined up beneath the ten-foot-long mirror, were occupied. Many of the older men rested, their chins on their chests, having been lulled to sleep by the snip, snip, snip of the scissors. An occasional snore would necessitate a poke in the ribs. A few onlookers leaned against the walls. As usual, only about eight of the twenty or so occupants were paying customers.

Two young boys sat on top of the brown Coca-Cola cooler, until they had to jump down so someone could remove a 6-ounce bottle from the long track. One of the boys was holding a bottle of pop, his pudgy, dirty fingers wrapped around the top. He had just poured his pack of Planters peanuts into the bottle, and was letting the salty foam erupt to the top of the bottle, ready to suck the tan froth off the top of the drink.

Charlie looked over the ridge of his eyeglasses, which were in their usual resting place, halfway down his nose.

"Tater-bug, you let that Coke run over, you'll be mopping it up," he said matter-of-factly.

"Yes sir, Charlie, I'll be careful with it," the boy answered, knowing Charlie's bark was worse than his bite, but also knowing that the barber was serious.

"He would've brought us somethin' to be proud of in this hick town, 'stead of never having anything to look forward to, outside that damn Mill." Spunkie, as he was well known to do, was spouting off. He loved to hear himself talk, and didn't mind if he was usually a minority of one in his views.

Charlie, without revealing his vote but leaving strong indications, replied softly, "Well, those of us that lived in the coal fields of West Virginia, and through the Depression, know that sometimes a better quality of life means putting bread on the table."

Several older men nodded their heads and mumbled something in agreement, while some of the younger men ranted something about, "Maybe we'd be better off if they did close it down."

Spunkie wasn't about to be put in his place by the antiquated notions of the older men.

"Yeah, I wish they would close that damn hell hole down, then we'd have to find other jobs. That arsenal down in Radford pays four times the wages they do here, and you only work half as hard."

"Yeah, but when was the last time anyone got blown to smithereens in the Mill, like they do at the powder plant?" one of the older men retorted.

"Well, it's better than going deaf from the noise of them looms, or dying from all the Bromo Seltzer everybody takes just to stomach the work," Akers ranted. "No wonder half the old men in this town are looney tics, that mill is enough to drive anybody crazy."

"Well, just how would you know, Spunkie? You've never worked a full day in your life. All you do is set at home and spend your daddy's money," replied Rayford Adams in an agitated, high-pitched voice. The frail built man of eighty bent over to spit the brown juice from his chew of Red Man into the trash can.

Spunkie jumped up, his face turning as red as a Wildcat home football jersey, his fist clinched. "Well, you little…, if you weren't half- dead already, I'd beat the shit outta you! I may jes' do it anyway," the bully screamed as he started across the room.

The 6'1", 210-pound Spunkie was a head taller and 70 pounds heavier than Rayford Adams. The old man swallowed his wad of tobacco as he watched the raging bull-dog lumbering toward him.

Until that time, Harve Edwards had kept his mouth shut, almost amused by all the bickering. Harve lived outside the town, so he didn't have a dog in this hunt, that is, until his life-long buddy, Rayford Adams, was physically threatened. Even though Harve was now 55, he was still one of the most massive men in Fries. At 6'3" and 230 pounds, he had a chest the size of a whiskey barrel, and arms the size of small trees. The thirty years he had spent slinging 100-pound sacks of grain down at the Fries Mercantile were very evident in the man's physique. Harve lived by the creed, *Speak softly, but carry a big stick.* He stepped directly into the path of the infuriated Akers.

"I think you oughta reconsider that, Akers," Harve said, looking down at the out-of-control intimidator.

Akers looked up, fury filling his eyes, as he contemplated challenging Harve. After all, Harve was an old man now. Still, not many men had ever dared challenge him, not even young hotheads like Spunkie.

Harve was normally as mild-mannered as they come, but rumors were that about thirty-five years earlier, as a young man, he had killed another boy, broke his neck with one blow. The story was that the boy had been telling lies about Harve's sister, disparaging her vestal reputation. The gossip really caught fire when the young girl left town suddenly to stay with an aunt down the mountain in Low Gap. Supposedly, Harve had sent word to the young Casanova to meet him on the cliffs just outside the town. The boy's body was found, neck broken, at the foot of the rocks.

Harve was called in and questioned, but he had an alibi. It seemed he and his pal Rayford Adams had been down at Byllesby Dam fishing for the entire day. They even had a chain of catfish to prove it. Finally, the county sheriff declared the death was due to an accidental fall from the cliffs. The crime may have just been a fabrication, but few men had ever dared to challenge Harve since that day.

By this time, Charlie realized that this thing had gone from a good old boy argument to the verge of a brawl. He had heard all he wanted. Once, ten years earlier, some of the football players from Galax had shown up the day after the big game and had started something up with the Fries boys. The $125 mirror above the chairs got busted, and the cost came out of Charlie's pocket.

The barber wasn't about to let that happen again.

"Okay, that's it, get out, get out all of you," Charlie screamed out, as he jerked the white cape off the startled customer in the chair, leaving one sideburn untouched with the shaving cream still on it. "I'm closing down this shop until you guys can get this bickering out of your system."

The old men jerked upright in their chairs. The two boys tumbled off the Coke cooler. Everyone's eyes widened and mouths dropped open.

"I mean it, you ain't bustin' up my shop," the barber said, as he grabbed his crutch and began waving the occupants toward the door.

"I'm sorry, Charlie. I really am." Harve said to the barber as he walked past.

As Edwards was walking through the exit he turned back, and in a calm, dispassionate voice he said to the still huffing and puffing Spunkie, "If you want to get this out of your system, if you still want to have at it, I'll be out back of the post office to oblige you." He walked out the barber shop door, turned left and sauntered toward the end of the block.

Spunkie stomped out the door, his fist clenched by his side, his whole body trembling with his fury. The young myrmidons were urging him on, anxious to see their fearless champion fight.

"You can take that old man Spunkie, show'em who's boss."

"Give him a whoopin' he'll never forget, Spunkie."

"Open up a can of whip'ass on 'em, Spunkie."

The older men lagged quietly behind the youngsters. They weren't saying anything, but they surely hoped Spunkie would go behind the post office. This would be one humdinger of a fight. It was time Akers got his come-uppance.

Akers looked to his left at the departing broad shoulders of Harve. The older man now walked with a noticeable limp, one shoulder drooping lower than the other from being thrown from a horse. He spun his left arm in a wind-mill motion. Was he urging Spunkie to come on, or just stretching out his aching body? Without turning around, Harve rounded the corner of the post office, disappearing out of site.

Spunkie stood motionless, just outside the barber shop. He

took a deep breath, then turned to his right, and waved a dismissing hand at the departing Edwards as if to say he wasn't worth his time.

"Ah hell, I'd hit that old man one time, he'd keel over, and they'd throw my ass in jail." Spunkie said with a forced laugh.

He walked down the street, got in his pick-up, and sped out of the parking spot, nearly hitting a little gray-haired lady walking to the bank to cash her Social Security check. The boys watched his truck as it bounced over the railroad tracks and disappeared around the curve at the YMCA.

"Yeah, he's right. He'd murder that old man," they mumbled as they began walking back to their homes. But deep inside, they knew they had just seen Spunkie Akers walk away from a fight with a man twice his age.

After the last customer departed, Charlie shuffled to the door. Shaking his head in disgust, he swung the sign around so that CLOSED read to the outside. He lifted his stronger leg up to the foot rest, and then plopped down despairingly into the barber-chair nearest the window. He looked over at the other barber, Horace.

"I don't think I've ever seen this town so angry at each other. I don't like it; I don't like it at all." Charlie said, shaking his head slowly side to side.

"Yes, I agree; it ain't looking good. Maybe think everybody'll get over it by Thanksgiving though."

"I hope so. It reminds me too much of thirty years ago when Pauline Payne got murdered at the theater, and it took them so long to figure out who did it. Everybody was just pointing their finger at the other fellow, wondering who the killer was. This town's too small to have people going after each other like that. I just never thought I'd live to see the day an election would split everybody up this way."

The town experienced a few more small incidents over the next three days. Most of these were petty, almost infantile. Someone spray-painted the word *Basterds* on the side of the Mill office. Some of the bosses found flattened tires in the Mill office lot. Probably the worse incident was the one that involved one of the Mill's tractor-trailers that broke down on the interstate, two hundred miles away from home. The cause turned out to be sugar that had found its way into the fuel tank.

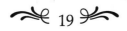

2
SPECIAL EDITION

MAYOR RECOUNT SHOWS TIE,
Legal opinion needed

was the banner on the November 19 edition of the *Fries Wildcat Spirit Weekly*.

For the second week in a row, Suzie Young was up late on a Tuesday night cranking out the newspaper on her mother's old typewriter. The clock showed it was almost midnight.

Oh no, I've gotten ink underneath my nails. I'd better get it out before Momma sees it, she thought to herself.

As always, she had painstakingly used a black marker and a stencil to print the half-inch letters to form the headline. She went to the bathroom and scrubbed the ink from under and around her short fingernails. Satisfied that it wouldn't be noticed, Suzie went to bed.

The next morning at 6:05, she jumped out of bed when her alarm clock began its clang-clang-clang. She quickly and quietly began to dress, hoping not to wake her mother. She failed. Her mother opened her bedroom door.

"Suzie, what in the world are you doing up so early?" her mother muttered, squinting through her sleep-laden eyes. "Are you sick, are you ok?"

"It's alright, Mom. I just need to head down to Mr. Turner's to print out the paper."

"What time did you get to bed last night?"

"Before midnight." Suzie didn't lie; it was a good five minutes before twelve when she laid down in bed to proofread the paper one last time.

"Suzie, now I didn't mind you doing this paper on the

weekend, but during the school week? I'm just not sure I like that."

"Oh Momma, I promise it won't affect my school work," the young girl pleaded, "and all the people are depending upon me. This is really important news I'm reporting."

Karen Young had accepted her daughter's new passion for writing three years prior because it had seemed to take away some of the pain of losing her father five years ago. Karen had to admit that it had never seemed to affect Suzie's grades. The girl had never brought home anything less than a B+ in her life.

Karen looked on the table where the newspaper lay, neatly typed out. She then looked at the trash can where a dozen or so balled up wads of paper had been thrown. Suzie was never satisfied until her paper was perfect. While Suzie finished dressing, Karen began reading the report of the previous night's Council meeting. She had to admit, it was making a lot of news in the town. Even though Mrs. Young didn't usually take interest in the political affairs of the town, it seemed as if everyone was talking about this election.

While she dressed, Suzie thought back to the night before, and the excitement she had felt as the events unfolded during the meeting. It electrified her so to know that she was the ears for the town, reporting the proceedings of the events that the citizens didn't have time to attend.

She let her imagination migrate from the little town of Fries. She was now in the far reaches of inner Africa, interviewing the chief of a long lost tribe for *National Geographic*. She could hear the steady pitter-patter as the raindrops fell from the jungle foliage to the vegetated floor. She could smell the exotic fragrance of the wild orchids. She could hear the bedlam from the menagerie of wild beasts that were roaming in the tropical forest, mere yards away from her. She then found herself in a large ballroom in a fancy New York Hotel, and could hear the announcement being made, *And now, the winner of the Pulitzer Prize for International Reporting in Journalism, Miss Suz...*

"Well, if you're going to Mr. Turner's you'd better get a move on," Karen said, interrupting her daughter just as she was about to go on stage to receive the prestigious Pulitzer.

The vote recount had taken place during the executive session of the regular Town Council meeting on the night before, which was Tuesday, November 18. First on the agenda was the recount, so the winner could then be sworn in and take over the meeting. The meeting was opened by Town Council Vice-Mayor, Buster Wilkinson.

"The um, first, item on the agenda is the um, the recount," Buster said, very uncomfortable in his temporary position. "We will need to go into executive session, so everyone will need to leave the room. Except the council. And Mr. Turner. We'll—, we'll let you know when y'all can come back in. Is that the right thing to do, Mr. Turner?"

"Yes, Mr. Wilkinson," the legal counsel answered, "that is the correct protocol."

The room full of attendees, including Herbie Bourne, Jonathan Armbrister, and Suzie Young, went out into the hallway.

"Shouldn't take long," someone said. "How long does it take to count 500 ballots?"

"Yeah, shouldn't take long," Spunkie Akers shouted from the back of the hall, having just shown up. "You might as well go home Armbrister, save yourself some embarrassment."

Even though he was standing twenty feet away on the steps, the musty smell of beer was very evident.

But it did take awhile, a long while. After thirty minutes, the people were still standing there, getting more and more impatient.

"What's taking so long? It shouldn't be taking this long," someone in the crowd complained.

"Unless someone's in there screwing with the votes," Spunkie said accusingly as he flopped down on the top step. He was no longer able to stand, the warmth of the hallway making him more intoxicated by the minute.

Fifteen minutes later, almost forty-five minutes after calling to order the executive session, a very pallid faced Buster Wilkinson opened the door. He looked out into the corridor, and immediately detected the smell of alcohol and saw Spunkie Akers, glaring through dazed, half-closed eyes.

"Herbie, go down the hall," Buster whispered to Herbie in a low voice. "Tell Bruce I think he might oughta come to the meeting. There might be trouble."

Herbie looked at Buster with a puzzled look, but saw the urgency in the vice-chairman's eyes. He turned and walked down the corridor, ignoring Spunkie, and knocked on Bruce's door.

"Sorry it took so long, folks," an evidently unraveled Buster Wilkinson said. "Come on in and set down."

After everyone settled down, Buster began to steal glances toward the back entrance. Leaning against the wall, next to the doorway, was a very volatile Spunkie Akers. Every once in awhile, he would sway, and then catch his balance. Buster pretended to be shuffling some papers, but was the whole time watching the door.

In a few minutes, Herbie walked in, followed by Police Chief Bruce Smith. The constable strolled over, and leaned against the wall near Spunkie. Akers at first did not notice who had walked up beside him. Then he recognized the policeman, and promptly teetered over to the corner, away from the officer. Buster then struck the gavel to the marble base, cleared his throat, and took a drink of water.

"The meeting of the Fries town council will now come back to order," he announced authoritatively, "Hmm, Mr. Turner, as legal counsel, would you announce the results of the, um, voting recount?"

Doug Turner was a very well-known and respected lawyer who kept offices in both Fries and Independence. He had attended Fries High School, then got a law degree from Wake Forest University. Although he lived just outside town, he considered himself one of its citizens, and provided free legal service to the council in addition to the free printing services for Suzie's paper.

He was also one of the town's largest benefactors, other than the Mill. It was Doug who would always step forward when the football team needed money for a special meal the night of the championship game, or the basketball team needed new uniforms. He was known to send spending money to many of the young people who had gone off to college. He often told the students he knew how they felt, not having had spending money when he was in college. He was also quick to point out his expectations of them, from the grades the students were expected to make to how long the boys should let their hair grow.

Doug raised a sheet of paper from the conference table.

"On November 18, 1969, at approximately 7:05 p.m.," the lawyer began in his polished baritone voice, "the Fries town council met for the purpose of a voting recount on the matter of the 1969 mayoral election. After three recounts, the final decision is that the final vote is...Jonathan Armbrister, 254 votes..."

The room immediately began buzzing; the vote was going to be reversed. Herbie Bourne was going to be announced the winner.

"Yeah, hell yeah," Spunkie shouted as he pumped his fist in the air, nearly falling out of his chair and onto the person sitting in front of him.

"Order. Order." Buster shouted aloud. "Let us finish."

The vice-chairman, now feeling more confident, looked straight at Spunkie, then at Chief of Police Bruce Smith, rolling his eyes toward Akers. Bruce edged over behind Spunkie, placed his hand on the young man's shoulder, and gave him a fatherly but authoritative smile. He then pulled up a folding chair, and firmly putting his hands on the young man's shoulders, pushed him down into the seat.

"The final vote is...Jonathan Armbrister, 254 votes," Turner read again, "Herbie Bourne...254 votes. One vote was dismissed for being improperly marked."

The room again erupted into a clamor. Spunkie Akers spit out an epithet, and side-stepping Bruce Smith, stormed out of the doorway, pausing just long enough to flash a parting glare and a middle finger in the direction of Jonathan Armbrister. Buster allowed the buzz to continue for about fifteen seconds, then realizing it was not going to diminish on its own, began banging the gavel.

"Order! Order! Get quiet or I'll clear the room!" Buster had learned that from watching Perry Mason and had always wanted to say it.

Then turning to legal counsel, Buster asked. "Okay, Mr. Turner, what is your advice on how we should continue?"

"Well, I must admit, I'm not prepared to offer advice," the lawyer said, as he actually scratched his head, totally perplexed. "And I do have a very heavy docket over the next two weeks. I would like to request three weeks to study precedence, and offer advice to the council on a special called meeting on Tuesday, December 10."

The council voted 4-0 to accept legal counsel advice, and scheduled another meeting for that date. After approving the invoices to be paid for the month, Buster requested that all other business be tabled until the next scheduled meeting. The Council agreed, and the meeting was adjourned.

The twenty or so attendees shuffled out of the town hall. Everyone was offering prognostications as to the outcome of the tied vote, everyone, that is, except Herbie Bourne and Jonathan Armbrister. Both of the candidates were strangely reserved and unknown to the other, were sharing the same thoughts. First, they wished they had not run for mayor, and second, each wondered if it would be best for the town if he withdrew and let the other be elected without any controversy. The two men actually looked at each other as they left the door, looking as if they were ready to say something. Then as the crowd spilled onto the street, everyone grew hushed. Parked on the street was Armbrister's new 1969 green Lincoln Mark II with red barn paint splashed across the hood, over the windshield, and along the roof. The paint was fresh, with drops still cascading off the hood and splattering onto the polished chrome bumper.

Everyone turned to look up and down the street. There was no one in view. Most obvious though was the empty space directly in front of the Lincoln. Most attendees had seen the old, beat up '55 Chevy pick-up that belonged to Spunkie Akers parked there earlier. About the only work Spunkie ever did was an occasional barn painting, a task for which he had an uncanny knack for stretching a week-long job into a month. One consolation to Jonathan was that the paint Spunkie used was of such poor quality that the first rains usually washed the coat away. He hoped the smear spreading over his car would come off as easily.

Jonathan turned, and with a dazed glare that hovered somewhere between anger and hurt, looked at Bruce Smith. The others just shook their heads, some turning to offer condolences to Armbrister.

"Why don't you come on up to the office, and let's have us a talk," Bruce whispered to him, placing a friendly hand upon Armbrister's shoulder.

"If you don't mind me driving your car," Herbie said to Jonathan, in a very conciliatory tone, "let me have the keys, and I'll run it down to the car wash. I think the paint might still be wet enough to wash off."

"Thanks, Herbie," Jonathan said, handing his challenger the keys. "I'll be upstairs with Bruce."

Sergeant Bruce Smith, about 65, had the professionalism and common sense of Andy Taylor, but the spit and polish of Barney Fife. His uniform, dark brown pants and tan shirt, was always neatly pressed. A black tie with its Windsor knot perfectly tied always ended one inch below the buckle of his polished gun belt and holster which housed his well-oiled, if not often used, revolver. Even at his advanced age, he still had a lean and muscular look about him. He had served as Chief of Police for almost 40 years, having succeeded his father. In those forty years, there had been one murder and one car fatality. The murder had occurred thirty years before in the local theater and was a true drama of romance, mystery, and suspense. The car fatality transpired in 1954 when the brakes gave out on Ethram Gramm's 1931 Chevrolet pick-up coming down the hill in front of the YMCA. He could not stop and the N & W train hit him. The truck was knocked over a thirty-foot bank in front of the White Flash Garage and landed on its top. Ethram died the next day from internal injuries.

Now Bruce was in his waning years, but still performed his duties admirably. His usual monthly crime docket consisted of two drunks-in-public, one inevitably being Spunkie Akers, and other various misdemeanors that usually went no farther than the offenders being taken to Bruce's office and receiving a reprimand. These misdemeanors usually consisted of such heinous and malicious crimes as the illegal use of a slingshot within town limits, excessive Halloween tricks, or reckless riding of a bicycle on sidewalks.

About once a year, usually during football season, the most odious of all misdemeanors would occur. This was when four or five young teenage boys would stand on the railroad trestle that was built over Route 94. There they would wait after a game for the bus hauling the departing visiting team. Then the boys would pee off the trestle onto the bus. If it was a warm and breezy August night, the youngsters could really have something about which to brag to their friends, because then the players would have their windows down, and if the wind was blowing from just the right direction, the opposing players would receive an unscheduled shower.

If Bruce ever set up surveillance for this act of chemical warfare, the young marauders would then hide in the woods just outside town and egg the bus, if at all possible using rotten eggs. After these atrocities, Bruce would usually just place the lads into the police cruiser, drive the juvenile delinquents to their respective houses, and turn them over to higher authorities; their parents. He knew the moms and dads would do much more than he would. Bruce seldom had a repeat offender, that is with the exception of Spunkie Akers.

The town's youth tended to not take the Chief seriously, though, and would ridicule the constable behind his back. Older men would quickly put the youngsters in their places with stories of Bruce's past accomplishments. Some of the actions had gone from myth to legend over the years, such as the one about the time that Federal Marshals were afraid to apprehend a fugitive holed up in Fries. Bruce, knowing the boy, promptly went up on the porch, kicked in the door, and brought the young man out by the neck of the shirt, the whole time chastising him for "embarrassing his mother." There must be some merit of truth to the story, though, because so many people have told it.

One story was not a fable, though. It was well documented in both the March 1942 edition of *Complete Detective Cases* Magazine under the article *Silent Killer and the Talking Pictures*, and later, in the June, 1942 edition of *Inside Detective* in their article, *The Secret Clue in Pauline's Diary*. These popular sleuth magazines told of Sergeant Smith's role in cracking the case of the aforementioned solitary Fries murder, that of Pauline Payne in the Fries Theater on August 16, 1941.

It seemed that Pauline and her new beau, a young man that was working at one of President Roosevelt's Civilian Conservation

Corp camps over in Baywood, had attended a show at the town theater that Saturday night. Suddenly two gunshots interrupted the movie. An unknown figure was seen rushing up the aisle, escaping into the night.

The beautiful young woman was found slumped over in her seat. Blood from a gun shot wound through her left side stained the new blouse she had bought for the date. The fatal bullet had found a resting place in her heart. Months later, the murderer was discovered to be the girl's uncle by marriage. Bruce received an accommodation by the State Police for his painstaking pursuit of the case.

Bruce's long, slow drawl seemed to make him likeable to the locals of this small southern town. He did, upon occasion though, have to show without question that he was the law. He left no doubts that he wasn't to be messed with, whether it be confiscating a sling-shot or breaking up a fight between two young knife-wielding punks.

"Take a seat," Bruce said as he pulled a chair up to the desk, "and make yourself comfortable."

The two men sat down. Jonathan had never in his sixteen years in Fries been in Bruce's police office. He looked around the walls. There were several certificates from various police training schools, showing Bruce had graduated from them with honors. One picture showed Bruce as Jonathan had never seen him before, in civvies, dark dress pants, a light gray dress coat, tie and hat, standing next to his beloved yellow Model-A he had named "Sunflower."

"Now, Mr. Armbrister," Bruce began, his drawl making the faster-talking Armbrister want to reach out and grab the policeman's words and yank them from his mouth. "You and me both know that it was probably Spunkie that did this. I will look around for witnesses, but I doubt I will find anybody willing to step forward."

Jonathan nodded his head in consensus.

"Spunkie is a hothead, and I've never seen him so riled up," Bruce continued. "I think he might be dangerous this time. I'm gonna phone the Grayson County Sheriff and advise him that we need to keep an eye on the kid. It may be time he needs to be sent away for awhile."

"Well, Bruce, I know you'll do what you can," Armbrister said, "I'll remember what you said, that he might be dangerous, and I'll notify the Mill security consultant."

What Jonathan wasn't saying was that as Mill superintendent, he had inside knowledge that things would probably get even worse. He knew that decisions had been made at the corporate level, and in spite of his strongly voiced objections, were about to be enacted. Bad news was coming, he just didn't know how bad it would be. He dreaded the day looming near when corporate decisions would be handed down that would certainly have adverse and possibly crippling ramifications on the town of Fries.

Bruce and Jonathan talked a few more minutes, and then Jonathan walked down to the street. There stood a beaming Herbie holding the keys. All traces of the red paint were gone from the Lincoln.

"Hey, I'm surprised it washed out," Armbrister said, obviously relieved.

"Well, there were a few spots left after the washing," Herbie said as he handed over the keys, "but Dave was able to buff those out down at the White Flash."

"What do I owe you? And owe Dave?"

"Not a thing. Dave wouldn't take anything, and I certainly won't."

"Well, I appreciate it Herbie, I really do. Cynthia would have been very upset to see the car damaged."

"Well, Mr. Armbrister, you're a good man. You don't deserve stuff like this going on. I certainly wish we could go back and change things."

"Thanks, Herbie. That means a lot to me. And I know what you mean, I feel the same way."

Everyone knew without a doubt that Spunkie had committed the vandalism. There was even a $100 reward offered, but no one stepped forward as a witness. Spunkie was usually very cautious when he did his devilment. If he was seen, most people would be reluctant to speak, not wanting to confront Spunkie's wrath. Not even for the equivalent of a week's pay.

For the next two weeks, the divisive wedge between the town

was driven deeper and deeper. Neighbors began to go out of their way to avoid speaking to each other. Children were forbidden to play with their best pals. Life-long friends were no longer able to talk because the subject of who should be mayor always arose. Even the two major churches began to feel the friction.

Jonathan Armbrister belonged to the Fries Baptist Church where he served in many capacities. Those at the church knew a very different man from the hard-line Mill superintendent some of the other people in town thought Armbrister to be. For some reason, it seemed most of the Mill management attended this church.

Herbie was born in Fries and had attended the Fries Methodist Church his whole life. Even though he had only finished high school, he had studied the Bible faithfully. He taught the youth group, where he had an uncanny propensity for being able to take any event in a young person's life and turn it into a parable. Although thirty years older than most of the kids, Herbie was able to relate to them on their level. They never felt that he was talking down to them. He also served as team chaplain to the Fries Wildcat football team. It was easy to understand why he was the youth's choice.

Each church had always had its own sense of pride and direction, though. This was the town's founding fathers' intention from the beginning. The Baptist Church attracted the more hard-line followers, many of whom had evolved from the old Moravian faith that dominated the religion of the Winston-Salem area. The Methodists were more ecumenical, bringing in the rural churchgoers, many of whom whose grandparents had never attended an organized church. Like the Bourne family, they had been brought into the fold by the hell-fire and brimstone preaching of Reverend Sheffey in the late 1800's. But the town's founding fathers had never envisioned that a town election would result in building a Berlin Wall between the two places of worship.

Everyone hoped that Thanksgiving would heal the strife between opposing forces in the town. After all, wasn't Thanksgiving the time for peoples of different beliefs and cultures to sit down together in peace and harmony?

3

Suzie Young and her mother Karen shared the dresser mirror in their modest two-bedroom house on Third Street. The daughter watched her mother as she carefully applied her pale pink lipstick, the only make-up she usually wore. Suzie was brushing her long blonde locks. Both were dressing for the Thanksgiving service.

"Momma," Suzie said, in a very disappointed tone, "I can't believe the churches cancelled the joint Thanksgiving's service."

Every year the two churches had always alternated in hosting the annual celebration. The pastor from the visiting church would provide the service, while the choir from the host church would supply the music. This year though, the two pastors met and discussed holding separate services. This was a very difficult decision because Pastor Hamm of the Baptist Church and Reverend Lyons of the Methodist Church had been friends for years, but the final decision came down from the respective church boards. The third church in town, Pastor Young's church, which the blacks attended, had never been invited to join in the joint service, so their service went on as always.

"I've always liked it when the churches do things together," Suzie continued. "That way I can do the things I enjoy at the Baptist church, but at the same time do things with Herbie's youth group at the Methodist church."

Karen looked down at her daughter who at thirteen was almost as tall as she was. She got her father's height, the mother thought to herself. Karen put her arm around Suzie's shoulder and hugged her.

"Yes honey, I know it's hard to understand why adults act the way we do sometimes."

"Why do we go to the Baptist Church?" Suzie asked her

mother. "It seems like all the people there dress better than us, and most of them are bosses in the Mill. I really feel more comfortable with the kids at the Methodist Church."

"Well, my parents and grandparents always went to the Baptist Church," her mother disclosed. "Your great-grandfather, my grandfather, was actually a big boss in the Mill. The company had brought him up from Winston-Salem when the Mill was first built."

"Did Daddy go to the Baptist Church before you married?"

"No, your daddy wasn't much of a church-goer before we married," Karen answered with a chuckle. "It took me about six months to talk him into going to church with me; then he began attending maybe twice a month."

"Momma, was Daddy a Christian?" Suzie asked, as she looked up at her mother with hopefulness in her eyes. "Will I see him in heaven? He never talked much about being a Christian."

"Suzie, some people talk about being a Christian, and some people live their life as a Christian." Karen's eyes moistened as she began speaking. "Many times he came home from a three-day haul without a dime, and had missed his last meal because he ran into someone at the truck stop that he felt needed his meal-money more than him."

"I think I'd do that too," Suzie said.

"Yes, I think you would. Your daddy gave his life to the Lord the week you were born, and he lived the rest of his life as a Christian."

"The week I was born? Why then?"

Karen was silent for a few seconds. The mother had often thought about the day she would have this discussion with her daughter. She didn't know why she had been so reluctant, but felt the time had come to share the story with the young girl.

"Okay, sit down. I'll tell you what happened," her mother continued. "I've waited until I thought you were ready. I guess this is a good time."

Suzie sat down, baffled by the gravity in her mother's voice.

"I went into labor with you a month early. I knew something was wrong, and when we got to the hospital, the doctors said you were in distress, as they call it. They thought your cord might be wrapped around your neck."

"That means I could've died?"

"Yes, they thought you might. They said the only way to save you was by doing a cesarean. Do you know what that is?"

"Of course, Mom. I've read all about it."

"Oh, okay," Karen said, not sure she wanted to know just how much else the girl had read. "So they did the cesarean. Honey, when they removed you, I could see you, your face was as blue as..." Karen pointed to the sofa, "...as that afghan."

"Wilson was outside when the doctors and nurses came running out of the room with you, and he could tell it was bad. They wouldn't even take time to tell him what was going on. I kept waiting for Wilson, but it was almost fifteen minutes before he came in. I could tell he had been crying, but he tried to convince me everything was fine. For a day and a half, they had you on oxygen. Then they came to us, and said you were all right, and would live. Your daddy and I hugged each other so. We had never been happier in our lives."

Suzie began smiling at the thoughts of her dad and mom hugging. She could still recall how much she used to love to watch her father come home after making a haul. He would first pick her up and swing her around in circles, then he would take her momma, and dip her, hugging and kissing her just like they do in movies.

"Well, that evening, the Pastor at the Baptist church came by. His name was Pastor Lineberry. Wilson sat there, but didn't say much."

"He left, and then Pastor Young came by to see us. He actually got to hold you Suzie. You should have seen him smile. Those big white teeth were just a shining. You were so small. He actually held you in just one of his big hands."

Suzie beamed. She had always loved Pastor Young, who she referred to as "Uncle Buster." She felt happy knowing he was one of the first people to ever hold her.

"When Pastor Young said he had to leave, Wilson asked him if he could speak to him for a few minutes. They left, and in about twenty minutes Wilson came back to the room. He had this radiant smile on his face. I asked him why he was smiling so."

"He said...," Karen began to cry. She took a couple of whimpering breaths. "He said that he had made a promise to God when the doctors went running out when you were first born because he just knew they thought you were going to die. He swore if God would let you live, he'd serve Him for the rest of his days. He had gotten Pastor Young to lead him to Christ. So to answer your question Suzie, yes, if you stay the same sweet wonderful girl you are now, one day many years from now, you will be seeing your daddy in heaven."

Suzie knelt down beside her mom, and placing her head against her, she hugged her around the waist.

"Thank you for telling me this, Momma."

"Your father used to tell me that to hear you call him "Daddy" made him feel like he was in heaven on earth."

Karen knew she needed to tell the complete story.

"But the doctors did tell me that I would always have problems delivering, and should not have any more babies, so I had an operation. They tied my tubes to keep me from having any more children. But your daddy said this would be fine, because no other kid could ever be as perfect as you."

Suzie smiled, lifting her head to look at her mom. Karen put her hands on both sides of her daughter's face.

"Your daddy would have been so very proud of you."

Suzie stood with her head pressed to her mother's chest for a few minutes, then decided to lighten the moment.

"So who did you vote for in the election? Herbie or Mr. Armbrister?"

"Oh, I didn't vote for either one. I wrote in the name of Suzie Young for mayor." Karen winked at her daughter as she grabbed her purse. "Now you get ready to go, or we're going to be late."

"So which church are we going to tonight?"

"Well, to be honest, I haven't even decided. I thought God might answer that for us before we get there."

When Karen got to the door, a light drizzle had started to fall. She looked to the sky where several large, ominous black clouds were cloaking the stars. It was at times like this she wished she had a car.

"Oh, we'd better go back and get our rain coats and bonnets;

it's going to rain." Mrs. Young warned.

After slipping on rain gear, the mother and daughter started back outside. Just then a familiar black Ford Fairlane pulled up in front of the house. It was Herbie Bourne and his wife.

"Hey," Herbie called out, rolling down his window. "I didn't want the two prettiest blondes in town to melt in this rain. Hop in and we'll give you a ride down to your church."

"Herbie Bourne," Karen said laughing as she opened the rear door of the car, "Ellen'll pull your hair out flirting with other women like that."

"Well, now that's why I said 'blondes'," Herbie laughed, as he patted Ellen's hand. "Cause she's the prettiest brunette in town."

"Mind if Suzie and I go to the Methodist Church with you tonight?" Karen asked, as she winked at her daughter.

In a way, the dissension was opportune. Most years, the communal service only attracted about 125 attendees because most people claimed they had been out of town when the reason was simply too much turkey and football. However, this year, each congregation was determined to outdraw the other and to take up all the available parking spaces. Usually the Baptist Church parked in an adjacent lot that belonged to the high school, and left the on-street parking for the Methodist Church. Word had been disseminated though, and the Baptists arrived thirty minutes early for the service, taking up all the on-street parking. This required the Methodists to walk an extra 200 yards from the school lot in what was now a heavy rain.

There was a minor auto accident with an ensuing scuffle when a Methodist and Baptist both approached the last on-street parking spot at the same time. When the Baptist pulled up alongside the car in front to parallel park his 1969 Buick Riviera, a Methodist in a '65 VW Bug sneaked headlong into the space. The Bug lost a front headlight, and the Buick lost a tail-light lens. The Baptist lost a coat button, and the Methodist suffered a torn shirt pocket.

Chief of Police Smith was not in attendance at the beginning of services. His '62 Ford Galaxie police car idled in the alleyway between Main and Vaughan Streets. About thirty minutes after the services started, a familiar Chevy pick-up truck turned off

Hilltown Road, losing a couple of beer cans as it turned right onto Main Street. It slowly drove down the car-lined street. Spunkie turned into the adjacent parking lot. As he did, Sergeant Smith shifted the police car into drive and eased out of the alley. Once Akers was out of sight, Bruce pulled onto Main and slowly made his way toward the parking lot.

Apparently Spunkie either saw the police car, or decided there weren't any cars that warranted his attention. He continued through the parking lot and out First Street, merging back onto Main at the west end of town, and then left. Bruce followed him to the town limits, then turned around at the river overlook, and returned to town.

Satisfied that Spunkie would not make another appearance, he then drove back to the Baptist Church and parked in the private high school lot where he could leave in a hurry if necessary. Then he went into the church to take communion.

The members of both churches spent time before and after the service discussing the election, and what could be done to ensure the right person, that is to say, *their* person, was elected. After all, it was Divine Intervention that a true man of *their* God should be leading the town. Both congregations came up with the same idea. By the next day two separate petitions had been started to "encourage" the existing town council to select each church's endorsed candidate. A veiled threat hinted that if a council member did not heed the desire of who they wanted chosen, that member might find himself defeated at the next election.

The consequence of the split Thanksgiving was that the animosity had escalated.

4

FREE SPECIAL EDITION

The Story of the Almost Thanksgiving

was the heading of the November 29th edition of the *Fries Wildcat Spirit Weekly*.

For one of the first times in her life, Suzie's literary juices had dried up and she could simply not find any real news to report. Besides, she was much too depressed and disappointed to report the only news that she could think of, that being the fact that the townspeople were acting like a bunch of spoiled brats. For the first time in three years, she thought of not publishing a newspaper. Instead, she decided to write a parody and offered the edition free.

The Story of the Almost Thanksgiving

Three hundred years ago, on the banks of Ancient River, there was a beautiful Indian village. Chief Kidslikealot and his people lived in harmony hunting animals and growing vegetables. The men would hunt all day while the women worked the gardens and tended the children. At night the tribe would all sit around big campfires. Their chief would then tell the young children stories about the stars and the moon, and about the Great Father. He would teach them to take care of their earth and to love one another.

Then one day the Pilgrims, with their leader, Pilgrim Armsinblister, came into the land and saw the river. They knew it would be the perfect place to begin a factory for manufacturing Pilgrim hats. They were able to make cheaper hats because the other companies made the hats from leather, but the new village made them from cotton. The cotton was grown right there in the village, along with a lot of vegetables. The men grew and picked it, then the children spun the cotton into cloth, and the women sewed the hats.

For the first few years the two groups could not get along. The Indians would sneak into the Pilgrims' settlement and steal the hats, tear them up and use them to make loin cloths, or put them up on top of their totem poles. The Pilgrims would sneak into the Indian village and throw paint on the teepees, or run their ponies off. Both sides were acting like juveniles.

But then the two groups began behaving like grown-ups instead of children, and lived in peace for ten years, although they never had anything to do with each other. They just went about doing things on their own, and never joined together in each other's celebration.

On the tenth year, the Indian chief and the Pilgrim leader decided to have a big feast to celebrate the ten years of peace. They decided to hold the feast at the end of the Indians' hunting season and the Pilgrims' harvest. The women from the village and the settlement met and decided what they would eat. The Indian and Pilgrim children got together to decide what games to play. Both the women and children got along just fine, and had everything important worked out.

All the men from the two groups had to do when the day arrived was to decide upon the seating arrangements, but they discovered they only had one Chair of Honor. The Indians felt their Chief should sit there since the Indians had been in this land since the beginning. The Pilgrims thought their leader should sit there because the Pilgrims had discovered cranberry sauce and sweet-potato casserole to go along with the wild turkey that the Indians were going to provide. So the men got into a big fuss. The Indian men grabbed their wives and children and stormed out, telling the Pilgrims they could forget about eating any wild turkey. The Pilgrims told the Indians they could forget about ever getting the recipe for cranberry sauce and sweet-potato casserole.

The two groups continued fighting for many more years. The Indians never got to experience how delicious the wild turkey tasted with the cranberry sauce and sweet-potato casserole. The Pilgrims, on the other hand, had to make their cranberry sauce in the shape of a wild turkey, because the Indians would not allow them to go into the forest to hunt the wild birds.

And that is why we don't have Thanksgiving today.

Suzie received several comments regarding her story. Some thought it was cute, some thought it was dumb, and some thought it had pretty much hit the nail on the head. But it did little to silence the bickering in Fries.

On Friday, December 5th, what little joy that was left in the town was sucked dry. The first payday in December was always very special to the employees. The Mill gave a $50 Christmas bonus plus a certificate for a country ham from the company store. For some of the employees, the cash bought the bulk of the Christmas presents for their children. The ham usually served as the Christmas dinner.

The 3 o'clock whistle blew, and the first shift rushed to pick up their checks and bonuses. The employees could feel the extra paper in their envelopes, and hastily tore them open. Instead of a bonus check or a ham coupon, they found the following letter:

Dear Fries Employees,

Due to severe international competition in the textile industry, the Washington Group must close operations at its Fries plant until further notice, and cancel all Christmas bonuses. We will be evaluating all possible scenarios and exploring possible solutions that might allow us to resume operations in the very near future.

Robert Livingston, Washington Group Chairman

The mixed reactions were emotion-packed. Some of the women broke down and began to cry uncontrollably as they saw their dreams of a white Christmas turn into a nightmare of a blue Christmas. Most of the households in the area had both parents working. It was generally accepted that the husbands worked and paid for the basics of life: mortgage, car, insurance, food. The women then worked to take care of clothes, pay school expenses, and buy gifts.

Some of the men began swearing. Even those that had never been heard to utter an oath were spitting out expletives of what they would do if they could get their hands on this Robert Livingston guy, whoever he was. Some of the more hot-headed men turned to go back into the mill. Apparently the security guards had been warned, and tried to restrain the angry men. Most of the watchmen, though, were old men who should have retired ten years earlier, but who could not afford to lose the income. All the security personnel could do was try to appeal to the good-nature of the employees, but right now, there wasn't any good-nature to be found. These were defiant workers that were not going to be suppressed.

The irate men pushed by security, and thought about storming into the Mill offices, but found the building closed and locked. The fuming men then contented themselves with throwing rocks at the superintendent's third floor office. Only one rock reached the height, crashing through the plate glass window. The men were rewarded with a shower of broken glass raining down on them. The man who threw that rock was congratulated with hoots and slaps on the back.

Several of the troops assailed the Mill, telling the second shift what would be waiting for them in their paycheck envelopes that night at eleven o'clock. Within thirty minutes, every employee had demanded his check from the foreman, and had stormed out of the plant.

By this time, Chief of Police Smith and two deputies had pulled their patrol cars through the factory gates and sat just outside the front door of the Mill office. Their lights were rotating to make sure their presence was known, but the sirens were turned off.

Bruce approached the men who were standing beneath the broken window.

"I know you're mighty upset, but I think you'd better just go on home before you get in trouble because that's just not going to do anybody any good." Bruce told them in his slow drawl. Bruce's twang was like molasses. It took awhile to begin dripping, and then it just kept pouring, in an agonizingly slow dribble. "Now fellers, I'm gonna let this broken glass go as an accident, but anything else is going to be dealt with to the fullest extent of the law."

The reason Mr. Armbrister was absent from his office wasn't because he was taking vacation or that he was afraid to be in the plant following the shut-down order. The Mill superintendent was in Winston-Salem at the Washington Group Headquarters arguing his case. He was fighting a losing battle. The Washington Group Board of Directors kept throwing figures at him—negative, condemning statistics.

"The freight cost at Fries is higher than at any of our other plants," one director pointed out.

"Yes, but that's because the town is farther from an interstate highway system than the other plants," Armbrister defended. "This company chose to locate the Fries plant there so they could build the hydro-electric dam. The railroad offered inexpensive transportation at that time. It's not the town's fault that the railroad's priced themselves out of business, and over-the-road hauling has taken over."

"Well, foreign imports are killing us with their lower prices," another director argued. "In order for this company to survive, we have to cut costs and eliminate some facilities, and Fries has the highest production cost."

"The reason our plant has a problem with production cost is because three years ago you shifted the higher quality cotton material to the North Carolina plants and furnished those plants with new equipment," Armbrister retorted, fighting to hold his temper. "Some of our equipment is sixty years old. Give us new equipment, and let us produce the higher priced cloth, and we'll beat *any* of the other plants."

Jonathan Armbrister was on the verge of totally exploding, something he had not done in years. He was becoming really frustrated trying to reason with these young upstarts. Until five years ago, the Board of Directors had consisted of engineers who knew the textile industry inside-out, or businessmen who had cut their teeth on the making of cloth. But the Board was now comprised of tenderfoot lawyers and MBAs who had never had any real-life experience. The only member of the old guard was David Danielson, but he was now senile and slept during half the meetings. The other members would wake him up just to take a vote. He would look around to see how the majority was voting, then follow their lead.

Armbrister, in the past, had been able to persuade the board to make concessions in order to keep the plant alive. He knew there would be no acquiescence today.

"Okay," Armbrister asked, realizing he would need to compromise, "so what do we need to do to keep the plant open?"

Robert Livingston, the 31-year-old chairman, slipped his gold-rim glasses back on his nose and reached up to adjust his expensive European silk tie. He puckered his lips. On the chairman's already small, oval face, the gesture made him look even more like the carp people back in Fries enjoyed catching on balls of dough. Most people couldn't stomach eating the fish. The carp had such a thick skull and were so slow to die; the locals had to hit the animals in the head with a hammer to kill them. Jonathan Armbrister found himself thinking how good it would feel to do that to this young, arrogant jackleg. Robert Livingston may see himself as a wunderkind, but Jonathan knew the Washington Group Chairman was just a charlatan that was going to run the company into the ground.

"Well, it's our evaluation that in order for this facility to contribute to the overall profitability of this corporation, we will need to see a…," Livingston hesitated, as he flipped through some papers pretending to look at detailed analysis, "…a 15% reduction in overall payroll."

Armbrister became livid.

"So this is what the whole thing is about?" Armbrister screamed, slamming his fist on the table. "The Fries people already earn 10% less than the average employees of the other plants, and you want to reduce it by another 15%? How much have you asked the other plants to reduce their payroll by?"

"Johnny," Livingston said with a smirk, using a familiarity he had not earned. He stuck his finger into his collar as if it was tight, which was impossible since the chairman's neck looked to be about the size of a half-gallon mason jar. "We're not here to discuss the other plants. We're here to discuss the Fries plant, and its apparent inability to keep up with the rest of the plants in the Washington Group."

Jonathan Armbrister wished he had that ball-peen hammer in his hand right now, because he was too angry to respond. All he could do was glare at the chairman.

"I think I speak for the Board," the chairman said as he looked around the table, and each member shook their head in awkward agreement, except for Mr. Danielson, who was just nodding his head up and down on his chest. "We will give you until February 1, 1970, to convince the work force at the Fries location to accept the salary cut."

Jonathan, still standing up, placed his hands on the big mahogany conference table. He leaned over until his face was three feet away, and looked straight into Livingston's eyes.

"They are called employees, *Bobby!*" Jonathan said slowly and forcefully. "They are called *employees.*"

Armbrister's face by now was a glowing, fiery red as he realized that the lay-off, here at Christmas, was nothing but a ploy to cut wages. The board felt they could break the employees' spirit over the holidays, and then the desperate workers would accept anything to return to work. He turned quickly and stormed out of the room, unconcerned that the door slammed behind him.

He stood there in the ornate lobby of the Washington Group Headquarters. He looked down at the marble floors, their waxed surface reflecting the pressed copper ceiling overhead. He felt a gentle breeze on his face, helping cool his anger somewhat, as someone entered through the eight-foot, hand-made mahogany doors, studded with their heavy brass hardware. Jonathan heard the sound of tinkling glass as the wind whispered through the chandeliers. He looked up at the aureate crystals as they diffused the last of the daylight sun that had reflected off the ceiling.

Jonathan counted the chandeliers. *Twelve. Each one probably cost half as much as the average Fries employee makes in a year*, the Superintendent thought to himself.

For a moment, he thought about going back into the board room and telling Robert Livingston where he could stick the Fries superintendent's job. The only thing that stopped him was the realization that he was the only member of management for Washington Group that cared enough to save the plant and the town of Fries. He didn't know how, but he knew he had to find a way.

For the first time in his life, Jonathan Armbrister felt old and tired. He had worked for the company since graduating from Wake Forest 26 years ago. The Board of Directors had always respected his opinion until now. He knew he was a dinosaur and would soon become extinct in the textile industry. The new board had no respect for the workers, just the bottom line. He could not impress upon them that the employees of the Fries plant had the best work ethic of any plant in the corporation, and that they were the most dependent upon the mill for a living. If they closed the Mill, they'd cripple an entire town; a town that was created by Colonel Henry Fries and bore his name. What would the Colonel think if he knew how his creation was being treated?

It was a long, dismal ride back to the town that Armbrister had grown to love. He knew that most of the townspeople thought he was just a corporate puppet with Washington Mills controlling the strings, but this wasn't the first time he had laid his career on the line to keep this plant open. He admired the work ethic of the people, so similar to that of the Moravians of Winston-Salem from whom he was descended. He knew that many of the families in the Fries area shared the Moravian background because they had migrated to Fries at the turn of the century with Colonel Fries.

Armbrister arrived back in town around six p.m. He was not surprised to see the Mill idle, the parking lots empty. He had a feeling there would be a very strong reaction to the lay-off. There were several men gathered just outside the Mill gates. They were surprised to see the green Lincoln pull into the lot. If they had had previous warning, they probably would have thrown some rocks, in spite of Bruce's advice. Instead, they just hurled insults and oaths, some questioning the superintendent's maternal ancestry.

As Jonathan Armbrister entered the deserted office, he found only his personal secretary, Miss Leonard, still at her desk.

"I'm sorry, Imogene," he said in an apologetic voice. "Were you afraid to go home?"

"Oh, no sir. Are you kidding? They don't scare me any. I knew you'd be coming back this evening. I asked all the security guards and the supervisors to file a report before they left to go home."

"Thank you. Thank you very much," Armbrister said as he slumped into his office chair. "Here, let me phone Bruce to come escort you home."

"No, that's okay. They're not going to do anything. They're just letting off steam. I did phone Bruce though, and he is keeping an eye on your house. Mr. Armbrister," the secretary started, and then hesitated, not knowing how to ask, "did you know that Mr. Livingston phoned after you left and told us to cancel the Christmas bonuses and the ham coupons?"

"He what?" Armbrister jumped to his feet with such vexation that it startled the secretary.

"Yes sir, he told us to pull them from the checks. We had already sealed the envelopes. He also sent a different memo to add to the envelopes." She handed the revised directive to him.

He read the memorandum. The wording had been changed from the compassionate, hopeful letter he had painstakingly composed, promising that all possible endeavors would be taken to re-open the plant.

"I can't believe that! If I had known…"

"I'm sorry. Should I have phoned you?"

"No, no, it's not your fault," he said as he let out a forced laugh. "It might be good you didn't phone me, or I might have just taken that weasel-faced Livingston by his gaudy silk necktie, and hung him from one of those fancy chandeliers at headquarters."

Imogene laughed with him —not that the comment was funny, but hoping it would ease the stress she knew her boss was feeling. The young lady had worked the last seven years for Mr. Armbrister as his personal secretary. After graduating from Fries High School, she had applied to replace the previous secretary who had retired after almost ten years with him. She needed the job very badly as both of her parents had become disabled. She was shocked when he offered her the job over other applicants with business degrees from Wytheville Community College.

Armbrister had hired her on one condition, however. She had to take time off at least two days a week to get an associate's degree from the community college. He said that the company would pay for tuition and books. One day she had incorrectly addressed an envelope he had given her containing the check and tuition invoice. She opened the envelope and removed the contents to transfer them to a new envelope. It was then that she noticed the check was written on the account of Mr. and Mrs. Jonathan Armbrister, not on a Washington Group corporate check.

If he had not been so good to her she would have quit. The

other women in the office were very jealous of her getting the position just out of high school. It didn't help that Imogene Leonard was, without doubt, the most beautiful girl in Fries. Although she wore the most conservative of attire—dresses and skirts down to her knees—when the other girls were wearing mini-skirts, even the most moderate clothing could not conceal the perfect figure the girl possessed. Her naturally wavy ebony hair hung halfway down her back. In the sunlight it glowed like coal that had morning dew covering it. Her eyes were like chestnuts, bright brown, with small amber flecks. Her facial features, her cheeks, her eyes, her lips, looked as if God had hand-picked all of His flawless components to place them on one perfect face.

It wasn't surprising that a rumor started within the first year that the young girl was having an affair with the older man. She was always leaving work for hours at a time, then staying in the office with the superintendent as late as 7 p.m. What the others didn't realize was that she was traveling to Wytheville for classes, and had to work the late hours to finish her work which always had to be perfect. This office scuttlebutt was quickly squelched when it reached Mr. Armbrister's ears. The next day Mrs. Armbrister showed up at the office, carrying a dozen red roses. The wife, without saying a word, marched up to the secretary's desk.

"Imogene, these are for you my dear," the wife said loud enough for all the ears that were turned in her direction to hear. "I just can't thank you enough for all the things above and beyond your duties that you do for my husband. He used to come home stressed every evening. But you do your work so perfectly, and a lot of his also. He is so relaxed now in the evenings. I just don't know what we'd do without you."

Jonathan was glad he had taken his wife, Cynthia, with him that day to stay with relatives in North Carolina for awhile. It would be best for her not to be here, she'd just be one more thing for him to worry about. She had a way of speaking her mind.

The superintendent then noticed a half sheet of plywood covering the opening where a window pane had been broken.

"Mr. Armbrister, I'm sorry," Imogene said apologetically. "They did it this evening. They just don't realize how much you have done to keep this mill open. I had Buster put the plywood up. He's ordered a piece of glass from Vass-Kapps Hardware."

"Thank you, Imogene, but I'm afraid there's not much I can do now."

"Well, we'll pray about it; I'm sure God won't abandon us."

"Imogene, I'm sure I haven't told you enough how exceptional you have been. If I had a daughter, I would hope she'd be just like you. I know you don't have an easy job, working for me. I appreciate all you have done. If things don't work out, I promise I'll get you a good job in Galax."

"Mr. Armbrister," the secretary said, her eyes reflecting the moisture in them, "I can't imagine ever working for anyone but you."

Imogene got her purse and walked out the door. Jonathan watched as she strode toward the men. She stopped and said something to them. The men lowered their heads, awkwardly kicked their feet in the gravel, and then began walking down the sidewalk toward town.

The superintendent began reading over the very detailed report his secretary had prepared for him. He stopped half way through.

I can't believe that Livingston cancelled the bonuses and ham certificates, he thought to himself, then finished the reports.

He spent the next four hours looking through the year-to-date payroll reports. He just couldn't see how to eliminate 15% without crippling production, but he could not stand the thought of asking the employees to take a cut in pay. Even cutting his own salary in half would only generate a 1% reduction.

He dropped his head into his hands, and began diverting his attention to what could be done to make this as good of a Christmas as possible for the citizens of Fries. At midnight, he cut off the lights. Jonathan remembered what Imogene had suggested. There, with the darkness of the room pierced only by the moon reflecting off the river, he bent his head and began praying. Surely God would help him find a way.

He thought about driving across the street to his home, but instead pulled a worn blanket and pillow from the closet and stretched out on the sofa in the office.

5

NO HAM, NO BONUS, NO JOBS

announced the December 6 headlines of the *Fries Wildcat Spirit Weekly*.

No one could remember any year in which the Mill had not paid a bonus or given a Christmas ham. The employees realized it was a gift, but it had grown to be expected and needed. If they had just been given some advanced notice, they could have prepared for not receiving it.

About half of the eight hundred Mill employees lived in the town. The rest lived in the surrounding communities, bearing such names as Eagle Bottom, Stevens Creek, Providence, Hawkstown, Hilltown, Windytown, Brush Creek, Cripple Creek and Scratch Gravel. The employees who lived in the outlying communities had to drive to work, but they also usually had homes that sat on an acre or more of land. They usually put out large gardens that not only supplied fresh produce for the summer months, but provided enough surplus vegetables that they could can and freeze for the following winter. Many also raised one or two hogs in a pen as far from the house as possible. These pigs would be fattened with any scraps left over from the kitchen table mixed with grain bought from the local stores. This "chop" came in brightly printed cotton sacks that, once emptied, would be used to make everything from pillow cases to dresses for the young girls. The county families, even though poor, were fairly self-sufficient.

The town folk were quite different though. By the mid 1950's, residents were no longer allowed to keep livestock within the town limits. Most of the houses were built in close proximity, with no more than forty feet between them, not enough for a suitable garden. Occasionally two neighbors were either exceptionally good friends, or perhaps kin, and would pitch in together to put out a garden between them. The small plot would usually have some tomato, potato, cucumber, lettuce and corn plants.

Yes, the town was very dependent upon the Cotton Mill. This was not anything new. That was the plan from the very beginning.

In that beginning, the country had just welcomed a new century. In the spring of 1900, Colonel Henry Fries had stood on the cliffs overlooking the river beneath him and knew he had found the location for his third textile mill. Colonel Fries was of Moravian descent, a religious sect emphasizing that a strong, undying faith combined with a dedicated, untiring work ethic guaranteed a successful life. Colonel Fries had reached success at an early age and had already proved himself as an entrepreneur. His enterprises would become a string of textile mills to produce much of the cloth needed by this country, a railway line to move the cloth, and subsequently Wachovia Bank to manage the finances generated by his various business interests. When he made a decision, he acted on it and Katy-bar-the-door on anyone who should get in his way. By 1901 he had purchased the Bartlett family farm and started building the huge red brick building on the northern bank of the New River that would become the Cotton Mill. The reason he built there was that it was the perfect location for a hydro-electric dam to furnish electricity not only to this mill, but also to the town that would follow.

The Washington Mill would be ready to open in 1903, but the businessman knew he had to have a work force that lived nearer than the surrounding communities. Few workers would be willing to travel by horse or wagon for an hour or two, each way, to work a 10-hour day, so he began building three hundred houses that would be rented to the workers, and a town to offer the goods necessary to the survival of the residents.

Within a year, both experienced and novice workers from a 100-mile radius, from the mountain region of Coalwood, West Virginia, to the piedmont region of Winston-Salem, North Carolina came to this newly planned community. Before the year was out, two new churches and a company store had been built by the company, and people were settling into the boom town known as

Washington Mills Village. By 1903 the name was changed to Fries, in honor of the man who had made it all possible.

But Colonel Fries' vision was more than just a capitalist's dream. He had a sincere dream of creating a Utopian society, a community based upon the Moravian concept of faith and hard work. To be sure that his perfect society nurtured, and the "young children" of the village were kept in line, Colonel Fries made sure the town was managed and run by his hand-picked disciples. The town owned the houses, the churches and the store, so the employees/citizens had to stay in line. Anytime there were dissidents, just as in the religious sects of the 18th century, they were cast out of the village. They lost their job, and hence their home, and had to leave behind the security of the sanctum. These serfs usually left with no training or education for any other work, and usually without savings for the town was an experiment in modern day serfdom.

This type of monarchy was necessary in the beginning to create a town of this type, blending in people of different morals, faiths, and attitudes. Three generations had accepted the parental guidance of the Mill. Now it was time for the fourth, and they did not want to be treated like baby chicks being watched over by a mother hen. They were ready to fly the coop.

So the one positive thing the layoff did was create a new sense of independence among the newer generation. Many of the younger people were already making plans after the New Year to move to Roanoke or Greensboro to work in some of the new industries springing up. Parents were already using the layoff to emphasize to their children why they should study hard in school and go to college so they would never have to face problems like this.

It seems that in times of adversity, some people will turn to faith while others turn away. That Sunday the two main churches showed a larger-than-normal attendance, even though many of the regular members were absent. There was a joke that there were two types of members in churches; there were the pillars, and there were the caterpillars. The pillars were there Sunday after Sunday, supporting the church. The caterpillars crawled in on Christmas and Easter. On this Sunday, most of the pillars stayed at home, while the caterpillars showed up. Both pastors were kept for a long time after Church, counseling these families as to how they were going to handle the current economic crisis. They needed to find some thread of hope, and the two pastors did all they could to help find this hope.

Spunkie was again observed driving up and down the street, looking at the cars. As before, Bruce sat in his concealed patrol car in the alleyway between Vaughan and Main Street, observing him. Spunkie, apparently not finding the car or whatever he was looking for, again departed.

"That boy's gonna get himself in a heap of trouble," Bruce mumbled to himself.

On Dec. 9, the specially-called council meeting was opened by Buster Wilkinson.

"First on our agenda," said the vice-mayor, "will be a report by legal counsel on the status of the tied mayoral vote." He was now becoming more comfortable with his position as vice-chairman, and was already entertaining thoughts of running for mayor in the next election.

"Well," Doug Turner started, and then hesitated to scratch his head, "I have to admit, I've never had a trial case this puzzling. The town code doesn't address it. There is precedence from other towns, from flipping a coin, to continuing to have a special election until someone wins, to council voting on the winner. I'm not ready to recommend any of these over the others though."

The four council members looked at each other. They certainly did not want the responsibility of determining the winner. Suzie Young slowly arose from her chair, and lifted her hand.

"Suzie," Wilkinson said with obvious aggravation after noticing her, "we're not ready for questions. We haven't decided anything yet."

"No, sir," Suzie replied, "I don't have a question; I have an idea."

"So what is your idea, Suzie?" Buster asked in a condescending tone.

"Well, when my daddy was alive, if I had a question about

money, I went to him. If I wanted to go somewhere, or do something fun, I went to my mom. Both were my bosses, but they handled different things."

"Suzie," the vice-mayor asked, "just what in the world does that have to do with our problem of deciding who will be mayor?"

"Well, I just thought—" Suzie started to reply, but hesitated, seeing that Buster Wilkinson was not welcoming her suggestion.

"Wait," Doug Turner injected. "I think Suzie might just have something. There's nothing that says we can't have two people serving in the same position, a mayoral committee of two I guess. Jonathan is excellent at finances, and Herbie is excellent at finding creative ways of improving the quality of life of the townspeople. Sure, sometimes the concept might clash, but the town would have an excellent checks-and-balance system in place." The attorney turned to the two candidates in the audience, "that is, if the two are agreeable."

The two deadlocked candidates looked at each other. Both shrugged their shoulders as if to say 'why not?' Then both men broke into smiles and began nodding in agreement.

"That's fine with me," Jonathan said.

"Well, if Suzie thinks it's a good idea," Herbie said as he looked at Suzie, "I'm sure it's going to work."

A motion was quickly made, a second added, a vote taken, and, within five minutes, Herbie Bourne and Jonathan Armbrister were sworn in as co-mayors. An extra chair was brought to the council table, and the two men sat down, both smiling broadly. They conferred for awhile, then Herbie announced.

"Jonathan will be presiding over the meetings; I never did like the thoughts of that part of the job," he said with a grin.

The specially-called meeting was adjourned, with the agreement that the two co-mayors would begin presiding at the next scheduled board meeting on December 16.

6

Special Edition

Two heads are better than on:
The town chooses co-mayors
read the December 11 copy of the *Fries Wildcat Spirit Weekly*.

The reaction of the town was slightly optimistic, and a glimmering candle of hope began to flicker that the harmony of the town would be revived. Conflicting factions actually began speaking to each other on the street, with an occasional "Merry Christmas" being exchanged.

Charlie's Barber Shop began receiving a slow stream of customers and loafers again. Business was still far slower than usual though, so Horace took this opportunity to take a couple of weeks off to visit family in Georgia.

Mr. Phillips, the local banker, walked by on his way to the post office. Looking into the shop's window he saw Charlie's chair open. He stopped and entered.

"Okay for me to get a haircut, Charlie?" he asked.

"Sure, Rex," the barber answered, rising up from the chair where he had been resting. "I'm always glad to have the best head of hair in town in my chair."

The banker laughed. His hair was thick and curly, and everyone was always telling him he had the best head of hair in the world, with the exception of Jeff Chandler.

Mr. Phillips settled into the chair, looking forward to the next fifteen minutes. Like most men in Fries, a haircut from Charlie was more than just personal hygiene; it was both physical and psychological therapy.

"Well, Rex," Charlie started, "do you think the town's about to get back to normal?"

Rex had almost dozed off from the hypnotic effect of the sharply edged scissors beginning their rapid-fire snip, snip, snip through the thick hair.

"Yes, you know I think things might be starting to look up a little bit," Rex said in a low, drowsy voice. "Word's gotten out about both Jonathan and Herbie being named co-mayor, and I think that's satisfied most of the people. I've noticed most coming in the bank seem a little happier. I think they've decided that they can have a good Christmas; it might just be a little different than in the past."

"Yeah," agreed Charlie, "other than for the hotheads. They're just not happy unless they're stirring up trouble."

On Saturday morning, December 13th, the phone rang at the superintendent's house. Jonathan Armbrister awoke, startled, and looked at the clock. It was 6:50 a.m.

Hope there's nothing wrong with Cynthia, he thought as he quickly grabbed the phone.

"Hello," an anxious Armbrister answered.

"You company bastard," said a muffled voice, obviously disguised. "I'd be mighty careful when you set down to start your car this morning." The phone then went dead.

Armbrister was sure he recognized the voice as that of Spunkie Akers.

It was then that Armbrister decided that perhaps Chief of Police Smith was right. Maybe things could get ugly. He looked in his address book until he found a name and telephone listing. He dialed the number.

"Hello, this is Piedmont Security, John Helmsman speaking." It was evident that the speaker was partially asleep, but trying to sound professional.

"Hi John. This is Jonathan, Jonathan Armbrister, how are you? I'm sorry I woke you up."

"Hey, Jonathan. That's no problem. How are you? I haven't heard from you for awhile. What can I do for you?"

"Well, John, the corporation's finally decided to shut down the plant here in Fries, maybe for good, and well, it's gotten a little ugly here. I've sent Cynthia to stay in North Carolina. Are you working on anything now?"

"Nothing I couldn't reschedule to head up to Fries." John answered. "Give me about an hour to take care of some things. I should be there by ten."

"Great! I'll meet you at my house. By the way, you might bring something to check my automobile. The phone caller mentioned a car bomb."

John Helmsman's biggest client was the Washington Group. John had known Jonathan and Cynthia Armbrister for several years, and considered them as two of his closest friends, if one could say John actually had close friends. After returning from Vietnam, the former Army Ranger liked to keep a wall separating himself from those around him, even those he considered friends. After hanging up the phone, John yawned and dropped his head into his hands to rub the sleep from his eyes. He jumped when he felt a soft hand touch the middle of his back. He had forgotten he had company.

"Who was that, honey?" a soft, kittenish voice asked.

John turned around and looked down into the half-closed eyes of a most fetching blonde. Even at this early hour, the woman looked breathtaking.

"Oh, it was a client." John began to explain. "I'm going to have to run up to Fries for a couple of days. They shut the mill down, and there have been some threats."

The squinted lids opened, revealing a set of eyes that always reminded John of the blue coral as seen through the crystal-clear waters in the Bahamas. A pout came to the girl's full luscious lips.

"Oh John," she purred, "I thought we were going to be able to spend the whole weekend together. You promised."

"Yes, I thought we could too," he said. "But Washington Group is my biggest account. I don't say no to them."

The shapely blonde, sat up in bed, letting the blanket drop to her waist as she began to stretch seductively.

"Are you sure I can't change your mind?" she whispered into his ear. Her warm breath swept over his lobe and down his neck. The arousing touch of her wet lips to his jaw brought back the memory of the previous night's activities. Her fingers were now curling, her French cut nails sliding down his back-bone, leaving a sensual trail that few men could resist, and she knew it.

Wow! She can be distracting, John thought to himself.

Jessica Trigiani was gorgeous, absolutely drop-dead gorgeous. She had almost become a model, but lost by a nose, a slightly oversized nose—at least by American standards. When it came to an alluring woman, the nose made her even more statuesque in a classic, Mediterranean way. But with the perfection required of a model, the facial feature made her less than flawless.

So instead of walking a runway, she was quickly hired to walk the aisles as a stewardess for Piedmont Airlines. Every Piedmont advertisement, from billboards to slick magazine ads, carried a photo of the long-legged blonde bent over a passenger; her eyes sparkling like blue sapphires, her snug uniform looking as if it had been painted on her, with the caption: *The Skies are More Beautiful When you Fly Piedmont Airlines.*

John looked at the clock and thought about calling his friend back and telling him it would be closer to noon before he'd be there. *After all, what was the hurry?* But then he remembered he never let pleasure, regardless of how titillating it might be, come between him and business. Realizing his responsibility, he laughed, shook his head, and leaned over to give the girl a quick kiss.

"Jessie, you're way too much," he said, just before slipping from beneath the covers and heading toward the shower.

Jessie gave a wolf-whistle as he crossed the room. This brought to his mind how the woman liked to surprise him in the shower. The first time, he was in the middle of shampooing. She startled him so badly he slipped and both of them went crashing to the floor. He knew he needed to take pre-emptive action.

"Jess, would you make some coffee-to-go for me, and maybe a BLT to have on the road?" John asked, trying not to sound demanding.

"Sure, baby."

That should keep her busy for the duration of the shower, he thought.

While showering, John began thinking about the last six months. He had met Jessie at "Renegades," a very popular nightclub in Winston-Salem which the young professional men and women frequented. He saw her on the dance floor with a much older man, who he later found out was a pilot. The older man never let her out of his sight, except once. The blonde started toward the restroom. John quickly made an excuse to his date that he needed to make a phone call. Picking up the phone just outside the ladies room, he pretended to talk. When the blonde came out, the phone next to John began to ring.

He clapped his hand over his receiver, turned to the blonde and said, "Excuse me Miss, perhaps you could answer the phone."

She looked at him, with a puzzled look, and then picked up the phone, "Hello?" she said.

"Hi, I noticed you are with someone tonight, and so am I." He turned slightly to reveal his moving lips to her. "But I'm not ever going to forgive myself if I at least don't go out on a limb and ask if I can have your phone number."

"Hmm, has no one ever told you it's dangerous going out on limbs, that someone might just cut it off?" She was giggling into the phone.

"Well, from the view I have from this limb, I'm willing to take that chance. I'm John."

"I'm Jessie, and actually I don't have a phone at the present. I'm a stewardess for Piedmont. Do you have a card with your phone number?"

"Yes, I have a business card."

"Well, leave it under the phone, because my date is coming in for a landing, about twenty feet away from you."

She then began to laugh on the phone, "No, ma'am, I assure you this is not the Renaissance Hotel. This is a night-club in downtown Winston-Salem."

By this time, the tall older man had reached the young blonde's side. She cupped her hand over the phone and whispered to her date. "It's a lady on the phone. I can't convince her this isn't the hotel." "Well, ma'am, try looking up the number again and redialing. I'm sorry, but I have to go now."

The blonde hung up, turned to her date, and added in a perky, professional voice, "And thank you for flying Piedmont."

John enjoyed the whole charade. He removed his business card from his coat pocket, and laid it on the shelf under the phone. He walked toward the Men's room, turning around in time to see the young woman reach over, and take the card as she walked by.

A week later, she had called him, and now they had been dating for the last half year. Not quite exclusively, but certainly more steadily than John was accustomed to. He soon finished his shampoo, shower, and shave, and picked out a blue striped oxford and pair of khakis from the closet. As he was dressing, he could hear and smell the sizzle of bacon and the coffee percolating in the kitchen. He removed three sets of pants, shirts and jackets from the closet, and slipped them into a suit bag. He pulled out a prepared overnight bag that carried socks, underwear, shaving kits, exercise clothes, and his "work uniform," which rounded out everything needed for a five-day trip.

He slipped on his oxblood loafers and a leather flight jacket. The jacket was well worn, and had more than one stain on it. It was a gift from a helicopter pilot who had crashed while serving with John as a "military adviser" in Vietnam before it had become a conflict. John had pulled him from a crashed bird. He left the bedroom and started into the kitchen.

Jessie was standing there, wearing nothing but one of John's shirt. Her legs were as long as his, and the tail of the shirt barely concealed her abundant curves beneath it. As he walked toward her, she turned around. The shirt only had the bottom two buttons fastened, and the top of the shirt nearly hung off the girl's shoulders. The blonde had found time between fixing coffee and a BLT to put on makeup. She bent over the countertop, setting the coffee travel mug down, and then placed her elbows on the surface. She framed her face with her hands, and in her most professional voice inquired enticingly, "Coffee, tea, or *me*?

"Well, let's see," John answered with a laugh. "How about coffee this morning, tea never, and *you*? How about the minute you walk through my door next week when you get back?"

"Okay, if that's the best offer I can get," she said. "I get back in from the Atlanta loop on Wednesday. I'll call you then. Sure you'll be back home?"

"Oh yeah, I'm sure it won't take more than a few days," he assured her. "And thanks for the breakfast."

He leaned over the counter to give her a quick kiss, knowing a long kiss and embrace would only encourage Jessie, and he would find himself not leaving.

"Hey, don't forget, we're going down to Mom's and Dad's this weekend," she reminded.

"Uh, yeah, okay."

John had tried to forget, hoping that the plan would be changed. He liked Jessie a lot, but meeting parents can take on a whole new meaning in a relationship, a meaning that he was not ready for.

Two and a half hours later, a '67 Corvette with a North Carolina license plate pulled into the rear of Jonathan Armbrister's house. A young man, early thirties, opened the door of the sports car and uncoiled his tall body from out of the low-slung seat. He stretched as he looked up at the house, owned by the company and provided to the mill superintendent. Even though his taste had always been more contemporary, he did find this house quite beautiful.

The house was a large, three-storey Queen Anne Victorian. It featured the steep-gabled roofs, each with a different ornate trim. A portico wrapped around the front and half way around both sides. Elaborate spindles connected with the top rails encircling the porch. From the house, one could see the entire downtown, but was partially blocked from the view of the factory by the Mill Office. There seemed to be a minimum of ten corners; John had never counted all of them. Each side had a bay window jutting out and the front had a bay window on each side of the entrance. The house was painted a bright sunny yellow with black trim. He never looked at the house without thinking about the gingerbread houses his grandmother used to make for him at Christmas. For John the sight of the house always brought back memories of the smell of gingerbread baking. This brought a smile to his face, but a longing in his heart for his grandmother who had long departed.

John Helmsman could see a few men at the mill gate across the road, but was able to sneak undetected to the rear door of the house. Standing there waiting was the Mill Superintendent.

"John, great to see you," Jonathan said as he greeted his friend.

"Same here," John said, then got straight to the point. "So

you've got some enemies? Tell me the events that have gotten you to this point."

Jonathan used to resent John's succinctness and his aversion to any closeness. He now overlooked the fact that the security consultant, even with an old friend, always seemed terse. Jonathan had once talked to a high school friend of John's who had told him that Vietnam had changed the man a lot, as it had a lot of soldiers.

Jonathan led the consultant into the living room and motioned for him to sit down. Jonathan spent the next fifteen minutes recapping the account of the last three weeks, starting with the election recount and the plant closing. John listened, taking notes, nodding occasionally. Jonathan finished with the most current event: the phone call with the car bomb threat.

"Let's take a look at your car," John said upon the completion of Jonathan's briefing.

John pulled a small mirror mounted on a chrome extension and a piece of carpet from his trunk. Lying on the carpet, he extended the chrome arm and thoroughly searched underneath the Lincoln. He got up, lifted the hood, and used the mirror to trace all the wiring. He opened the car door and lying down on the floor board, searched beneath the dash. He reached up and inspected the wiring to the ignition. He looked under the seats.

After fifteen minutes of scrutiny, he declared the automobile safe. To guarantee his work, John took the keys from Jonathan, slid behind the steering wheel, and turned the key on. The big V-8 roared to life. John let it idle for about sixty seconds, then turned the engine off and handed the keys to Jonathan.

"Looks clean," the security consultant said. "Usually if there's a phone call, it's just a threat. Want me to report it to the State Police?"

"No, no, let's not do that," said Armbrister.

"How well do you know the Chief of Police in town?" John asked.

"Bruce? Oh, I know him pretty good," Jonathan said. "Or as Bruce would say, 'fair-ly welllll'." Jonathan chuckled, using an exaggerated drawl.

"He's an older man," Jonathan continued after not getting the expected smile from his impersonation. "He's in his sixties, and does a good job as a small town officer."

"Phone him. Give him my name, and tell him I'd like to speak to him."

Jonathan looked at the front page of the phone book where he kept Bruce's number listed, and dialed it.

"Sergeant Smith, Fries Police Department," a voice answered.

"Hi, Bruce, this is Jonathan Armbrister. I have a gentleman here by the name of John Helmsman who would like to speak to you. I'm putting him on."

"Hello, Bruce. This is John Helmsman. I'm a security consultant from Winston-Salem. I hope you're having a good day."

"Yes, John, I'm having a fairly nice day, and I hope you are too." John heard the Chief reply in an extremely slow drawl and realized that Jonathan's impersonation had not been exaggerated. "What can I help you with?"

"Bruce, I do a lot of work for Washington Group," John began his vindication. "Mr. Armbrister contacted me this morning after receiving a threatening phone call. I don't think it's serious enough to contact the Sheriff's Department, but I would like to do a little investigating. I'll be glad to stop by your office, but I was hoping to avoid notice."

"What do you look like John?" the chief asked.

I'm 6'2", 220 pounds. I'm thirty-three years old. I have a military cut flat-top, black hair and brown eyes. I'll be wearing a brown leather jacket. I drive a red Corvette, but I'm leaving it parked at Jonathan's house, and will be walking downtown."

"Does Mr. Armbrister know who made the phone call?"

"He thinks someone by the name of Spunkie Akers."

"Yeah, that's what I thought."

"Chief Smith, I do have a pistol. I normally keep it in the car, not on me. Would you like to see my permit?"

"Naw, John, if Mr. Armbrister vouches for you, that's good enough for me. Let me know if I can be of assistance."

"Thank you very much. I will," John said, and then hung up.

"Any place in town that guys generally gather to talk?" John asked, turning back to Jonathan.

"Yes, there are two places. Either at Charlie's Barber Shop or Bud's Corner Drug store."

"I'm going to reconnoiter, see or hear what's going on. I'll be back in a couple of hours. Maybe you'd better just stay put here."

John walked the hundred yards down to the Mill entrance where the sidewalk began. At the foot of the hill, another fifty yards down, the sidewalk leveled at the beginning of Main Street. He walked first into Charlie's Barber shop, knowing this business location was often the best source of information.

There were two older men sitting in the chairs talking. John saw a man resting in the barber chair. He walked in.

"Hi, I'm passing through town," John said in a cheerful voice. "Could I grab a hair cut?"

Charlie reached for a crutch and moved to the back of the chair.

"Sure, just take a number," the barber said with a chuckle.

John climbed into the seat.

"I'm not sure if I can find enough hair there to cut," Charlie said.

"Yeah, I like it short and flat." John laughed, and then added. "The last time I came through, it seemed there was a whole lot more going on. Town seems kinda dead today."

"Yeah," Charlie answered as he studied the stranger's face in the mirror on the opposite wall. "They shut the Mill down yesterday. Everyone's trying to figure out how to make it through Christmas."

"Ouch, that's gotta hurt, this time of year. How's the people taking it?" John said, as he slowly began to pick up the local dialect.

"Well, some's taking it okay, but others are pretty ticked off. I've never seen the town so divided."

"Well, it seems a pretty peaceful town. I don't guess anybody will cause any trouble, will they?" John said, trying to not sound interrogatory.

John saw one of the older men, frail and slim; jerk his head up at the inquiry.

"Well, even peaceful towns have their hotheads," Charlie answered, then redirected the subject. "So what kind of work do you do?"

"I'm a business consultant." John replied in a well-prepared answer. "I travel through the surrounding states, trying to find locations to open new businesses."

"Well, if you can think of any businesses to bring to Fries, I think we'd be happy to see them," Charlie said as he looked over the top of his glasses at the young man, still not quite sure what to make of him.

"Yeah, I sure will," John promised.

"Well, there you go. I feel guilty charging you for no more of a haircut than that," Charlie said as he rubbed the spicy-smelling, soothing hair tonic into his customer's scalp.

"Looks good," John said, running his hands over the flattop. "You men have a good day."

"Yes, you too," Charlie called back as he began climbing into the idle chair again. "Come back and see us."

"So who are the hotheads I'd better not get in way of while I'm here?" John said with a short laugh as he was walking out the door.

"Well, I think you'll know them when you see them," Charlie said with a grin.

The frail old man that had been sitting almost asleep looked up and said, "Just ask 'em if his name's Spunkie."

Charlie watched John as he left. Charlie always had a sixth sense about people. Even though the young man seemed nice enough, although somewhat stiff, Charlie was sure there was more there than met the eye.

John strolled slowly down the street, studying the faces and movements of all he met. He could tell a lot just by observing people. This was a skill he had learned while in Special Forces Intelligence. By the end of the block, he could have told which of the six people he had passed would be capable of violence. He entered the corner drug store, noticing there were about eight people inside, mostly men.

"Hello neighbor. Have a seat. We'll be right with you," Bud greeted him.

John sat down at an empty table between two groups of customers. An attractive girl, pony-tail tied back, quickly rushed over to him, her pad and pen in hand.

"Yes, sir, what would you like?"

"Well, how about a ham and egg biscuit," John said, looking

down at the breakfast list, "with mayonnaise and a slice of tomato. And a cup of coffee, black."

"Yes sir, coming right up."

John began to study those around him, listening to several conversations at once. Then his adroit ears picked up the words, "He needs to be run out of town, maybe in a coffin."

John glanced over to the speaker, an unshaven man in his mid twenties, about his size, dressed in dirty jeans and sweat shirt.

"Well now Spunkie, I don't like what's going on either, but violence ain't the answer. I ain't even sure that Armbrister's responsible for this lay-off. I've heard tell that he..."

"What the hell do you mean? He's the damn superintendent!" Spunkie interrupted. "You need to decide which side you're on, Clarence."

"I'm just saying..."

"Here you go, sir. Is there anything else?" The young girl asked, setting down the breakfast order.

"No, this is all, thank you," John said quickly, anxious to get back to the conversation.

The man John identified as Spunkie then leaned over and lowered his voice. John quickly got up with his cup of coffee and walked to a corner display of post cards. He stood immediately behind Akers, and pretended to examine the cards.

"Well, you need to decide," Spunkie hissed. "We've got'em where we want'em. I tell ya, he's scared shitless. You could hear his knees a'knockin over the phone this morning. He's ready to haul his sorry tar-heel ass back to North Carolina for good."

Spunkie then stood up abruptly, bumping John away from the postcards.

"So if you're with me," Spunkie said in a low voice, "have you ass at the front gate at two. We'll show them they might push these old farts around, but they can't treat us like shit."

John moved further down the counter, as if he had to worry about Spunkie apologizing for bumping him, and then slowly turned back. He watched Spunkie exit, get into an old pick-up truck, and pull out amid a cloud of smoke from his tires.

John went back to enjoy his breakfast, at the same time scanning for other conversations. The diverse discussions ranged from how they were going to buy presents to if the unseasonably warm weather would change before Christmas. John felt he had heard enough and stood up to return to Jonathan's house. He stepped up to pay his tab, when an older man in uniform walked in.

"Hello, Bruce," Bud greeted the office. "Ready for your ice-cream cone?"

"Yes, guess I am, Bud."

Bud began dipping a single scoop of vanilla ice cream onto a cone.

Bruce surveyed the drug store, and then his eyes locked on John. The investigator gave a slight smile, and an even slighter nod of the head. Bruce studied the young man, turned away, as he gave a slight nodding of his head in recognition.

7

"Well, something's up," John reported as soon as he entered Jonathan's rear door. "They're planning to meet at the front gate at 2 p.m. I suggest we notify the State Police."

"No, no, I still think that would just make things worse," Jonathan said, shaking his head. "The town's been through enough already. I still think it's just a few hotheads. Mostly Spunkie Akers."

"Yes. He's definitely the instigator."

"I just don't think he'll get a lot of people to back him. Maybe just a few of the impressionable young kids. I know the Grayson County sheriff. Here let me call him."

Jonathan looked in his roller desk for the sheriff's home phone number and dialed. John listened as the superintendent talked.

"Hello," a voice answered.

"Hello, Herb. This is Jonathan Armbrister. How are you?"

"Well, hello Jonathan. I'm good. How are you?"

"Well, we might have a problem brewing here. I don't know if you've heard. We had to shut the Mill down, and a few rabble rousers have made some threats. I think we might have a few show up at two this afternoon to cause some mischief. I don't think it will be much, but do you think you could send a couple of deputies down to my house, about 1:15?"

"Yeah. I think I just heard on the radio where I have two deputies at Riverside investigating a wreck. I'll send them on down."

"That'd be great, Herb! You and Gladys have a great Christmas."

"Sure will, same to you and Cynthia."

"Let me give you some background information on Spunkie Akers," the superintendent said after he hung up the phone, and had turned back to John. "His mom died about two years after he was born. He had a really great dad, Chuck. Chuck drove a truck for us. One night, about five years ago, he and another driver, Wilson Young, were hauling a load of cloth to North Carolina down Fancy Gap Mountain. Wilson was driving—"

"I believe I remember hearing that story," John interrupted. "Wasn't it around Christmas?"

"Yes, three weeks before," Jonathan said and began again. "Where was I? Oh, yes, so the air-brakes went out on the rig. They probably could have made it down to the bottom of the mountain and got stopped except they met a station wagon in a curve. Instead of taking a chance on hitting that car, Wilson took the rig over the mountain. It killed both of them. The station wagon was carrying a family of six that would have died if the truck had hit them."

"So Spunkie thinks he needs to be a bad-ass for a payback?" John said in a non-sympathetic tone.

"Well, actually Spunkie was already bad by this time. After this he just didn't have anyone to keep him in line at all."

"Really?"

"Yeah, he was always getting in trouble as a kid, breaking windows, vandalizing, drove poor old Chuck up the wall. Spunkie, like his dad, was a pretty good baseball player. He could really throw that ball. Some people said pro scouts had clocked his fast ball at 93 miles per hour. His senior year, Fries was playing at Independence, our big rivals, and Spunkie was pitching. Some of the Independence players were really razzing him from the bench. They didn't know his mom was dead, or didn't care, and they kept calling him 'Momma's Boy.'"

John listened intently. From Jonathan's tone he could tell something somber was about to be revealed.

"Spunkie threw a fast ball, and hit one of Independence's players in the head. Cracked his batting helmet. Knocked him out cold. The guy laid there for several minutes, and then they had to take him to the hospital. Blood was actually coming out of his ear. It was pretty darn scary. Everyone assumed it was an accident. The whole time they were working on the batter at home plate, Spunkie was throwing to the third baseman to stay loose. But then, just before the ump started the game back, Spunkie walked over to the first baseline and hollered out to the Independence bench, 'So do anymore of you a-s-s holes want one in the ear?'"

"You've gotta be kidding!" John said in amazement.

"I kid you not. The benches emptied, and there was one heck of a free-for-all. They had to call the game. Coach Martin threw Spunkie off the team. Even though Spunkie was only four months away from graduating, and maybe looking at a pro contract, he dropped out of school. Needless to say, after that, no pro team would even look his way."

"He does sound like a mental case."

"He worked several jobs, never more than a few months at a time; just enough to keep Chuck off his back. But then, when Chuck died, Spunkie got the $25,000 life insurance settlement, and hasn't worked a day since. Well, he does do a little barn painting," Jonathan said, and then added with a laugh, "and once in while a little car painting. But he spends everything on beer and pot, so I hear. I understand the money's about gone, so he may be dealing now."

"Yeah, I recognized that glaze in his eyes this morning," John said in agreement. "You don't get that from beer."

The men's conversation was interrupted by the sound of a car pulling into the driveway. The two deputies had arrived in a single patrol car promptly at 1:15. As arranged, they pulled into the back of the Armbrister house.

John met them, and introduced himself. The older deputy, about 35, short, stocky introduced himself as Deputy Carrico. The younger officer, standing behind Carrico was in his early twenties, about 6', 180. He quietly identified himself as Deputy Honaker. John took them into the kitchen and initiated the briefing.

"Jonathan doesn't think it's going to be more than a few local punks," John said, "with a guy named Spunkie Akers as the ringleader."

"Yeah," the deputies looked at each other and began to laugh. "If anyone is going to cause trouble, it'll be Spunkie."

"If you agree," John offered, "I thought one deputy and I will go to the office. How about you and me, Officer Carrico?"

The security consultant had instantly sized up the two officers, the confidence they showed, the way they carried themselves, and easily identified Carrico as the person he'd want to have watching his back.

"Sure. Sounds good," Carrico answered.

Normally the ranking deputy would never have let a civilian make the plan, and expect him to go along, but Carrico could tell Helmsman had done his homework, and knew his way around a stakeout.

"From there we will have surveillance of the south and east side of the mill," John said, pointing to a map Jonathan had provided. "We can take a radio with us, and Deputy Honaker could set up base here at the house where he can watch the north and west side of the facility and the upper parking lot."

"Okay. Sounds good," Honaker answered, nodding his head in agreement, content to be in the background.

"Jonathan, will you dial Bruce again for me, please?" John requested, turning back to his friend. The deputies looked at each other. They had seldom heard anyone other than Mrs. Armbrister call the important man by his given name. The superintendent did so, and handed the phone over to John when it began ringing.

Bruce answered.

"Hello, Chief, this is John Helmsman again. It was good seeing you in the drugstore."

"Oh, yes, John. Did you find out anything?" Bruce asked.

"Yes, I did. It seems Spunkie Akers has planned some illegal action at the Washington Group complex around fourteen-hundred hours today. Deputy Carrico and I will be staked out in the main office building; Deputy Honaker will be manning the radio at Jonathan's house. You can coordinate with him."

"Ten-four," the Chief answered. "I'll park my unit at the southwest corner of the depot parking lot. I can observe anything going on east of the Mill, plus monitor traffic on Route 94 and Main Street."

John could sense the excitement in Bruce's voice. He remembered what Jonathan had said, and he felt confident if things got ugly, Bruce would handle himself admirably.

"We'll stay in contact," John said. He then hung up and conveyed the message to the deputies. "Bruce is going to be at the old train depot location to get a long range view. Does that sound suitable?"

Deputies Carrico and Honaker agreed that it did.

"The Sheriff told us it might be time that we stop putting up with this crap of Spunkie's," Deputy Carrico said. "He wants us to collect evidence and bring every charge we can on him. This boy needs to pull some hard time before he causes some real problems."

"Well, you guys get set up while I go change," John said, then went into the bedroom. There, he laid his overnight bag on the bed. He slipped into his "working uniform," which consisted of black paratrooper's pants, with side pockets, paratrooper's boots with a knife holster, a padded mesh shirt, his shoulder holster, and his well-worn brown leather flight jacket.

At 1:35, John walked outside where Deputy Carrico and Honaker were going over the final details. Jonathan unlocked the Corvette, reached beneath the driver's seat and pulled out a pistol. He started to slip it into his shoulder holster when he noticed the lead deputy staring.

"Want to see my permit," John asked.

"No," Carrico said. "I was just wondering what the heck you've got."

"It's a Heckler-Koch 9 millimeter semi-automatic. Bet you've never seen one."

"No, as a matter of fact, I haven't."

"Well, that's because they're not on the market yet. They only went into production this year. A friend of mine sent it to me to field test," John stated. "Want to look?"

He handed it over to Carrico, who began studying it, checking its balance, its weight, then sighting it.

"It's a beauty. So light, beats the hell out of these Colts we carry." Carrico was sounding like a kid eyeing a potential Christmas toy.

"Think you might want to shoot it after all this is over today?"

"Yeah, I think I might just like that."

The two men crossed the road and unlocked the small gate. Walking down a short sidewalk they were able to enter directly into the third floor of the office building. From this location, they had a bird's-eye view of the east and south section of the property thirty feet below.

"Surely they won't drive right up to the front gate," Carrico said. "I bet they'll come in the upper lot. You did remember to lock back the gate, didn't you?"

"Yeah, I did."

"Good." Carrico said with a smile, revealing to John that there must be a plan.

The two men went to opposite ends of the south-facing wall of windows to set up their makeshift observation points, which were straight back chairs set on top of desks. Carrico did a radio check.

"Deputy 4 to Deputy 25. Do you read me?"

"Ten-four Deputy 4. Deputy 25 reads you, loud and clear. Over and out."

Both of the men had found a naturalness with each other. They began exchanging life stories of high school and military. Neither yet felt the closeness to share more personal information.

Two o'clock arrived, with no events.

Ten after two, and still nothing was afoot.

Jonathan was beginning to feel a little relieved that nothing was going to happen, but felt bad that he had pulled the two deputies away from their other duties.

At 2:18 p.m., Deputy Carrico's radio crackled to life: "Deputy 4, this is Deputy 25. Do you read me?"

"Deputy 25, I read you. Go ahead."

"We have a dark-colored pick-up, Virginia plates 285-478, just pulling into the upper lot. Driver has been visually IDed as Spunkie Akers. Two unidentified males, late teens, in the bed, two more in the cab. Oops! There goes a beer can, looks like littering; possibly contributing to the delinquency of a minor if Spunkie bought the beer."

Silence followed for a few seconds, and then the radio began to transmit again.

"Suspect is getting something from the back of the truck. Looks like a burlap bag, and...hmm, can't make it out. Hmm, I do believe Mr. Akers has himself a pair of bolt cutters. Now I do wonder what he's planning on doing with those."

Ten seconds of silence.

"Oh my, my, my. Mr. Akers has just cut the lock on the gate. I do believe that is called breaking and entering."

"Are you logging this, Deputy four?" Carrico asked.

"Ten-four."

John allowed his usually stoic countenance to twist into a slight grin as he visualized the two deputies making listings of the violations that Spunkie Akers was piling up.

"So how much rope are you going to give him?" John asked.

"Well, I'd say we've given him enough already for the noose. Now, we need to get him to slip it over that thick head of his, and pull it tight," Carrico said with a laugh.

The radio came alive again.

"Suspect and four accomplices have entered the yards, and are headed toward the office building along the west side. I will lose visual in ten seconds. You should have visual soon after that. I do think we have a drunk in public charge here. Over and out."

A few seconds passed. John then saw some young boys walking quickly to the front of the office building below.

"Ten-four, we have a visual on the suspects," Carrico reported back to Honaker.

Just then John saw something out of the corner of his right eye. Something was happening down on the lower lot. A young girl with a wool cap covering her head had suddenly appeared and was walking across the lower lot, carrying something rolled up in her arms. She ran up the steps outside the main factory building. From there she stepped on to a ledge that didn't appear to be anymore than a foot wide.

What is she doing? Jonathan wondered to himself.

"Carrico, look over there on the east face of the mill building. What is that girl doing?"

Carrico took a pair of binoculars and began studying her.

"I—I can't tell. If she'd turn around—. She's, she's tying the end of something off to one of the windows. She's gonna kill herself. Think we should go after her?"

"Well, I'd hate to startle her and make her fall. She looks to be okay. Is that a sign? What does it say?"

"Can't make it out," Carrico said. Turning back to the scene below them, he asked, "What's our visitors up to now? Hmm, let's see what they have in that burlap sack. Oh, looks like some spray paint, looks like we have some vandalism going on here. He's getting something else out, some other bags. Oh, rocks. I guess I know what he's going to do with those."

Then, even through the glass windows, the two men could hear the whooping and the hollering, followed by the sound of broken glass down on the first floor.

"Come on. Come on Spunkie. Now break into the office," Carrico urged as he kept watch with his binoculars.

Just then, through the partially opened curtains, Deputy Carrico saw Spunkie wind up, and cut loose, like a centerfielder throwing a runner out at home. A second later, the glass pane just above Carrico's head shattered, covering the deputy with broken glass. He jumped off the desk, shaking the shards of glass off his uniform.

"Okay, sounds like destruction of private property," he said, then turned and grinned at John. "I'd say this will be enough to put our boy away for awhile. Would you testify to assault on an officer?"

"That's what it looked like to me," John agreed.

Peeking back through the pane-less window, they saw that the rock-throwing had halted. Spunkie caught site of the girl on the ledge, and had begun to walk toward her.

Carrico swept his binoculars to the young girl. She had just finished tying off a banner that read *"Peace on Earth,"* and carefully affixed in neat red letters was…*"And In Fries Too."*

John saw Spunkie approaching the wall, waving his hands threateningly. Now through the broken window, they could hear the perpetrator's voice more distinctly.

"Take that damn sign down you little brat" Akers screamed.

The girl answered, but neither of the two men could hear what she said.

"You take that sign down, or I'm gonna bean you upside that thick head of yurs!" To prove his point, Spunkie threw a rock that hit about fifteen feet away from Suzie.

"I'm going down there before he hurts her," Jonathan said.

"They may make a run for it, if they do, have Honaker waiting on them."

As John started down the steps, he heard Carrico speaking into the radio, "Deputy 4 to Deputy 25. Deputy 4 to Deputy 25...."

Just as John opened the door leading to the front lot, he looked up just in time to see a rock hit an overhanging eave, about five feet above the girl. The rock ricocheted and hit her in the head. Her legs wobbled, she took a step, began to teeter, and then toppled off the ledge. John's heart stopped, as he watched her fall about twenty feet. Halfway to the ground the girl's body crashed through some tree limbs. They partially broke her fall, but in the process flipped her upside down. The tough, hardened Vietnam Ranger felt his stomach knot up as he heard the girl's head hit the pavement with a sickening thud.

Within seconds John was by her side. Out of the corner of his eye, he saw the four younger boys begin to dash off. Spunkie was still standing there, his face twisted into a smirk.

"I didn't mean to hit her. The rock bounced," Spunkie said, but showed no remorse. "It was her own damn fault for being up there in the first place, putting up that stupid banner."

By this time Deputy Carrico was rushing out of the office building.

"Halt. This is Deputy Carrico. Stop where you are or I'll shoot," he screamed out without pulling his revolver, but the boys continued to run. He observed that they were running straight back to the pick-up truck where Deputy Honaker was waiting. He keyed the mic on the radio.

"They're on their way back there. Apprehend them, but first have Bruce call the rescue squad. We have a young girl hurt. It may be bad. She fell from the top of the Mill."

He raced over to John.

"How is she?" He asked as he leaned over John's shoulder, he then screamed, "Oh my God! Oh God, no! It's Suzie."

"You know her?"

"Yes. Yes. I know her real good. I'm close to her and her mother, Karen. She's like a daughter to me. Oh honey, hang on, hang on there. They're coming for you."

John heard the trembling in the officer's voice and looked over at him, seeing the tears glistening on the weathered cheeks of the deputy.

"She's breathing on her own. That's a good sign." John said as he pulled a white cotton handkerchief from his pocket and began to wipe the blood from the girl's forehead. He was whispering something to the girl. "I think all the blood is just from the cut on her forehead. I don't think we should move her though."

"We've already radioed for the rescue squad." Carrico said, then licked his lips and gathered his composure. "Yeah, I hear them now. Give me the key. I'll run and unlock the gate." The Deputy turned and gave a hard glare toward Spunkie. "You've done it now, Akers. You'd better hope and pray this girl makes it."

Akers just returned the scowl. After Carrico sped by him, Akers turned to leave. John had done all he could for the young girl lying there, breathing in short, shallow gasps. He turned his attention to Spunkie, who was almost to the steps leading up to the upper parking lot, and his truck.

"Hey, Akers," John barked out. "Just stop where you are."

"Yeah, and who'da hell are you to tell me anything?" Spunkie snapped back, after whirling around.

"I'm the man that's going to detain you until they haul your sorry ass off to jail," Helmsman answered, his patience quickly wearing thin.

Spunkie advanced toward John. Both men were about the same size, but that is where the similarities ended. Spunkie had bullied the boys and men around Fries for eight years. He had been in dozens of fights, usually against drunken boys smaller than he was. But even with guys his own size, he always won, because he had a jaw of steel. He could take three punches in the face, shake them off, and then land two of his own. He had never been beaten in a fight. Or at least none that he was sober enough to remember.

But John was different from anyone he had ever fought before. The security consultant wasn't a brawler; he was a trained fighter, even a killer. As a veteran of the Green Beret Special Forces in Vietnam, he was trained that a fight should last the minimum amount of time.

Spunkie took a wild right sidewinder swing at John's head.

John swept his left arm in front of his face, knocking the approaching blow harmlessly away. At the same time, his right fist, which had been cocked on his right hip, shot upward just as he stepped toward Akers. During the delivery of the punch, an instantaneous decision was made deep in John's trained memory. His fist went from being led by his knuckles, to being rolled backward toward his forearm, now being led by the heel of his open palm. Before Akers could even think about delivering another blow, his head shot back on his neck, as John's hand heel crashed into Spunkie's face, just above the upper lip where the nostrils flare. Akers' knees buckled, as he crumpled to the pavement. The thug's eyes instantly filled involuntarily with tears, as the warm salty taste of blood began to clog the back of his throat. The entire orchestrated attack of six motions took less than two seconds.

"You sonna bitch, you broke my nose!" Spunkie screamed as red bubbles rolled out of his mouth— like a mad dog foaming, and that's just what he was.

John wanted to do so much more than that. He wanted to stomp the face gawking up at him. His mind recoiled to one particular mission in 1965, one that he had tried to expunge from his mind's eye so many times. The memory was of a captured VC soldier who was being interrogated by John and one of his buddies. In an instant when his buddy had turned his attention, the VC pulled a concealed knife, and plunged its blade deep into the American soldier's heart. John had a haunting flashback of his own boot, pulverizing the enemy soldier's face time and time again until it was no longer recognizable. It had turned into a mass of mangled flesh, broken bones and tissue. The sight of the lifeless enemy soldier laying there was forever etched in the veteran's mind.

But John had changed; he would never allow himself to do that again. Besides, he thought to himself, this punk's not worth it, so he turned away. When he did, he saw the young blonde girl lying there, still bleeding, her long blonde hair now matted with blood on the left side. Her face had taken on a pale, ashen complexion, her breathing now undetectable.

"Damn kid should learn to mind her own business. She

deserved what she got," Spunkie mumbled through blood bubbles.

Rage raced through the former Ranger. He whirled around. Spunkie had risen up on his hands and knees, and was trying to stand.

John caught him in the stomach with the instep of his black leather paratrooper's boot. The wind swooshed out of Akers' lungs like the steam from an old locomotive; red spittle spewed as Spunkie crashed onto his back.

John rose up the right boot, bending his toes back to bury the boot heel down into the face of the still smirking Spunkie Akers. He would make sure Spunkie would never show that sneer to anyone else. Through the haze of the combat, almost as if at the end of a dream, John heard the sound of a siren, and a voice.

"John, no. No, John don't do it." He then felt a set of strong arms wrap around him, pulling him away from the prostrate felon.

He felt his body pulled backward until his boot fell back down to the ground. He turned to face a huffing Deputy Carrico. His first instinct was to deliver a disabling blow to the deputy and return to his attack on the scum lying on the ground. Then, an ambulance came screeching to a halt fifteen feet away.

"Did you see what that sonna bitch did to me?" Spunkie wailed, wiping the blood with his dirty t-shirt. "I'm going to sue his ass."

"This man came to the aid of an officer in distress." Deputy Carrico countered, gazing down at him. "And I'm still pretty distressed, so if you don't shut your mouth, I'm going to turn him loose on you again."

He then twisted Spunkie's hand behind his back, and slapped handcuffs onto him.

"Hey! That hurts! What the hell you doing that for?"

"Well, Spunkie, it seems we have about a half dozen charges against you," the deputy answered.

"What do you mean, what have I done?"

"Well," responded Carrico, "how about contributing to the delinquency of minors, drunk in public, disorderly conduct, breaking and entering, vandalism, destruction of private property, assault with intent to kill, and now, I just found out from my partner, that in pursuing your buddies, he had to drag them from the pickup, and in doing so, he found a bag of a very pungent smelling herb. Now, I wonder what that could be?"

"I don't know what'da hell you're talking about."

"You'll soon find out. Now you set down on those steps until I'm ready to take you to the patrol car."

By this time, John had made it back to the rescue squad. They were securing the young victim to a back board, being careful not to move her neck.

"How is she?" John asked anxiously.

"Not too good. The best thing we can say is that she's breathing on her own. Any idea what happened?" a rescue worker, with *Donnie* stenciled on his uniform, asked.

"Yes," John said and began giving an abbreviated recounting of the story of what had happened. "She was up there, putting up that sign. Spunkie Akers saw her, threw some rocks at her. One rock bounced off the eave there and hit her. I don't know if it knocked her out, or if she just fell. That's where the cut on her forehead came from. She hit that tree. That broke her fall, but also made her land head first. I sure hope she will be okay."

"Yeah, I do too," Donnie said solemnly. John thought he saw a tear running down the paramedic's cheek. "Her name is Suzie. She's probably the most loved kid in this town. They'd better put Spunkie in jail, because if anything happens to her, someone might just kill him. I'm not sure I won't do it myself."

They eased her into the back of the ambulance, and with lights flashing and sirens blasting, they headed toward Galax Hospital. John turned to Deputy Carrico, who was leaning on the handrail on the steps leading up to the parking lot, smoking a cigarette. John could see the officer was still quite shaken.

"I swore I'd given up these things. I had to bum one off of Honaker," Carrico said.

"Thanks, Deputy. For stopping me. I—I just snapped," John said.

"Let's just hope I won't be sorry that I did," the Deputy said, still fighting back tears as the ambulance turned the corner at the end of the street and started up the hill past the John Thorpe YMCA.

He flicked his half-smoked butt away, and then walked over to Spunkie, jerking him up by the belt buckle.

"Come on, Akers. You've got a long day waiting you."

Carrico and Helmsman scaled the steps to the upper parking lot, prodding the prisoner before them. The police cruiser sat behind the pick-up. As Deputy Honaker began pushing Spunkie into the back seat, the handcuffed man began spitting oaths at anyone within earshot.

"Now Billy," Carrico was saying in a fatherly tone, "you know your dad is going to tan your hide when he finds out about this. Now, if you can convince me, and the court, that Spunkie got you drunk, and talked you into this, then I bet I can get you off with just a slap on the wrist, and maybe probation."

"Yeah, he's gonna kill me. He'll whip me good." The young boy was blubbering, partially from the beer and partially from his trepidation. "That's what happened. He bought us beer. We've been drinking since this morning."

"How about the grass?" the deputy continued questioning. "Did he give you any grass? Be honest, 'cause I can give you a drug test to see if you're lying."

"Yes, Sir." The young boy was now scared to the point of telling everything. "But I only took one or two tokes; that's all. I didn't like it. I don't ever even smoke cigarettes."

"Well, Billy," Carrico said, squeezing his shoulders sympathetically. "You tell all this to the judge, and I'll tell him how helpful you've been. I'm going to let you go home now. Tell your dad you've gotten in trouble, but Richard Carrico is going to take care of you. You did know your dad and I played football together, didn't you?"

"Yes, sir, he talks about that a lot. Thank you, Mr. Carrico. I swear, I'm never gonna do anything like this again."

"I believe you, Billy. That's why I'm helping you out here."

The whole time Spunkie had been kicking the back seat, spitting on the rear window, and screaming profanities.

"Spunkie," Deputy Carrico said as he opened the back door, staring daggers at the prisoner, "I'm gonna tell you this once, and one time only. If you kick that seat, or cuss, or spit one more time,

I'm going to mace you, do you understand that? And then, just for good measure, I might just take this club and beat the ever-loving shit out of you. Do you get me?"

"Yeah, I getcha." Spunkie growled.

"Looks like I'm going to have a full evening booking this joker," Carrico said as he closed the rear door and turned to John, extending his hand. "I have a feeling he'll be looking at an easy five to ten. Can I get a rain check on shooting your H-K?"

"Sure. As a matter of fact, by around May, they're going to be hitting the market. Talk to your sheriff. See if he'd let me bring some up and have you guys try them out on the firing range."

"You bet I will. It's been great meeting you John, and call me Richard. I have to admit, I had never thought I'd have any use for a civvie in your profession, but you're an okay dude."

"Yeah, I guess we are misunderstood," John said, laughing. "I think the problem is that some guys are in this business just for the money. I do it because I love it. I served in the Green Beret and would probably still be in the military, but I took some shrapnel."

"Yeah, I kinda figured you had some kind of background, the way you handled Spunkie. It's taken three officers to restrain him before. It took you like, two seconds. Maybe when you come up, you could also show us a few of those moves."

"Well, I just hope the little girl, Suzie, makes it. I understand she's a charmer."

"Yes, she sure is. She means the world to me," the deputy said. He stopped, studying John's face intently, and then said, "John, would you do me a favor? Could you go by Karen's, the girl's mother, and tell her about the accident? Tell her I'm sorry I couldn't come. And maybe give her a ride to the hospital? Mr. Armbrister knows where she lives."

"Sure, I'll be glad to," John answered, detecting the officer's strong sense of affection for the mother.

John crossed the road to the Superintendent's house and filled Jonathan in on the details. The superintendent was very concerned about Suzie, only knowing she had fallen from the Mill building. John also told him of the number of charges they were filing against Spunkie, explaining he was sure it would be several years before he'd get back to Fries.

"I'm confident your need for my services are completed," John told his friend, "Does $500 sound fair?"

"That's very fair," Jonathan smiled. "I think you earned it."

"If it's all right though, I would like to stay overnight. Off the clock," John added.

"Okay. In case something flares up?" Jonathan questioned.

"Well, no," John began to explain. "Deputy Carrico, Richard, asked if we could go tell the girl's mother. He also wanted me to drive her to the hospital. I take it he's very close to the family."

"Yes, they are very close," Jonathan agreed. His voice then took a weighty inflection. "Yes, we'll go up and tell her, and then you drive her to the hospital. You might stay with her for awhile. She'll need someone. Suzie is everything to her." Jonathan then added, in an almost incoherent murmur, "Suzie is everything to all of us."

"I take it Suzie is the daughter of the man that died in the truck accident with Spunkie's father?" John asked.

"Yes. That's right. She is."

The two men pulled up in front of the Young house, located on Third Street. Railroad Street was the lane nearest the river and rested about twenty-five feet above the tracks. On the same elevation as Railroad Street was Main Street, which served as the only avenue in and out of town. From Main Street, a terrace of four narrow roads ascended up a steep mountain slope. The streets were in order; First, Second, Third, and finally Top Street.

Prior to 1955, when the town owned all the houses, a person's address also denoted their position in the town hierarchy. The local businessmen and Mill supervisors lived on Railroad and Main Street. The shift bosses lived along First and Second, depending upon their seniority. Then laborers lived along Third and Top Street, except for one large, impressive house at the very end of Top Street. It was a two-story built on this highest street, and had a breathtaking view. Mr. Ace and Miss Minnie lived in this house. As promotions were made, it was a coveted privilege to pack up your family and move down one street. Wilson Young's highly compensated truck driving position had earned the Youngs a Third Street address.

Jonathan and John walked to the front door of the simple, box-shaped house. As with most homes on the top three streets, the residences had no front yards, and meager back yards. A short walkway connected the front door to the sidewalk. Jonathan took a deep breath, let a sigh wheeze from his lips, then knocked on the front door.

The door opened. John looked at the short, slim, attractive woman and found it hard to believe she could have a teenage daughter. With her blonde hair pulled back into a pony tail, she didn't look a day over twenty-five. A white powder smudged her face.

"Well, hello, Mr. Armbrister. To what do I owe this honor?" she asked. "Excuse my appearance. I've been baking cookies. Come in, but please excuse the house."

"No, Mrs. Young," Jonathan uttered, as he took the woman's hands into his, "we don't have time. Umm, if you will, grab your coat. Suzie has had an accident."

Her face turned chalky, leaving the flour splotches barely noticeable. She partially collapsed, falling to the side against the door frame, using it for support.

"Oh my God, Suzie? My Suzie! What's wrong?"

"There was an accident," Jonathan said, trying to appear calm. "She...she was putting a banner up on the Mill, and well, John will give you the entire story, but well, she fell. She was, she was unconscious when the ambulance got there. I'm sure she will be okay. I'm sure she will."

Mrs. Young stood there, her hands clamped over her face for a few seconds, and then she inhaled deeply, turned around and with remarkable repose grabbed her coat from the closet. She started out to the car, but just as she was ready to close the door behind her, she stopped.

"Just a minute, please," she said as she went back inside, grabbed a small New Testament from the coffee table, and stuck it into her coat pocket.

Jonathan opened the front passenger door for her. Normally she would have insisted upon riding in the back and letting someone as important as Mr. Armbrister ride in the front, but she was too disquieted to consider her impropriety.

"This gentleman's going to drive you to the hospital. He's John

Helmsman from Winston-Salem, and is a very good friend of mine," Jonathan said as John slid behind the wheel. "He's going to drive you to the hospital and stay with you tonight. If there is anything you need, anything at all, clothes for you or Suzie, food, anything at all, you just let me know, and I'll pay for it."

"Thank you, Mr. Armbrister," Karen said as she took the superintendent's hands in hers again. "You are a good man, a truly good man. I'm so sorry some of the people in this town have treated you the way they have. They just don't know you like I do."

"Thank you, Mrs. Young. That means a lot to me," Jonathan said as he squeezed her hand. "I'll keep Suzie in my prayers. She is such an angel. I know she will be okay."

Mrs. Young just nodded her head.

"John," Armbrister said, "I'll walk home from here. You take care of her."

John Helmsman had never felt so inept. He simply could not think of the words to say, so he remained quiet. He knew the directions to the city, but when he got to the Galax limits, he asked how to get to the hospital. Karen, clutching the New Testament tightly in her hand, directed the security consultant to the Galax Memorial Hospital parking lot.

8

Once they pulled into the space marked *Emergency Room Visitors Only*, John quickly jumped out and ran to the passenger side of the car. By the time he arrived, Karen was already half-way to the hospital's glassed entrance. John trotted and managed to catch the woman just as she entered the lobby. Mrs. Young led John at a brisk pace to the elevator which took them to the Third floor. Karen rushed toward the Emergency Room Information desk.

"We're here for Suzie Young," the mother called out while on the run, still ten feet away from the information desk. "She was brought in with a head injury."

"Are you family?" the nurse asked, looking at the two of them.

"Yes, we are," Karen said, not wanting to take the time to explain.

"She is in surgery. We will take your information," the nurse in a starched white uniform said, passing the clipboard across the desk, "and then you can take a seat. We'll have a doctor come out as soon as possible."

The two sat in silence for what seemed an hour, but was actually only fifteen minutes, when a doctor, in scrubs, mask hanging off his face, approached them.

"Mr. & Mrs. Young?" he asked.

"Yes," Karen answered, as she and John stood up.

"Suzie has sustained a severe trauma to the rear portion of her brain, leading to a swelling of the occipital lobe," the doctor explained, a slight, re-assuring smile on his tired face. "We have arrested the swelling, but are concerned with the initial trauma. She is still unconscious. We do have her on a respirator, although she was breathing on her own when she was brought in. We hope to have her in a room within the hour. When we do, we will come get you and take you to see her. I'm not going to say that she's out of the woods, but I've seen much worse who have made it. We do have some fears that her vision will be affected, and there does appear to be some paralysis."

John felt Karen begin to crumble. He quickly wrapped his arm around her. She turned to hold on to him. The doctor looked down at the small New Testament clinched in Mrs. Young's hands.

"I see you've brought a higher power," he said. "Why don't you go down to the hospital cafeteria? You'll be more comfortable there. We'll page you when your daughter is out of surgery."

John and Karen retraced their steps to the elevator and stepped in. The door slid closed, leaving the two alone. John stole a glance over at the woman's profile. Even in her plain cotton dress, her hair pulled back in a pony-tail, no make-up, she was by far one of the most stunning women he had ever seen. Not beautiful in the classic, sculptured way Jessie was, but in a more natural, captivating breath-of-fresh-air way. John redirected his attention to the light panel until the door opened into the lobby.

"You find us a seat," John said, trying not to sound domineering. "I'll get us something. What would you like?"

"Oh, just coffee I guess, black," Karen replied in a subdued voice.

"You really should eat something," John said. "It may be a long night, Mrs. Young."

"Well, maybe just some dessert, you choose," the mother said, offering a slight smile to John, "and please call me Karen."

John welcomed making decisions, and seldom abdicated the responsibility, but he wasn't too keen on the challenge of choosing a woman's sweets. He examined the assortment of desserts through the display glass. He finally selected a blueberry pie, and then added a peach cobbler.

"Could you give me a bowl," he asked the young perky brunette wearing the white serving uniform, "with two scoops of vanilla ice-cream?"

"Sure, coming right up," the short, athletic-looking girl, about nineteen answered, as she smiled flirtingly at the handsome older man, "and would you like something else?"

Usually, he would not have let such obvious coquetry pass without reciprocation, but tonight for some strange reason, he had no interest.

"No," he said, smiling politely, "I guess that will be all."

He placed the desserts on a tray, poured two cups of black coffee, and paid the cashier. He turned around. The room was almost empty so it was easy to pick out the blonde pony-tail. Karen was sitting across the room by the windows, her face buried in her hands.

"I couldn't quite make up my mind," he announced as he set down the tray, "so I got both peach cobbler and blueberry pie, and thought we'd share."

"Both are my favorites, Mr.-," Karen began to reply.

"Helmsman," the security consultants finished, "but please, call me John."

John sat down and began dividing the dessert into halves. He then took a serving of ice cream and holding it over the top of Karen's desserts, lifted his eyebrows to her in a questioning gesture.

"Yes, please," Karen answered, allowing herself a slight giggle. "Thank you John. I'm not used to being waited on."

"It's my pleasure," John answered, a little surprised at his small act of servitude.

Both lifted their coffees to take a drink at the same time. Their eyes engaged for a moment. John looked into her soft, moist eyes, more beautiful than the bluest sky he had ever seen.

Karen gazed into his dark brown eyes. She thought how perfect they matched his strong, firm face. It was a face that showed no emotion though. Then, feeling strangely uncomfortable, Karen dropped her eyes and began to take a bite of the cobber a la mode.

"So tell me what happened, John. I need to know," the mother asked in a tone showing both maternal concern and a dreadful fear of hearing the actual details.

"Well, as Jonathan told you, I do security and investigation work," John began slowly. He knew that this account needed to be more sensitive than his usual "just the facts" briefing. "He had phoned me when things got a little ugly. I spent this morning investigating. I found out that Spunkie Akers was instigating some suspicious activities involving a small group of young boys. He wanted them to meet him at fourteen…at 2 o'clock at the mill 'to get even,' as he said."

"Did Mr. Armbrister tell you about my husband and Spunkie's father?" Karen questioned.

"Yes, he did," John answered, and in a moment of compassion, unconsciously reached over and placed his hand on Karen's. Her hand tensed, and he realized what he had done. She made no effort to move her hand though.

John smiled, patted her hand, and began to take a bite. He slowly chewed his blueberry pie, giving himself a few seconds to collect his thoughts.

"We phoned the Sheriff," he continued. "And he sent down two deputies, Carrico and Honaker." John noticed a slight smile of recognition at the mention of the first officer.

"Suzie actually showed up before Spunkie and the four teenagers. She had climbed onto the narrow ledge at the Mill Building, and was tying up a banner. At first we couldn't read what it said, but when she finished, we saw that it said 'Peace on Earth, and…' John stopped talking. He was suddenly finding it difficult to control his emotions. He was usually more professional than this.

"'And in Fries too,'" Karen finished. "I saw her working on that banner last night; I think she might have gotten it from the Church."

"Well, Spunkie and the four teenagers showed up," John started speaking again, determined to report the happenings without losing control. "They started to throw rocks at the windows, and then he, Spunkie, saw Suzie and the banner. It really pis…, it really made him angry. He started screaming at Suzie to take it down. She refused, and he began throwing rocks at her. I don't think he meant to hit her. He was just trying to scare her, but…"

"Spunkie doesn't always make the right decisions," Karen said, shaking her head almost as if in a trance. "That's for sure."

"Well, I began running down the stairs, hoping to stop things. Just as I ran out onto the front lot I'm sure I saw a rock ricochet off the eave of the building, bounce down, and hit Suzie somewhere around the head. I'm not sure if it actually knocked her out, or just scared her, but that was when she fell off the ledge."

Karen put a hand to her mouth as she fought to hold in a scream, and instead, exhaled a low, moaning whimper. John reached over, took her other fist in both of his hands and continued.

"Just before she got to the pavement, her feet got tangled in a tree limb, and it broke her fall. I really think that saved her life, Karen, I really do." He did not tell her that the tree limbs also flipped her so that she landed head first.

"I was the first to get to her. I made sure she was breathing, but I knew not to move her. Within ten minutes, the rescue squad was there. They did a good job, a great job. As good as I have ever seen. So that is when Officer Carrico asked me to come tell you, and take you to the hospital. He really seems to care a lot for you two."

"Yes, Richard does like to take care of Suzie and me," Karen said with a smile. "Sometimes he tries too hard to be a substitute daddy, and it aggravates Suzie"

"Karen," John said, as he softly patted her hands, "I know that everything is going to be okay. I just know that it is."

John now wished he had more faith, or any faith, so that he could say the right words to her. Words that would make her feel comforted and give her hope. They both grew silent as they ate their dessert and drank their coffee.

When they finished, Karen pulled her hand from John, temporarily disappointing him. Then she took his hand in hers. He felt her small fingers, so soft and delicate, fold around his large hands.

"Thank you so much for what you've done," she said, squeezing his fingers.

"I've done little, but I will do whatever you need. You just let me know."

Just at that moment, the speaker announced *The parents of Suzie Young will be allowed in the recovery room in 10 minutes.* Ten seconds later the message was repeated.

The smile left Karen's face as the reality of the mishap returned to her. She quickly gulped the last drink of coffee, and stood up. She reached over, and took John's hand, not in a romantic way, but rather in a plead for support for what she was about to face.

Just as they left the dining room, she saw the chapel. Karen stopped, and looked inside the dark sanctuary, lit only by a few altar lights and candles.

"We still have a few minutes," she said, looking up at him. "I'd like to pray."

John just nodded his understanding and followed her.

The mother quietly, reverently entered the small chapel, totally empty until now. She walked to the short rail at the front and knelt, clasped her hands, and placed the laced fingers before her face. She immediately began crying as her lips moved in a silent, fervent prayer. John knelt beside her and closed his eyes, uncertain of what to do next. After a few seconds, he opened his eyes. He was looking up at a stained-glass window. The scene was of Christ, His left hand on the shoulder of a young boy, His right hand on the head of a blonde-haired girl. Tears begin pouring down the tough, seasoned Vietnam veteran's cheek. He felt a rush of despair begin rumbling deep in his gut, threatening to make him pass out or at least vomit. Then, it felt as if the anguish was being forced out of him by a replaced feeling, a feeling of...hope, and promise. He cupped his hands together and began praying silently.

God, you know I don't have much practice. I don't know the last time I prayed, maybe not since I was a kid. I've not been much of a Christian. I've killed people, and even today wanted to kill someone. I've done wild things that I know are not right. I don't know much about what it takes to be a Christian, but I do know upstairs is a young girl who is an angel. She is everything a Christian should be. And Karen is everything a Christian and a mother should be. Please God, please don't take her away. I don't deserve anything, but if you will just spare her life, then I'll become a better person. I'll become what ever you want me to become, if you'll just let Suzie live. I don't know what else to say. I don't even know if you listen to someone like me. Maybe I have to prove myself to you first. But I will do what ever it takes. I guess that's it, God.

He opened his eyes again, and looked around the room. There he saw another stained-glass window displaying a lofty mountain, with a glorious sunrise, or sunset, golden streams of light breaking over the ridges. The scene revived a Bible verse his grandmother used to recite to him. He recalled it had something to do with looking up at the mountains and getting strength from God.

John then felt Karen's hand take his. The two stood up. They looked into each others eyes, purposefully. Then Karen wrapped her arms around John, hugging him to her, her cheek pressed against his shoulder, the pony-tail tickling his chin.

"Thank you John," she whispered. "Thank you so much for being here with me."

She raised herself up on her tip-toes, and kissed him on the cheek. They walked out of the chapel, and with no more communication, returned to the third floor recovery room.

She stopped at the information desk and asked for Suzie Young's room.

"She's in room 314," the nurse said with a compassionate smile.

"Thank you. Thank you very much," Karen replied.

They walked down the hall. Just as they were passing Room 316, the doctor left Room 314. Recognizing them, he stopped and greeted them just before they reached the room.

"She came through surgery fine. Don't let all the IV's, monitors and the respirator scare you. Most of it's just for precaution. She is unconscious. The next 24 hours are very important. If she wakes up by tomorrow night, chances are very good. If she doesn't…well, she will probably slip into a coma, and then it's just wait and see. There's not really much you can do for her now," the doctor continued, "but there is a very nice chapel near the dining room."

"Yes, we've already been there," Karen answered, with a little hitch in her voice.

"Well, do feel free to talk to her," the doctor encouraged. "She may not respond, but there is a good chance in a few hours she will be able to hear you."

"Thank you, doctor," Karen said, shaking the surgeon's hand.

"You're welcome. I'll be checking back with you in the morning. If you need anything at all, just let the nurse know," the doctor said. As he started out the door, he turned to John and said, "I'll have someone bring you an extra fold-out chair."

Karen took John's hand, squeezing it tightly as she rounded

the doorway. Even after the warning, the sight of her precious daughter laying there, her hair partially shaved and numerous probes and IV's running to all parts of her body was more than she could stand. She turned around and all but collapsed in John's arms.

"It's okay. It's okay Karen," John whispered as he wrapped his arms around her, supporting her as he patted her back. "Like the doctor said, all of this is just for precautions."

He led her over to the left side of the bed. Suzie's left hand was one of the few areas that didn't have something connected to it.

"Oh, Suzie, oh my baby, please don't leave me. I couldn't stand losing you. Oh God, please don't take her away from me," Karen pleaded, bending over the motionless body, the tears streaming down her cheeks.

A beam of light flashed into John's eye, and he turned to look out the window. The view was breathtaking. The sun was just setting over a distant mountain and the whole sky was a kaleidoscope of swirled oranges, blues, and reds. John took Karen by the shoulder and turned her so she could witness the sunset. Karen sniffed to stop her crying, as she gazed in awe at the majestic site. She then began softly reciting, "I will lift mine eyes unto the hills, from whence comes my strength…"

John's memory rushed back to his Christian grandmother's favorite scripture. He totally enveloped Karen with his arms, as an angel's wings surrounds the one he is guarding. Then in unison, the couple concluded the verse, "…my strength comes from God."

The couple stood there, awed by the sunset. Karen could feel John's heart pounding against her head. She tried to remember the last time she felt so safe. Even though her daughter was lying in the bed, unconscious, Karen had never felt more certain in her life that all would be well. She thought back to the sunsets she and Wilson used to watch from the back porch of the house. At a certain time of the year, the sun actually looked as if it had fallen into New River, and had left a flaming trail all the way down and over the dam. So many times over the past five years, she had wondered if she would ever feel as contented as she had those days on the deck, with Wilson's strong, comforting arms around her.

John wondered if Karen could feel how hard his heart was pounding. His eardrums were pulsating from the thumping. He was conscious of not letting his arms hug her tightly. Instead he wanted her to feel comforted, to know that he was there for her. He again felt the strange emotion sweeping over him that he had experienced in the chapel. For the first time in many years, he felt ready to open his heart to someone.

Just then a voice at the door interrupted John's and Karen's thoughts. They turned to the doorway to see a nurse enter.

"Mrs. Young," she said "there are three men in the waiting room. They said they are pastors and were hoping they could see you."

"Oh, okay. I'll be right out," she said to the nurse, then turned to John. "Please come with me. I want you to meet them."

Karen entered the waiting room, John by her side. The three pastors stood, and the mother took turns hugging them as each whispered a comforting thought into her ear. She acknowledged each with a nod and a smile. She then turned, and placing a hand on John's arm, introduced him.

"This is John. He's a friend of Mr. Armbrister, and he helped Suzie when she fell," Karen said, wondering if she was blushing as much as she feared. "He also was kind enough to drive me here."

"John, this is Pastor Hamm, from the Baptist Church we attend, and this is Pastor Lyons from the Methodist Church where Suzie goes to youth fellowship" she said, then smiling she turned to a massive black man, as big as most NFL football linemen, "and this is Suzie's Uncle Buster Young. He's the pastor of our black church in town."

John couldn't conceal his discombobulated double-take, which brought a big laugh from both the black pastor and Karen.

"That is a long story," Buster said as he wrapped a huge hand around John's. "I'll let Suzie tell you later."

"How is our little Suzie?" Pastor Hamm asked in a low soothing voice.

"The doctor says if she wakes up in the next 24 hours, she should be ok, so we just need to keep praying that God will bring her to."

"Well, we just wanted you to know that we…, that all of Fries, is praying," added Pastor Lyons, who if standing beside anyone beside Buster Young, would also look like a NFL lineman. "We know we can't come to the recovery room, and we just wanted you to know we are with you in prayer."

"Thank you so much," Karen said softly, reaching out to take the hand of the two pastors closest to her. "Will you pray for us before you leave?"

The three ministers, Karen and John joined hands in a circle. Each pastor then prayed for healing powers through the hands of the attending doctors and for strength that would carry Karen through the night.

The clergymen then shook John's hand and gave Karen a departing hug. Pastor Young was the last of the three pastors to leave. He stopped and wrapped his tree-limb sized arms around John in a big bear-hug.

"You look like a good man, a strong man," the black man whispered into John's ear. "Miss Karen needs your strength right now. Take care of her and my precious Suzie."

"I will," John said. "I promise you I will."

"Let's go get another cup of coffee. It may be a long night," Karen said after Pastor Young had left.

"I think you should tell me your life story," John said as he returned to the table and set down the two coffee cups.

"Are you sure you're up to hearing such an exciting story?"

"I know I will enjoy it," he assured her.

"Well, I've always lived right here in Fries. My mom and dad both worked in the Cotton Mill. I was a pretty good student and really hoped to go to college, but I fell hopelessly in love with Wilson Young when I was twelve years old. I told everyone that I was going to marry him. We were next door neighbors, but Wilson was a star quarterback on the football team and barely noticed this skinny little kid next door. He left for the Navy right out of school. They put him in the Seabees. That's where he learned to drive big trucks."

She stopped to take a drink of her coffee. John watched her intently, seeing the conflict between anxiety and nostalgia wage a battle in her eyes. He wondered if they sparkled this much at a time like this, how they must radiate when she was elated. He found himself hoping he could see that firsthand one day.

"When he came back, I had grown up. I'll never forget the day he came home. I baked him a carrot cake. I knew that was his favorite. He couldn't get over how much I had grown up."

John watched the woman's blue eyes begin to gleam with a faraway expression. He studied her small delicate fingers as she wrapped, and then unwrapped, them around the handle of the coffee cup.

"For the next couple of weeks he dated every girl in town and half the ones in Galax. Then he asked me out, and he never dated anyone else after that. A few weeks later, he asked me to marry him. I was only sixteen, and my mom threw a hissy-fit. I was a good girl, but she knew if she stood in the way, we might just run off to Sparta and get married. So she and Daddy finally gave me their blessing a few months later. I was 16 1/2 when we married. I had promised Momma we would wait to have children, but, well, I got pregnant two months later." She stopped and took another drink of the hot beverage. "Am I boring you yet?"

"Not at all, I'm enjoying this," John told her. "I could listen to you talk forever. I love your voice. It reminds me when I was in the Army, out West in Kansas, on temporary duty. I used to call information for North Carolina just so I could hear a southern accent."

Karen laughed, and then continued her story.

"Well, as you know, girls 'in the family way' don't attend school, so I had to drop out. I did go on to get my GED. Since then I have worked in the payroll office at the Mill."

"Suzie seems to be quite a remarkable young lady," John said.

"Yes, we could tell Suzie was going to be smart. She was reading at the age of three and making up and writing stories by the time she was four. She has always made straight A's." The mother said it matter-of-factly, with no trace of boasting.

"But when Wilson got killed in the truck wreck five years ago, it devastated Suzie," Karen said, as she began looking down at her cup, unconsciously using her fingers to trace its rim. "He used to take her on trips in the truck, or down on the river fishing, or just for long walks in the woods."

John saw a retrospective smile find its way to Karen's tense countenance.

"She was just lost when he died. I was so worried about her for almost a year. I wasn't sure if she was ever going to snap out of it."

"Then when she was ten, she started writing. Her first stories were, I guess like therapy for her. They were about the things she and her dad used to love to do. One story was actually published in the *Reader's Digest*. She has the article framed in her room. I'm sure she'll want to show it to you."

"I can't wait to see it." John said, discovering that he wanted to learn more and more about the Youngs.

"When she was ten, she wrote an article on the Fries 4th of July parade and sent it to the local newspaper in Galax. They didn't print it. This was one of the few times I ever saw her angry. She stomped her foot and said, 'I'll show them, I'll start my own paper, and put them out of business.'"

This brought a laugh from John.

"Don't laugh, because that's just what she did. For the last three years she has written a small, one-page newspaper, well, two pages because it's on the front and the back, called *The Fries Wildcat Spirit Weekly*. And if what I hear is true, the *Galax Daily* subscriptions in Fries are half what they were before. In fact, Suzie has more subscribers than the Gazette has in town."

John delighted in watching Karen, her eyes now gleaming with pride. He could not stand the thought of what it would do to Karen if anything happened to her daughter.

"So, for the last five years, my life has been filled with keeping Suzie happy. And she deserves it. Not just because she is mine, but she really is a wonderful kid. She never gives me any headaches. She studies hard and never gets into trouble."

"The worse problem I have with her," Karen said, letting a soft laugh infringe upon her stoicness, "is that she doesn't understand why she can't stay out late covering council meetings and the such. So now, I just go with her so she can stay till they end."

Karen took another long drink of her coffee, smacked her lips, and set her coffee cup down with an emphatic gesture of finality.

"So, I guess that's it! That's my life.'

"That's interesting, but all you've told me is about Wilson and

Suzie."

"Well, that's been my life," she answered.

"Tell me Karen, if you could do anything you wanted to, what would it be?"

Karen sat for what seemed like a full minute. John couldn't tell if she was trying to decide, or was merely hesitant to share a dream with a near-stranger.

"Well, I'd love to go to Radford College and get my teacher's degree," she finally answered emphatically.

"Then why don't you?"

"Oh, I don't know; I have some money," Karen said in an almost repentant voice. "I still have about $21,000 left from the settlement and from a small life insurance policy from when my dad and mom died a few years ago, but I'm saving it for Suzie. She'll probably want to go to somewhere like Harvard or Yale."

John looked at her. Even with all she was going through, Karen still had such radiance. He had never known anyone like her before. She was so delightfully different than the superficial women he had dated in North Carolina. He thought back to the $100,000 trust fund left to him by his father. He had never felt worthy of using it to support his frivolous lifestyle, so he had never drawn a cent from it. He had never allowed himself to think of how much joy it might be to have someone he really cared about, and to be able to make her dreams come true.

"Well," Karen said, interrupting John's musings, "I guess it's time we get back."

Karen and John walked back to the room, each absorbed in his and her own contemplations.

Meanwhile, on their drive back to Fries, the three Pastors were making plans for the next day's Church service. It had been a long time since the three men-of-the-cloth had been brought together under such a common cause. It had actually been two weeks since the Methodist and Baptist Pastor had even spoken, although they had been lifelong friends. But all the disunity of the last few weeks was now cast aside because the only thing that was important right now was that Suzie had to live.

As Karen and John walked into the room, they saw that someone had brought in an extra fold-out chair. Two blankets and a pillow lay on the makeshift bed. John anticipated Karen's wish and pulled the mother's lounger to the left side of Suzie's bed. He watched Karen kiss her daughter on the cheek. Then she took the girl's hand into hers, and began kissing it.

The chaotic day had turned into a relatively quiescent night. With the door closed, only an occasional swishing of the nurses' rubber-soled shoes could be heard from the hallway. Inside the room, the low-pitch rhythm of the respirator and the constant humming buzz of the monitors were becoming hypnotic to the two adults, both fatigued from the day's events. The serene solitude suscitated a review of the day.

Karen had not even thought of dating since her husband had died. But tonight, in the abyss of the second worse tragedy of her life, she enjoyed so much having a man there for her, to support her when she needed someone. It didn't matter that he was a stranger, or at least was until five hours ago. Now it almost seemed she had known him for years. She warned herself not to get too carried away because John was a worldly man—so handsome, so strong. How would he ever been happy with her, or with Fries. Their lives were as different as…, as night and day.

Oh, Karen, get a grip, he's just doing this because Mr. Armbrister told him to, she thought to herself.

On the other side of the room, John sat partially upright, pondering. He had never imagined that he would be capable of settling down. He enjoyed his bachelorhood too much. But here he was in a room, with a woman and her daughter he had known for only a few hours, and he was questioning if his current lifestyle was truly what he wanted. Karen was so different from what he had always stereotyped as the woman who would make him settle down. Up until now, his romantic life had been filled with stewardesses, female lawyers or other professional women.

But how could someone like her, so pure, so perfect, ever be interested in someone like me, he reasoned.

She would be horrified if she knew how many men he had killed in Viet Nam, or that he could have murdered Spunkie earlier in the day without batting an eye. What would she think of his many casual relationships with women, never concerned with the consequences? Or that he had only prayed once in the last twenty years? Well, there were those few times in 'Nam, but they were just spur of the moment reactions. Foxhole prayers they call them. Could he convince her he could be different? That in many ways, he already had changed?

John continued to reflect upon the occurrences of the day. The unfamiliar emotional volcano that had erupted over the normally reserved, hard-as-nails ex-GI, first in the chapel, then while he watched the sunset with Karen, simply could not be identified. As they say on *Lost in Space*, 'it does not compute.'

Was it passion, not the kind he felt for Jessie, but a passion for living, and a passion for having someone to care for?

It almost felt like exhilaration, or as some of the French advisors that had served with him in 'Nam would say, *joie de vivre*. He didn't know what it was, or what caused it, but he did know he liked this new feeling. He could hear Karen breathing slowly. John thought she might be already asleep, and if so, he did not want to awaken her.

"Good night, Karen," he said softly.

In a stifled, drowsy but oh so syrupy voice, Karen replied, "Good night, Wilson, I love you."

Soon the two were asleep. Throughout the night every noise woke Karen, and startled, she would look hopefully at Suzie, praying she would see her daughter's beautiful blue eyes flickering open. Instead, she would realize it was just some noise from the hallway, transcending the monotone of the respirator and monitors.

9

Karen awoke to light streaming through the window. She lifted her head from atop Suzie's cold, lifeless hand. The crisp, white sheet was still damp from her tears of the night before. She remembered why she was there, and her heart grew heavy. She looked at the clock. Almost 7:30. Slowly she began to regain her senses.

It's…, Sunday, the…14th, she thought to herself. The mother turned to look into the little girl's face, praying to see a sign of life, any indication of consciousness, but she saw none. Sitting upright on the edge of the chair she realized that John was gone. She was disappointed but admitted she wasn't surprised.

How many total strangers would stay in a room sleeping upright in a chair, if they could be elsewhere? Then a sad thought swept over her. *What if he had decided this was too much and had gone back to North Carolina, never to be seen again?* But before she could fret further, John walked into the room carrying two cups of coffee and two ham biscuits.

"Hi," he said with a sheepish grin. "I thought you might be hungry when you woke up."

He rolled the hospital-bed tray to her lounger and set their breakfast down. She smiled up at him, and slid over in an implied invitation for him to join her.

"How did you sleep?" she asked, her eyelids puffy.

"I don't think I've slept so badly since I was in a fox-hole," he said with a laugh.

"Well, I've never slept in a fox-hole, but I can't imagine it could have been any worse," she agreed with a smile. "But I'm sorry, I should have told you to drive back to Fries and spend last night." She hoped she was sounding more convincing than she truly felt.

John, setting his coffee down, took her left hand in his right and began patting it.

"Karen, I was exactly where I wanted to be."

Karen turned away to conceal the drop of happiness gliding down her cheek. It had been a long time since a man had gotten to her like this. As the two sat there, side by side, sharing their coffee, they both sensed a refreshing closeness. They began sharing stories of the happiest parts of their childhoods. Karen related stories about her parents, and about growing up in a small southern cotton mill town. John detailed his cheerful reminisces of summers with his grandparents on their tobacco farm in Elkin, North Carolina. Karen could sense his sadness as he told her about his parent's divorcing when he was twelve. His mother had died six years ago, his father just last year.

John's retrospections were interrupted by a startled Karen, as she spilled her coffee in her haste to turn to a motion from the bed.

Back in Fries, it was 10:45, and worshippers were arriving at the two churches. They were surprised to find a sign on their doors.

CHURCH SERVICES HAVE
BEEN RELOCATED
TO THE HIGH SCHOOL GYM
FOR A JOINT SERVICE

As the church goers entered the Home of the Wildcats, they found several members of Pastor Young's congregation already sitting on the wooden bleachers. Pastor Young, Pastor Lyons and Pastor Hamm stood in a circle deep in conversation. Over the next five minutes the wooden bleachers began to fill. Each family would walk in, find someone from their congregation, and go join them. Soon a Babel of conversations consumed the make-shift church as everyone questioned this change in scheduled services. The only people not talking were the ones who sat with somber faces, for they knew the reason for the united service.

Three chairs had been set up at the end of the gym, nearest the entrance, under the basket. A podium rested on the free-throw line. At promptly 11 o'clock, Pastor Lyons walked to the podium solemnly. The Methodist clergyman was a strong, powerful individual, standing about 6'4" and weighing about 240 pounds. His physique, even though he was in his fifties, divulged the outstanding athlete he once was. He had been offered a professional baseball contract out of high school as a pitcher but opted instead to marry, raise a family, and preach the gospel. Part of his magnetism was his baldness that made a perpetually present toothy smile even more electrifying. All he needed was a gold earring to be a double for Mr. Clean.

"And from the tenth chapter of Mark," Pastor Lyons said, as he opened his Bible and began reading "starting with the thirteenth verse, 'and they brought young children to him, that he should touch them: and his disciples rebuked those that brought them. But when Jesus saw it, he was much displeased, and said unto them. Suffer the little children to come unto me, and forbid them not, for of such is the kingdom of God. Verily I say unto you, Whosoever shall not receive the kingdom of God as a little child, he shall not enter therein.'"

"From the Book of Matthew, the eighteenth chapter, we read," the preacher continued in a softer voice than usual, "'At the same time came the disciples unto Jesus, saying, Who is the greatest in the kingdom of heaven? And Jesus called a little child unto him and set him in the midst of them, and said, verily I say unto you, except ye be converted, and become as little children, ye shall not enter into the kingdom of heaven. Whosoever therefore shall humble himself as this little child, the same is greatest in the kingdom of heaven. And whoso shall receive one such little child in my name receiveth me.'"

The towering clergyman then straightened from the podium and elevated himself to his full height, studied the congregation on both sides of the court for a very seconds, and then, with his deep compelling voice, emphatically announced, "'but whoso shall offend one of these little ones which believe in me, it were better for him that a millstone were hanged about his neck, and that he were drowned in the depth of the sea.'"

Pastor Lyons then closed his Bible. His eyes scanned the congregation, as if challenging them to immerse themselves in the scripture that he had read.

"Blessed be the word of the Lord, and Blessed be those ears that hear, and heed His words," the cleric said, and then slowly walked back to his chair.

Pastor Hamm then stood up and limped to the podium. If not for the lameness, Pastor Hamm would have been imposing. He was tall and muscular in a gangly Lincolnesque manner. Most people assumed the polio outbreak of the early 50's was responsible for his infirmity. Few knew the many various afflictions that had befallen this man of God on a daily basis. God alone gave him the strength to get out of bed every day so he could continue to spread the Holy Word.

"'And he shall send a child to lead them,'" Reverend Hamm read in his soft, sometimes almost inaudible voice. Whereas the Methodist preacher's voice was usually booming and powerful, the Baptist preacher's voice was, well, Christ-like. It was filled with humility and benevolence.

"Throughout the Bible," he said, "we are told about how God used children to do the things that adults should do, but so often we lack the faith, or maybe we're just not humble enough. God sent David, because the older brothers and other soldiers lacked the faith that God would protect them against the enemy, even wearing their heavy armor. He sent the baby Jesus to earth to give us an earthly figure so we would be able to have faith. Adults are constantly needing to be more childlike."

"Yesterday afternoon, a child stepped forth to lead this town. God had given her the strength to show us the folly of our childish behavior. She hung a banner on the Mill that read 'Peace on earth, and in Fries too.' A rock was thrown at this girl and she was hit, and she fell from the Cotton Mill ledge."

The crowd took a collective deep, anticipatory breath.

"This morning," the preacher's tenderhearted voice began to break, as he took a handkerchief from his pocket and began to wipe his moistened eyes, "Suzie Young lies unconscious in a hospital bed in Galax."

The gym almost became a vacuum as those who had not heard the news gasped. Pastor Hamm waited a few seconds to allow the cacophony of *whats*, *hows*, and *whos* to die down.

"The doctor does not know the severity of her injuries, but if she has not gained consciousness by this morning, he fears she will slip into a coma." Pastor Hamm said, then took a few deep breaths, and continued, the whole while, wiping his eyes. "Friends, why did it have to come to this? Most towns would feel fortunate to be led by a good, honest, God-fearing man, and we have two, and either would make a wonderful mayor. Why have we let politics tear us apart?"

Repentant sighs began to escape from clinched lips. A rumbling of sniffle-filled moans echoed off the masonry walls of the basketball arena.

"God provided manna to millions of children wandering in the wilderness. Why are we so faithless to think that he would let us starve just because the Cotton Mill closed its doors? Why did we let the brightest light in this town, Suzie Young, be…, almost extinguished, before we realize we are not living alone in darkness?"

By this time, the Pastor, his body already weak, was stricken with such grief that he began to totter. The other two pastors quickly rushed to Pastor Hamm's side, steadying him by his arms. Pastor Hamm hugged the other two pastors to him. Such a contrast stood before the union of believers. A large, strapping, robust preacher, tanned from his youthful outside activities, a fragile, weakened pastor, pallid because it took all his limited stamina just to make it through a day to collapse upon the sofa at his home in the evening, and then another pastor, black as the darkest night, as big as an oak, but crying like a child in the arms of his two brothers in faith. The congregation too was turning to each other, tearfully embracing each other, when Pastor Hamm began to speak again.

"So after we are dismissed by Pastor Young, I hope each of you will spend the rest of the day searching your hearts that we will return our faith to God, and to pray that God does not snuff out this angelic light we call Suzie Young."

Pastor Young, still holding onto the other two pastors, began to speak between tremors of emotion.

"Oh Heavenly Father, we come to you to beg your healing of our lovely, precious Suzie. Your heaven has so many angels already, beg you to leave this one with us. Our town needs her so very much. As we enter this Christmas season, and celebrate the birth of your son, Jesus Christ, who was our greatest gift, we beseech you for one more gift. We ask that you give us back our Suzie. And it's in Christ's precious name we pray…

Pastor Young stopped without saying Amen. After a few seconds, the assembly looked up and saw the minister having a conversation with a tall, dark-haired stranger. Only a few knew him to be John Helmsman. The Pastor then grabbed John, hugging him, lifting him completely off the floor. He then turned to the gymnasium congregation, lifting his arms into the air, as he began to shout jubilantly.

"Praise God, Praise God Almighty. He has heard our prayers. Suzie is awake, and the doctors say she's gonna be fine!"

The congregation was quiet for a few seconds, and then an uproar erupted. The people emptied out of the bleachers onto the floor and began a celebration like the Fries gymnasium had never seen. No game-winning basket by a Wildcat had ever evoked such a celebration. Blacks hugging whites, Methodists hugging Baptists, Bournenites hugging Armbristernites. No longer were there three congregations in attendance. It was now one body of Christ celebrating the answer to their prayers. The celebration lasted for about ten minutes and then the people began slowly exiting, hugging and wishing each other a Merry Christmas. John saw Jonathan in the crowd and came up to him.

"Jonathan, is it alright if I keep your car for a while longer? I want to wait, to bring Suzie home when she gets to come."

"Sure, John, that would be fine. I'm really enjoying driving that 'Vette of yours anyway." Jonathan said as he slapped his friend's shoulder, a big smile on his face, "As a matter of fact, it would sure make a nice Christmas present for Cynthia. Sure you don't want to sell it to me?"

John thought about the need for a larger car, at least temporarily. He also didn't seem to have the same infatuation for the sports car as he had just last week.

"Well, I don't know. Let me think about it over the next couple of weeks, I'll make a decision by New Year. It could always be a New Year's present," John said with a laugh.

Jonathan tried to remember the last time he heard his friend seem so at ease or happy. John's entire countenance had taken on a new demeanor. Jonathan was excited for his wife to see this change in their friend.

John waited until Pastor Young was finished slapping backs and hugging. When the pastor went to get his overcoat, John approached him.

"Pastor, do you have a moment?" John said, as he placed his hand on the pastor's arm.

"Sure, John, of course I do. Wonderful news, glorious news isn't it?"

"Oh, yes, it is!" John said with a beaming smile. "Hmm, Pastor Young, I made a promise last night, to God, a promise I intend to keep, but well, I don't know how, and I was hoping you could help me."

So it was there, on Dec. 14, in the bleachers of the Fries High School Gymnasium, John Helmsman kept his promise and gave his life to God.

An exuberant new Christian drove back to the hospital, greatly transformed from the sullen man that had arrived in Fries just two days earlier. He now had a life purpose, a plan that included more than himself, or when to trade cars or girlfriends. It had been many years since he had felt such undeniable joy and peace. John whipped the Lincoln into the hospital parking lot, screeching to a jolting stop. He jumped out and walked briskly to the recovery room. He was excited to see Suzie, but also apprehensive. She didn't even know him. She had just awakened at 10:45 a.m., and her eyes were just beginning to focus when John had rushed out to get the doctors. John and Karen had been asked to wait outside until the doctors had finished examining her at 11:30. As soon as the medical team had given him the wonderful news, John had immediately dashed out the door to tell everyone before church let out.

How would she feel about him? What would he say to her? How much should he say to her?" The questions were rushing through his head like a whirlpool, a new question popping up before he could find an answer to the prior one.

He entered the elevator and pushed the button for the third floor. He thought Karen felt the same attraction for him that he felt for her, but what would Suzie think about a new man in her mother's life. He was so different from her father? *Father*?

Could he actually be thinking about taking that big of a step? The elevator door squeaked open, and John stepped into the hallway. He heard the chime, and then the door closed behind him. He started down the hallway, and then stopped. A shivering palpitation overwhelmed him, almost dropping him to his knees. He wondered if he was having a heart attack, and leaned against the wall. He then realized he was experiencing what was known as an anxiety attack.

"My God, what am I doing," he said under his breath. "I can't just change my life overnight this way. I barely know this woman."

He abruptly turned and began walking hastily back toward the elevator. Just before calling for the elevator, John looked out the window at the end of the hall. The mountains were awashed in sunlight. The memory of the previous night's sunset that he had shared with Karen made his body radiate, like the tingling warmth one feels from a fireplace after coming in from the cold. He remembered how the hair on his arms stood on end at the touch of her fingertips. He could smell again the strawberry fragrance of her hair as he leaned his cheek against her blond locks. He remembered the pounding thud in his ears from his heart as it raced as if he had run a marathon. And he remembered the total, absolute, unequivocal delirium he felt knowing he had never experienced this bliss before. John Helmsman then realized he would never find anyone else like Karen Young anywhere in the world.

He took a deep breath and headed back toward Room 314. From ten feet away he could hear adolescent giggles usually heard only at teenage girls' pajama parties. He rounded the corner, ready to introduce himself. As soon as he entered the room, Suzie looked up. Only one IV was now connected to her. She was sitting upright, leaning over a serving tray, eating from a large bowl of ice-cream. John opened his mouth to speak, but the little blonde girl spoke first.

"Hi," Suzie called out. "Let me guess, you're John, the guy that has brought such a sparkle to my mom's eyes."

"Suzie!" Karen exclaimed, blushing.

John laughed, pleased at the thought that he must have been the object of discussion for the past few minutes.

"It's the sparkle in *your* eye that I'm glad to see," John said as he walked to her right side and took her small, delicate hands into his large fists. Suzie squeezed slightly. John could tell the young girl was trying so hard to look strong for her mother, but she was still very weak.

"I was just asking Suzie if she remembered anything about the fall," Karen said from the other side of the bed. "She said the only thing she remembered was lying on the ground, like she was dreaming, and she kept hearing a man whisper, 'Don't worry, you will be okay. Don't worry, everything will be alright.' Was that you telling her that?"

"Yes. Yes it was," John answered, with a smile, as he remembered saying those exact words to the young girl as he was wiping the blood from her forehead, "but I didn't think she could hear me."

"Well," Karen said, with a hitch in her voice, "Suzie, tell John what else you told me."

"I can remember hearing those words," Suzie's began, her eyes moistening, "but I remember that when I opened my eyes, and, and…" her voice began trembling, "I looked up and saw,…I saw my father."

"Did she…, did she ever open her eyes?" Karen asked as she fought back her own tears.

"No, she never opened them, I'm sure of that." John said as the back of his hand swiped quickly over his eyes. He realized he needed to change the tone of this conversation, or he was going to lose control, which is something he never did.

"Suzie," John said, adjusting his voice to overcome the emotion he was feeling, "you should have seen the celebration in the gymnasium when Pastor Young announced you were awake, and were going to be alright."

"In the gymnasium?" Suzie asked, arching her brows questioningly. "Why was Uncle Buster in the gymnasium?"

"Are you kidding?" John answered in a dramatic voice. "Why, young lady, it seems you have single-handedly brought the entire town back together. You have brought peace to the town of Fries."

"Really?" she said, a big smile sweeping her face.

"Yes, all three churches, the Methodist, the Baptists, and Pastor Young's, all three had a joint meeting in the gymnasium. And when I told Pastor Young, and he announced that you were going to be okay, well, I promise you, there's never been a celebration like that after any old basketball game. Everyone was hugging and slapping each other on the back."

By this time, Suzie had pushed her ice cream away and was sitting upright in the bed. Flashing a wide smile, she turned to her mom.

"You don't need to get me a Christmas gift now, Mom. This is all I wanted."

"Oh, and by the way," John continued, "a Mr. *Bourne* sent you a message."

"You mean Herbie? What did he say."

"Let's see, if I can remember exactly," John said as he expressively puffed up his chest and deepened his voice. "He said, '*Young Lady, don't think just because you got a bump on your head, you're getting out of reading the Christmas Story scripture again this year. . I've sent it to you; I want you to practice it while you're lying there in bed with nothing else to do, and by tonight be able to read it to your mom and John.*'"

"Leave it to Herbie to make sure I keep up with my Youth Group work," Suzie said with a giggle.

John just grinned and winked at Karen. Karen smiled, but then got very somber, and with a dispirited voice said, "Well John, I guess you probably need to be getting back to your work, now that everything is good here. I can't tell you how much I appreciate what you have done."

"Well, if it's okay with you and Suzie, I was kinda hoping to spend a few more days." John answered, searching Karen's face and eyes for acquiescence. "I thought maybe you and Suzie could show me what a Fries Christmas is all about. I mean, if I'd not be in the way."

Karen's mouth curled into a smile as she looked down at Suzie, who was smiling back up at her, anticipating her mother's excitement at hearing the request.

"What do you think Suzie? Think we will have enough of those

Christmas cookies and custard for an extra person?"

Suzie took her mother's hand in her left hand, and pulled it over to couple with John's hand.

"Well, if we don't, we can always make more," the young girl said with a laugh.

Karen looked across at John. He squeezed the two small hands with his long fingers. Their eyes met, and then almost instantly they both looked down at Suzie, who was watching the two adults with amusement.

"So John, tell us about some of your past Christmases" Karen said, "maybe your favorite one."

John tilted his head, rolling his eyes back as he thought for a few moments, and then started.

"I'd have to say it was, hmm, when I was about six, I guess. That was before my father and mother had divorced. Mom had an emergency surgery at Bowman Gray Hospital and wouldn't be home for Christmas. Dad took me over to stay with Grandpa and Grandma Darnell over in Elkins. Do you know where that is?"

"Hmm, yes, it's down in North Carolina, not too far from Mt. Airy. We also had relatives that lived there," Karen answered, as she sat down on the edge of the hospital bed, still holding Suzie's hand in hers. The two listened intently.

John's expression began to drift into a nostalgic visage, his dark eyes taking on a new sparkle.

"We had a wonderful, traditional Christmas. Grandpa and I went out on the farm, cut the tree, and brought it back with the tractor. Oh yeah, I also cut a little small tree, only about this high," John said, placing his hands above each other, about eighteen inches apart. "I was going to decorate it to take to Mom's hospital room. Grandma popped popcorn to decorate it with, and let me put the other decorations on the tree. On Christmas Eve, Grandpa hooked up the hay wagon. All the kids from Church jumped on, and we rode around States Road singing Christmas carols to everyone. Then we stopped at the church and drank hot chocolate and ate cookies. I was almost asleep by the time we got home, and grandma put me to bed. I always slept in the back room where there was no heat. It was cold, and I remember Grandma holding a big quilt up in front of their pot-belly stove in the living room.

Then she had me run and jump into bed, where she had pulled back the covers. She then put the hot quilt over me, and then pulled the other covers over the hot quilt. I remember feeling like a turkey roasting. The sheets were cold in a nice crisp sort of way, but the blanket kept the top of my body toasty."

John's countenance then took on a slightly forlorn, distant look.

"But I remember then I began to cry because I remembered that my mom would not be there for Christmas. The next morning I woke up to the wonderful smell and sound of Grandma cooking breakfast. No one could cook a country breakfast like her. I jumped up out of bed, ran into the living room, and there in the chair, sat my mom."

John's lips began to quiver as he felt his eyes become moist. He sucked in his bottom lip, biting it to regain his composure. He looked away for a few seconds and then turned back and smiling at Suzie, while he squeezed her hand, continued.

"They had let her out of the hospital for the day, and Dad had picked her up at 5:30 that morning and had driven her to Grandma's. You know, I can remember Christmases all the way back since I was three or four, but I cannot remember a single thing that I got in all those years. But I will always remember like it was just yesterday the joy I felt when I saw my mom sitting in that chair."

Suzie turned loose of John's hand, and reached up to him. John leaned over the bed as the girl hugged him. Without thinking, John kissed her on the cheek. It would never have been something he would have thought of intentionally doing.

"Okay, now it's your turn Momma. What was your favorite?"

"Hmm, okay, let's see," Karen said with a finger to her chin in a contemplative look. "I'd have to say it was the year your daddy came back from Viet Nam and got out of the service. He got back on October 17th, a Friday."

"As you know, I had loved your father since I was your age, but he was four years older, so I was just a pesky little kid when we were growing up. You know kinda like you are now," Karen laughed as she mussed her daughter's bed-hair. "But I had grown up a lot during those three years, and he began to notice me. The first few weeks back, he dated a different girl every night, but I took him another plate of peanut butter cookies or slice of carrot cake almost every day. Then, he invited me to the Halloween Party at the YMCA. He said I was so skinny, he was taking me as the scarecrow in The Wizard of Oz. Not to be outdone, I told him we'd make a good match, because he was the one that didn't have a brain."

This brought a big laugh from Suzie, who had always loved to listen to her parents' good natured teasing.

"Well, we had a wonderful time, and he stopped dating anyone but me. The week before Christmas, he asked your granddaddy to ride with him to the store to get soft drinks. When they came back, my dad had been crying. I could tell. I wondered what Wilson had said to him. Then, on Christmas morning, when I woke up, he, Dad and Mom were sitting in the living room. I was embarrassed. My hair looked terrible, and I was in an old torn house coat. I fussed at him for catching me that way. He laughed and said I could never be anything but beautiful, and…"

Now it was Karen's turn to get emotional.

"…and that he hoped soon he'd be seeing me every day dressed that way. He knelt down…," Karen said as she lowered her chin to her chest and turned to look out the window, "…he knelt down on one knee, and asked me to marry him. He then slipped the engagement ring on my finger."

"Oh wow!" Suzie said excitedly, "You've never told me that story. What did Grandma say?"

"Well, she was quick to remind him that we would wait until I graduated, but I talked her out of that real soon, and we were married a few months later. Then 10 months later, I had this little stinker!" Karen said as she tweaked her daughter's nose.

"Momma," Suzie said, her voice suddenly very serious, "is it true you had never dated any other boys besides Daddy?"

Karen knew that Suzie had started developing an interest in boys, especially Jason Campbell who had been a star quarterback for the Fries Wildcats the year before, and was now attending VPI.

"That's true," Karen answered. "I'd met some boys at dances, at church, and yes, I'd even kissed a few, but I had never gone out alone on a date, besides with your father."

"So Momma, how do you know, when you've met the right person?"

By this time John was wondering if he should leave the room, but instead opted to sit down in the chair and begin to idly leaf through a magazine, trying to appear inconspicuous.

"Well, honey," Karen said, "you know it's the right boy when you are in a room full of people, but he is the only one you see, or hear, or smell. You know it when you are away from him for even a day, and might even be so busy you barely have time to think, but he's the only thing you can think about. He's the one that you just can't imagine living your life without. But I think the most important thing is that he's the one, when you are at the lowest point of your life, who is there with you, and you know, that with him by your side, you can face…"

Karen suddenly realized what was about to come out of her mouth. She looked over, blushing, at the man sitting in the chair on the other side of the bed who was smiling contently toward her.

"…you can face anything." Karen quickly looked down at her daughter, hoping the incriminating flush had faded away from her cheeks.

"Okay, Stinker," Karen poked her daughter in the ribs gently, "now it's your turn."

"Well," Suzie began immediately, having had the time to think of her best Christmas, "I think the best one was the year Daddy got caught in the blizzard up in Pennsylvania." She turned and looked at John. "His truck broke down, and he wasn't going to make it home, but at the truck stop he was at, he ran into someone from Fries, and caught a ride home. I was so happy to see him on Christmas morning. He felt so bad because he hadn't had a chance to buy me anything, but that was fine. Just having him was all I needed."

"Yes, honey," Karen said, lifting her daughter's hand to her lips and kissing it, "that was also special for me."

"But, you know, Momma, I really, truly feel like this year's Christmas is going to be one of my favorites."

"Now honey, you know that money is tight this year. You might get some clothes, but I'm not sure about skates or the record player and records."

"No Momma, that's fine. Those aren't important. I think this is going to be the best because I think the people in Fries will learn the true meaning of Christmas."

"Well, I hope you're right, honey. We'll just have to wait and see."

John looked at his watch. It was nearly 3:15. He picked up the piece of paper Herbie had given him at the church service that morning and handed it to Suzie.

"Hey kiddo," he said, "you need to start studying your scripture reading. I expect you to recite it by heart to us tonight. Umm, Karen, why don't we go get a cup of coffee so she can study."

"Well, actually John, I was hoping you could drive me to the Roses store. I need to get some things to freshen up. We could get us some coffee there, at their snack counter."

"Oh, okay, that would be great. I could use some things myself," he said.

When they got outside, John put his arm around Karen's shoulder, and pulled her head over toward him. She was pleasantly surprised at his show of affection. He then began whispering.

"Just wait until I tell you what the pastors came up with after the service this morning."

John opened the door and let Karen slide into the passenger side of the Lincoln. He slipped behind the big steering wheel and started the powerful V-8 engine. On the way to Roses, John began telling Karen the idea the pastors had for that evening. The two spent the next fifteen minutes finding the things they needed at the store. While Karen was checking out, John went to the snack counter and bought the coffee.

"Do you think she'll be up to doing it," Karen asked, wrinkles of concern creasing her forehead. "I mean, standing in front for all that time?"

"Yes, I think it will be good for her. Umm, Karen, I've been meaning to ask you something."

"Sure John, what is it?"

"Well, umm, how long have you and Richard been dating. I assume it's serious."

"What makes you think Richard and I are dating?" Karen said, her eyes opening widely as she began to laugh.

"Well, I assumed, I mean, he just acts so close to you, and to Suzie."

Karen begins laughing so hard she had to set her coffee down to avoid spilling it.

"John, Richard is my cousin. He's close because we have always been almost like brothers and sisters. I have no brothers and he has no sisters. Now that Wilson is gone, he just likes to think he takes care of us."

"Well, I just thought...I mean, it's because he said," John stammered, but then he felt a tremendous sense of relief, and seeing the humor of the situation, began to laugh himself. "Well, I guess that's what I get for assuming."

At 3:50 p.m. Karen returned to the room carrying several bags with Roses Department Store written in red script across the front. Suzie lay upright in the bed, holding the sheet of paper in front of her, as she recited the Bible verses.

"Hi, get everything you needed?" Suzie asked.

"We sure did. It's sure going to feel good to brush my teeth and put lipstick on," Karen said as she gave her daughter a kiss on the forehead.

"Where's John?"

"Umm, he...had some things to do downstairs," Karen answered, trying not to sound evasive, then redirecting the questioning, "so how are you doing with the verses?"

"I've got them all memorized. I can't wait to read them to you and John tonight."

"Well, in about an hour, you'll be able to do just that."

John met the pastors and Herbie at the front door of the hospital. Pastor Young introduced John to Herbie Bourne.

"Is there anything I can help with?" he said as he held the doors open for the men, who were carrying some boxes.

"No," Herbie answered, "I think we've got it all. Does she know?"

"No, we were going to let it be a surprise."

The five men, four women, and ten youth walked to the cafeteria and began the process of turning the dining room into a stable.

At 4:15 the PA system began to crackle, and then an announcement echoed throughout the three floors of the hospital.

May we have your attention please? May we have your attention please? We will be having a special Christmas presentation followed by refreshments in the cafeteria at 4:30. Everyone—patients and visitors, and staff, is invited. If you need assistance, please page your nurse. If you would like to assist patients, please report to the information desk outside the cafeteria. We could use your help. Thank you and we hope to see you there.

"Oh Momma, that sounds like fun. Can we go to it?"

"Are you sure you feel like it?" Karen asked with an impish grin. "Do you feel like walking, or should I get a wheel chair?"

"No, Momma," Suzie said with excitement, "I'll be fine. I'm just a little weak, but you can help me."

Karen removed from the Roses bag a new robe she had just bought and slipped it over Suzie's hospital gown. They started out of the room toward the elevator.

"Won't we be early Momma? They said it didn't start until 4:30."

"Well, we do want to get a good seat, don't we?"

Even before the two Young girls reached the cafeteria, they could hear laughter and the sound of tables and chairs being scooted over the tile floor. Just as they walked through the doorway, a voice called out, "There's Suzie!" All the heads then turned toward her. Suzie began to recognize who was doing the work. There were Janice, and the twins Teresa and Marie setting up the stage. Johnny and Jimbo from her youth group were moving tables to the side and arranging chairs. And there was Nacine and two girls from Pastor Young's church. A couple of kids from the Baptist Church were arranging plates of cookies alongside paper plates and napkins on a table. Herbie and the three pastors stood at the front of the cafeteria. All scampered toward the young girl. Karen held onto her daughter to keep the onrush from knocking down the convalescing teen.

"What are you guys doing here?" Suzie asked, barely able to stand in one place she was so thrilled at the sight of her friends. She wanted to hug each of them at the same time.

Nacine, her dimples sunken deeper than ever in her round chocolate face smiled, showing the most lovely white teeth you have ever seen.

"Suzie," the young girl said in her soft, angelic voice, "we didn't know how long you might be here, so we decided to come give a Christmas play for you tonight."

"You're kidding! You're putting a play on here?"

By that time the pastors and Herbie had arrived.

"Yes, Suzie," Herbie said with a gentle hug, "and you're going to be reading the Bible scripture. Are you ready?"

"Yes, sir. I know it all by heart."

"Well, Suzie," Karen said, "we'd better get you in the back room then, because we have to get you dressed."

Taking her in a storage room to the left of the cafeteria, Karen pulled from a drycleaner's bag a long, flowing white gown that Herbie had left hanging on the door. The mother removed the terry cloth robe, and then slipped the gown over Suzie's head. A pair of white cardboard wings was slipped over her shoulders, and a halo made from tinfoil and a coat hanger was placed on the young girl's head, completing her transformation into a cherub.

"Ah, I always told you that you were an angel," Karen said as she hugged Suzie, and kissed her on the forehead, nearly knocking the halo off.

10

John had given Karen the play's agenda on their way to Roses earlier that afternoon. The mother opened the door a bit to watch the people as they began to file in. Patients, some in hospital gowns, some in pajamas walked into the room. Others were rolled in wheel chairs. Visitors were taking their places among the patients. There were even some doctors and nurses standing along the walls, in their scrubs and white uniforms, ready to answer pages and rush off at a moment's notice. At 4:40 p.m., Herbie Osborne walked to the front of the cafeteria. Karen motioned for Suzie to come to the door and watch.

"May I have your attention please?" Herbie asked. After about thirty seconds the scraping of chairs and buzz of conversations quieted enough to allow the introduction to continue. "My name is Herbie Bourne, and I'm the youth leader at the Fries Methodist Church. As most of you know, Fries has had a hard time the last month, and the thoughts of a Merry Christmas seemed far away. We didn't think things could get any worse, but yesterday they did. Our own angel, a sweet, vivacious teenager by the name of Suzie Young had an accident and was brought here to the hospital. Our prayers were answered, and she is okay, so we decided to bring an early Christmas party to her, and we want all of you to be our guests. Our angel, Suzie Young, will be reading the scripture of the Christmas story. We have handed out copies of the songs we will be singing, and our music director, Mrs. Jennings, will play the piano and lead us in the songs. We hope you enjoy our Christmas gift to you."

Herbie then looked over to the door, and waved for Suzie to come to the front.

"Honey," Karen said to Suzie as she opened the door, "go stand where Herbie is standing, and begin reciting the scripture.

Do you need the copy?"

"No, Momma, I know it all by heart."

"Okay, speak slowly. Herbie is going to hold his hand up when he wants you to pause, and then nod his head when he wants you to start back. This is so the others can come in and do their parts."

Suzie made her way slowly to the front of the room without her usual bounce. The long dress touched the floor and gave her the appearance of gliding. Just as she took her place, the sun began to glimmer through the window. The combination of the tinfoil and the young girl's golden hair created an aureole encircling her head. She looked at the audience, smiled and began speaking in her luculent, melodious voice.

Luke, second chapter, first through the eleventh verses.

And it came to pass in those days, that there went out a decree from Caesar Augustus, that all the world should be taxed. And this taxing was first made when Cyrnius was governor of Syria. And all went to be taxed, every one into his own city. And Joseph also went up from Galilee, out of the city of David, which is called Bethlehem, because he was of the house and lineage of David…

Suzie saw Herbie hold up his hand, and she stopped speaking.

Just then, from the rear of the cafeteria a young black girl began walking up the aisle. It was Nacine. She was dressed with a long white robe, made from a sheet. A white towel was draped over her head, held in place by a safety pin, and hung over her shoulders. All that could be seen was the young girl's dark face, with dimples deep enough to bury a finger. Her big chestnut eyes gleamed, white-wide not with fear, but excitement. Along side her walked a young boy, about a foot taller than she. His skin was a dark bronze, appearing Hispanic. His eyes flashed side to side, not quite as happy to be here as Nacine.

Herbie nodded his head, and Suzie resumed her narration.

…To be taxed with Mary, his espoused wife, being great with child. And so it was, that, while they were there, the days were accomplished that she should be delivered…

The young couple walked to the front of the cafeteria. A young boy, Caucasian, sat at a table that had been pulled to the left front of the room. He was dressed in a brightly colored robe, with a sunflower yellow towel wrapped around his head. He appeared to be entering something in a ledger and counting coins. The pretend Joseph with his pretend wife by his side knocked loudly on the table top. The Caucasian boy unintentionally jumped, dropping some of the coins. The audience emitted a small chuckle, and then restraining themselves, again became quiet. Nacine gave the bungling thespian a reproachful scowl.

*...And she brought her firstborn son, and wrapped him in swaddling cloths, and laid him in a manger; because there were no rooms for them in the inn...*Suzie again saw Herbie's hand go up.

Mrs. Jennings began a prelude and started the audience off in her flawless soprano voice, *Away in manager...*, By the time the music director got to *"no crib for a bed"*, the audience had joined in timidly.

While the strains of the song rang throughout the room, the Caucasian youth stood up, and facing the young couple, vigorously shook his head no, pointing for the couple to go away. He gave a very redeeming performance, for the glare he gave to Nacine/Mary appeared genuine. Joseph showed his wife to the Innkeeper, pointing to her belly, very pronounced with the pillow stuffed beneath her gown. The innkeeper then pointed to the other side of a room, where a manger had been placed, and waved them away, turning his back on them.

The young couple walked to the plywood manger, and knelt. A baby doll had been placed in the manger before the play started. A diaper had been wrapped around the doll served as the swaddling cloths. The new mother picked up the baby and lifted it toward the ceiling.

And fit us for Heaven to live with Thee there. Just as the final resonance of the piano died out, Herbie again nodded.

And there were in the same country shepherds abiding in the field, keeping watch over their flock by night. And lo, the angel of the Lord came upon them, and the glory of the Lord shone round about them: and they were sore afraid. And the angel said unto them, Fear not, for behold, I bring you good tidings of great joy, which shall be to all people.

Just as Herbie's hand started up, the music director began the opening bars of "The First Noel." The congregation had now begun to sing with more enthusiasm.

The first Noel the angel did say
Was to certain poor shepherds in fields as they lay;
In fields where they lay tending their sheep,
On a cold winter's night that was so deep.

Several young boys began walking down the aisle in their bath robes. Each carried a makeshift shepherd's hooked staff. The least boy, no more than six years old, carried a white stuffed lamb in his arms. When he reached the manger, he leaned over and laid the lamb in with the baby Jesus. This elicited endearing "ahs" from the audience.

Suzie continued.
From Matthew, Second Chapter, first and second verses;
Now when Jesus was born in Bethlehem of Judaea in the days of Herod the king, behold, there came wise men from the east to Jerusalem, Saying, Where is he that is born King of the Jews? For we have seen his star in the east, and are come to worship him.

Mrs. Jennings led in with…
We Three Kings of Orient are,…

Then three grown men, Herbie, Pastor Lyons, and Pastor Buster Young began a promenade down the aisle, each carrying a box decorated with multi-colored foil wrapping paper.

Luke, second chapter, thirteenth and fourteenth verses.
And suddenly, there was with the angel a multitude of the heavenly

host praising God, and saying, Glory to God in the highest, and on earth, peace, good will toward men.

Suzie then lifted her arms, and stood on her tiptoes, like a ballerina, stretching her body upward, her head thrown back, looking heavenward. Karen clasped her hand over her mouth with a gasp. Certainly her daughter would fall backwards. John swore for a moment that the young angel had actually levitated. Three little cherubs, more like fairies than angels, came from the side and stood beside Suzie.

"Will you all please stand up and lift our voices to God as we sing "Joy to the World?" Mrs. Jennings requested from the piano bench.

The walls of the cafeteria resounded with the voices of the fifty or so people singing, their faces glowing, for they had truly gotten their first anointing of Christmas Spirit. As the final words were ended, Pastor Hamm shuffled to the middle of the room.

"Rejoice for born to you today is a savior, who is Christ the Lord," the humble pastor proclaimed in his obsequious voice. "He is truly my savior, and if He isn't yours, I pray that you will find Him this holiday season. So please bow your heads as I dismiss us with a prayer. I would also like to invite all of you to join our youth for hot chocolate provided by the hospital, and fresh cookies made by our teenagers just today."

For the next forty-five minutes, everyone enjoyed a time of refreshments, and rejoicing in the season. Suzie barely had time to eat a single cookie, or drink a cup of hot chocolate because of all the strangers wanting to hear her story and to compliment her on the wonderful job she had done with the recitation.

John, Suzie, and Karen returned to the hospital room. The experiences of the evening had fatigued the young girl somewhat, but once lying down, she was still very excited and kept the two adults up talking until after nine o'clock. Then, like a light switch, she closed her eyes and fell asleep. Her mother came over, tucked the covers around the daughter, and kissed her goodnight on the forehead.

Karen turned to walk by John, who was sitting in the chair, a blanket over him. She stopped, turned back to him and proceeded to tuck the blanket around him. She then bent over and kissed him motherly on the forehead also. John smiled, took Karen's hand in his and kissed it.

"Goodnight, John."

"Goodnight Karen. Last night you called me... umm, nothing." John decided this wasn't the time to tell her about her calling him by her husband's name the night before.

The three spent the next morning sleeping soundly until the breakfast was brought in by the orderly. Karen started over to the tray.

"No, Mom," Suzie said, motioning her mother away. "I feel great; I can eat by myself today."

John and Karen exchanged slightly awkward smiles, each waiting for the other to say something first.

"Hmm, I think I'm getting used to this chair," John finally spoke. "I might have to buy it and take it home with me. I may not be able to sleep in a bed now."

"Yeah, I know what you mean; I slept pretty good last night, too."

At nine that morning, a doctor walked in.

"Hello young lady," he said with a strong Spanish accent. "I'm Doctor Gonzalez; you did a wonderful job yesterday. My son Ricki played Joseph. He attends church with you."

"Oh, yes sir," Suzie answered. "Ricki's a very nice boy. Everyone likes him.'

"He had a very difficult time when we first arrived from Mexico. He tried two, maybe three churches, but they did not receive him well. You received him very nicely in Fries, so I drive him there each Sunday."

"Well, we are all God's children," Suzie said with a smile.

"Okay, young lady," the doctor said as he put the stereoscope ends into his ears, "let me examine you and see how you are doing."

Fifteen minutes later, after thoroughly examining the young girl, he sat down on the edge of the bed.

"Well, you have truly had a miraculous recovery. I think you are ready to go home. Would you like that?"

"Yes, Sir!! I'd like that very much."

He turned to John and Karen.

"I do not see any future concerns, not even with her vision," he said in a soft voice. "Everything looks very good. If she should begin to have the headache, or her vision, it become fuzzy, you call me and I will meet you here at the hospital."

"Thank you, doctor," Karen said as she wrapped her arms happily about Gonzalez.

"I am glad we could help. She is a very special girl. We'll have someone come here soon with the discharge papers."

By noon, John was pulling up in front of the Young's house. As requested, he had phoned Herbie before leaving the hospital. As John was helping Suzie get out of the car, her youth sponsor met her with a vase containing three red roses. His wife carried a cardboard box with the top cut off.

"Ah, there's my favorite girl," Herbie said as he handed the flowers to Suzie and gave her a welcoming hug.

"Oh, Herbie, thank you so much. No one's ever bought me roses before."

"And here's some food some of the ladies from the churches prepared," said Herbie's wife Ellie as she handed the box to Karen. "There's even one of Mrs. Young's pies in there."

"Thank y'all so much," Karen said, her eyes beginning to moisten. "You shouldn't have done this."

"We just wanted to let Suzie know how happy we are that she's okay," Herbie said, then turned to the girl again, "and, young lady, I forgot to tell you what a fantastic job you did with the scripture last night. I can't believe you recited it all from memory."

Suzie beamed from the man's approval. Her youth counselor affirmation's had brought her through the grief of losing her father.

"Well, won't you come in?" Karen asked the Bournes.

"No, we just wanted to drop this off and give you our love."

"Now you take care of these Young girls," Herbie said to John as he smacked him on the shoulder. "We don't trust just anybody with them."

"Yes," John replied with a smile, "I plan on doing just that."

Once inside the house, Karen and John began preparing lunch from the food that was brought while Suzie looked for a place to put her roses. The three sat down to a lunch of freshly baked rolls, ham, potato salad, green beans, and, of course, some of Mrs. Buster Young's chocolate pie.

Mrs. Young's chocolate pies were known throughout the county. The chocolate was so rich, some people said it was sinfully decadent. When he heard this, Pastor Young would always correct the speaker and say, "Oh no, it's Heavenly rewarding." The rumor was that after slowly melting chocolate bars in a double boiler, she then dropped ice cubes in it, and whipped the chilling mixture with a special wooden spoon. The crowning touch though was the meringue topping. It looked like stormy ocean white-caps, topped with golden brown foam. In addition to the egg whites, vanilla extract and extra fine sugar, there were other ingredients. Some speculated it was cream of tartar. Probably the delicious taste came from the fact that like the chocolate itself, Mrs. Young spent a full fifteen minutes whipping the meringue by hand, instead of two minutes using an electric mixer. The result was truly a culinary masterpiece, both delicious to the taste and pleasing to the eye.

"Momma, I'm feeling great," Suzie said to her mom between bites. "I want to go report on the council meeting in the morning."

"But if you feel like going there, you should be back in school."

"If I call Mr. Weatherman, and he says it's okay for me to come to school at lunch, will it be okay."

"Well, if your principal says it's okay, then I might let you go."

Five minutes later Suzie came running back into the kitchen.

"Mr. Weatherman said that if I make up my class work, it will be okay for me to come in at lunch. He also said I had to promise not to be climbing out onto the side of the school to hang up signs, but I'm pretty sure he was joking about that."

"What time is the meeting?" John asked.

"It's at ten."

"Oh, okay. If your mom says you can go, then I'll come up at 9:30 and drive you down."

After the meal, John stood at the sink and helped Karen wash the dishes. They were quiet, contented with just feeling each other's closeness. Every few minutes Karen would look up at John and give him a smile. Sometimes words just simply aren't needed.

By the time the kitchen was cleaned, it was almost 3 p.m. John knew there were things that Karen would need to do, and he had paperwork he needed to complete also.

"Well, I'm sure you have a load of things to do, and I need to do some paperwork, so I guess I'll head home," John said.

Karen felt a tinge of sadness. Standing there at the sink, she felt such a familiarity to him that she had forgotten it was only temporary. She forced a smile.

"John, I just can't tell you how much you helped me make it through this. I don't think I could have made it without you."

"Well, I'm glad I was there, and I'm happy if I did help." John tried to read into what Karen had said. Was she hinting that his role was over, that he was no longer needed?

"Would it be alright if I pick Suzie up in the morning then?"

"Oh, yes, of course. I would appreciate that."

John still could not determine what Karen was feeling, but then she took his hands in hers, brought them to her chest and said, "You never need to ask to come here. I'm always happy to see you." She stood on her tiptoes and gave him a quick kiss on the cheek.

John gave her a hug then walked through the living room to the door. Suzie had fallen asleep on the sofa, so he just gave her a kiss on the forehead.

Thirty minutes later a car squeaked to a stop outside the house. Karen, who had fallen asleep in the armchair quickly turned to look out of the window, hoping to see that John had found an excuse to return. Instead she saw a police car with the words "Grayson County Sheriff's Department" printed on the side. She smiled at the familiar officer and walked to the door to meet him. Suzie, by this time, was sitting up on the sofa, trying to rub the sleep from her eyes.

Before Karen could reach the door, it swung open.

"Hello, Uncle Dickie," Suzie squealed at the sight of the officer.

"Hey, how's my girl doing?" the deputy asked as he reached over to hug her. "I'm sorry I wasn't able to make it to the hospital to see you, but I had to work a double shift over the weekend."

"That's alright. We understand."

"So how have you been?" Richard said, turning to Karen, "I know it's been rough."

"Yeah, it was pretty scary for about eighteen hours."

"So, umm, who drove you to the hospital?"

Karen knew that her cousin wanted to get the lowdown.

"Oh, let's see. What was that guy's name that drove me, do you remember Suzie? You know the one that dropped me off in the parking lot and I never saw him again?"

Suzie saw a chance to play along with her mother's game.

"Yeah, wasn't it Bimbo, or John-Boy, or something like that?"

"Are you sure it wasn't John-Boy, as in John Helmsman," the deputy said with a twinkle in his eyes.

"Oh yeah, I do believe that was his name."

"So, um, what did you think of John? Pretty good guy, isn't he?"

Karen couldn't hold herself back any longer, and with a laugh confessed, "Yeah, he's a very nice guy. I really enjoyed having him there with me."

"So you did get to spend enough time together to get to know him?"

"Well, almost every minute between Saturday afternoon and a half-hour ago." Karen then added with a laugh, "he opened up a lot, after he found out you and I aren't dating."

"Dating?" Richard said. "What in the world gave him that idea."

"Well, apparently he gathered it from the things you said."

"Yeah, come to think of it, I guess maybe I never told him you were my cousin," the deputy said with a laugh, and then added, "so I guess it's not a surprise that he would think you'd be hung up on a good looking hunk like me."

"Well, you're a hunk, but I won't say of what."

"Umm, could you come outside to the patrol car? I need to…um…show you something," said the Deputy.

Once they got outside, Richard leaned against the patrol car.

Karen could tell that he just wanted to get her away from Suzie so they could talk.

"Karen, I know you don't like me sticking my nose in your personal life. Heck, you've told me that enough times," the cousin said with a laugh. "But well, it's strange how you can get to know someone better in a matter of minutes, during a stressful situation, than some people you've known for years."

Karen looked at her cousin with a puzzled expression. She had no idea where this was going, but she had never heard him talk with such seriousness in the years she had known him.

"John Helmsman is unusual. You can tell there's a lot about him that he doesn't let anyone know about. A lotta guys that came back from 'Nam act that way. But I can tell you this. If he tells you something, you can take it to the bank. He is one of the finest men I've ever met. And I only realized today why I think so."

"And why is that, Richard?" Karen asked.

"Because John Helmsman..." Richard looked deeply, sincerely into his cousin's eyes, "...is exactly like Wilson Young. I saw that when he went after Spunkie. He wasn't a paid private investigator doing his job; he was a father protecting his child. I saw the same thing when I saw him wiping the blood from her forehead, and telling her everything was going to be alright."

"Richard," Karen asked, eying her cousin suspiciously, "is that why you asked him to take me to the hospital?"

Richard grinned that impish little boy grin that made everyone like the deputy. In spite of his foolhardiness, Karen had always been able to see right through him though.

"Yes Karen, that is exactly why I had him drive you to the hospital. There was no one in this world other than myself that I would have trusted with that job, other than maybe Wilson."

John woke up the next morning, still stiff from the past two nights' contorted sleep. It had been entirely too long since he had worked out. He took a quick shower, and then pulled a shirt and pair of pants from the suitcase. This was his last change of clothes. He was going to have to drive back to Winston-Salem, or maybe just go to the laundry mat. He hadn't done his own clothes since college. He could imagine pulling out from the machine pink underwear. On second thought, he would take everything down to the Fries Laundry he had seen down past the Corner Drug. He walked into the kitchen.

The mill superintendent had a plate of eggs and bacon in front of him. The *Roanoke Times* was spread out, making it easy to read while he was eating.

"Hello Jonathan. I didn't see you before I went to bed last night."

"I stayed late down at the office, going over the records," Armbrister said. "I just keep hoping I can find some way to make the cuts headquarters want so we can reopen the Mill. I keep looking, but just can't seem to find any fat. So, how's Suzie?"

"I think she's going to be fine. She's still a little weak, but considering what she went through...She's a tough little cookie," John said with a laugh.

"That's good to hear. So what are your plans for the day?"

"I'm going to pick Suzie up in about...," John said as he looked at his watch, "thirty minutes, to go to the council meeting. I guess you'll be heading down there, too. Then I guess I'll hang around town, maybe take some clothes to drop off at the cleaners."

"You know, I'm seriously thinking about just withdrawing as co-mayor. Herbie could do a great job, and if there's no Mill, I'm not going to have much influence anyway."

"Well, Jonathan, I've never known you to walk away from a battle, and I know you are the best man. Besides, I think the town's about to settle down after this weekend."

"I made some extra eggs, ham and toast. They're on the stove. Help yourself and read the paper," Jonathan said as he passed over several sections of the newspaper. "Wake won again last night, I think they're going to have a good team this year."

John drove up to Third Street. He pulled in front of the house and was ready to go to the door when Suzie came running out.

"Mom rode over to Galax this morning with the Lawsons," Suzie said, and then smiled. "I think she may be going to buy me Christmas presents."

"Oh, you think so?"

"I think so, but it would be okay if she doesn't. I don't really need anything."

John wound his way down the terraced streets until he reached Main Street. Going to the three-way intersection at the trestle, he then made a U-turn and pulled into a parking spot in front of the Mick-or-Mack. Suzie hopped out of the car.

"What are you going to do this morning?" she asked.

"Well, I have some office work to do. I also need to take my clothes down to the cleaners, I'm just about out of anything to wear."

"Are you coming to eat dinner with us tonight?"

"Well, maybe you'd better wait and let your mother ask that," John said.

"Oh, I know it's okay. She's hoping you come. I know because she was going to buy something special to fix for dinner."

"Well, in that case, tell your mom I'll be there around five."

"Okie-dokie, see you later, alligator," the girl said with a giggle as she jumped out of the car and began rushing up the steps to the Council Chambers.

11

The regularly scheduled meeting of the Fries Town Council convened with a historical beginning. Herbie and Jonathan jointly took the gavel, and symbolically opened the meeting. Jonathan quickly went through the agenda in his very efficient, organized manner. Then he got to the last item on the agenda that was simply denoted as "Christmas Committee."

Jonathan hesitated, cleared his voice, and began.

"As we all know, the town is looking at the possibility of a dismal Christmas this year, due to…," he hesitated, feeling an added pang of anguish at the cause, "due to circumstances. But that doesn't mean we have to accept it. This town has always had a sense of spirit. From the carving out of the rocky banks of New River a dam that would spawn an industry, to an industry that begat a town—a town full of spirit—from the work ethic of the employees, to the athletes who participate at the high school. I challenge us to call upon that spirit to give this town the best Christmas ever. A Christmas based not upon lots of expensive toys, but based upon the true meaning of the Season."

At that point, Jonathan's speech was interrupted by an uproar of applause. Jonathan was somewhat taken back, for he had not intended for this to become an oration.

"So," the co-mayor continued, "I would like to suggest that we form a Christmas committee of about six members. Do I hear any nominations? I have discussed this with Herbie, and he and I would like to volunteer to represent the council on this committee."

The other members quickly agreed on a committee of six and began discussing who would make up the remaining four.

"Hey, I think our two pastors from the Methodist and Baptist Churches should be on it," Ruth Catron, the only female member of council, suggested.

"Okay, we need two more."

"Well, I think we need to be sure we include the black families from…" Dickie Smythers caught himself as he almost used the derogatory term for the section where the blacks of the town lived. This disparaging term had been used for the first 65 years of the town's existence, but in the last five years, was being eliminated by the younger generation as blacks had been easily and comfortably integrated into the Fries school system.

Dickie continued…"From the Hollow. I think Pastor Young would be a good member."

All the board members readily agreed. Pastor Buster Young was one of the most beloved members of the town, black or white. He had worked for forty years in the Maintenance Department of the Mill. Every child in town grew up loving the giant black man as he led his crew of young white boys throughout the town cutting the grass with the long-bladed scythe. It was reported Buster had once lifted a Buick off a mechanic when the car had fallen off the jack. Buster's chest was the size of a large tree, but it had to be to hold his enormous heart. His arms were bigger than tree's limbs, but they had to be to lift the spirit of all those around him. In spite of his size, he was still one of the most humble, compassionate men who had ever lived.

"Well, that leaves one more member," Jonathan said, "and I'd like to suggest who I think would be the most valuable member of the committee. I'd like to nominate," he turned and smiled at the little blonde girl setting on the front row, busy taking notes, still looking frail from her hospital stay "Suzie Young, if she feels up to it."

Suzie glanced up quickly from her notepad, eyes wide with surprise. She instantly looked at the table of council members. Each quickly broke into a smile, and nodded in hearty agreement.

"What do you think Suzie?" Herbie asked, smiling at his favorite youth member. "Do you feel up to it?"

"You bet I do," the girl answered.

Herbie knew she would. Although Suzie had attended the Baptist Church with her mother since she was a child, for the last five years she had attended the Methodist Youth Fellowship meetings led by Herbie. He knew she was the most responsible, ambitious young person he had ever seen come through the MYF in his twelve years of serving as youth leader.

"Okay, it's set," Jonathan said. "Let's see, that should be the committee. Either Herbie or I will be phoning the members for a meeting. We will try to have two more before our party. I encourage everyone though, to be thinking of ideas, and places we might look toward for assistance with toys, gifts, donations, things like that."

The meeting was dismissed. Suzie wasn't sure if her mom would be home yet, but she still bounded up the 100 plus steps to her home to tell the news to her mom. Suzie came running in the back door, just in time to see Karen quickly stuff some items in a shopping bag, which she then placed on top of the refrigerator.

"Momma! Momma! They put me on the Christmas Planning Committee, with all the other adults!"

"Really? Well, I guess they know what a fine job you'll do." Karen said as she gave her daughter a loving pat on the head, "umm, did John not drive you back?"

"No, he had some things to do, but I invited him to come up tonight to eat."

"Oh, okay, but I'm sure he's getting tired spending so much time with us." Karen said, but she certainly hoped not. She then added, "I thought you were supposed to have gone to school after the meeting."

"Yes ma'am, I promised Mr. Weatherman I'd be there by lunch time. I just wanted to tell you the good news first. I'll be home at 3:30 to help you with dinner."

After watching Suzie run up the steps to the council chambers, John had dropped his clothes off at the Fries Laundry. He later went by Jonathan's office, and using the superintendent's typewriter, wrote up the final draft of the security report. He suggested some additional security policies that the company should consider if they decided to reopen the plant.

He wanted so much to head up to Karen's but it was only 4 p.m., and he didn't want to wear out his welcome. He began driving up Route 94 toward Independence. He had only been to

Fries once before, and then only for a day. Jonathan had often told him of how beautiful this drive was as it often ran parallel to the New River. He never quite made it to the small town of Independence, county seat of Grayson County. Instead he stopped at a wayside park at Riverside. There he sat for nearly half an hour, watching the river as it flowed lazily between the rocky cliffs. He thought about how life is so much like the river. Storms came along and washed sediment into the stream, making it muddy. Sometimes heavy rainstorms even made the river overflow its banks. The river continued to flow though, and soon the waters are back within its banks and it is again running cool and clear. His life had seen many storms, and often it felt muddy and overflowing its borders. For the first time in nearly five years, he felt as if his life was ready to flow clear and cool.

John headed up to the house on Third Street at five o'clock. He was excited to find what special meal Karen was cooking for him. He knocked once, heard a cheerful *Come in* and opened the door to walk into the living room. The moment he opened the door he could smell the appetizing aromas wafting from the kitchen. He could hear the two Young ladies laughing gleefully while they worked.

"Umm, something smells delicious," John exclaimed as he started toward the smell.

Karen met him at the door leading from the living room and kitchen. She reached up and placed both hands against his chest, pushing him backwards.

"Hey, you can't come in here," she said. "We're having spaghetti, and this sauce is a close family secret, you'll have to marry me to see what's in it."

As soon as the words were out of Karen's mouth, she regretted saying them. She turned an instant blushing red, and clamped her hand over her mouth. She turned quickly on her heels to start back into the kitchen so John could not see her embarrassment. John grabbed her by the apron stings, and pulled her back to him.

"Hey," he said with a laugh, "how did you know that's what's kept me from getting married, finding a woman with a good spaghetti recipe?"

He leaned around her, and kissed her softly on her cheek.

Karen closed her eyes, loving the tactility of his closeness, wishing she could deduce what was in his heart, but when she was with him, she lost all sense of reasoning. To make it worse, the feelings she held for him frightened the heck out of her.

"Well, you'd better let me go, or we'll be having burnt sauce. You go and sit down in the living room and watch the news."

John did as he was told and turned on the TV. He dialed in to one of the only two stations that could be picked up in the town. The girls continued to cook and giggle in the kitchen, their conversations just low enough that he could only hear a few words now and then. Whatever they were talking about seemed to be making them happy.

In a few minutes Karen called from the doorway, "Dinner's ready."

John jumped up. He did not have to be asked twice. He had noticed that the kitchen light was turned off. When he got to the doorway, he saw two lit candles on the table atop a white lace table cloth.

"The candles were my idea," Suzie called out. "And I'm going to serve you and Momma, just like you were in a fancy restaurant, so please come take your seat."

John came to the table, helped Karen with her chair, and then took his seat. Suzie poured ice tea in the three glasses. She then brought a platter containing toasted and buttered garlic bread. Following that was a tossed salad. Then she brought three plates of spaghetti. The rich, meaty sauce had at least five different spices swimming in the rich tomato base.

The two quickly reached out, each of them took one of John's hands, and then joined their own.

"Dear Father," Karen prayed, "we thank You for this food that You have so generously provided for us. We continue to thank You for making Suzie better. We ask Your blessings on all those in Fries who may not have much this Christmas, and most of all, dear Lord, we thank You for bringing John into our family for this holiday season."

She lightly squeezed John's hand. He opened his left eye just enough to look over at Suzie. She had a most happy, contented smile on her face. Her lips revealed that she was finishing a prayer of her own.

"For it's in Christ name we pray, Amen."

The three began eating the food before them. With the first bite, John stopped, closed his eyes, and leaned his head back as he expressed his delight.

"Umm, this is delicious. You girls sure outdid yourselves."

They just looked at each other and smiled. Two heaping plates of spaghetti later, John finally slid his chair back from the table.

"Oh, I am so full," he said, patting the flat muscular stomach that showed the slightest hint of a bulge, "I don't know the last time I enjoyed myself so much. Now what did you say that spice was that made it so good?" He said in a conniving voice.

"I told you, it's a secret family ingredient."

"Let me guess," John said with a twinkle in his eye. "Oregano!"

"No, you silly thing," Karen said, "but I see you watch Andy Griffith also."

He walked over to the pot of sauce on the stove. He used his finger to swipe a taste of the mixture from the ladle. Lifting it to his mouth, he licked his finger as if he were a gourmet food critic. He then pulled a pasta strand from the side of the pot and walked over to Karen's side. Dropping to his knee, he took her left hand in his, wrapped the noodle around it, and looked up into her eyes.

"Karen Young, will you marry me and share your recipe," he said with mock sincerity, "I mean your life, with me?"

They all laughed uproariously.

"So, you'd only marry me for my cooking?" she said with mock indignation.

"Well, that along with about a hundred other reasons," he said with a wink.

"Okay," Suzie said to the adults, "you two go in and sit down on the couch and watch TV, and I'll do the dishes."

"Thank you, honey," Karen said, taking John by the hand and starting into the living room. "That's sweet of you."

"And I promise not to peek," the daughter said with a giggle, "in case you two love-birds decide you want to do some smooching."

"Well, what would you want to watch?" Karen asked John as

she turned on the early 60's model Magnavox black and white television.

"To tell you the truth," John said with an almost apologetic smile, "I don't watch that much TV anymore, so I don't even know what's on. So whatever you want to watch is fine with me."

"We don't really have much choice; we only pick up the two Roanoke stations. I usually like to watch "Julia." Diahann Carroll stars in it, you know, the singer."

"Oh yeah, I like her, sure, let's watch that."

"I like it because it's about a single mom, working to raise a child, in her case, a son. She's a nurse. Her husband got killed in Vietnam."

John felt his throat restrict, making it difficult to swallow. He hoped Karen would not ask him about his time in the Hell called Vietnam. He just wasn't ready to talk to her about that part of his life. The two began watching the show. By the first commercial, Karen had leaned her head over slightly onto John's shoulder. He lifted this arm, and she laid her head over on his chest. John had not felt so unsure of himself since high school. He wished he knew his boundaries, something he usually didn't worry about.

Twenty minutes later Suzie started back into the living room.

"Okay, you have to stop your kissing now because there's a kid in the room," she said as she plopped down on the couch on the other side of John. The three then began watching *The Tuesday Night Movie*. Halfway through the movie, a commercial came on advertising the next episode of "Columbo." There stood the every fumbling Peter Falk in his trench coat that looked as if he had slept in it.

"Now, John," Karen said teasingly, "you're a private investigator. Why don't you dress that way?"

John laughed, and then stopped. He couldn't believe it. He had been gone from his apartment for four and a half days, and he had not once checked his messages. He hadn't even given Teresa a number where she could reach him in case of an emergency.

"Hmm, well, it's getting late," he said, anxious to get back to Jonathan to check his answering service "I'd better head out and let you ladies get to sleep."

"Oh, we'll probably not go to bed for another two hours,"

Karen said, not wanting to give up her shoulder-pillow. Suzie had almost fallen asleep, and raised her head slowly from his lap.

"Well, I really need to take care of some things tonight," he said as he stood up and reached for his jacket, "I'll call you tomorrow."

Karen was surprised, and concerned. John had changed his mood now, and seemed so different. Had she said something to offend him? Was he uncomfortable with her and Suzie's coziness on the sofa?

John slipped on his leather bomber jacket as Karen followed him to the door.

"John, are you okay?"

"Yes, sure why?"

"Well, you just seem like you decided to hurry off on the spur of the moment."

"Oh, I just remembered some things I have to do, that's all. Thanks again for that dinner. It was fantastic," he said as he gave her a quick kiss on the cheek, then looking over his shoulder at Suzie he added, "see you later Suzie."

With that John rushed out the door.

"I'm going to bed, honey. Come on, you need to go too," Karen said as she woke Suzie up again.

Once Karen reached bed she continued to try to understand what could have caused such a change in John. The mood shift seemed to occur just when she made a joke about Columbo. Could he possibly have gotten offended about that? She thought about calling him at Mr. Armbrister's, but did not want to chance waking up the Mill superintendent.

I'll call him tomorrow morning and talk to him, she thought to herself.

As soon as John got back to Jonathan's house, he immediately went to the phone and dialed his answering service. For the last three years, whenever he left town, he switched his phone over to Teresa Patton.

"Tri-City Answering Service," the very perky, but professional voice answered. John had never met Teresa, and had so often wondered if she looked anything like her voice sounded. He had concluded she probably did not.

"Hi Teresa, this is John Helmsman. How are you? I hope it's not too late."

"Oh no, not at all," Teresa answered, somewhat surprised because John had often called her much later than tonight, and never felt the need to apologize.

"I have totally forgotten to call to check my messages, things just got—well, a little crazy," John said, not wanting to go into detail about what had held his attention for the last four days. "Got anything important for me?"

"Well, let's see what we've got," Teresa said as she started reviewing the call sheet. "You've had three calls the last three evenings from Ray Gardner, just wanting to know if you wanted to go to Renegades for drinks. Two calls from the dealer to remind you it's time for scheduled maintenance on your Corvette. You've had two calls today from Jessie. She said she'd see you tomorrow. And you had a call from a Edward Jones, Security Manager from Piedmont Airlines. He said it's important he talk to you. He said he had an opening at 10 a.m. tomorrow morning if you can make it."

His heart raced when he heard the words, "Edward Jones, Security Manager from Piedmont Airlines." He had been waiting a year for this message.

"Okay, phone the number Jessie gave you. Tell her that I'll meet her at my apartment at one tomorrow afternoon," John said, took a deep breath, and then continued. "Phone Mr. Jones. Start trying at 7:30 in the morning, keep trying until you get him. Tell him I'll be there at 10 a.m. sharp. I'll phone you again from my apartment, to see if you have anything else for me."

"Okay, John, will do. Have a good night."

"You too, Teresa. I probably don't tell you enough what a great job you do, and I really do appreciate it."

"Oh, you're welcome," Teresa said, her voice suddenly more bubbly than professional. She wondered if John had been drinking. She had never heard him so—, well, nice. She also wondered if he looked half the hunk that he sounded on the phone. She decided he probably didn't.

John sat there in the chair. He was very excited about the appointment with Piedmont. He had been trying for two years to get a meeting to discuss doing work for them. He had done a few small jobs for Mr. Davis and a couple of the other members of the board. They always seemed happy with his work and promised to keep him in mind in the future. He always felt they thought he was too inexperienced. So now, after two years of wanting this opportunity, he questioned if he was going to have a difficult decision to make.

After fifteen minutes in the chair, it was evident he wasn't going to get to sleep, so instead of taking a chance of oversleeping in the morning, he decided to go ahead and drive the ninety minutes to Winston-Salem tonight. He quickly scribbled a note to Jonathan, laid the Lincoln car keys on the table, and grabbed the Corvette keys from the rack.

Opening the door, he slumped down into the low bucket seat. As he rubbed his hands over the wood-grain steering wheel, he was reminded just how he had enjoyed the Vette. When he bought it, it seemed the most important thing in his life. It was his baby. He washed it at least four times a week, and had it detailed at least monthly. The tarp went on at the slightest indication of rain. The oil got changed every 2,000 miles. But oddly, tonight, it only seemed to be a way to get him from Virginia to North Carolina. The best thing about it was that it would also get him back to Fries fast.

He shifted the 4-speed into neutral and freed the emergency brake. Keeping the door ajar, John stuck his foot out and began to push the car forward. The car soon began to drift down the driveway, avoiding the roar of the engine just outside Jonathan's bedroom window. Once at the bottom of the driveway he turned the key, shifted into second gear, and eased out the clutch. The big V-8 rumbled to life, and the driver pulled slowly out onto Route 94 toward Riverside.

The night was beautiful. John thought seriously about stopping to put the top down, but instead drove non-stop until he arrived around midnight at his apartment in a stylish part of Old Salem. For the last six months, the normal pattern would have been to phone Jessie's apartment and let her know he was back in town. If she wasn't on a flight, she would be at his apartment in thirty minutes because she would probably not take time to do more than slip her stewardess trench coat over her nightgown. Instead, he was now dreading his meeting with her on the next day, and was thinking of how to word what he would say to her.

John set his alarm for 6 a.m. He wanted to be at a high level of alertness, in the zone as athletes like to say, for his meeting with Piedmont. This meant a trip to the gym for a two-hour routine. John lay in his bed for the next half-hour, wondering what Karen was doing right now, and rehashing in his mind how wonderful the last few days had been.

The next morning John was awakened by the alarm clock. His last few mornings had been more relaxed, sleeping late until seven most mornings. But he awoke with adrenalin-fueled energy, excited to do the best sale job he had ever accomplished. Before, he had hoped to have a meeting with the Airlines to sell them on himself. Now he knew he would have an even more difficult job of selling them on his newly-revised business plan.

He slipped into his favorite workout clothes, matching WFU football shorts and t-shirt. He pulled on a pair of black jogging pants and hooded sweatshirt as the early morning temperatures were hovering around freezing. He then went to his closet and looked at the several suits, jackets and pants, looking for the perfect combination. He thought about the blue suit with the faint burgundy pinstripe. If he was going to be meeting with the President of Piedmont, Mr. Davis, he would wear this suit. Instead he was meeting the Security Director. Chances were that Edward Jones had a background very similar to his own. If he were interviewing someone for a job, what would he want to see him wear? He thought for a while before removing a pair of tan khakis. He took a navy blue blazer and placed it on the rack with the slacks. Instead of a freshly laundered and starched white shirt, he opted for a more casual white oxford. Flipping through his ties, he finally settled on his lucky tie, a red, white, and blue diagonally striped polyester tie. No silk jobs today. A pair of black loafers should complete the garb. He reached in the closet and grabbed a gym bag that was already packed for a workout. He poured a glass of orange juice and headed out the door. He was excited about making it to the gym. The fitness center was really all he had missed while being away from Winston-Salem.

"Hey stranger, I've missed you," said a tall red-head with a very athletic figure that was teasingly emphasized by a pair of tight pink short-shorts and t-shirt that read "Piedmont Fitness Club—Home of the Hard-bodies." "Where've you been?"

"Hi Penny, been up in Virginia for a few days."

"So what's your pleasure for today?" the girl asked in a most provocative voice, her tongue quickly licking her pale pink lipstick, making her lips glisten.

"Oh, I think I'll do three miles on the track, hit the weights for a few sets. Then, how about scheduling me for a massage at 8:30?" John said as he grabbed two towels.

"Want me to get someone to replace me at the desk? I give a pretty good massage; of course I'm sure you remember that." The two had dated a few times, just before he met Jessie, and Penny never hesitated to let John know that the fun times could continue any time he chose.

"Hmm, maybe I'd better get Cecil today. I need a deep-tissue massage. I haven't worked out in a few days. He's good at working the kinks out."

"If I didn't know better, I'd swear you had forgotten about how much fun we had," said the redhead as she poked her bottom lip out in a pout. "So what's the chance of us having dinner and you catching me up on things?"

John had to hand it to her. The girl was persistent and wasn't about to give up. John just started toward the locker room.

"Not sure how long I'll be in town," John answered, not completely lying.

"Well, just remember, my number's in the book."

"Sure will, Penny. Take care."

John quickly hung his clothes and gym bag in the locker, slipped off the jogging pants and hooded sweat shirt, and ran up the steps to the indoor track. As usual, he ran the first five minutes at half-speed, and then went all out for ten minutes, half speed for five, then all out for ten minutes. By the time he got to the weights, he had his heart rate in the optimal work-out rate of 140 beats per minute. He never strayed from his work-out routine, same order, same number of reps and sets. John was satisfied with his build and just wanted to maintain it. He knew he was quickly approaching the age when that would become more and more difficult. By the end of the weight session, John was much more exhausted than usual.

It's amazing how easy it is to get out of shape in a few days, he thought to himself. This convinced him that he would never again go four days without a good workout.

He looked at the clock. Almost 8:20, just enough time to take a quick shower before his massage.

As usual, Cecil's fingers performed magic. The masseur was a stocky former airman who had lost his eye-sight during the Korean War. The man's fingers were short but powerful. John swore the man could crush a coconut with them. After thirty minutes, all the kinks had been removed from the security consultant's body. By 9:30 John had re-showered, shaved and dressed. He was feeling toned, relaxed, and ready to take on the world. The Piedmont Aviation office building was just two blocks from the gym, so by 9:50 John was standing in front of the receptionist desk. He had learned how valuable it can be to be friendly with a front desk person.

"Good morning, Ms. Henderson," he said, looking down at the name plate as he handed her his business card. "I'm John Helmsman. I have a ten o'clock appointment with Mr. Jones."

"Yes Mr. Helmsman, is that Mr. Edward or Mr. Thomas Jones?" the lady asked, barely taking time to look up from the telephone message pad on which she was writing.

"That would be Edward, Director of Security."

"I'm sorry, but he's on the phone right now," the middle-aged woman said with a slight acknowledgment. "I'll beep him as soon as he gets off."

"Thank you very much," John said, never letting the smile leave his face, even if she wasn't noticing. He then saw a snapshot of a young boy in a football uniform on her desk. "Nice looking young man. Your son?"

"Yes, that's my son Jacob," she said, her eyes suddenly

illuminating. "He'll be sixteen this fall."

"Number twelve. Does he play quarterback?"

"Yes, he was second string this year, but should start next season. Did you play football, Mr. Helmsman?"

"Yes, I played quarterback at RJ Reynolds, and please call me 'John.'"

"RJ Reynolds?" she said, her eyes widening, "You're Johnny 'Ringo' Helmsman."

"I haven't been called that for awhile," he said with a laugh.

"My younger brother played tackle with you, Preston Wilson. I'm Rachel."

"You're kidding; Tiny Wilson was your brother? He was a fantastic blocker. I don't think I ever got hit by anyone he was blocking."

"He's always telling Jacob about you. He said you threw the tightest spiral he's ever seen. As a matter of fact, Jacob keeps an old high school picture of you on his wall. Would it be too much for me to get you to send him your autograph?"

"Well, I'd be glad too, or if you'll give me your address, I have some old photos of my freshmen year at Wake Forest, I'll send one of those to you. And please call me John."

"Oh, thank you Mr...., Johnny..., John." she was almost giggling by now. "He'll love that. He's a huge Deac's fan. He hasn't missed a game since they opened Groves Stadium."

"It'd be my pleasure, Rachel."

"Oh, he's off now. Let me just slip in and tell him you're here."

John sat back in his chair and waited. It was at least five minutes before Rachel opened the door and waved him in.

"Mr. Helmsman, Mr. Jones will see you now," she said in her best professional voice.

"Thank you, Rachel. Have a nice day, and give my best to Tiny."

"You too, sir, and I will. I'll have that address for you before you leave."

John walked into the office, and instantly smiled. Edward Jones was wearing almost exactly the same outfit he had on. He immediately extended his hand.

"Mr. Helmsman. Thank you for coming," the security director

said as he stood from behind the desk. Jones appeared to be in his early forties. John could tell at a glance that he was a man who had worked his way to this position, and had not had it handed to him merely because he was one of the director's sons.

"Mr. Jones," Helmsman said as he took the man's hand, giving it a healthy grip and shaking it enthusiastically. "I was delighted to receive your phone call. I've looked forward to being able to discuss my company with Piedmont Aviation for a long time."

"Well, we thought since you were going to use our name, maybe we should give you some work, and call me 'Ed,'" the director said with a chuckle.

John echoed the laugh and then handed a brightly colored folder across the desk.

"Ed, I've taken the liberty of preparing a prospectus of what you can expect of my company."

The director rolled his chair away from the desk and leaned back. John liked the casualness the interview was taking. He mirrored Jones' informality by unbuttoning his blazer, and crossing his legs.

"Well, John, let me tell you why we contacted you," the director said after he had spent a few minutes looking over the prospectus. "We like the fact that you do good work, and you're a one-person operation. We have, umm, a situation that needs to remain very confidential. Can I depend upon your silence, even if we don't decide to work together?"

"Yes, I assure you of that."

"Okay, this is the situation. It's been brought to our attention that there are possible items being smuggled in through our freight handlers. This may be with their knowledge, their serving as accomplices, or they may just not be observant enough. We want to find out internally and take care of it before it becomes a real problem. We need someone to infiltrate the carriers. We would send you to a different airport every week. You'd spend an average of three days a week working undercover there. It should take about six months, and we would pay you $35,000, plus expenses."

John tried to conceal his reaction to the offer. The six months of part-time work was as much as he normally made in an entire year.

"Again," we like you because you have worked for some of the board members, and they like your work, and you're a one-man operation. We don't want this leaking out"

John then took a deep breath. The time had come for him to promote his company, his new company.

"I assure you that my company will give you the quality service you want, and with the confidentiality that the job demands. I do need to make you aware of an organizational change in my company. I am in the process of adding an extra field agent. I will be conducting operations from the main office, while he will be doing most of the field work."

Edward Jones pulled his chair back to the desk, stuck his finger in his shirt collar that barely buttoned around his size 17 neck, and squinted.

"Hmm, that might be a problem. We assumed we'd be using you personally."

"Well, I assure you that the man I put into the field will represent me completely. I promise you will not be disappointed."

"Are you quite certain it would have to be this way?" The security director's face was no longer showing its previous affability.

John's mind began to race. The opportunity of a lifetime was waiting. Opportunity had finally found his door and was knocking it off its hinges. Was he going to throw it away because he thought he might want a different lifestyle? A lifestyle that he did not know for sure Karen wanted to share?

He was never more sure of anything in his life.

"Yes, Ed, I promise you that *my company*, whether it's me or my agent, will give you the service you deserve."

Edward Jones folded his arms across his chest and looked over the desk at John with a cold icy stare that seemed to last for minutes. Then John noticed a slight upturn of the edges of the lips, and then a smile replaced the glare.

"Well, before you came in, my secretary spent five minutes telling me what a great guy you are, that she's known you for years, and I never second guess Rachel. If I have your assurance, then you have the job."

John felt as if his feet never touched the rich tile floors of the Piedmont Airlines lobby as he departed. He glanced at his Rolex Oyster Perpetual Explore. He then thought about the dire straits the townspeople of Fries were facing here at Christmas. For the first time since he had purchased the $200 watch, he felt guilty for this extravagance.

An $8 Timex could have just as easily told me it was 11 a.m., he thought to himself.

That would leave him about ninety minutes to stop at his favorite deli for a tuna salad croissant before leaving for his apartment. The food was great at Andre's Deli, but even more important, it was usually quiet. This would give him an opportunity to arrive at an answer to two questions.

What was he going to say to Jessie and
Who the heck was he going to hire as an agent for Piedmont Security.

Karen finally left her bed at 7:30 a.m. She had only slept a few hours during the night. She wished she had phoned Mr. Armbrister's house the night before.

Just what could have brought the change over John?

After Suzie left for school, Karen turned on the rear stove eye, and then set the pot on it to warm up the coffee left over from the day before. She went to the bathroom and used a washcloth to clean the sleep from her eyes. She stared at herself in the mirror.

I'm glad John's not here to see me look like this, Karen thought to herself.

She soon heard the bubbling of the percolator telling her the eye-opening beverage was ready. She poured a cup, dropped in two teaspoons of Domino sugar, poured in Silver Cow Evaporated Milk, and stirred, transforming the coffee from her usual 10W—30 motor oil black to a more appealing light tan.

Karen took her coffee onto the back porch and set down on a weathered wooden chair with a woven reed seat. She could almost see the Armbrister house from there. She wondered what John was doing right now. She hoped so strongly that he would phone her. She decided if he had not phoned by 9:30 a.m., she would call him.

After finishing her coffee she went back inside and began doing housework, not because the home needed it, but because she needed to stay busy. Twice the phone rang, but it was not John, just friends. She quickly offered excuses for leaving the conversations so the line would remain open. Soon the wall clock read 9:35. Karen sighed, looked up Mr. Armbrister's number, picked up the phone and dialed. She heard someone pick up the phone.

"Hello, Jonathan Armbrister speaking."

"Umm, yes, Mr. Armbrister, this is Karen, umm, Karen Young. I'm sorry to bother you. May I speak to John, please?"

"Oh, I'm sorry. He's not here; he's gone back to Winston-Salem."

Karen felt a lump the size of a soft-ball spring up from her chest that made it as far as her throat and then stuck. She swallowed hard.

"Oh! Okay. Did he, umm, did he say when he might be coming back?"

"No, I was already asleep when he got here last night, and he must have left during the night. He was gone when I woke up at six. His note just said he had business to attend to in Winston-Salem."

Karen felt a shudder of dread sweeping over her body. She could tell something was wrong last night. She guessed all the events of the last four days had just piled up on him, and it was too overwhelming for him.

"Oh. Okay. Thank you, thank you Mr. Armbrister."

"Do I need to give him a message?"

"No. No. That's okay. Thanks anyway. Have a...have a good day Mr. Armbrister." Karen said quickly, as she was anxious to hang up the phone because she felt a sudden weakening in her legs. She dropped to the sofa. Soon she was pulling the end of her dress up to wipe the tears that had started to flood her eyes.

What was she thinking? Couldn't she tell the difference between a man just being considerate and romance?

At noon the front door opened and Suzie came running in.

"Hi Mom," Suzie said cheerfully. "I forgot to take my lunch so I had to run home. What do we have for a sandwich?"

The young girl then saw her mother quickly wipe her eyes.

"What's wrong Momma?"

"Oh, nothing's wrong, honey," Karen answered, forcing a lighthearted tone.

"Has…has John been by?"

When Karen heard the words, it was as if the Fries Dam gates had opened up, as the tears began cascading down her face like the New River over the dam. She quickly pulled a chair from the kitchen table, sat down, and laid her head on her arms, her body convulsing.

"Momma, what's wrong?" Suzie repeated as she came running to her mother's side.

Karen fought to regain her composure then turned to Suzie.

"Honey, umm, John has gone back to Winston-Salem. I don't think we'll be seeing him again."

"Oh Momma, you're so silly. Of course he's coming back. He loves you."

"Now, Suzie, how can you say that?" Karen asked as she hugged her daughter to her side.

"Because I see how he looks at you Momma, just like Daddy always looked at you. And besides that, he's your paladin."

This brought a smile to Karen, for she realized Suzie was using one of her recent vocabulary additions, so she continued with their game.

"Paladin?" Karen answered with an exaggerated puzzled look. "You mean he runs around in black, shooting bad guys."

"No Mom, he's your knight in shining armor."

Karen pulled her daughter to her and hugged her tightly. To be so young, Suzie always knew just what to say to make her feel better.

"Okay, you pour yourself some milk while I fix you a peanut butter and jelly sandwich."

John stuck his key into the apartment door lock. It was 12:45, so he should have time to change clothes before Jessie got there. When he started to turn the key, he could tell the door was unlocked. He turned the knob and walked in. Regretfully, he could hear soft music playing on the eight-track player in the bedroom. He slowly, reluctantly, walked to the bedroom. There, lying spread out on the bed, in a black lace teddy was Jessie.

"Today you don't have the option of coffee or tea," the girl giggled as she rose up and knelt at the end of the bed in her best Yvette Mimeaux impersonation.

The long blonde locks hung alluringly over her shoulders. She tossed her head, flipping the hair to her back to expose the cleavage barely covered by the low-cut lace negligee. She grinned kittenishly, slowly tracing the outline of her pink lips with the tip of her tongue, as she wriggled her matching pink fingernails toward him in a "come-hither" motion.

This may be more difficult than I thought, John thought to himself.

He quickly turned away and walked back toward the kitchen.

"Umm, Jessie, we need to talk. Umm, want to slip a robe on and come into the kitchen?"

John walked to the refrigerator, took a beer from the bottom shelf, popped the cap and sat down at the small table. In a few minutes a robed Jessie walked into the kitchen, a very put-off expression on her face.

"So what's the problem, John?" the girl asked, her voice showing no attempt to conceal her vexation.

John looked at her. She was beautiful, no doubt about it, but for the first time since the night they met he had no desire to make love to her.

"Jessie, I like you very much; you are a very beautiful woman…"

"Something tells me that there's a 'but' coming up," the blonde said as she turned around, reached into her purse and pulled out a cigarette. She knew how John hated to have her smoke, but she was now sure she had nothing to lose.

"I just think it's time we both move on, Jessie."

"So, who is it John? What's her name? Let me guess, PENNY!"

"No, it's no one from here. You don't know her. Her name is Karen, she's from Fries."

"Are you sure this is what you want?" Jessie put the cigarette out, and turned back toward John, a seductive smile on her face, as she quickly slipped her robe up and sat down on his lap, her lips rushing to his. She devoured his mouth with hers. After a few seconds, she realized that she was getting no response from the man. No longer did her kisses spark the heat they once did. He slipped his fingers beneath her thighs and lifted her up from his lap. She now knew that it was over.

Without another word, she walked to the closet, took out her stewardess trench coat and replaced the robe with the coat. She slipped her feet into the black sandals. As she walked by, she threw the robe at John, spilling his beer. Her only acknowledgement of him was a flash of the middle finger just before she slammed the door behind her.

At 3:45 the phone rang in the Young's living room.

"Hello, Young's residence," Suzie answered, listened for a few seconds and then continued, "Yes she is, one moment please."

She then turned to her mother, and placing her hand over the receiver said, "It's for you, something about vinyl siding."

"Hello, this is Karen," the mother said, ready to inform the pushy salesman that she had no interest in his product.

"Well, you don't have to be so professional," John said with a laugh.

Suzie began giggling as she mouthed the words to her mother, "I told you so, I told you so."

"Well, hi John, I understand you went back to Winston-Salem."

"Yeah, when I saw the commercial for Columbo last night, it reminded me. I've gone four days without even checking my messages. When I got to Jonathan's, I found some important messages and left at midnight to come down here. I had some, emm, loose ends that needed taking care of."

"So, umm," Karen was almost afraid to ask, "are you planning on coming back?"

"Well, yes, of course," John said, not able to understand her doubt, "I have a lot of things to talk about. Some, umm, great things have happened. Or at least, I hope you'll also think they were great. Besides, I was promised a Fries Christmas. Have you forgotten?"

"And you're going to get one," Karen said, her heart now pounding with happiness.

"I've got just a little more business left to do. I hope to be back up to Fries by Thursday, around noon. You won't forget me by then will you?"

"Well, you might have to remind me what your name is," she said teasingly.

"Think you could do me a favor? Could you give me Richard Carrico's phone number? I need to discuss something with him."

Karen recited the number from memory, wondering about what he could possibly be wanting to talk to Richard.

"Well, I'll see you Thursday. I'll call you when I get there. I'm already missing you," John said.

"The same here," Karen said.

"Bye."

"Bye."

Karen just stood there for a few seconds looking at the phone, with a very contented smile. She then stuck a finger into her hair, began twisting a curl, as she began to hum, "Love is a Many Splendored Thing."

Suzie just giggled.

12

THERE WILL BE A CHRISTMAS

read the headlines of Suzie's December18th edition of the *Fries Wildcat Spirit Weekly*. In it she gave the highlights of the board meeting, then tried to repeat verbatim as much of Mr. Armbrister's speech as she could recall. It was times like this she wished she had one of those tape-recorders that she sees the journalists on TV use. She reported who the six Christmas committee members would be, after the three pastors had been asked and had accepted. She tried to report her nomination as casually as possible, without letting her pride show through. Her mom had always told her it's okay to be proud, but wrong to have pride. Sometimes she could not understand how to have one without the other.

Friday, December 19th was an exciting day because this was the last day before the Christmas break. She thought the day would never end. All the kids had wanted to know what she would be doing on the Christmas committee. She felt like a celebrity. When Suzie left school at 3:15, her mom and John were waiting for her. They drove to Galax where they had hamburgers, milk shakes and onion rings at Kenny's Restaurant. Afterwards they stopped at Roses. As they entered the department store, John leaned over to Suzie.

"Here, use this to buy your mom some Christmas presents," he said as he slipped a twenty dollar bill into her hand.

"I'll meet you up front in thirty minutes," Suzie said, turning to her mom as she disappeared into the store.

John and Karen began walking through the store aisles. Karen ran into several friends who made a point of coming up to her under the pretense of wishing her a Merry Christmas. She knew it was because they were dieing to know who the striking stranger was. Karen did not disappoint them, as she would place her hand on John's arm, and introduce him as 'my friend John from Winston-Salem.' John offered Karen money for the holidays, but she assured him that she had already bought Suzie some clothes.

The three returned to the Young house that night about 9:30. Just as they entered the door, they heard the phone ringing. Suzie ran to answer it.

"Hello, Youngs' residence."

"Suzie?"

"Yes?"

"This is Herbie. Can you attend a Christmas committee meeting tomorrow morning at ten in the council chambers?"

"Yes sir, I'll be there."

She hung up the phone and turned to the adults.

"That was Herbie. We have a committee meeting tomorrow morning at ten."

"Do you want me to drive you down?" he asked.

"I think that would be great, see you at 9:45."

"Why don't you make it 8:30, for breakfast?" Karen said, then quickly tiptoed up and gave John a kiss on the cheek before he could leave.

On Saturday morning, Jason Campbell sat at his mom's kitchen table having fresh pork tenderloin and gravy. Jason had graduated from Fries that June where he had been an All-State Quarterback. He had received several offers for scholarships, but on the last play, of the last game of the season, he had suffered a knee injury that had ended his football career. He was now at VPI studying Civil Engineering.

"I see in Suzie's newspaper that the town is trying to put together some kind of a Christmas for the kids," Jason's mom Leah said.

"That's great," Jason said, not looking up from the sports page of the *Roanoke Times*, "leave it to Suzie to make sure something gets done."

"Yeah, that's quite a little girl," Leah said. "I saw her mom the other day at Piggly Wiggly, and she was asking about you. You know Suzie still has a huge crush on you?"

"I'm just the big brother she never had," he said.

"Karen said that Suzie has the copy of the paper she wrote about your career at Fries, the one you signed for her. She has it framed along with your senior photo on her wall, right next to her picture of Davey Jones, or whatever the kid's name from the Monkees is."

"Well, she's a neat kid, but she's a tad too young for me."

"Well, when she grows up, she's going to make some man a good wife."

"I wish there was something I could do for the party," Jason said, trying to change the subject.

Even though the Campbells lived about five miles away from Fries in a small community called Brush Creek, they felt a real kinship to the town. This was true of all the surrounding areas. Fries lay in the middle of Carroll and Grayson County. Even though the school was technically for the citizens of Fries, students from the surrounding counties of Carroll, Grayson, and even Wythe County often chose to come to Fries High School. It wasn't because of the facility itself, for Fries High School was the oldest in the area. It was more a matter of pride, and tradition. Many of the parents had gone to Fries, and went on to work in the Cotton Mill, before moving to the country. It was only natural that the kids would go to school there too.

"Well, it's not much," Leah said, "but I am giving several jars of tomatoes and several bags of green beans and corn for their dinner that night."

"Well, maybe I can think of something to do, too."

"So how's the job going?" Leah asked. Jason was on his Christmas break from VPI, and was staying in Pulaski with his sister Lisa and her husband Jeremy. He was working at the local IGA grocery store over the holidays.

"It's going good. I kinda enjoy it. Reminds me of when I worked at Shepherd's."

"Well, we sure miss you. You haven't been home but a few times since you left for college."

"Yeah Mom, sorry about that. It's really been busy. I've had to study on weekends."

Jason didn't explain that the reason he had to study so much on weekends was because he and his buddies, Don and Roy, were spending almost every night at the Hokie House, drinking beer and eating Hokie Burgers. This explained the ten pounds he had put on during his first quarter.

"So how are you doing in school?"

Jason took a deep breath, wondering if he should admit to the terrible grades that would be arriving in the mail within the next two weeks. He thought perhaps he should prepare his mom for them.

"Well, my grades aren't going to be very good."

"You mean B's and C's?"

Jason didn't volunteer that the only courses he had passed was a C in English Lit, and a B in Phys. Ed.

"Well, or maybe even worse."

"Jason!" his mom gasped, "You've never made bad grades, you're not partying too much are you?"

"No mom, it's just that I can't handle the subjects. I never had calculus, advanced chemistry and physics at Fries. I'm in these classes with those rich kids from northern Virginia. They had those classes in high school, so it's like repeat courses to them, but I never had them."

Fortunately, about that time Jason's father Colin walked in. Colin had worked in the Cotton Mill for thirty years. Even though the lay-off was going to be rough on him, it was not as bad as the people who lived in town. Most of the "out-of-town" workers raised small gardens, even livestock to keep them fed. Most had basements or cellars full of jars of food, and freezers full of frozen food. It also helped that Jason's mother Leah worked in a sewing factory in Independence. Colin had also found temporary work doing overnight stocking at a local grocery store.

"Hi Jas, good to see you, son. I didn't know you were coming." Jason met his dad at the door, and the two hugged.

"Yeah. Sis offered me the car for the day, so I drove up last night after work. Mom said you had just left when I got here."

"How you liking the job?" the father asked.

"Great. Mr. Powers is a really nice man. I'm doing a little stocking, but mostly packing groceries and carrying them to cars. I even got a dollar tip this week. So how does it sound on the Mill starting back up?"

Colin was a loom fixer in the Mill, and, as a skilled mechanic was one of the higher paid hourly workers. He also stayed "in the loop" of the people who had contact with the management.

It doesn't look good, not good at all," Colin said, his usual smile dissipating. "The rumor is, the Company is going to play hard ball. They're going to starve us for a few weeks, then offer us our jobs back at lower pay, about a quarter an hour less."

"Do you think the people will take it?"

"I don't know. People like us, we can make it, but the people in town, I don't think they could go weeks without a job. I think they'd go back for whatever the Mill offers."

"Do you think there might be a strike?"

"No. I don't think so. This area's a lot different from the coal mining towns. Remember we tried that strike a couple of years ago, and nothing good came of it? Plus, for some reason, the Union don't have no interest in us. I guess we're just not big enough for them to set down with."

"I understand Mr. Armbrister has been made out to be the villain in all this."

"Well, I think just by some of the younger workers, and some of the trouble makers. The rest of us know that the guys down in Winston-Salem are calling the shots."

"Yeah, it sounds like Spunkie really stirred up a hornet's nest, but I guess he'll get what's coming to him now."

"I heard they might sentence him to five years. He had just better be glad that nothing happened to Suzie Young, or someone would have killed him."

Jason enjoyed talking to his dad so much. His father had only finished the eighth grade. He had dropped out of school at fourteen when his father had medical problems. Being the oldest son, he had gone to work in the Mill to support the rest of the family of eight. But Colin had read his whole life, anything from *Life Magazine* to Zane Grey novels. He had learned a world of knowledge through the written word and could discuss most anything.

Jason's mother, Leah, wasn't as knowledgeable in worldly matters, but she was unbelievable at managing money. Thanks to her financial skills, in fifteen years the family had gone from living in a small rented three-room tobacco farmer's house in Danville, to a nice 1500-square foot brick house with a basement, setting on four acres of rich, creek-bottom land. The parents had helped put one daughter through business school, one through nursing school, and were now putting him through college.

"So what are you going to do today?" the father asked his son.

"Well, mostly just lay around," Jason answered. "I had thought about going down to Jess and Myrtle's tonight. But I'll probably wait and go down Christmas night. Ruby and Linda will be there then, and I'll get to see Linda's new baby I guess."

He noticed his parents gave each other a strange look when he mentioned Christmas night.

The Campbells had lived in their house the last eleven years. From the first day they moved in, Jason, as a six-year-old, adopted the Marshes as his second family. While growing up on Brush Creek, he would spend some of almost every day at their house. He would help with errands, such as carrying water and collecting eggs. His most enjoyable time was with Jess in his shop. Jess, much like Colin, was uneducated, but was a self-taught mechanical genius. He could take scrap parts that he had collected from the junk barrel at his job at the Mill, bring them home, and make something useful. Jason felt honored, because he was the only young boy on the creek that Jess would allow in his shop.

The two daughters Ruby and Linda, were both older, but were just like sisters. Jason's older sister Josie had married and left home when he was six, and his other sister Lisa had left home when he was nine. The two Marsh girls had very quickly become his siblings by proxy.

"Oh, that reminds me. Betty Jean Morrison saw me the other day and said to be sure to have you come by and see her on Christmas day. She wanted to show you something."

"Hmm, wonder what she's up to now."

"I don't know, but she sure seemed excited to see you. She always seemed like she liked you as much more than a neighbor."

Jason was glad his mother didn't know just how much more the young girl did like him than a neighbor. He felt it was time to redirect the conversation.

"Wow Mom, that tenderloin was delicious. Thanks so much." Jason gave his mom a kiss on the cheek. "It's been a year since I've had it."

"Glad you liked it. If you'd come home more, you'd have it more often," she chided.

"Well, it's been difficult without a car," Jason offered as an excuse.

Leah looked at Colin, then back to Jason.

"Well, we were going to talk to you about that," she said. "Are you sure you don't want to get a car? You've not had one since you blew your Mustang on the 4th of July. I'm sure Mr. Wall wouldn't mind you using some of the money he left you to buy one."

"Well, I can't have a car my freshmen year at Tech anyway, so I thought I'd wait and get one in the summer."

"Well, then during the time you're on break, you can take the Buick back to Pulaski."

"But that only leaves you with the one car," he said. Jason would love to have a car to drive while in Pulaski, but would never want to make it difficult on his parents.

"That's alright," his mom said. "We'll be okay with one car until next month when you go back to school."

Jason had to admit, he liked this idea. There was a very cute blue-eyed blonde who was working in the pharmacy snack counter next door to the IGA. He had been dying to ask her out, but didn't want to have to beg his sister to borrow her car.

"Well, if you're sure. But what about Lisa's car? I drove it up."

"Well, we were wanting to go talk...to see, Lisa this weekend," Leah said, as she turned her head slightly away, her voice sounding somewhat strained, "so we'll drive two cars down, and drop off hers."

"Well, I'd appreciate that. Thanks, Mom," Jason said as he gave his mother a thankful hug. Jason noticed that his father had not participated in the discussion and had turned his head away, looking out the window at nothing in particular. *Was he upset that Jason was taking the car?* Jason took his cup of coffee and walked into the living room. The Mill may have lain off, but you'd not know it by the presents under the tree. But then the lay-off would not have affected gift buying in the Campbell household, because his mother always had her presents bought by Thanksgiving.

Jason may be a college student, but he still had enough of the little boy in him to take his foot and move wrapped presents around, trying to pick out the ones that belonged to him. This reminded him that he had not yet bought his parents' presents, but he was sure he knew what he wanted to get them. He had found one of the new Polaroid 360 Land Cameras that he thought his mom would like. His dad was always complaining about his razors, so Jason was buying him a Remington electric razor.

"Well, at least I won't have to worry about buying a present for a girlfriend," Jason then thought to himself. He tried to laugh, but knew that he was fooling himself trying to pretend it didn't bother him. He began to get depressed. For the last three years, a big part of Christmas was finding just the right gift for Katy Lynn. He always saved at least $75 from his summer jobs to do this.

"Hey, I think I'll take a walk," he said as he picked up a windbreaker. "Be back in an hour or so."

The day was very nice, sunny, about 65 degrees, even though it was mid-December. Maybe it would be a perfect day to take a walk and try to figure things out. Jason walked first down to the edge of Brush Creek. This stream started about six miles above his house and ended about six miles beyond his house. There it flowed into the New River at a point about five miles north of Fries. New River was one of the oldest rivers in the world. Some say only the Nile was older. Jason had always heard this was why the river flowed north, starting in North Carolina and ending in West Virginia.

Jason had read once that the New River flowed into the Kanawha River, which flowed into the Ohio River, which flowed into the Mississippi River, which flowed into the Gulf of Mexico. As a kid, Jason would make small boats using left over pieces of wood from Jess's shop. He would write his name and address in big script letters on the makeshift boat, and throw it into the creek during the spring floods. He always hoped to receive a letter from someone along the Mississippi who had found the boat, but he never did. It did make him think though how he too, could be swept away from Brush Creek, figuratively, to a place bigger and better.

Jason began to reminisce about how much fun he had growing up on the creek. Route 94 ran across the stream on a three-span concrete bridge. Even before the young man decided on engineering as a career, he used to study how the overpass had been constructed. He spent hours locating the seams where the concrete had been poured, searching for birds' nest in the weep holes that were formed to let groundwater drain from behind the abutments, or to study the vibrations and deflections of the steel beams as large trucks drove overhead.

He thought back to the first fish he caught at the age of seven from the creek using the bamboo pole his dad had bought him that day from the Western-Auto in Galax. Actually he didn't really catch it. He snagged the minnow in the side. He recalled how he ran up the steep bank to Oscar's store to weigh the trophy, and Oscar laughing as he laid the sardine size fish on the scales. Jason was now sure that the store-owner must have put a thumb on the scales to get the little 4" long silver-side to weigh even three ounces. He caught larger fish, mostly red-eyes, using the long tubular tin cans that the luncheon meat came in that Oscar cut into custom made slices. He was reminded of the crawdads and how he would grab them just behind their big pinchers. He could hear himself begging his mom to cook the crustaceans, because he had heard they tasted just like the lobster that rich people ate. He had promised himself that one day he would go to fancy restaurants and eat things like lobster. He knew he'd even eat snails, if it was shown as escargot on the menu. He wanted to try everything life had to offer.

He recounted, as he got older, going up the creek to the various fishing spots with names like Maude's Hole and Little Rock. He laughed as he remembered the best fishing site, The Blue Hole, which was off limit because Jason's dad and his cousins' father, Hershel, felt it was too dangerous. He thought of the time he, Junior, and Ravin had disobeyed and gone to the forbidden location. He relived how he had caught the biggest bass he would ever catch, just to be caught in a rainstorm, and how they had climbed into a cave, built a fire to stay warm, and had cooked the fish over the fire. Then, how their fathers, concerned with the flash flooding from the rainstorm, had come looking for them, just to find the boys in the cave, warm, dry, and fed, while their fathers were soaked to the bone. His dad had given him the only whipping he had ever given the boy, if three smacks across his jean bottom with a switch could be called a whipping.

He walked down along the bank of the creek, along the garden, now barren with the rumble and remnants of the harvesting. Tomato vines had been laid to the ground by the earlier snows. The corn stalks lined like defeated soldiers, broken off six inches above the ground, but whose deep roots kept them from being totally blown away by the winter's icy gusts. Jason knew this was all part of life and nature. By spring, the barren, lethargic plants that had months before borne such wonderful vegetables, would be plowed under, new seed planted, and the hope of new fruits of labor, or in this case, vegetables of labor, would take sprout, and spring forth. What was now so colorless and stark would by summer be alive and vibrant. Death follows new birth; new birth is then followed by death in a perpetual cycle.

Mr. Campbell took great pride in his gardens. Jason could remember the good-hearted bragging between his dad and the other men as to the astronomical number of bushels that one potato plant had furnished, or how many ears of corn one stalk provided. It wasn't lying; it was just stretching the truth. He remembered all the times he was to help hoe the garden, but something would come up, like a ball game or swimming at the YMCA pool, always something. Colin would fuss for awhile, but then would always relent, and let Jason leave the garden to go have fun.

Once Jason got to the edge of the garden, he looked up into the woods. The level plane of the garden rose into a steep slope, covered with a mixture of pines and hardwoods like oak, maple, and hickory. With the leaves gone from the hardwoods, Jason could easily view the big rocky bluff that jutted out from the mountainside. Jason had spent many happy hours there. The bluff was flat on top, about ten-feet by six-feet. From the time he was about ten until he turned sixteen, he spent hundreds of hours on the elevation. He would take his Boy Scout knapsack with him. From it he would pull matches to build a fire, cans of pork-n-beans, and Vienna sausages, sardines, and crackers, with a canteen full of grape Kool-Aid. After cooking, or eating a raw dinner, he would unroll his sleeping bag and pull out adventure or history books to read.

He would then stand up, and look out over the horizon. No longer would this be Jason Campbell from Brush Creek. Now it was Daniel Boone, exploring the wilderness of western Virginia. Or maybe Meriwether Lewis, as he studied the raging Mississippi for a safe crossing point. Or perhaps he was Colonel Henry Fries, standing on the rocky cliffs, overlooking the waters of New River, planning the location for a cotton mill, and a town to support it.

The dreams were still vivid in his memory. Then he thought to himself, *as long as you have dreams, you have hope.* He was about to lose hope, though. He then felt a pang of guilt as he remembered how he had been blaming the lack of preparation at Fries High School for his failing grades. But it was those teachers who had given him dreams. It was Mrs. Davis in the sixth grade who had encouraged him to overcome his speech impediment, to overcome his insecurities and speak up in class, and to develop a passion for reading. It was Freddie Jennings in the 9th grade who had convinced him that a 95-pound scrawny kid could play football, and even though he came from a very modest family, this kid could grow up and go to VPI and major in Engineering. His teacher Mrs. Fender, and Mr. Fender, her husband and the principal, had taught him a hunger for learning that could be satisfied through books. Later in high school it was teachers like Mrs. Lyons who had never lost her patience, or her faith, in him in spite of his shortcomings. It was teachers like Mrs. Jenkins who had given him the confidence to be a public speaker. It was men like Coach Martin and Coach Statzer who taught him there's nothing wrong with getting knocked down, just as long as you wipe the blood off and get back up.

These teachers had given him all he needed to succeed. For sixty years people from Fries had survived not because they were smarter, but because they worked harder. Fries sports teams had won, not because the athletes had more talent, but because they had more heart. The towns on the west side of the Blue Ridge mountains had not come from the fancy-pants English noble class, but had instead come from the hard working European middle-class, such as the Scots, the Irish, and the Germans. He had come from good stock.

Jason looked around him, at the creek flowing on its way to the Gulf of Mexico, to the garden that kept the family fed, to the forests sinking their roots into the steep mountain slopes. He knew he was going to have to make a decision during the break whether or not he should admit that he didn't have what it took to be an Engineer, and to go into another easier major. Jason looked down at a clod of dirt, loosened from the roots of a corn stalk that had been pulled from the ground. He picked it up, studying it, before throwing it into the creek. The hardened brown dirt soon became soft, and within moments, and within feet of where it had hit the water, had dissipated into several smaller clods, leaving a brown stain on the water. From its point of splashdown, there resonated several concentric water ripples that were growing steadily larger and larger. Some of the dirt from the clod of soil would probably flow into the Gulf of Mexico. It would find a way to go to somewhere bigger and better. Jason turned and walked back to the house with determination. Entering the front door, he hung his windbreaker in the closet.

"Hey, if you need me," he called to his parents, "I'll be in my room, reading."

He entered his bedroom, unchanged since he had left it in September. He scanned the books in the bookcase his Uncle Emmitt had given him for Christmas three years before until he spotted the small paperback book for which he was looking. He carried the book back to his bed, slid his shoes off, sat down on the bed with his back against the headboard, opened the book up, and began reading the book that he had first read in the eighth grade at Vaughan Intermediate School. The title was "Your Career in Civil Engineering."

13

John showed up for breakfast Saturday morning at 8:30. Karen was still in her housecoat.

"I'm getting entirely too comfortable with you," she said with a laugh, "I can't believe I'm letting you see me in my housecoat, without any makeup."

"I'd enjoy seeing you like that every day," he said. She gave him a puzzling glance.

"Hi John," Suzie said as she came running in, giving him a kiss on the cheek.

"So how long do you think your meeting will last?'

"Oh, probably a couple of hours."

"Well, unless your mom has something planned, I was hoping this evening, we might all drive to Galax, have dinner, watch their parade, and drive through town to see the decorations."

"Oh yes. Momma, can we do that. Please?"

"Oh, okay. And maybe when you guys get back from town, we'll go cut a tree."

After breakfast, John and Suzie left for town, where he dropped her off on Main Street at 9:45.

"If you finish early, just go to the Corner Drug. Here's a couple of dollars; get yourself a shake. Don't eat too much though, or your mom will skin my hide."

Suzie scuttled up the steps to the council chambers and the meeting.

Herbie, feeling a little more confident in a smaller group, called the meeting to order and asked members if they had any ideas.

"Well, I think this would be the perfect time to get back to a traditional Christmas, one where family, tradition, and the birth of Christ take precedence over a room full of presents," Pastor Hamm said, starting off the discussion.

"Yes, I totally agree. Perhaps we could have several events at our churches, or maybe in the auditorium as a group," offered Pastor Lyons of the Methodist Church.

"The children of my church usually don't get a lot of presents, but parents spend the year around making toys and clothes for them. I think sometimes something that the child knows comes from the parent means even more than store-bought toys," Pastor Young said.

Herbie spoke up, "I know of two wonderful Mennonite Ladies, Miss Zarfus and Miss Hess, who spend all year preparing big manila envelopes with Bible pictures, bookmarkers and the such. I bet they might have some left over. Wonder how many kids we have in the town?"

"I got a count from the town clerk," Jonathan said. "She gave me a list of nearly 200."

"I think we need to agree on something from the beginning," Herbie said. "Anything we discuss remains a secret, so it will be a surprise."

Everyone agreed.

"So that means no special editions, Suzie," Herbie said with a wink. "And we haven't heard from you. What do you think?"

"Well, I do know there's not much money," she said, in deep thought, "but I do hope we can find a way to give some presents. I also like the idea that we should try to go back to the traditional Christmases. Maybe the MYF could go caroling, Herbie."

"Excellent idea, Suzie," Herbie agreed. "Anything to bring back a little Christmas spirit."

"You know," Jonathan said, "there are lots of people that have moved away. I bet if they knew about what has happened, they would help with small donations. Who would like to try to make some contacts with me?"

"Well, I'm not busy right now, Mr. Armbrister," Herbie said with a laugh. "I'll be glad to help."

The whole committee recognized the significance of the statement said in jest. It was made with good humor, with no animosity, and showed that wounds had healed.

"And we are still having Sunday night for our Christmas plays at the churches, right?" Pastor Lyons said more as a statement than a question.

"Maybe if we could raise some funds, the theater would be reopened, and on Monday night two free movies could be shown with free drinks and popcorn. I'll take care of this," Armbrister said, because he already knew of who he was going to ask.

"Okay, so on Tuesday night," Herbie said, "the combined youth of the three churches can go caroling and hand out invitations for a grand Christmas Eve party on the 24th, at the school gymnasium. Suzie, we'll discuss this after MYF Sunday evening, okay?"

"Yes, sir, that will be fine."

"Well, things are about to look up," Jonathan said, "but you know, we're about to forget one of the best parts of Christmas, the parade. I know usually we get lots of floats entered, trying to win the big prize money given out by the Mill, but that's no reason why we can't have a smaller one. As a matter of fact, I've gotten so optimistic, why don't we plan on putting together a last minute Christmas parade at 6:30 that would end at the gym for the Christmas party."

The others agreed enthusiastically.

"Hey, my brother-in-law is the band director at Galax," Pastor Lyons said. "I bet I could get him to bring the band over."

"Yeah," Herbie said, "and I bet Pete would be glad to get the Boy Scouts in it."

"School's already out, so we can't have them vote for a snow queen," Herbie said, then looked at Suzie, "but I bet we could all agree on who we'd want for a Snow Angel."

Pastor Hamm, picking up the cue, said, "I nominate Suzie Young as snow angel. All in favor say 'aye.'" Five ayes rung out before Suzie had a chance to say anything.

"Of course, we want to get the fire trucks and the new rescue ambulance to be in the parade," Pastor Young said.

"Do I get to ride in it?" Suzie said with a laugh. "I can't remember anything about the last time I rode in an ambulance."

"Well, that leaves us with Santa," Herbie said. "Any idea who to get for Santa?"

"Well, let's think about Santa and decide that on Tuesday," Jonathan suggested. "Will someone ask Bruce Smith about wearing his police uniform and hauling Santa in his old car?"

"Yeah, I'll ask him," Jonathan said, "I have a meeting with him on Monday."

The committee decided that most of the work would center on the Christmas party at the school. Each member would be thinking of more ideas for this, and they would discuss them at the next meeting, set for Tuesday morning at ten.

"Well," Herbie said looking at his watch, "a quarter after noon. It's been a very good, very productive, two-hour meeting."

After dropping Suzie off, John had gone back to Jonathan's house and called his answering service for his messages of the last three days. After collecting the messages, he began phoning friends, associates, clients in North Carolina to let them know:

No, I haven't fallen off the ends of the earth, I'm, well, rather involved with something in Fries.

No, I won't be back in time for all the Christmas parties, and won't be taking any new jobs for at least the next week or so.

There was also a message from Jessie, but he did not respond to her request to *"call me, if you want to."*

About ten before noon, he drove down and parked in front of Bud's Corner Drug. He walked through the door, smiled and waved at Bud, and began to look around for Suzie. He did not find the little blonde girl, but he did see a familiar face, Karen's cousin, Richard Carrico sitting at a table. The deputy was turned around in his chair, arms resting on the back, talking to Chief of Police Smith, who was sitting at an adjoining table enjoying his vanilla ice cream cone.

John went to the counter. Although he wasn't hungry or thirsty, he always felt uncomfortable sitting in a business, without patronizing it.

"Hi, Bud, how about a cup of coffee? Maybe a piece of that apple pie, too."

Bud began pouring a cup of coffee.

"Enjoying your stay John? You know, one more week, and you become an honorary citizen of Fries," Bud said with a chuckle.

"Really? Do I get free coffee and pie then?"

"Heck no. We begin to charge you double then," Bud laughed,

as he slid the pie and coffee over the counter to him. Bud recognized a noticeable difference in the young man, not as stiff and aloof as he had seemed a week earlier. "Guess you're having a long, involved case you're trying to crack," Bud continued, with a wink.

"Yeah," John said, smiling back, "I'm afraid it might be the toughest case I've ever had to crack."

When the John turned around, Deputy Carrico was motioning him over. John approached the county deputy. Bruce was just leaving and John quickly thanked him for his assistance on the Saturday of the accident.

"Mind if I join you Deputy?"

"Sure, boss," Carrico said with a wink. "Especially now that you're practically a part of the family. Understand you've changed your address to 105 Third Street."

"Well, not quite yet," John said, "but I have to admit, I like the idea."

John lowered his voice as he whispered to the Deputy.

"So if everything works out, does February 1 still look good for you?"

"Yep, it sure does. I'm really excited."

"Well, I'm not excited," John said with a laugh, "I'm scared to death."

At 12:20, Suzie, accompanied by Jonathan Armbrister, came into the diner. Suzie came running over to hug her second cousin's neck.

"You're looking good as new, sweetheart," Richard said.

"Hey John," Jonathan said, leaning on the table, "Suzie said she thought you might be here. I wanted to drive down to North Carolina, to pick up the missus. Do you mind if I take your car?"

"Sure, of course. Could you do me a favor? Go by my apartment and pick up my mail? The key is the brass one, first on the key chain."

"Sure, be glad to. We'll be back tonight. Want to have dinner?"

"Well, Jonathan, you know how I enjoy your company, but the truth is, tonight, I'm having dinner with the two prettiest blondes you have every laid eyes on."

This brought a giggle from Suzie, as she stood at the counter, ordering a strawberry milkshake.

"Well, I guess I can't beat that offer. We'll see you tonight when you get back to the house."

"Sure thing, Jonathan," John said. "Have a safe trip. Hey, and watch out for radar down on Route 52 there at Pilot Mountain. I think they have it in for that red car."

"I don't think they could catch me. That car really scoots," Jonathan said, his face loosening up from its usually rigidness. "Oops sorry, Deputy Carrico, you didn't hear me say that."

"Now Mr. Armbrister, I'm quite certain you'd never exceed the posted speed limit," the officer said.

"Ready to go, Suzie Q.?" John said as he pushed his chair away from the table.

"Yes, can't wait to go get the tree."

"Keep your fingers crossed," John said with a smile as he leaned over to shake Carrico's hand. "I'll let you know how Wednesday night goes. It all depends on that."

"Well," the deputy returned with a wink, "I don't think you'll need it, but you've got my vote."

"Stay by your phone incase I need a tie-breaker."

John turned around, and putting his hand on the blonde head, said, "let's go kiddo."

As the two walked in, Karen looked at them, her hands on her hips, with a mock serious look on her face. "You were sure gone a long time, I have a feeling someone had a barbeque down at Bud's."

John and Suzie looked at each other guiltily, and then laughed.

"Nope, wrong-o, just a shake." Suzie said with a chuckle.

"Well, I didn't fix anything, in case you had. So we'll just have tomato soup and cheese sandwiches while we are decorating the tree."

John searched his memory for the last time he had decorated a Christmas tree, much less gone into the woods and cut one. Then the memory of his grandparents came back to him.

"Where will we go for the tree?" John asked, wondering how he was going to haul a tree in the back of the Lincoln.

"Oh, just across the street, and up into the woods," Karen answered. "A friend of ours owns the land there. He lets some of us cut the white pines for Christmas trees, then Suzie and some of the other kids get pine seedlings from the 4-H, and replants them."

"Well, that is a good idea. How will we cut it down?"

"I brought a saw up from the basement," Karen answered, but then looking at John's dress pants, "but, I'm afraid you're going to ruin your dress pants. I've laid a pair of Wilson's pants and a shirt on the bed. Why don't you change into them?"

John looked at Karen. She had an interesting expression, something between a smile and grief.

"Thank you, I'll do that."

John was amazed at how closely the clothes fit him. The shirt was a little tight through the arms and chest. The pant's waist was a size too large, but nothing a belt wouldn't solve. The way he was eating, by the end of the week the pants might fit perfect. The length of the pants reached the instep of his boots.

When John entered the room, Karen clasped her hand to her mouth and let out a low whimper.

"I'm sorry Karen. Let me go change back into my clothes."

"No. No, John," she said, with an approving smile, "please, it's okay."

Suzie looked at John, starting at his head, then combing downward. She also smiled, then came and took her mom's hand and squeezed it.

Karen handed John the saw, and they all walked out the door, Suzie still holding her mom's hand. When they got outside and started across the street, Suzie reached over and took John's hand also. John looked down at the young girl and smiled warmly. This whole experience was so strange to him, feeling almost surreal. But it also, at the same time, possessed a very natural quality. It was beginning to feel like a Norman Rockwell painting.

"Oh Momma, I forgot to tell you," Suzie said as they started up the set of steps across the street, "we are going to have a Christmas parade just before the party Wednesday night, and I'm going to be riding in it, as the Christmas angel. They don't have time to elect a snow queen."

"Well, that is great, honey. Wonder where we can get you a

convertible to ride in?"

John laughed to himself.

"So, Suzie," he said "if you had a choice, what kind of convertible would you want to ride in?"

Suzie thought for awhile, the answered, "Oh, one of those fancy sports cars, a red one, like maybe a Corvette or Camaro."

"If I got you a red Corvette Stingray convertible to ride in," John whispered in her ear, "would you put a good word in for me to your mom?"

"Oh yes, I sure would," Suzie said with her eyes opening wide in excitement. "Do you know someone that has one?"

"I sure do," he said. "ME!"

"You're kidding!" the girl squealed. "Momma, John has a red Corvette convertible that he is going to let me ride in, in the parade."

"John, are you serious?"

"Yes, Jonathan has been driving it because I needed a bigger car to bring Suzie home."

"So Suzie," the man said, turning back to her, "if your mom's real good, you think we should let her ride in it too?"

"Yes, I think she'd look really neat in it."

The three walked for about ten minutes into the woods when Suzie eyed a white pine about six feet tall.

"Oh, Momma," the girl said, motioning to her mother to come to her, "this one's perfect."

John looked at the tree critically with arched eye brows. It was probably the ugliest tree he'd ever seen. Apparently a storm had struck one side, and several branches were missing. The growth of the other branches had also been stunted. Karen noticed his puzzled look, and began laughing.

"What's wrong, John?" the mother said with a chuckle. "Don't you like Suzie's choice?"

"Well. Yes. Sure. It's, it's fine," John answered, trying to conceal his disapproval.

Karen and Suzie both began to laugh.

"Suzie always picks out, well, the tree that doesn't quite look like a Christmas tree is supposed to look. She says she knows a less pretty tree loves to be dressed up for Christmas also, and it has every bit the right to look as pretty as any other tree in the woods."

"Suzie, you never cease to amaze me," John said, shaking his head. "Okay, I guess this will be the tree then."

Fifteen minutes later, they were back at the house. While John began slipping the tree-holder onto the trunk, Karen began preparing the soup and sandwiches. During this time, Suzie began getting the decorations from the attic. Within fifteen minutes, the soup and sandwiches were on the table, and the decorations were laid out.

Suzie was too excited to sit at the table to eat. She began taking the decorations from the boxes and placing them on the tree between bites of sandwiches and spoonfuls of soup. First, the three strands of multi-colored lights, then the various colored balls, then the silvery garland. By the time the bowls were being scraped empty, and the last crust of the sandwiches had been devoured, the tree was almost complete.

"John," Karen said, "would you put the angel on the top, and then we can light the tree."

Suzie slowly, gently lifted the exquisite angel from its box. John could tell that it must be very special, and he felt honored to be placing it.

"Remember us telling you about the night Daddy wasn't supposed to make it home but he did?" Suzie said, as she handed the adornment to him. "Well, he bought this at the truck stop."

"Thanks so much for letting me place it," John said, feeling a lump swell in his throat.

"Oh," Karen said, to break the somberness, "that's just because you're the only one around who is tall enough to do it without a step-ladder."

Just after John had placed and adjusted the angel, Suzie took the extension cord in one hand and the Christmas light plug in the other hand.

"Ten, nine, eight," Karen began the count down, and the others joined, "seven, six, five, four, three, two, one!"

Suzie connected the plugs into the extension cord, and the small living room was illuminated in bright, festive colors. The angel atop was bathed in a luminous corona.

"I do believe, Suzie," John said as he examined the creation, "that you *did* pick the prettiest tree in the whole woods."

Karen then brought in steaming cups of hot chocolate that she had left simmering. Going to the record player, she put on the Christmas album by selected artists. The three sat bunched together on the sofa, admiring the tree, while hot chocolate warmed their bodies, and Christmas music fueled their spirits.

After the album had played through twice, John looked at his watch. It was 4:35.

"Hey," he said looking at the ladies, "ready to head to Galax for dinner?"

"Yeah, let's go!" the feminine duo answered in unison.

"Would it be alright," John said, and then hesitated; not sure he should finish, but finally decided to, "for me to wear this shirt and pants? I really feel comfortable in them."

"Sure," Karen said, as she rubbed his chest through the thick cotton fabric, "you look good in them." Then she added with a grin, "not so much like a city slicker. Let us go change though. We'll be back ready in ten minutes."

While the girls were changing, John began walking around, exploring the house, since he now felt comfortable to do so. He looked at the books on the shelves. There were several novels, books on writing, history and geography, and boxes that enclosed *National Geographic* magazines, dating back for the last three years.

He then began to study the photos on the various shelves. He eyed a man, assumedly Wilson, in his uniform, standing at a proud, erect attention in front of the steps that John recognized as being the ones across the street. Next was a picture of a young blonde bride with a young groom, looking very uncomfortable in his three-piece suit. He looked much thinner than his clothes would indicate. *I guess that's what Karen's cooking does for a man,* John thought. *Gosh, how Karen looks like Suzie in the picture!*

John smiled as he looked at a picture of proud parents holding a tiny new-born.

Then there were various photos of older people. Were they parents, grandparents? Sometimes at that age, it's so difficult to tell.

Then the sound of the bedroom door opening broke him from his study, and he turned, and let out a low approving whistle.

"Now," he said, bringing his thumb and index finger up to pinch his chin, "I don't know for the life of me which of you is the most beautiful."

"He's quite a sycophant," Suzie said to her mother with a giggle.

"A sick elephant?" John said with a mock look of shock.

Karen began laughing as Suzie just stood there with a smug expression on her face.

"Suzie learns two new words each day," Karen began explaining, "she then likes to work them into a conversation when you least expect it."

As John was helping the two ladies with their coats, he noticed how worn they were. Soon they were in the car, had turned east onto Main Street and were headed toward Galax. Just before reaching the railroad tracks a mile from Galax, John looked to his left at a tall, towering Victorian Mansion, even more impressive than Jonathan Armbrister's home.

"I noticed that house on our way back from the hospital Monday," John said, nodding toward the house as he slowed to an almost stop. "What's the story on it?"

"Oh, that's the old Cliffside Mansion," Karen said, "It was owned by Mr. Felts who ran the detective agency. Did you ever hear of him?"

"I bet it was the Baldwin-Felts agency," John answered reflectively. "They became famous, or infamous, I guess it depends upon who you talk to, for the things they did in the West Virginia coalfields in the 20's. I also think they tracked down the Allens after the Hillsville Courthouse shootings sixty years ago."

John turned to Karen, a sparkle in his eye.

"Think you'd ever want to live in that house?" he asked.

"I'd be happy to live in the barn," Karen said with a chuckle, but she did not realize how serious he was.

"I heard that the house is haunted by the miners who were killed in West Virginia," Suzie said with excitement. "Sometimes at night they say you can see lights up in that top part, even though no one can get into there."

"Well, we'd better get out of here before they come and get us," John said as he gassed the big Lincoln and squealed away.

After reading *Your Career in Civil Engineering,* Jason began looking through some of the other books on the shelves. Then finally, he took down his Fries Highs School annuals, *The Echo,* and began looking through them. The first was his sophomore year at Fries High, the 1967 Annual. He looked at older friends, guys that played on the football team, when he did little more than play on kickoffs and punts, with some mop-up duties as the back-up quarterback.

He then turned to the baseball pictures, and there was his photo, Jason Campbell, outfielder. It did not reveal that he never got to play at all that year. He gathered more splinters from the bench than found in a box of toothpicks. He laughed as he remembered telling everyone that the closest he got to the field that season was when he got to take the pitcher's warm-up jacket out to first base whenever the starting pitcher got a hit.

He knew what followed the baseball pictures and almost closed the book, but he didn't. He turned the page slowly, and looked down. It was a full page picture of Katy Lynn, with the caption, "Miss FHS." She had won as a freshman, the first one to ever do so. He had met her that summer at a school dance at Vaughan. Even though he lived five miles away on Brush Creek, they had found a way to see each other almost every week. Katy Lynn would either come to visit her cousin on Brush Creek, or Jason would find an excuse to hitch hike to Fries. He had often said that Chiney Alderman picked him up and gave him enough rides that summer to claim him as a dependent on his taxes. Then fall came and Jason started to school at Fries. But it was football season, and football players can't be distracted by girlfriends during the season, or so he thought, so the two of them had drifted apart. He remembered having to sit in the auditorium during pep rallies, and watch her sit with other boys. Football season was soon over, and in November she won Miss FHS. Jason walked up to her in front of her boyfriend who stood a head taller than he, and asked the beauty queen if he could walk her home.

"No Jason, Eugene is walking me home," she said as she smiled politely.

Jason remembered how devastated he was. He caught a ride home with a buddy. About fifteen minutes after he got home, the phone had rung. When Jason answered, it was Katy Lynn. She proceeded to tell him that she had promised Eugene he could walk her home, but she had told him that she would not be seeing him again. She told Jason that she would save a seat for him on Monday, if he wanted it.

Monday morning Jason rushed into the auditorium as soon as the bus let him off. Sure enough, half way up the auditorium, sat a petite blonde, with an empty seat next to her. He continued to fill that seat pretty much the rest of his high school years.

Jason then began looking at the other annuals. His junior year, when the starting quarterback had gone down with a broken leg, and he started the last six games, setting a new Fries record for passing yards. He looked again at the baseball pictures, where now he had actually lettered.

Then he moved on to his senior annual. The white shirt and narrow tie in his senior picture. The football pages showed that the Wildcats had won the District Championship with a record of 9-1. His full page picture, holding the football up in a passing pose, doing his best Johnny Unitas impersonation, with the caption, *Jason Campbell, All-State*, and the eight records he had broken at the school, and the one record, Most Total Yards, for the state. Nine and one. The thought of that last play flashed back in his head. If they won, they would be named the top team in the state. Only a yard to go for eternal fame. This would be the play that he had run at least fifty times that year and had never been stopped for no gain. Then the memory of the excruciating pain as Tinker Reed's helmet hit the inside of his knee. Then he remembered the frustration of spinning, as if in slow motion, trying to thrust himself forward a yard; trying to will himself over the goal line. He then remembered the heartbreak of looking forward after he hit the ground, and the ball rested less than a foot from the goal line, less than twelve inches from victory, from a college scholarship.

He had no pictures in the '69 baseball section because his knee had not healed enough to play. At least that was his excuse. He did not want to admit that he had felt defeated; he had lost all hope. He then turned to the page at the end of the annual, and he looked at the picture of him and Katy Lynn, at the prom, on the Homecoming Court. Even though the pictures were black and white, Jason remembered that she wore a pale-blue gown. Her long, blonde hair hung in rivulets down over her shoulders. He had won King of the Homecoming Court, and she had placed second. He had told her on the way home that she would always be his Queen. He had hoped she knew what he had meant. He had then made up his mind that as soon as he graduated from college, he would marry Katy Lynn.

Jason closed the book. His chest felt heavy. He had not seen Katy Lynn since they broke up on the fourth of July. He had given her diamond earrings, but apparently she had hoped for a diamond ring for her finger. They had split up three times before, but it had never been for more than two or three weeks. Jason felt certain this time it was for good.

"Jason, lunch is ready," his mom called, breaking him from his funk.

Jason placed the annuals back on the shelves, took a deep breath, gathered his composure, and walked into the kitchen. Sitting in the middle of the table was a big pot of homemade vegetable soup and grilled cheese sandwiches. Jason loved his mom's vegetable soup. Everything but the macaroni came straight from the garden. Jason was quiet for a few minutes until his dad interrupted the solitude.

"Well, if you weren't planning on doing anything this afternoon," His dad said, "Let's watch the bowl game; it's the Bulldogs and the Sooners."

"Sure, that'd be good." Jason said to his father. The truth was he would enjoy doing *something* with his father, but watching football still reminded him of how his life might have been had he not had his knee blown out.

"Well," Leah called out from the kitchen, "while you two are watching the game, I'll be doing some laundry. Did you bring your dirty clothes home Jason?"

"Yes ma'am," he answered from the den, "they're in the car, I'll run and get them."

"What time do you think we should leave to head back to Pulaski, Mom?" Jason asked as he handed her the dirty clothes, "I promised I'd be in at the store by seven tonight and help stock for tomorrow."

"Oh, we don't like driving when it's too late, so we'll leave when you do, around six."

"Do you think VPI will ever play in a major bowl game?" Jason's dad asked during halftime.

"Well, I don't know, teams like Nebraska and Georgia get a lot of the great players. They have over a hundred scholarship players on the team. Their subs could beat most colleges. I'd like to think one day things will be made more equal, and we'd be able to get some good players where we'd be able to play and beat some of those teams, though. We made it to the two Liberty Bowls in the past three years, but then this year we struggled again."

"Do you ever think," Mr. Campbell said, then hesitated because he and his son had not discussed the subject he was bringing up, "about if you hadn't hurt your knee, and would have played for the Hokies?"

"Well Dad, I wouldn't have played for VA Tech, probably VMI, because I would have never gotten a free-ride at Tech." Jason said, still not comfortable discussing the disappointment.

"You know, one of Tech's coaches was setting there in front of us watching you that last game. He told me that you were one of the best he had seen."

"Frank Beamer was twice the player I was, and he didn't make it as quarterback, so I doubt I could have played for Tech. But things worked out for the best for me; I really think that."

Jason had truly enjoyed his day at home. It was always wonderful spending time with his parents, but today he had really gotten his head back together. He really felt confident about being able to improve his grades. He would just need to limit his trips to the Hokie House. There, and to the donut shop to see Janice and have her free coffee and donuts. But soon it was almost 6 o'clock, and time to go.

"Guess I'd better hit the road. Now, Mom, are you and Dad sure it's okay, that you won't be needing the car next week?"

Mrs. Campbell looked at Mr. Campbell, who then turned away. Jason thought he saw his dad's chin quiver.

"Jason, we won't be needing it, because,...because I have to go to Roanoke next week to have eye surgery."

"Eye surgery? What's wrong?" Jason said as he felt an uneasiness spreading over his body.

"They're not sure. It may just be something simple, or, well, it might be cancer."

"Momma, what...How...?"

"Don't worry about it yet, though. They'll do the surgery on Tuesday morning at ten and know something within a few days."

"A few days? When will you be coming home?"

Jason heard a low whimper coming from the direction of his father, who had his back turned to everyone.

"Well, they think I should be able to come home by the 26th or 27th, if everything looks alright."

"You'll...you'll miss Christmas?" It was all Jason could do to keep from joining his father in crying.

"Yeah, it looks like it," she said, forcing a smile, "but that's okay. There will be other Christmases; you guys just enjoy this one without me. We're going to go down to Pulaski to tell Lisa now, and then call Josie. But don't worry. Everything'll be fine. I know it will."

Jason grabbed his mom, and hugged her. Leah felt her son's tears running down the side of her face. She kissed her son and patted him on the back.

"Okay now," she said, "you get along, or you're going to be late, and be careful."

Jason hugged his dad and went out to the 1963 Buick Wildcat. He started the engine. The 401 cubic inch engine, with its 325-horsepower engine growled to life. Jason loved to drive this car, even if it was a four-door, had a 3-speed automatic instead of a straight, and got about eight miles to the gallon of gas. But tonight, his heart just wasn't in it. Before pulling out of the driveway, he bent his head over the steering wheel.

Oh God, please don't let anything happen to Momma, please don't.

He sat there, his head over the large steering wheel for about sixty seconds. He then wiped his face with his shirt sleeve and drove to Power's IGA in Pulaski to stock shelves.

14

Jason arrived ten minutes before time to start his shift. He noticed that Mr. Powers' office door was opened, so he looked inside. There sat the owner, going over paperwork.

"Mr. Powers," Jason said after lightly tapping on the doorframe, "do you have a couple of minutes?"

"Sure, come in," Mr. Powers said with the ever-present smile on his face.

"Mr. Powers, I'm Jason Campbell."

"Yes, you're my college boy. What can I do for you?"

"Well," Jason said hesitantly. The store owner, although very personable, still intimidated the young college student. "I noticed in the storage room a box of the Christmas candy canes that had been damaged in shipping. What were you planning on doing with them?"

"Well, usually the shipper just pays us a fraction of the cost, and we sell what we can. Why do you ask?"

"Well, Sir, I'm sure you don't know, but I'm from Fries. Well, actually just outside Fries, on Brush Creek."

"I know Fries well. And Brush Creek. I used to deliver goods there. As a matter of fact, that was one reason I hired you. I saw you had worked at Shepherd's. I always thought a lot of John and Haswell. When I phoned them, they gave you an excellent reference. Haswell did say you liked to drive a little faster than you should, but I promised him I'd not be loaning you my car."

Jason had to grin at this, thinking back to the time he wrecked his car with his boss's two sons with him. Fortunately, there were no injuries, except to Jason's wallet when his father made him pay for the damage.

"Well, Fries is having a rough time this year. The Mill shut down the first of the month, and it doesn't look like much of a

Christmas for the people there. They are giving a party though for the kids, about two-hundred of them, and I thought I'd like to donate the candy canes, if you'll sell them to me."

"Well, Jason, yes, if you don't mind that they're broken. I'll make you a good deal. It speaks highly of you that you'd do that."

"The town has always been very special to me."

Mr. Power's pulled a work schedule from his desk and moved his finger down the list until he located Jason's name.

"Jason, what were your plans for Christmas Eve?"

"Well, that kinda brings me to another question. I was to be off Christmas Eve, but my mother is having eye surgery Tuesday. It..., it may be cancer. If I could change, I'd work Christmas Eve if someone would work for me Tuesday."

"I don't think we'll have any problem finding someone to do that. I'll keep your mom in my prayers.'

"Thank you, sir, I'd appreciate that."

"Jason, you do have experience doing inventory, don't you?"

"Yes, sir. I did it all the time at Shepherd's."

"What if I let you off Tuesday and schedule you to come in at noon on Wednesday. We are due to close at five, but we have to do inventory after closing. It usually takes about three hours. I'm always having people phone in sick that day, and I never have enough working. Would you be willing to stay until about eight to help me with the inventory?"

"Sure, yes sir, I'd be glad to. I've always enjoyed doing it," Jason said, although truthfully he had hoped to go to Brush Creek and attend the Christmas Eve service at Mt. Hope Church.

"Good." Mr. Powers said, then pushed his chair back from his desk, and with a smile added, "I'll tell you what. For doing this for me, I'll sell you the fifty pounds of candy canes for $20, and I'll throw in about 25 pounds of nuts, and 200 oranges. How does that sound?"

"That...that sounds fantastic, great," Jason said, not believing what he had just heard. "Thank you so much. Umm, could I also buy two hundred of the 5-pound bags from you?"

"You drive a hard bargain, Jason," the store-owner said with a deep belly laugh. "You should be taking business instead of engineering at Tech. Sure; you can have as many bags as you need.

As a matter of fact, I'm sure we're going to have some of the Christmas bags left over, and it has 1969 printed on them, so go ahead and use those up."

"Thank you so much, Mr. Powers," Jason said as he shook the older man's hand. "The kids will love this."

Jason ran out to begin his shift, happy that thanks to the generosity of the storeowner, the kids in Fries would have a little more Christmas than they previously thought.

That evening, Horace Hawks sat down at the dinner table reading that week's edition of the *Fries Wildcat Spirit Weekly*. Bringing in the food was his wife, Elicia. Around the table sat the Hawks' boys, Tater, 21, Lump 18, and Cabbage, 15. Horace hauled coal for the citizens of the town and surrounding areas, and also for the Mill, which was now no longer placing any orders.

The three boys all went by nicknames and no one other than close family knew their real handles, not even their best friends. Tater was the oldest, and had worked for his dad since he was sixteen, starting by unloading and loading coal, and then moving on to driving trucks. His nickname came from his extreme fondness of the edible starchy tuber. If Tater had his way, a typical meal would consist of potato soup, ham with fried potatoes, mashed potatoes, and potato salad, and maybe a potato cake for dessert.

Lump was the middle child, and his moniker came from his big brother who, upon seeing the newborn baby, said, *Why, he's no bigger than a lumpa coal*. The nickname stuck. Lump would be graduating that year from Fries where he had been a star football and baseball player. Much to his father's chagrin and his mother's consternation, Lump was leaving home to go into the Air Force at the end of school. Mrs. Hawks' trepidation had been compounded by the recent death of Raymond Harrell in Vietnam. Raymond had grown up next to the Hawks, and had been like a fourth son.

The baby, Cabbage, got his name from his two older brothers because until he was six years old, he believed that his dad and mom had found him in the cabbage patch. Cabbage was the studious member of the family, and father Hawks already had plans for him to attend the Wytheville Community College to get an Associate's Degree in business.

Horace sat there perusing the weekly newspaper while Elicia brought in the dinner. When she joined them it was the signal for the family to join hands, and for Horace to offer the blessing. After the prayer, Elicia began passing the bowls around. Horace cleared his throat and spoke up.

"Suzie wrote a nice article about the hope of having a decent Christmas in town."

"Yes, but it's going to take a lot of work," the wife answered. "No one has any money after being out of work for three weeks."

"You know, Elicia," Horace said as he took his reading glasses off and laid them on the table, "this town has been good to me, to all of us. We would have never been able to afford this house, or the other things we have if it wasn't for them doing business with us."

The wife looked at her husband. She could always tell when something was churning in his head.

"So, what do you have in mind?" she asked.

"Well, everyone in town uses coal to heat with. Some even to cook with. I think I'll go pick up a load of coal with the Big Mack, it can legally haul ten tons, and give each family two 50-pound bags of coal for Christmas."

"Well, that's a very charitable idea," Elicia said, but then began laughing.

"So what's funny about it?"

"Well, it's a great idea, but it reminded me when we were kids, our parents always told us if we were bad, all Santa would bring us was a lump of coal. Now you're going to give them a hundred pounds. Just how naughty do you thing they have been?"

The whole family laughed at the joke made by Elicia who seldom attempted humor.

"But how are you going to haul it?" Mrs. Hawks asked. "You promised that you would drive me to Winston-Salem to shop"

"Well, Tater, can you make a run?"

"Gosh Daddy, I have to haul the rest of the coal in the bin to the Mill. That was the last of the order, and I promised I'd have it there by Tuesday, and it'll take two days."

Mr. Hawks turned to look at Lump.

"No, now you're not sending Lump," she said before the husband could say a word. "He just hasn't had enough experience to drive over those mountains all the way to Coalwood."

"Well, what can we do then?" Mr. Hawks asked to all within earshot.

"Hey, I bet if you phoned Chiney," Tater suggested, "he'd go just to get to drive Big Mack."

Chiney Alderman was the only other coal hauler in the area, but he drove a twenty year old Reo that only had enough power to haul about three tons. He would buy small loads from Horace, and then haul them to people who lived outside of Fries. It would typically take him about eight hours to deliver loads to two houses. There would be two hours of driving time, three hours of repairing the truck on the side of the road, and three hours of unloading the coal and talking at the houses. Ask anyone what they thought of Chiney, and they'd laugh and reply, *He's a good ole soul*, because that is exactly how Chiney described everyone he knew. Chiney's other constant statement was instead of a greeting such as 'hello,' he would instantly offer the remorseful greeting, *It's a cruel old world, a cruel, cruel world*, but then if he knew you well enough he would flash his engaging smile and add, *but the girls are lovely*.

Horace phoned his old friend.

"Chiney? Hey, this is Horace. How are you? Merry Christmas."

"Ah, Horace, it's a cruel world isn't it? A cruel, cruel world."

"Yeah it is, Chiney, but let's me and you make it a little better."

"How's that?"

"Well, I will pay for the coal, if you'll take Big Mack up to Coalwood on Monday to get a load. Then I'm going to give a hundred pounds to each town family."

"Well, ole buddy, I'd love to do that, that's a great idea, a right neighborly idea, and well, I would be more than happy to do it, I'd be right honored and privileged to do it, but I have to deliver coal on both Monday and Tuesday." Chiney never believed anything should be said in a couple of words when it could be said in a couple of dozen.

"Hmm," Horace said, knowing Chiney would find a way, "wonder who else we could get to drive Big Mack? I just don't know if I trust anyone but you."

"Well, now, let me ponder this, you know, if I'm not being paid for this, and you're giving it away as a charitable thought, then I don't think the Good Lord would consider me as working on the Sabbath if I went up there tomorrow and got it, right after I get out of church."

"No, Chiney, I don't think He would hold that against you at all. I'll phone them today, and let them know you'll be there around 3 p.m. Big Mack will be parked down at the coal yard, all gassed up, and rarin' to go. The keys will be in the usual place. Just leave it parked there tomorrow night. Thanks, buddy, I think we'll make some families happy."

While the Hawks enjoyed their meal, John, Suzie and Karen were enjoying a prime rib. This was a new experience for the two girls who had never enjoyed anything more than a T-bone prepared on the back porch grill. Suzie used this occasion to have John describe some of the restaurants where he had eaten in New York, Paris, and other major cities of the world. John tried very hard to give the inquisitive girl the information she wanted without sounding puffed-up.

After finishing their peach cobblers with ice cream, they drove into town and found a good parking spot for the parade. Karen had brought two quilts. They laid one on the hood to sit on, then after sitting down, Karen spread the other quilt over them, as they watched the parade go by.

Following the parade, they drove through town, winding in and out of the nicer residential areas, to look at the decorated homes. To Karen, Galax, with a population of 7,000, was a large city. John, having been to cities with populations in the millions, found it a nice quiet alternative.

"Why don't we drive back by Riverside?" Karen suggested. "Some of the houses along the river have some beautiful decorations."

"Your wish is my command, my lady," John said as he flashed her a smile.

Karen slid across the leather seats to snuggle against him. The three of them reveled in the various decorations that adorned the homes. There were phone poles decorated with colored foil to look like candy canes and Santa with reindeer pulling a sleigh on the ridge cap of houses. There were Nativity scenes, one even with live lambs in a pen.

By the time the three had reached Third Street, it was almost ten. John walked Karen to the door as Suzie sleep-walked her way into the living room.

"Why don't you come to church with us in the morning?" Karen said, just as he was about to tell her goodnight.

John had not stopped to think that since accepting the Lord the week before, he had not been to church. This would be a good beginning.

"I think I'd like that. When should I pick you up?"

"How about 10:30? We'll skip Sunday School," she said, sensing that church-going was a new experience for him, so she thought she'd ease him into the routine.

"That sounds wonderful, see you then."

She tiptoed up, and gave him a short, but sweet kiss on the lips. She then hurried into the house before he could see how closely the red glow on her cheeks matched the lights on the tree.

When he got home that night, the Armbristers had arrived from North Carolina. Cynthia met him at the door and gave him a big hug.

"Thanks for taking care of my husband while I was down in Winston-Salem."

"Oh, you're welcome;" John told her, as he winked in the direction of Jonathan "he wasn't too much of a problem."

"Jonathan filled me in on everything on our way back. Sounds like it's been a real roller coaster, but hopefully things might be looking up now."

"Yeah, I believe so," John agreed, gratified that he wasn't going to have to keep the events a secret.

"And Jonathan also tells me that North Carolina's most eligible bachelor has gotten up here and gotten smitten. Now I want to hear all the details."

"Yeah," John said as he felt an unfamiliar blush come to his face, "I think you might say that. She's quite a lady."

"Yes, she really is, John. I know you've had your share of

women, but believe me, you'll never find a better woman than Karen Young."

"I fully agree, and that Suzie, Cynthia, I swear, she is unbelievable. People keep saying *What's this younger generation coming to?* Well, if she is any indication, then I think this country has a great future. But enough about me. Tell me about you. It's been almost a year. The last time we talked, you and Jonathan were excited about taking a Caribbean Cruise next year. Are you still going?"

Cynthia looked at Jonathan, and they both grinned.

"Interesting you should ask," Cynthia said as she looked at Jonathan and the two began to grin. "That was the subject of most of our conversation coming home. We've saved almost $2000 for the trip. We hope to leave around June."

"So where all will you go?"

"We fly to Miami to catch the ship." She began to recite the itinerary with a dreamy look on her face. "We'll have stops at St. Thomas, St. Marten, San Juan, Barbados, Jamaica and Aruba."

"I bet you're excited."

"Oh, yes, it will be our second honeymoon."

"More like our first," Jonathan said with a chuckle. "Our first honeymoon was to the Biltmore Hotel in Greensboro and we ate at the Burger-Bee. I was fresh out of Wake. That was the most we could afford."

"Well, you guys deserve it. I hope it goes well. Oh, by the way, I'll be going to Church with Karen tomorrow. I think she said she goes to the Baptist Church with you."

"Wow! The surprises keep coming," Cynthia said with a pleased expression. "I've been trying to pray you into church for three years."

"Well, I think you might like this news. When we took Suzie to the hospital, while she was still in surgery, I stopped by the chapel with Karen. I found myself making a promise to God. The next day, when she came out of the coma, I had to keep my promise. Pastor Young helped me because I had no idea how to be saved."

"Well, you had a fine one to lead you. All of our pastors have more education than Pastor Young, but few know the Bible, or love God any more than him."

The three old friends sat and talked until after midnight. When Cynthia began yawning, they all agreed it was time to retire for the night.

"I'll have breakfast ready at nine. You should still have time to get dressed and to Karen's in time."

"Good, umm, what are you going to fix?"

"Well, if I remember correctly, you've always been partial to my Belgian waffles with about half a pound of bacon on the side."

"You have a most excellent memory," John said.

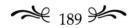

15

John awoke Sunday morning to the smell of country bacon being fried and fresh coffee brewing. Over the low, muted voices of Jonathan and Cynthia, he could hear the sizzling of the meat, as it popped in the skillet, and the bub, bub-bub of the java as it bubbled in the glass globe of the stainless steel percolator.

John loved Cynthia's waffles. He had first had them almost three years earlier on New Year's morning in Winston-Salem. Jonathan and Cynthia had spent the night at John's apartment. The night before, they had celebrated New Year's at a local restaurant. In addition to the three, there was also Denise, a 26-year-old kindergarten teacher who was a friend of Cynthia's. This was the first of many girls that Cynthia had tried to match up with John. All the girls were very nice, moral girls, a trait that John just wasn't sure he was looking for at that time in his life. John had to smile to himself. *Who would Cynthia use her matchmaking skills on now that he was no longer eligible?* Or, at least, he hoped he wouldn't be.

Jonathan was sitting in the living room, drinking a cup of the previous day's coffee while the fresh brewed, and reading the *Roanoke Times*.

"Charlie Davis had another great game," Jonathan informed John from behind the sports pages. "To be a sophomore, he's a heck of a player. I bet he makes the All-ACC team."

"Do Wake and VPI play this year? If they do, let's get four tickets and take some of your Hokie buddies to the game."

"Yeah, you're right, that would be fun. I'll check and see. I even know who I'd want to take, Birddog and Wade."

"Umm, Jonathan, I need to talk to you, about Karen. Let me tell you what I was thinking about, and tell me what you think. But be honest."

The two men talked quietly for ten more minutes when

Cynthia called from the kitchen.

"Well, are you two going to talk all morning, or come in here and eat these waffles before they get cold?"

"Thanks, Jonathan," John said, as the two men stood up, and shook hands. "Now keep your fingers crossed for me."

"I sure will, John. I sure will."

The two men then raced into the kitchen, both demanding, "Where are those waffles?"

After eating, John took a shower, and then dressed in his freshly laundered blue pinstripe suit with his stylish burgundy and blue striped tie.

At 10:35, John picked up the two Young girls, and they drove to church. He was afraid he would be uncomfortable with such an unfamiliar experience as going to church. Instead, he felt a refreshing exhilaration.

Just as they were parking, the Armbristers arrived in the flashy red Stingray.

"Is that your car, John?" Suzie asked, her eyes as large as quarters.

"Yes, it sure is."

Suzie went running to the car before the Armbristers could even open the doors. Cynthia got out, saw Suzie, and gave her a big hug.

"You gave us quite a scare, young lady. Are you okay now?"

"Yes ma'am, I'm fine. I'm going to get to ride in John's Corvette in the Christmas parade."

"You are? Well, I can't wait to see that."

The five walked in together. Karen felt very self-conscious as it seemed every eye in the church turned to watch her walk in with the tall stranger. Or was it because she was walking in with the Armbristers?

"Here, sit with us," Jonathan said. "There's always plenty of room on this pew."

Karen was somewhat awestruck. *It was one thing that everyone in the church was watching her walk in with this strikingly handsome man, but now she was going to sit with the Armbristers?* She felt the warmth as her cheeks began its reddish blush.

That morning, at the three churches, all the pastors had agreed to preach about the joy of giving. They used the example of The Fourth Wise Man, who had spent thirty-three years searching for the Christ child to give Him three precious jewels, but before finding the grown Savior, had given the rare gems away to help the unfortunate. They all were encouraged to heed God's teaching that *wherever you have given unto the least of these, you have given unto me.*

"Did you have plans this evening?" Cynthia asked Karen as they walked to the street, arm-in-arm. "I left a ham cooking on the stove. Why don't all of you come over? The men can sit in the living room and watch football, and we can talk. You can get me caught up on all that's happened the last few days."

Karen was almost too shocked to speak. She looked at John, who was nodding his head and giving her an encouraging smile.

"Well, yes, if you are sure that will be okay," Karen answered.

"Oh, we'd love it. We'll see you about 1:30." Cynthia said as she gave Karen a hug.

"Chiney, would you like to have Sunday dinner with the wife and me?" Pastor Hamm said as he shook Chiney's hand prior to exiting the church. "The kids always love having you around to tell your stories."

"Well, now Preacher, normally I would love to come visit with you and the missus and the little darlings, but I've got to make a trip today. Yes I do. I've gotta drive up to Coalwood, to get lumps of coal for all the good boys and girls."

"You mean for the bad boys and girls, don't you?" the pastor said with an almost inaudible chuckle.

"No sir," Chiney said as he gave him a wink, "this year it will be for the good boys and girls."

"Will you be back in time for the play tonight?"

"Well, I surely do hope so, Parson, but they're calling for a smidgen of snow, and you know how those mountains get once'n they get them a little bit of that white stuff on them, but if I can, I surely will."

So Chiney drove his old pick-up down to the coal yard and climbed up into the front seat of the '67 Mack Dump Truck. He smiled, and hesitated, rubbing the leather seats, and the dash without a single scratch or dent. He turned the key, and listened to the powerful diesel come to life, shaking the entire truck with its power. He eased out on the clutch, and felt a surge forward. He loved the opportunity to drive this truck. This would only be his fourth time to drive the big rig. It gave him a sense of pride that, other than the Hawks themselves, he was the only other person ever allowed to drive Big Mack. He pulled out of the lot and started on the three hour trip to Coalwood.

He made great time, as the diesel, unencumbered with any tonnage, chewed up and spit out the numerous mountains between the Cotton Mill Town and the Coal Town.

Normally he would not have been able to pick up a load on a Sunday, but the mine superintendent's oldest, Sonny, was home on Christmas break from Virginia Polytechnic Institute and was more than glad to make an extra $10 loading the truck. By 3:45 p.m., he was fully loaded with 10 tons of anthracite coal.

As he pulled out of Coalwood, and headed south on Route 52, he had to turn on his wipers as large, nickel-sized snowflakes began hitting the windshield. By the time he got to Bluefield, there were six inches of snow on the ground, and he had to slow to 30 MPH to let the wipers keep up with the snow that was smothering his windshield. He had finished the treacherous Welch Mountain, but still had the equally dangerous East River Mountain and Big Walker Mountain looming ahead of him. There were rumors that they would be starting an interstate highway from Wytheville to Bluefield that would have tunnels through both of these mountains. Chiney would sure have liked to have those tunnels today.

He had only driven Big Mack during summer weather, once in the rain. He was not afraid of any physical injury from sliding off the road, but he would sure hate to put the first dents into the unblemished truck.

Chiney began to sing to spend the time, and to steady his nerve by making up a song to the tune of "Jingle Bells."

Dashing through the snow,
In a 10-ton big old Mack,
I'm not slowin down for notin,
Not even Santa with his sack,
My diesel horn will blast,
Anyone that gets in my way
I'm on my way back to Fries,
With free coal for Christmas Day.

He breathed a sigh of relief as he pulled off of Route 52 onto Interstate 81 at Wytheville. By now it was already 8 p.m. and there was a full foot of snow on the road. He thought about stopping for coffee as he passed the two truck stops, but then saw their lots totally full of vehicles, so he continued.

As he headed north on I-81 he had the road all to himself.

Ah, another hour or so, and I'll be home.

He continued at a speed of 35 MPH, the weight of the truck providing excellent traction. He may not even have to stop and put on chains, he thought to himself. Another two miles, and he would be leaving the interstate for Route 94, which would lead him home to Fries.

Through the hazy veil of falling snow, he saw two red brake lights appear suddenly in front of him. The lights, in an eerie display, rotated to the right, disappeared, then rotated to the left, disappeared and then two bright head lights, aimed their beams straight at him, rotated clockwise to the left, and then left the road at an angle. Chiney began to slowly tap his brakes, checking in his mirror to make sure no one was behind him. He turned the emergency flashers on and eased to the left as slowly as possible. Through the winter-wonderland mist, he saw the silhouette of a car, trunk first into the median. He could see Arkansas tags peeking from the snow-crusted bumper. He pulled along side just as a middle aged man opened the door cautiously, almost into the lane of traffic.

"Howdy, neighbor, are you okay?" Chiney asked, as he rolled down the window.

"Yeah, yes, I…I think I'm alright," the man answered. "Do you think I can get it out?"

Chiney looked at the nice big Buick, about a '65 he thought, sunk up to the door panels in the snow.

"No ole pal, you're stuck mighty tight. Grab what you need, turn off the car, and jump in."

The man, fighting to stand up in the foot of snow, looked at the head with the big toothy smile stuck out the truck window, looked at his beached Buick, and decided that would be his best choice. He reached back in, turned off the switch, grabbed a small suitcase from the rear seat, locked the doors, walked around to the right side of the cab, and pulled himself up onto the seat.

The man, wearing a nice dress shirt, a tie loosened at the neck, dark wool dress pants, and expensive leather shoes, now covered with snow, climbed into the cab.

Chiney reached over, extending his hand to help him in.

"Ah, it's a cruel world we live in, a cruel, cruel world," Chiney said, the smile never leaving his face.

The man looked at the figure behind the wheel, thought about if he should close the door, but then decided it would be safe.

"Yeah, especially tonight," he said, laughing back.

"Glad to meet you neighbor; my name is Chiney, Chiney Alderman."

"Glad to meet you, my name is Sam, Sam…, well, just Sam, and I really appreciate this."

"No worry, neighbor, 'cause that's what neighbors are for. The Good Book says to 'do unto others as you would have them do unto you,' so I'm always glad to do unto others, just like the good book tells me to."

They traveled another half-mile, then Chiney pulled off onto Route 52 that would take him to Route 94 and then to Fries. At the top of the ramp, they pulled into Blair's Exxon service station. Chiney crossed the four-lane and pulled the big Mack into the last available space in the lot.

"Come on in, Sam, just Sam, and we'll see what Claude can do for you, but I have a feeling it might take a spell."

They walked into the main room of the station, overflowing with weary travelers. There were families with small children, young college students on the way home for the holidays, and ironically, even a van filled with a church group going on a skiing trip.

"Hey, Claude, my buddy Sam here decided to park butt-end-first in the median about half a mile south. How long before you could get him out?"

"Oh Chiney," Claude said, rubbing the dirt from his hands onto his coveralls, "I'd say at least ten or twelve hour. We got us over twenty cars on the list in front of him. I've called the boys in to help, but it's still gonna take some time."

"Yeah, that's what I thought," Chiney said, nodding his head slowly.

"Well Sam," the truck driver said, turning back to his new friend, "why don't you just head back to Fries with me. I can bring you back tomorrow after Claude gets you pulled out. There's no motels around here, and I have a extra cot at my house, and you're mighty welcome to it."

"Well, I was supposed to be in Pennsylvania by noon tomorrow," Sam said deep in concentration, "but I guess I can forget that. Are you sure it won't be any trouble?"

"None, at all, love to have the company, just give old Claude your keys and write your license plate number on the tag. Claude, I'm gonna get us a couple of cups of coffee. Here's a dollar."

"Oh no, here let me pay," Sam offered.

"No sir-ree, you're my guest. Give me just a minute to place another call."

The phone rang at Horace Hawk's house.

"Hello." A very anxious truck owner answered.

"Howdy, Horace, just wanted to letcha know everything's okay, I'm just really running behind cause of the snow. Got here at Ft. Chiswell, and found a guy in the median, he's comin' home with me and we oughta be there by midnight. I'll bring the truck down tomorrow."

"Okay, thanks for calling. I was getting worried about you."

By the time the two men climbed back into the cab of the coal truck, the snow had stopped. The full moon cast a surreal shroud upon the surrounding landscape. Bright Christmas lights that hung from house eaves flickered through the frosty coatings. The pine trees along the road looked like Christmas trees with the sprayed-on artificial snow covering their boughs. Sam, being from Arkansas, had only seen pictures that came close to this natural beauty.

Route 52 looked clean of snow, so Chiney decided he would not need to put on the chains. On the cleared road, the chains would wear quickly, and Horace would not like that. The road trucks in Carroll County though, had not been able to keep up with the snowfall and Rt. 94 still had half a foot of snow. Chiney thought about pulling over and reconsidered putting on the chains, but could not find any road-sides that had sufficient room. He decided to continue.

This full load of coal will be enough to get me over the mountain, he thought to himself.

"Ever seen anything like this in Arkansas?"

"No, never have," Sam said, clinching the armrest on the truck door, his fingers as white as what was covering the ground.

"Well now, don'tcha worry, I've driven in much worse than this. It's just a matter of taking her easy, and not havin' to do any quick braking."

After being on the road for about forty minutes, Chiney started up a long steep mountain.

"Well, this is Brush Creek Mountain, if we make it up it, we'll be home free," Chiney told Sam.

"Have you ever had problems getting up it?" Sam asked, hoping to be reassured. "Has it ever been this bad?"

"Well, this truck's a whole lot better than mine. I don't think mine would make it up here tonight, this is the worse I've seen it since the bad snow in '63. I did have to back my truck up the mountain once though, with a full load of coal. That was a hoot."

"You're kidding. The snow was that bad?"

"Nope, the weather was fine, it's just that the low gears went outta my transmission, so I had to turn her around, and back up the mountain. After I got to the top, I just backed her right up on the side ova bank and was able to drift off and use my high gears to get her home."

Sam laughed at the thoughts of Chiney backing a coal truck up this mountain. It was enough to relieve some of the stress Sam had been feeling. His fingers took on a less pallid pink color.

Chiney did "take her easy," and after reaching the top of the mountain, found much less snow had fallen. Thirty minutes later, he pulled into his small, boxed-shape home about a half-mile outside of Fries. Sam looked at his watch. It was now midnight. He should be very sleepy, but the tension of the last three hours had him on a three-cups-of-black-coffee high.

Sam wasn't surprised, or put off, by the appearance of the small, simple bungalow. He had seen many like it while growing up in the rural section of Arkansas. He judged it to be maybe 800 square feet in size. Gray speckled shingle siding covered the exterior walls, with black rolled roofing on top. In Arkansas, it would look a little different and be called a shotgun house.

"That's the johnny-house there behind the house," Chiney called out just as they started in the front door, "if you need it before you go to bed. Give me a minute, and I'll turn the back porch light on for ya. If you need to do more than pee, then there's a Sears and Roebuck catalog for you to use."

Chiney entered the unlocked house, turning lights on as he worked his way into the kitchen where he turned on the back porch light. Sam disappeared into the small wooden structure thirty feet to the rear of the house. Fortunately, he only needed to urinate; because the thoughts of sitting down on the icy wooden seat gave him a flash of movies he had watched where the kid on a dare would stick his tongue to a flag pole in the dead of winter. He thought back to childhood memories when he used to visit his grandparents on their farm, and used the out-house, as they called it. He laughed to himself at the memory that it was bigger than this one, it was a two-seater. He could never believe two people would ever want to use it at the same time though.

Sam waded back through the snow, his feet nearly frozen as the dress shoes offered little protection. The leather shoes, as were his socks, were now soaked. He entered the kitchen.

"Warmed up some coffee." Chiney said as he handed a steaming cup of the thick black beverage to the guest, "Why don'tcha set yourself down by the stove, take those wet shoes and socks off, and thaw them out."

"Thanks, I'll do that," Sam said as he sat down in the first of two chairs Chiney had placed a couple of feet away from the big Warm Morning stove.

The shoes and socks were quickly removed, and his bare, numb feet were placed on the second wooden chair. Within minutes, a warm tingling sensation began in his toes, and soon spread through his feet, and then throughout his legs.

"Good coffee. Between the java and the stove, I soon should be thawed out," Sam said between sips.

"Yeah, it's H & C; don't know if you have that down south."

"No. I don't think we do. It's really good. Wonder where it's made."

"Just right down the road, in Roanoke. About two hours from here. They got them a big ole neon sign of a coffee pot that advertises it."

"Really? Hmm, I need to check on it." Sam said as took a notepad from his pocket, and wrote a note to himself: *Check on H & C Coffee, Roanoke, Va.*

"Want something to eat? I have some biscuits and ham in the warmer."

"No, no, I'm fine. Thank you, though. Actually now that I've thawed out, I'm getting a little sleepy. It's been a long day. I had been on the road since eight this morning," Sam said, then looking at his watch to see it was after midnight, "or I guess I should say yesterday morning."

"Where did you come up from?"

"I had left Nashville, was on my way up to Pennsylvania."

"So what do you do, Sam?"

"I have a few stores I run, selling household merchandise."

"Really? I always thought I'd like to buy a store, with gas pumps. I like to talk, and I could just set there talking to my customers all day. I'd have a big pot-belly stove, with lots of chairs, maybe a checkerboard."

In spite of the strong coffee, Sam felt his eyes growing heavier.

"Well, if it's okay, I think I'll turn in," he said, standing up and placing the coffee cup on the table.

"Yeah, think I will too. Come on in and I'll fix up the couch for you."

Sam followed Chiney into the living room. Chiney reached

into the closet and got down a pillow and three hand-made quilts. The pillowcase had a familiar pattern. Sam recognized it as the old flour sacks that his grandma used to sew into pillow cases. It had been adorned by hand-stitched embroidery. Chiney doubled over the first cover and laid it down on the couch, then laid the other two across the back.

"Nice quilts. Hand made, aren't they?" Sam said, studying the patterns.

"Yep, they were my mom's. She and another dozen or so ladies used to meet every month or so for a quilting bee. They'd make them about fifteen quilts a year. Sell a few to pay for the material, although lots of the material was scraps from the sewing factory up in Independence."

"My grandma made quilts until she was in her 90's," Sam said. "We could tell when she began feeling bad because she quit making her pieces."

"Here, let me put some more coal in the stove. You'll probably only need the one quilt until the fire dies down, then you can use the other. I've got a pair of long johns you can wear if you want to."

"No, that's alright. I'll be fine."

"Well, Sam, have yourself a good night sleep, I'll see ya in the morning."

"Yeah, you too, Chiney. Thanks again for all you've done."

"Hey, you've done thanked me enough, I enjoy your company. I don't have myself neer' enough guests."

Sam pulled off his wet pants and shirt and laid them over a wooden back chair. He usually was much more careful with his dress clothes, but felt being casual with them wouldn't be any worse for wear than what they had already been through. He lay down on the couch, folded the first quilt and placed it over him. After awhile, he began looking at the coal stove. In the darkness, he could see the burning glow, with intermittent combustion through the open ash door. Once in a while, a glowing ember fell down into the ash. He could smell the pungent aroma of the coal burning in its musty, but natural fragrance. He could hear the popping and crackling of the combustion process. He recalled that he had once read that coal was fossilized peat, made from the decaying plants that had sunk to the bottom of swamps a million years ago. He had always wanted to visit a coal mine, because he heard you could often see fossils embedded in the coal bed. The combination of fatigue and the soft soothing stimulations to his senses served as an ideal sleep-inducer. Within minutes he was snoring.

In spite of the snow, the churches had held their Christmas plays. The snow had reduced the attendance somewhat, with the out-of town visitors not making it in, sure that the snow was going to be worse than it actually ended up being. As so often occurred, the heaviest snow didn't make it over Brush Creek Mountain.

16

John woke up Monday morning. He could hear the sounds of breakfast being prepared. He slipped on his jeans and Wake Forest sweatshirt and went in to join the Armbristers for breakfast.

"Remember you asked Saturday night about our cruise?" Cynthia said, looking at John over the coffee cup she held in both hands.

"Yeah, sounds great. Wish I could find someone to join me, and go with you," John answered with a mischievous grin.

"Well, that's just it," she said, "We will probably be putting the cruise off for awhile."

"Really? Why?" John said with a puzzled look.

The couple looked at each other, then reached and took each other's hand.

"Well, last night" Jonathan said, "after we went to bed, we began thinking about Pastor Hamm's sermon. It really hit us, and, well, we decided to put the cruise off, and do something else, something better with the money."

"Oh, and what might that be?" John asked, but was sure he had an idea of what it was.

"Jonathan is going to announce at the Christmas party Wednesday night that the Mill is furnishing hams for everyone, and the $50 bonus."

"You've got to be kidding? You've saved that for years, and now you're going to give it away, and not even let people know it's from you?"

"Well, yes, because we think the people would consider it charity from Jonathan, but from the Mill, they'll think they deserved it."

"Well, I guess, but still, that's quite a gesture."

"We think that is what God wants us to do," Cynthia

continued, "and we know He will bless us for it."

"Well," John said with a chuckle, "I'm just too new to all this to hear what God is telling me, I guess."

Meanwhile, half a mile up Route 94, there were sounds of life in the Alderman house. Sam opened his eyes, glinting to block out the bright sun crashing through the front window. The worn yellowed curtains offered little resistance to the glaring early morning beams. Sam's first recognition was that of a popping, sizzling sound coming from the kitchen. Then he began to salivate as a mouthwatering aroma wafted through to his nostrils. This stimulated an electrical impulse that coursed through a mile of circuitry until it triggered a pinhead portion of the cerebral cortex that released a childhood memory from his grandmother's kitchen. *Country ham!* Sam's hippocampus screamed at him. *Chiney's frying up country ham.*

He got up to put on his clothes. The cold floor sent shivers through him as his feet first touched the worn linoleum. He quickly sat down in the chair and put on his stiff socks. He felt his shirt and pants, and found them totally dried. Almost too dry because he had placed them a little too close to the stove and he could smell a slight singe emanating from the wool pants. He looked at his watch. Nine o'clock! He could not remember the last time he had slept this late. He quickly slipped his shirt and pants on and came into the kitchen.

"Good morning, Sam," Chiney called out cheerfully. "Grab yourself a cup of that coffee from the stove while I finish frying up this ham and these eggs."

"Boy, that smells good," Sam said as he poured his coffee. "There's nothing like ham and eggs to start the day, and, is that what I think it is? Is that...sausage gravy?

"It sure is. You like gravy?"

"I sure do, but I travel a lot, mostly up north. I don't get gravy very often."

Chiney opened the oven door and removed a tray of biscuits, steam rising from the buttered tops. Grabbing a plate, he pulled opened a biscuit then using an old coffee cup, ladled a heaping serving of gravy over it."

"How ya like your eggs?"

"Oh, with this gravy, over easy would be great."

Chiney carefully scooped up two eggs, their golden centers resembling a blazing noon-time sun. He slowly eased the twin orbs onto the gravy so as not to break the centers. Then on the side of the plate he laid a piece of golden brown ham.

"Fresh ham, I'm sure?" Sam said as he broke through the first egg yellow with his fork, watching the yolk flow into the gravy biscuits.

"Sure is, just killed it this past Thanksgiving. She was a good one too, dressed out at nearly 250 pounds, just like I like em."

Sam looked down at his plate, savoring the moment, because he could tell this was going to be the best breakfast he had eaten in a long time, maybe since his grandma's. He brought the first bite to his mouth.

"Umm, delicious," Sam said, not the least bit embarrassed that he was talking with his mouth full of food.

Chiney laid a pie pan of biscuits on the table, alongside a bowl of fresh butter.

"Here's some strawberry jam if you like it," Chiney said. "The ladies at the church made it just this spring. Here's some homemade apple butter, too."

Chiney fixed himself a matching plate, and sat down across the table from his guest.

"So, Sam," Chiney said just before taking a bite from his jam and butter biscuit, and right after a large clump of strawberry oozed out of the biscuit and dropped to his plate, "do you travel very often across this big old country of ours?"

Sam waited to finish his chewing, then answered, "Yes, Chiney, this year I've been on the road about twenty days out of every month."

"So what do you sell on the road?

"I don't sell. I'm actually looking for the best markets, the best quality items for the least prices at my stores."

"Oh, so you have more than one store, eh?"

"Yeah, I have a few, but I'm looking to triple the number of stores over the next few years. That's why I'm have to find new markets for buying merchandise."

"Well, that doesn't leave you much time for your family, if you have one."

"Yes, I'm married to a great little lady and have four wonderful kids. I guess I'm working hard now so they will have a good life in the future."

"I've never married, myself," Chiney said as he finished his jam biscuit and started on his gravy and eggs. "Guess I just never met the right woman. Always thought I would like to have had kids, though. I do love having kids around. I really like it when they have me tell Bible stories to the kids down at the church."

Sam finished the last of his gravy and egg biscuit by turning his fork on the side and scraping the last of the mixture from the plate. *Just as I remembered, it's always better to run out of biscuit before you run out of gravy and egg*, Sam thought to himself. He then grabbed one of the biscuits. As he split it open with the ends of his fingers, a release of steam with the heavenly aroma of freshly baked bread greeted him. He spread some of the fresh butter on one of the opened halves, and watched as the yellow cream began to immediately melt and spread over the textured surface, filling each crevice. He then took a spoon and slapped a generous helping of the strawberry jam onto the buttery biscuit.

"Have you always lived here?"

"Sure have," Chiney said as he got up to refill the coffee cups. "I was born right here in this house and I'm sure I'll die here. Our local high school team's called the Fries Wildcats. We have a song that goes, 'We're Wildcats born and Wildcats bred, and when we die, we'll be Wildcats dead.' I guess that's me."

"What did you say was the name of the city?"

"It's Fries, like freeze, but it's spelled F-R I-E-S. Now, I know it's spelled like it would be said like french fries, but it's not, because it was named after the guy that started the Cotton Mill, and the town, Colonel Henry Fries. People here abouts have the joke, 'It's freeze in the winter, and fries in the summer. And it's not really a city, just a little town on the banks of the New River, with only about 800 people. Some people say the town's so small, we have both town limit signs on the same post."

Sam began to laugh so hard at the good old boy humor he was listening to that he spit his coffee out onto the table.

"Oh, I'm sorry", he said as he began cleaning the liquid from the table with a dish towel. "Well, I'm sure it's a nice place if everyone's like you. So have you always hauled coal?"

Chiney stopped long enough to take another bite of the gravy and biscuits, while he began sticking a thick slice of ham inside another biscuit. The plate that had previously held nearly a dozen was now down to just four.

"Nope, I did lots of things before I went into the service during W W two. When I got back, the Mill was hiring, so I went to work there. Around 1950, things begin to slow down, so I found myself laid off. My mom and pop had died, left me just enough money to buy an old dump truck, and I begin hauling coal to people.

"Well, that's a nice truck you've got now."

"Oh no, now that's not mine, that's my friend's, Horace Hawks. He's got himself a big business. I'm just small time. I buy from him, and deliver to homes out in the country. He only hauls big loads."

"So why were you out on a Sunday in such bad weather?"

"Well now, Sam, our town has found itself between a rock and a hard place. The only work here is the Cotton Mill, almost everyone works there. Here at Christmas time, they up and decide to shut her down and I don't know if they're going to open her back up. So everyone is really down and out about now."

"That's a tough break," Sam said with sincere sympathy. He had known firsthand what it meant to be unemployed and not know how you are going to feed your family their next meal.

"Yeah, it is, the people are really hurtin' right now. Well, my old pal Horace, he comes up with this here idea that he would buy a truck load of coal, and give each family a free supply of coal so they can heat their homes and maybe use their money for other things, like buy a toy or two for their kids."

"Well, that was very nice of him, so you offered to go get it for him?"

"Yeah, it was the least I could do. Those of us that's got right now, needs to help them that don't have, especially here at Christmas time. The thoughts of a child not getting' any Christmas presents might neer' breaks my heart."

Sam detected an abrupt change in the man's normally lively

and upbeat manner. He looked at Chiney, who had turned away and was wiping a towel across his eyes.

"Well, that's mighty generous of you, and the other fellow," Sam said. "So why did the Cotton Mill shut down?"

"The company, they claim the Mill is losing money, and there's not much demand for American-made cloth. It's got so much cheaper to buy it from across the ocean. I don't know about that. I just know that the town is only here because of the Mill, and without the Mill, the town'll just dry up and blow away."

Just then a grinding noise was heard outside.

"Sounds like they're finally getting around to cleaning the road," Chiney said as he pulled the curtain back from the kitchen door. "The county seat is over at Hillsville, about forty-five minutes away. They always make sure they have that part of the county cleaned for' they finally get around to us."

Just then, the phone rang. Sam looked in the direction of the unfamiliar clanging and saw a black rotary dial phone, at least thirty years old. He hadn't seen one like that for ages, other than in some antique shops.

"Hello, neighbor, cruel old world, isn't it?" Chiney answered, before he heard the caller's voice.

On the other line was Mr. Blair, the Service Station owner at Ft. Chiswell.

"Hey, Chiney, I got your buddy's car hauled in, but I've got bad news. It's got a broken tie-rod. It will probably be tomorrow, maybe Wednesday, before I can fix it."

"Okay, let me tell him."

Chiney turned to Sam and put his hand over the bottom of the phone.

"This is Claude from the service station. They got your car towed in, but it broke a tie-rod when you went into the ditch. He might not get it ready until Wednesday."

Sam frowned. This was really going to get him behind on his schedule, but he saw no other way.

"Oh, okay. Well, tell him to do the best he can," Sam said, the disappointment evident in his voice. "If he does get it finished earlier, I'll pay him extra."

Chiney conveyed the message, and Claude promised to do the

best he could, but explained that he just had so much work piled up from the blizzard."

"Chiney," Sam said as he slid back from the table, rubbing his stomach, "that was a fantastic breakfast. You're as good of a cook as my grandma was."

Sam went to the stove and poured himself a third cup of the coffee, surprising himself at how comfortable he had made himself in the home of this person he had known for barely twelve hours He picked up the H & C Coffee bag on the counter and studied it. He took a pinch of the coffee, smelled it, rubbed it between his fingers, tasted the grounds, and gave it an approving, *umm*.

He walked to the window. The sun was now glistening off the snow-capped trees in an almost blinding haze. Across the road, he could make out a small winding stream, still flowing, the edges frozen. He could see that the water gave way to what appeared to be a water fall.

"Is that a waterfall down the stream?"

"Yeah, that's called Little Bartlett's Falls. That's where the town gets their water from. The Bartletts, they owned mite neer' all the land around here around 1900. That's when Colonel Fries found the Big Bartlett's Falls, and realized this would be a dandy place to built a dam and start his mill. He bought up a whole heap of land from the Bartletts."

"So the Mill has been here since 1900?"

"Yep, up till about fifteen years ago, the Mill, they owned everything. The houses, the stores. Then they sold the houses to the people renting them, them that didn't have the money, they just had to move out of town. But I guess that was okay, cause it gave the people a sense of pride, owning their own home."

"How many people does,...did the mill employ."

"Oh, at one time upwards of about 2000, biggest place around, but now, around 600. Think you might want to see the town?"

"Yeah. I think I would," since he wouldn't be getting back on the road for a couple of days, and had just remembered that he hadn't even gotten his briefcase with his paperwork from the trunk of the car. *Maybe I can get Chiney to drive me down later today to get my briefcase,* Sam thought to himself.

They loaded into the big coal truck, and drove the half-mile into town. They drove beneath an old rail-road trestle.

"So they have a rail system here?" Sam asked.

"They used to, but tractors and trailers got so cheap, the Mill started hauling with their own trucks. The trains, they quit running about eight years ago."

Sam looked to his right, and saw the expansive cotton mill facility looming as a ghostly apparition in its snow-white shroud. It was void of all activity. The pick-up stopped and then turned to the left, starting through the downtown. Once on Main Street, Sam could see on the left a fifteen-foot high embankment that led up to the old railroad line. In the middle of the town block was a row of steps leading from the street level to the abandoned tracks. They then appeared to continue up the slope to houses built on the side of the mountain. On the right a perfectly straight row of buildings lay.

"Okay, now there's the Washington Inn, most people call it the Boarding House there on the right. For a long time, it was an inn house only for the women teachers they brought in to teach at the school. They used to keep a guard there to keep the local boys away, although I personally knew about a stairway from the coal room up to the second floor," Chiney said with a rascally chuckle.

"Chiney," Sam said as he looked over at him, trying to decide how to make his request without offending his new friend, "I've really enjoyed your hospitality, but I think I'll get me a room there tonight. I hate to impose upon you."

"Well, now you're not imposing on me at all, I mighty enjoy your company, but I will be gone most of the time, and you'd be better off here in town, since you don't have a vehicle. I'll be glad to take you down to get your car on Tuesday though, or haul you anywhere you need to go."

Chiney continued with his informal tour.

"Now, there's the post office, next is Jack's insurance office, then there's Charlie's barbershop, that's where you go for all the local gossip, and even sometimes to get a haircut," Chiney said with a deep chortle.

Sam was enjoying the tour, but was getting a little anxious because Chiney had not looked at the road in front of him since the excursion had commenced.

"Okay, now there's the First National Bank of Fries. Mr. Phillips, he's the President, a fine fellow, really helped out a lotta people out here in this town. Okay, there's the clothing store, Harold Andrews runs it. There's the grocery store. It used to be run by the Company, but now Mick or Mack runs it. And there on the corner is the Corner Drug. Bud runs it. He doesn't sell much medicine; it's mostly a meeting and eating place. He serves a mighty good lunch."

That brought them to the end of the block, and just as they started to turn right, Chiney pointed up the hill where the street began an ascending sweeping turn.

"Now there's the John Thorpe YMCA, named for one of the Mill general managers that used to be here. It's a really nice place for the young people to come play games, to swim. It's better than anything they have in this area, even in Galax or Wytheville."

Sam then watched Chiney turn into a graveled lot. A concrete pad, about 100 feet by 100 feet was covered with black coal dust. Sam, who in his life had driven a semi a few times, was impressed with the ease with which Chiney maneuvered the big rig, shifting from reverse to forward gears without a single indication of scraping.

Chiney backed to the rear of the pad, lifted the bed, and as it began dumping, moved forward, spreading the coal evenly along the pad, to make it easy to load into 50# burlap sacks. Chiney made a sweeping U-turn to park the dump truck next to the pad.

"Come on, I'll let you into the office while I clean off my pickup," Chiney said to his friend as he stepped down off Big Mack's stainless-steel running boards.

Sam grabbed the travel bag he had retrieved from his snowbound Buick, and followed Chiney. Unlocking the door to the office, Chiney then used his boot to kick the drifted snow from the door before opening it. Sam sat down in a worn leather-backed swivel chair. Chiney took a broom from the corner, and a windshield scraper hanging on the wall, and went to his pick-up truck, no longer a faded black, but now white from six inches of snow. In about ten minutes, the old coal hauler came back to the office.

"Wanna take a walk through the downtown?" he asked.

"Yeah, I'd like that a lot," Sam said, jumping up eagerly.

"Okay, I'll give you the nickel tour, down to the end of the street, to the Boarding House."

Along the way Chiney recited several tales of local interest to Sam, who was very keen on hearing about the quaint little town of Fries. The streets had already been cleaned by Buster Young and his maintenance crew. Just then a sedan pulled up, blew its horn and quickly eased into a parking space.

"Hey, Chiney," called out a tall, slim fortyish gentleman, wearing glasses, "this would sure be a good day to go bird hunting."

"Hey, Birddog, how are ya?" Chiney said, sticking his head into the passenger window. "Well, that might be fine, I don't think I'll be able to deliver any coal today, I'm sure the back-roads haven't been plowed yet."

"Great, meet me back down here at two with Cotton."

"I will most certainly do that, Birddog."

"So you like to shoot birds huh?" Sam asked excitedly.

"Sure do, do you like to hunt, Sam?"

"I LOVE to bird hunt. It's my greatest thrill in life."

"Oh, so you hunt a lot?"

"Well, actually, I don't think I've been hunting at all this year. Just been too busy."

"Want to go with us?"

"You bet I would," Sam answered with a smile that seemed to double in breadth to all former smiles he had previously exhibited. "Sure your friends don't mind?"

"Of course not, more the merrier," Chiney said, slapping Sam on the back and almost knocking him off the side walk. Then he added, "that Birddog's a fine man. He's actually a college professor, smart as a button. But you'd never know it. He acts no better'n me, and I never finished the tenth grade."

"So Cotton is another hunting buddy?"

"No, Cotton is my bird dog. Some people say he's the best in the United States, but the scriptures tell us that when pride comes, disgrace will follow, so I'll just say he's the best in the three counties."

They soon arrived at the Washington Inn and entered the front door. Chiney led Sam back to the kitchen where Myrt was cleaning up after breakfast.

"Good morning Myrt, it's a cruel, cruel world, isn't it?"

"Oh, hi Chiney," an older woman of about sixty answered, as she wiped her hands on her yellow flowered apron. "Yeah, it can be, but we just have to keep trying to make it better, don't we? So who's your buddy?"

"Myrt, this here's my good buddy Sam, just Sam, all the way from Arkansas. He got stuck over on the interstate, and I brought him home with me."

"Mighty glad to meet you, Sam," Myrt said extending her hand.

"Sam's needing a place to stay tonight. Can you put him up?"

"Sure can. I won't be able to get it ready until after lunch, but he's welcome to leave his stuff behind the counter here."

"That would be fine," Sam said. "I need to buy some hunting clothes in the mean time. Think they'd have some at the clothing store?"

"Oh, yeah, you'll have no problem there," Chiney said, then added with a laugh, "but you might have trouble buying some of those fancy dress pants like those you're wearing now."

"So I'll be seeing you after 1 o'clock, Sam." Myrt said as she reached for the bag.

"Yes, Myrt, I'll see you then," Sam answered.

"So come on then and let me introduce you to everyone," Chiney said.

The first stop was at Charlie's barbershop.

"Howdy, Charlie, how are ya? Want you to meet my good buddy Sam from Arkansas."

Charlie, twisted his body to one side, then slowly got down from his padded seat attached to the side of the barber chair, took his crutch from the counter, and walked toward Sam, his free hand outstretched. Sam quickly surmised that the barber must have had polio as a kid.

"Glad to meet you Sam from Arkansas. Any friend of Chiney's is surely a friend of mine. If you have a few minutes, come on back for a haircut. Things are slow today."

"I might just do that. Good to meet you Charlie," Sam said as he finished shaking the barber's hand. Sam noticed that there was no weakness in Charlie's handshake. His hand was still throbbing from the firm grip. They walked outside, as Charlie resumed his conversation with two men setting in the straight back chairs.

"Charlie's usually full, but the layoff has everyone a'skeered to spend money."

Sam stopped outside a store front considerable more ornate than the others.

"Now here's the bank, if you need a check cashed, or anything like that, just go in and tell Mr. Phillips you're a friend of old Chineys, and that I'll vouch for you."

They then walked down the street another fifty feet. Chiney pushed open one of a set of glass doors. A very well dressed older man, early 50's; wearing a black wool suit, with a stylish red bow-tie greeted them.

"Good morning Mr. Alderman., I hope you are having a wonderful day and a Merry Christmas."

"Yes, I surely am Mr. Andrews. I want ya to meet my good buddy Sam from Arkansas, he's gonna be needin' some huntin' clothes, and such, you will take a check from him want you?"

"Yes. If he's a friend of yours, I'm sure that will be acceptable."

Chiney then took his friend into the last store on the block, Bud's corner drug.

"Hello Chiney. Come on in, you good old soul," Bud called out before Chiney was even half way through the door.

"Well thank you kindly Bud, thank you kindly. Want you to meet my good buddy Sam from Arkansas."

"Yeah, Sam I hope your car will be okay," Bud said, his grin letting the half-smoked, but now unlit cigar dangle from the corner of his mouth.

"Oh, how did you know..." Sam started to ask.

"News travels fast in a small town like Fries," Bud said with a deep belly laugh.

"Now Sam's gonna be in for one of your delicious lunches in about an hour Bud, you take care of him," Chiney said.

"I sure will Chiney," Bud said with a nod. "Birddog tells me you guys are going hunting. Hope you have good luck. If you get more than you can eat, you know where I live."

"Now I will surely do that."

"So," Chiney said as he turned to Sam, "think you can keep yourself busy until I pick you up at two?"

"Yes, I'm looking forward to seeing more of the town."

"Good," Chiney said as he grabbed Sam's hand for a hearty goodbye shake, "let me go take care of a few things. I'll pick you up at the boarding house at two. And don't worry about getting any boots, looks like we wear about the same size, I'll bring you a pair of mine."

"Well," Sam said as he turned to Bud, "I'll be seeing you in about an hour for lunch."

"See you then Sam, good meeting you."

Sam retraced his steps down the block, and walked into Charlie's Barber shop. There was only one person in the chair, but the two elderly men still set in their chairs, nodding sleepily.

"Say you think you can work me in?" Sam asked.

"Sure," Charlie said, then added with a facetious smile, "just take a number."

"Jonathan, this is Sam," the barber said, as he turned to the customer in his chair, "he got stuck in the snow over at Ft. Chiswell, and Chiney brought him home."

"Yeah, that sounds like Chiney, he's a good old soul," Jonathan said, extending a hand from beneath the apron around his neck, "glad to meet you Sam."

"Sam, this is Jonathan Armbrister, he's the superintendent of the Mill, and one of our co-mayors."

"Glad to meet you Jonathan."

Sam thought about asking about the mill closing, but thought that would probably be a sensitive issue.

"So Sam, what do you do?" Jonathan asked.

"Well, I run some stores down south. I was on a buying trip when I got caught in the blizzard. Then fortunately for me Chiney came along."

"So how's the Christmas Committee planning going?" Charlie said, as he turned back to his customer in the chair.

"Well, we had our first meeting last week. I'm sure you read Suzie's article. Right now we are trying to contact Fries graduates and former residents who might want to help with donations. We hope to give the kids at least one or two presents."

"Yeah, it breaks my heart to think of them not getting anything," the barber said as he turned around and opened the cash register drawer, and removing a bill, placed it in Jonathan's hand. "How about donating this for me. I'd like to do more, but, well, you can see that business is a little slow."

"Thanks Charlie. Yes, I know this is a sacrifice."

"Jonathan, I know it's been rough on you, being the superintendent and all, but I want you to know that those of us that have any brains know how hard you have fought to keep the Mill open. If anyone can get them to reconsider, it will be you."

Jonathan was silent for a few seconds, and then simply said with an emotion-filled voice. "Thanks."

Sam pretended to be reading a *Sports Illustrated* article, but was taking all the conversation in. He had learned years before, that one of the secrets of success was to let others talk, while you listened.

"So when is your next meeting?" Charlie asked.

"Actually tomorrow morning at 9 a.m." answered Jonathan. "If you want to come, we'd love to have some public input."

"Would it be alright if I came?" Sam asked, as he looked up from his magazine.

"Sure, love to have you," Jonathan said, the added with a chuckle, "it will probably be the most exciting thing going on in town this week."

Charlie dusted the powder onto the soft-bristled brush and swept the loose hair strands from Jonathan's neckline. He splashed the tonic on his hand and rubbed it through the customer's hair, then used the comb to add a wave. He untied the cloth from around Armbrister's neck, and like a matador waving a bull past him, Charlie waved the cape to the side, allowing the customer to depart the barber chair.

The Mill superintendent handed Charlie a ten, and when Charlie turned to make change, Jonathan said, "No, keep it. I didn't have a chance to buy you anything, Merry Christmas Charlie."

"You too Jonathan," Charlie said as he handed the customer a 1970 Fries Barber Shop calendar.

"Okay Sam. Climb aboard."

"Just a good trim," Sam said as he settled into the seat and leaned back.

The barber chair was adjacent to a big cast iron radiator. The circulating hot water heated the room a toasty 75 degrees to offset what usually would be the cold draft from the front door opening and closing every few minutes. As the rhythmic clipping of the scissors began, Sam felt a slow, comforting unconsciousness sweeping over him. He closed his eyes and relaxed. The fusion of smells swept through his nose, the Red Rose hair tonic, the oil on the clippers, and the leathery smell of the strop— all acted to sedate him.

It seemed he had just sat down in the chair, when he jerked his head up, feeling the soft sensation of the brush across his neck line.

"Oh, sorry. Guess I must have fallen asleep," Sam said with a startled jerk, as saliva dropped from the corner of his mouth.

"That's okay," the barber said. "It happens all the time."

Charlie splashed on the hair tonic, although Sam's hair was too short to comb. The barber then untied the cloth, and took it off. He then turned the chair 180 degrees so Sam could check the haircut in the mirror.

"Great job," Sam said as he looked at his reflection in the mirror. "It's as good as my own barber does, and he's cut my hair for thirty years."

Sam reached into his wallet to pull out a five-dollar bill to hand to Charlie.

"Oh, guess Chiney didn't tell you," Charlie said, "we don't take out of town money. Just consider it an early Christmas present."

Sam thought about insisting, but saw Charlie was very serious, "Are you sure?"

"Yeah Sam, just want you to feel welcome in our town. Glad fate brought you to us, and I hope it will bring you back again."

"Merry Christmas to you too, Charlie," Sam said with a departing handshake, "I also hope we will be seeing each other again."

Sam walked down the street, and then saw the sign *First National Bank of Fries*. He realized that he had less than $100 in his wallet, and knew that it might be difficult to cash checks in the town. He opened the heavy wooden doors with brass hardware and entered into the bank. He walked up to a very pretty young teller behind the placard identifying her as "Phyllis".

"Hi, Merry Christmas. May I help you?" she asked with a smile that would chase away the clouds from the darkest day.

Phyllis had the smooth, milky complexion of so many country girls. Her face was very attractive, but what really caught Sam's attention were the dark, sparkling eyes. She would have been cute even if she had not been wearing the Santa Claus hat. Her rural accent made her even more charming and the warm friendly smile instantly made Sam feel right at home.

What a perfect person to welcome a customer into a business he thought to himself. Sam made a science of identifying the right kind of people who make good representatives. He wished Phyllis lived in Arkansas. He'd offer her a job on the spot.

"Yes, I'm from out of town, I was hoping…"

"Let me guess. Your name is Sam, from Arkansas." Phyllis said with a giggle.

"Well, yes, how did you know that?"

"Well, Chiney was in here earlier cashing a check," she said, "and he said if you came in, to take good care of you."

"Is there anybody in this town that doesn't know Chiney? Sam said with a laugh.

"No, and Chiney has never met a stranger. So what can we do for you, Sam from Arkansas?"

"Well, what would I need to do to cash an out-of-state check?"

"Just follow me into Mr. Phillips office. He'll be glad to take care of you."

She opened the pass gate to him, and led him along a small hall to a door marked, *Bank President.*

"Mr. Phillips, this is Sam, Chiney's friend. He'd like to cash a check," the teller said.

Mr. Phillips stood up, walking from around his desk. He was middle-aged, with salt and pepper curly hair. Even without his dress jacket, he still looked very professional.

"Hello, Sam. I am very glad to meet you," he said, offering his hand. "How much would you want to cash it for?"

"I was hoping $500. Would that be too much?"

"I'm sure it won't be. I'll just need to see your driver's license."

"Sure," Sam answered as he took out his wallet, and removing the Arkansas license, handed it across the table to the Bank President. This was much easier than he thought it would be. He'd had more problems than this cashing checks in Arkansas before.

"Thank you," Mr. Phillips said as he looked down at the name on the license. A wrinkle creased the banker's forehead as he looked back up at the man sitting across from him. He then looked down at the cover-photo on the *Life* magazine on his desk.

"Yes, *Sir*," the banker said with a grin, "I think we'll be glad to cash a check for whatever amount you like."

Sam glanced at the magazine and smiled. "You know, I'm really enjoying being just Sam. You will help me keep it that way, won't you?"

"Yes sir, of course I will. Here, I'll cash this myself," Mr. Phillips said as he went to a separate till, deposited the check, and removed ten crisp $50 bills, and counted them out to his visitor.

"I hope you enjoy your stay in our town, Mr…, eh, Sam, have a Merry Christmas."

"Thank you. You too."

"Merry Christmas Sam," Phyllis called and waved as he left.

Sam then walked down the street to the clothing store.

"Hello Mr. Andrews, I'm back."

"Yes sir, Sam," the older man said. "But please call me Harold. Only Chiney calls me Mister. It's a delight to see you again. Now what may I help you with?"

"I understand you carry hunting clothes?"

"Yes, we do. Please, follow me to the back of the store."

As they reached the rear of the store, Sam saw a large assortment of brown hunting pants, jackets with oversized pockets for placing game and elastic loops for storing shells and various colored plaid flannel shirts. Mr. Andrews pulled the omnipresent measuring tape from around his neck, and took some quick measurements.

Within fifteen minutes Sam had bought a pair of flannel-lined hunting pants, a matching green and red flannel shirt, insulated socks and a hunting jacket.

"I notice most people here aren't much for wearing dress pants and dress shirts," Sam said, "so give me another pair of jeans, and a couple of shirts that would blend in with the locals."

"Yes, a lot of the men your age in town wear the gray and brown corduroy pants, with flannel shirts, let me pick out a pair for you."

Mr. Anderson brought the purchases up and laid them on the counter along with the hunting clothes.

"Do you think you might need some underwear, or socks?"

"Yes. Good idea. Give me a couple pair of underwear, a t-shirt, and maybe three pair of socks, one black, one brown, one gray," Sam said as he studied the man and thought what an excellent salesman he was.

"So would there be anything else Sam? Do you need a belt, or a hat?"

"No, I think that's all for now. I appreciate your help. You're an excellent salesman."

"Well, tell you what. Let me throw in this hunting cap as a Christmas present. It has the turn-down flaps that keep your ears warm. That wind is a little brisk today."

"Thank you, Harold, thank you very much."

"Thank you, Sam, for letting me be of service to you. I hope you enjoy your time in Fries and will come back soon to see us. And have a very Merry Christmas."

"I think I'll do that very thing."

Sam picked up his large bag and walked to the Corner Drug. He stopped outside to study the assortment of posters being displayed in the window; the Fries High School Wildcats' basketball schedule, several announcements for church fund raisers, and something about a lost calico cat. He then entered the café.

"Hello Sam," Bud greeted him heartily. "Have you worked up an appetite walking around our huge metropolitan commercial center?"

"Yes Bud, I sure have," Sam said trying to match Bud's enthusiasm. "Let's see, now what was it Chiney told me I should try? Oh, yeah, I want one of your barbeques with everything, French fries, and one of your cherry vanilla sodas."

"Well, you just sit down over there next to the window, and watch our busy Main Street, and we'll have it to you in a few minutes. So are you looking forward to your bird hunting?

"Yes. I'm really looking forward to it." Sam said as he glanced around the room. "Not very busy today, is it?"

"No, hasn't been too busy the last few weeks. Since the Mill shut-down. Everyone's pinching pennies for Christmas."

"Soon his order was delivered to his table by an attractive, but very shy waitress bearing the nametag, "Juanita." Sam wrapped his napkin around the bottom of his sandwich, forgetting that he wasn't wearing one of his expensive suits, and took a bite.

"Umm," Sam said with a long, drawn-out sigh of contentment, "Chiney was right. "This *is* a delicious barbeque."

"Thanks, Sam, glad you like it. We make it ourselves. Buy fresh Boston butt, grind it, and cook it right here. I wasn't sure a city-slicker like you would like it," Bud said with a grin.

"Oh, I'm far from a city slicker," Sam retorted with a laugh, "My folks lived in the country and we were so poor, we had to rent fatback to go into our pinto beans."

"Really?" Bud said. "Well now my folks were so poor, they made us stand up in bed to turn over so we wouldn't wear out the sheets."

The businessman was enjoying this camaraderie very much. For the last fifteen months he had been traveling, dressing in expensive suits, to talk to venture capitalists and Wall Street financial analysts, trying to convince them that a small-town businessman from Arkansas could develop a successful plan to build a nation-wide retail store chain. It was good to take a break from those know-it-alls, and just be plain Sam with the people he considered to be the salt of the earth. It was this kind of people, hard-working, price-conscious consumers that would make his dream successful.

Sam loved to watch people, study them, and it had made him a very good business man. He felt confident in being able to look at a person, and know what he was like, what he wanted out of life. He just didn't have very many subjects to study in this diner. Several people wandered in and out without catching Sam's attention.

Toward the end of his meal, Sam saw an attractive young couple come in. The lady was wearing a pair of jeans, not the designer kind, just plain ones, and a black wool jacket. Her blonde ponytail hung from beneath a red, white and green crocheted hat. Her male companion was a full foot taller. He wore no hat, and his short military style hair cut glistened with a few snow flakes that had blown from surrounding awnings. He wore khaki corduroy pants. Even under a leather flight jacket, the man was obviously very muscular. Sam loved to study the clothing styles of different areas, and just from the clothes, he could tell this man wasn't from, or lived in, this area. He had more of a metropolitan look.

"Karen," Bud said, "it is so good to see you. Is Suzie still doing okay?"

"Yes, she's back to her old self. She's all wrapped up in this Christmas Committee stuff. She has poor old John running her all over the place."

Karen then began to blush when she realized she had so casually referred to John.

"Oh, I'm sorry, Bud. Have you met John Helmsman? John, um, was here working for Mr. Armbrister, and he was the first to get to Suzie. John drove me to the hospital. He has been a great support to me the last couple of days," she said, as she turned and grinned up at him.

"Oh yeah, John and I are good old buddies by now. He's been in a few times," Bud said. He had not seen Karen look so happy since she had lost her husband. Bud then turned toward the investigator and added, "But it is good to see you again John. It looks like you've decided to do more than just pass through."

"Yes sir," John said returning the smitten smile toward the woman, "Karen and Suzie have been kind enough to invite me to celebrate a Fries Christmas with them."

"Oh, by the way," Bud said, "Deputy Honaker was in here earlier today, asking if I had seen you. You made quite an impression on him. Seems you handled Spunkie better than two deputies usually do."

"Well, Spunkie was so drunk," John answered with a chuckle, "I'm sure Karen could have taken care of him."

"So what can I do for you Karen?" Bud said, turning his

attention back to her.

"Oh, we just stopped by to pick up some aspirin for Suzie. I don't think it's anything to worry about. She's probably just been reading and typing too much."

"Well," Bud said as he handed a box of Bayer's over to Karen, "we don't want her to not feel like attending the Christmas Committee meeting tomorrow morning. If anyone can save Christmas in this town, it will be her. Give her my love."

"I'll tell her that Bud. You and the family have a Merry Christmas."

"Yes, you guys have a merry one also."

Sam had become attentive at the reference to the meeting. It did sound like this meeting was a very important event and that Suzie must be the town darling. He looked at his watch. It was nearly one o'clock. He needed to get back to the Boarding House and change if he was going bird hunting. He wiped his mouth a final time with the napkin and came to the counter to settle his bill.

"That was delicious Bud. What do I owe you?"

"Tell you what Sam. Just bring me a pheasant if you get an extra one, and we'll call it even."

"Sounds like a deal, see you later."

17

Sam stopped after exiting the Corner Drug, allowing his eyes to adjust to the bright midday sun reflecting off the snow. Much of the snow that had been plowed to the side of the street was now melting slush. Sam began his walk back down the street, his bag of new clothing in hand.

As he passed the clothing store, he waved at Mr. Andrews who was adjusting some suits on a rack. Sam thought about how the clothing in the store was of good quality, but even in a relatively economically depressed town like Fries, was overpriced. He was sure that Mr. Andrews wasn't overcharging, but there were just so many 'middle-men' between the merchant and the producer. Eliminating those could eliminate 30-40% of the cost, allowing a larger volume to be sold, due to the lower price. Middle-income Americans would reap the benefits of this retailing plan. It would be almost like selling to the retail market at wholesale prices.

Within two minutes he had finished the 400-foot walk. As he started into the seventy year-old inn, he looked up to the idle cotton mill. Across the front of the building, even at this distance of 500 yards, he could make out a banner hanging loosely from the building. He squinted, barely able to read it, but could tell it said something about Peace, Earth, and Fries.

He entered the front door, and immediately Myrt came out of the kitchen to greet him.

"Hi, Sam, your room is ready. Need any lunch?"

"No, thank you," he said, not wanting to tell her he had eaten at the corner drug.

"Well, how about a cup of coffee before your hunting trip?"

"Oh, that would be good, actually great, thank you," he said, and then asked. "And also, could I borrow a telephone? I'll reverse the charges."

"Sure, use the one right there at the counter. I'll bring your coffee to you."

Sam placed the collect call. Fortunately, his wife was at home and quickly accepted it.

"Hi, honey bun," Sam said, using his favorite pet name for his wife, "how's everyone doing?"

"Hi Sam," his wife answered, "Well, we got the tree up over the weekend. The kids are getting excited. Are you in Pennsylvania now?"

"That's what I'm calling about. I got to Virginia, somewhere near Roanoke, and ran into a snow storm. I slid off the road and got stuck, but I'm alright. I broke a tie-end rod, and they're having to replace it, so now I'm in a little town called Fries. It's spelled f-r-i-e-s, but it's pronounced freeze. It was named after a guy that started the town about a hundred years ago."

"Sounds quaint, a lot like home."

"Yeah, it reminded me a lot of home. The people are really nice, in spite of their problem."

"Really? What kind of problem?"

Myrt brought the cup of coffee and set it down on the counter with a bowl of sugar and a small pitcher of cream. Sam covered the receiver with his hand and whispered, "Thank you."

"Well, they all work in the same place, a cotton mill, and it's been shut down, right before Christmas. Doesn't look good for the families here."

"So how long will you be there before heading up to Pennsylvania?"

"Well, I'm not sure. Hopefully, I'll only lose a couple of days."

"Are you still going to be able to make it home by next week?"

"I hope to," Sam said, but his wife could hear his hesitancy, "but it's going to be tight. I…I may not make it."

"Oh, Sam," his wife answered, not even attempting to conceal her disappointment and frustration, "the kids will be so disappointed. They were even discussing postponing presents until New Year's, to wait on you."

"Honey, I'm sorry, but we've discussed this before. If we are going public next year, I have to have everything in place, suppliers, networks, transportation. There's just not enough time left. After this summer, we'll have more time for family things."

"Sam, for some reason, I doubt that," she said in a tone that made it clear that this conversation was over.

"I'll be home as soon as I can," Sam said after a few moments of icy silence. "Tell the kids to go ahead and enjoy Christmas, though."

"Okay, Sam. Be careful and get home soon. I love you."

"I love you, too. I'll call Christmas Morning."

Sam hung up, feeling guilty but knowing he was doing what had to be done. Thirty years of hard work had led to this opportunity, and he knew he had to make sure nothing went wrong.

"So you say the room is ready?" Sam asked, trying to force a smile.

"Yes. Here's your key. It's room 221."

"Thanks. See you this evening."

Sam walked up the creaking steps to the second floor until he found the room. He walked in, laying the overnight bag and the clothing bag on the dresser. From the foot of the bed he had an excellent view of New River. He watched as huge pieces of ice were breaking up and shooting over the dam, crashing and breaking up into smaller pieces on the rocks below. He watched as the miniature icebergs floated out of sight around the bend in the river.

Sam checked his watch. It was 1:35. He decided to wait until after the hunt for his shower, and like an excited kid trying on his new clothes on the first day of school, he began changing into his new hunting clothes. *Even the feel of hunting clothes is exhilarating by itself,* he thought to himself. Sam slipped on the heavy wool socks, hoping that Chiney remembered to bring the extra boots. He then pulled the cap over his head, twisting it to get that just-right feel, picked up his jacket, and walked out the room, locking the door behind him.

By the time he got out to the front lobby of the Boarding House, Chiney was sitting there holding a pair of boots. One glance told Sam that these are not an extra pair of boots, but practically new.

After sliding on the new boots and lacing them up, they

walked outside to the truck. Chiney had added a wooden dog box to the pickup. As Sam neared the truck, he could hear a low moaning sound from a dog. Just as Sam started to look into the box, Birddog opened the truck door from the inside, and began to slide over, moving his legs to the right to clear the floor gear shift.

"Good to see you again," Birddog said with a big smile as he extended his hand to Sam, both for a shake and also to help pull him into the pick-up.

"Hey, good to see you too," Sam said. "Thanks to you guys for letting me tag along."

"Glad to have you. Chiney says you love to bird hunt. I do too."

"Yes, I do. I can't believe I haven't been for more than a year. I'm really looking forward to today.'

"Yeah," Chiney added, "it's gonna be a perfect day, warm enough for Cotton to pick up the scent, with a nice white background to shoot against. Old Cotton is dying to get at it."

"I'm anxious to see this Cotton."

"Yep, Sam," Birddog said nodding his head as if in deep meditation, "today you've got the honor of hunting with the best bird dog in the three counties, maybe even the entire state. He's a true miracle of nature. Why, he might even be the Eighth Natural Wonder of the World."

"So why the name 'Cotton?'"

Chiney and Birddog laughed and exchanged a wink to each other.

"Well," Chiney said with an impish grin, "you'll soon find out."

"Oh, by the way, Chiney, I happened to remember. I don't have a Virginia hunting license."

"Yeah, old buddy, I've already thought about that. Today you're not Sam, you're Chiney Alderman."

"Oh, well, but what if you need to show yours?"

"I don't hunt much anymore," Chiney said, as Sam detected a glint of remorse in the man's usually effervescent visage. "My eyes are going. I can still drive fine, but I can't aim a gun very good anymore."

"Oh, really? Yes, I'm going to need to get glasses myself. I just keep putting it off."

"The doctors, they say glasses won't help, it's from an injury. I..., um, got some sand in my eyes during the war."

"Oh, where did you fight? I was in the war, but never left the states. I really admire you guys that did the real fighting."

"Most of the action I saw was fighting in the Desert, in the Northern Campaign, back in '43. A shell went off about fifteen feet in front of me, blew my blasted helmet off. I thought I had been hit by shrapnel, but it was just sand. Felt like a thousand bb's hitting me, they was hot as hell. Well, the sand did a lot of damage to my eyes. They said I might go blind one day. I was in the hospital for about four months, and then they sent me home. I was fine until about ten years ago, then I've started having stabbing pain, like little lightning bugs going off in my eyes, and I've slowly but surely been losing my eyesight ever since."

"But doesn't that affect your driving?" Sam asked, as he noticed how Chiney was leaning over the steering wheel, squinting.

"Lawd no," he laughed, turning his head and closing only his right eye that was visible to the other two to make it appear he had both eyes closed. "I could drive these roads with my eyes closed."

"So how did you get your name, 'Chiney'?" Sam asked.

"That was in the war, too," Chiney said as the old sparkle returned to his countenance. "Some of those Yankees from up north, they was making fun of how I talked, but I told them, I was talking right, they was the ones talking funny. But one of them said that I couldn't be from America, I must be one of them Chiney-men. One of my buddies from Fries was serving with me, and he come back and told might neer' everybody about it, and that's what everyone has called me, ever since."

Sam was really enjoying the companionship of these two down-to-earth men. It was hard to believe they seemed so alike, but were actually so different.

"So Chiney tells me you're a college professor," Sam said, turning to Birddog.

"Well, I never really considered myself a professor," the man answered in a soft voice, "just a teacher mostly, and a coach, over at the community college in Wytheville. Most of the kids around here can't afford to go off to VPI, or to Radford, or to East Tennessee State, so they stay at home and go to Wytheville for two years, then transfer. It costs about half as much. I really enjoy watching the kids come through our system, then go on to finish their degree."

"Well, that's great, Birddog. You're really to be commended."

"As a matter of fact, the president of the Community College is an old Fries boy named Wade Gilley." The college professor said, as he directed the attention away from himself. "I've heard he's the youngest college president in the whole country. That fellow will go somewhere, mark my word. But he's still just as down to earth as anybody. That's kinda something our parents build into us here in Fries. No matter where we go, and what we do, we're still just plain folk, and need to not get too big for our britches."

"Got any more home town heroes?" Sam asked. Also being from a small town, Sam always enjoyed hearing true stories of "home-town boy does well."

"Well," Chiney replied, "we have a mighty fine baseball player that was drafted by the Giants last year, I think he'll make a good one. Name's Ed Goodson, lived down the road there in Ivanhoe, but played all his ball here in Fries, and up at East Ten-e-see State. He's got the prettiest swing you've ever seen. Just a skinny ole thing, but he can hit that ball a mile. They had to put a net over the right field fence at the ball park because he kept knocking balls into the river, and the bass kept choking on them." Chiney said, as he stole a look over to see if Sam had caught his tall tale. He then continued. "He'll be playing in the big leagues by next year, I'll betcha."

"You know," Birddog said in addition, "I think any of our men and women that fought in the wars are our heroes. My own brother Freddie, he's a local teacher, was highly decorated in the Korean War. And then there was Russ Gilley that died in the second World War, he was quiet a hero."

"Yes, I'd second that motion," Sam said with a solemn nodding of his head. "We owe our veterans a lot."

About that time Chiney pulled off the hard surfaced road and stopped at a gate. Before the old tired engine stopped wheezing, he had jumped out, and was running in a slow trot to unlock the gate.

"That Chiney is a hoot," Birddog said with a chuckle. "Everybody in town loves him, but he is a strange one. Talks to himself a lot. You'd think he was a little touched, but actually, he's smart as a whip. Really knows his Bible, too. He teaches Sunday School at times and does almost all of the readings at the Baptist Church because he knows all those hard words." Birddog said, but then began laughing zestfully, "or at least we all figure he knows them because he never hesitates in pronouncing them. He may just be making them up though."

"Yeah, I don't think I've ever met anyone quite like him," Sam said in agreement, "tell me more."

"Well, talk about being frugal. He tapes his state inspection sticker onto his vehicle windshields and switches it and his license plates back and forth from his truck to his car. He only puts a gallon of gas in his car at a time, always the cheapest grade, because he said if you keep more than a couple of gallons, it evaporates. But everyone loves him. He's Fries' Good Old Soul. Oh, and the story he told you about how he injured his eyes in the war? Well, he actually saved three of his men by pushing them into the fox-hole and he took the blunt of the blast."

By that time, Chiney had unlocked the gate and was sliding back into the truck. He pulled through the gate, leaving it unlocked.

"Well, we're here." Chiney said as he stopped in the middle of the field. "Let's go shoot us some birds."

The day had warmed up to a comfortable 50 degrees. In the hectic pace of the last year and a half, Sam had forgotten how absolutely wonderful it was to forget about everything, and lose himself in a good bird hunt.

"Sorry, Sam," Chiney said as he pulled a gun from behind the seat, "but the only bird gun I have is this old double barrel Winchester. Hope it will be okay."

"Sure you don't want to use it?" Sam asked, "I don't want to keep you from hunting. I'll just act as a blocker to keep the birds from running on the ground. I'm happy to just be out here in the open."

"Oh, no, I really was serious about not shooting anymore."

"Okay, if you are sure."

Sam lifted the gun to his shoulder and made an imaginary sweep of a pheasant taking flight.

"Oh, this will be great. This was the same model of gun I used to hunt on my granddaddy's and grandmother's farm in Arkansas."

"What do you hunt with now?" Bird-dog asked.

"Well, I just bought a recoil-operated Browning A-5. It looks like it might be good for both pheasant and geese. But truth told, I haven't even used it yet."

"Yeah, I read about that gun in *Outdoor Life*," Birddog said as he pulled a Winchester pump action from its case. "That's supposed to be a fine gun."

Sam turned as he heard Chiney unlocking the dog cage in the bed of the pickup. The dog had been so quiet, Sam had forgotten about it.

"Come on, Cotton," Chiney called out, smacking his hands together and whistling. "Come on, old boy."

Then, like a shot out of a cannon, flashed a snow white buddle of fur from the box.

"Well, I'll be...," was all Sam could say.

The dog had the appearance of an English Setter, but was totally white, with almost a pink tint. The dog jumped all around and against Chiney, shaking its tail. The dog's body became a convulsion of twists and turns, tail wagging, head jerking up and down. "Come on, Cotton," Chiney said as he finally took he dog by the collar, and turned its head toward Sam. "Say 'hello' to my buddy Sam."

Sam was just shaking his head from side to side, his eyes opened wide in amazement. Cotton looked up at Sam, panting to be rubbed. Sam looked down into a face of pink eyes, pink nose and pink lips. There was even a pinkish glow beneath the white fur.

"It's...it's an albino." Sam said finally, just as Sam and Birddog began to laugh.

"Yeah, sure is. His dad and mom, they was just as normal as could be, but they was older dogs. This was the only pup born in the last litter."

"Chiney wanted to call it 'Albino,'" Birddog said, "but I

suggested instead we call it 'Cotton.'"

"Yeah, I can see why," Sam agreed, "what with his color."

"Well, not just that, but Chiney always keeps parts of the cotton bales from the Mill as bedding in his dog houses. The pup was three days old before Chiney saw him lying in the back of the dog house, in the cotton."

Chiney pulled the dog back to him and began tying a long strip of what appeared to look like film negative around the dog's head.

"Why are you doing that?" Sam asked.

"Well, Cotton's nearly blind, but his eyes are still really sensitive to the sun and with the snow, it would be real bad on him."

"Oh, I see."

"He's also deaf," Birddog said.

"Deaf? Umm, Chiney, I don't mean to offend you, but how can a deaf, almost blind dog find birds?"

Chiney and Birddog both began laughing uproariously.

"Well," Chiney began explaining, "it's just an instinct with him. I guess he's made up for his disabilities by having a higher than average sense of smell."

"Yeah, we've got several people like that in Fries." said Birddog. "Like Charlie, the barber. He's had polio ever since he was eight, but still does everything the rest of us does, and works ten hours a day, six days a week in the barber shop."

"Yeah, and there's Mr. Pless who owns the furniture stores. He's only got one arm, lost the other as a kid, and he plays baseball with the old-timers. And he's killed every type of big game found in the U.S. and Canada."

"Yeah," agreed Sam, "I think the good Lord gives each of us extra abilities. We just have to learn how to find them."

Chiney placed his hand in front of the dog's nose, offering his scent, and the dog began to follow him. The men walked for about five minutes until they were in the middle of a large field, amid five large piles of cut pines.

"Doug Turner, our local lawyer owns this land," Chiney said. "He lets everyone bring their old Christmas trees here and pile them up. He even imported these pheasants. It makes a great place for birds and rabbits to spend the winter. This is about the only place we could hunt birds during the winter, especially with a snow."

Chiney squatted down next to Cotton, and began rubbing the dog behind his ears. Cotton yelped a couple of times, began swishing his tail at a rapid rate, and then licked his owner's face.

"Okay, ole boy," Chiney said, his mouth pressed to the dog's ear, "now I want you to put on a show for Sam here. Show him what a special dog you are."

With that, Chiney nudged Cotton's shoulder, urging him in the direction of the discarded pines. Chiney then smacked Cotton on the rump and the dog started off at a slow trot. He first headed just to the left of the first pile, stopped, lifted his head, his pink nose twitching, then began to hone in on a scent in the direction of a mound of brush. He stopped about ten yards away, sniffing. He then began to circle the pile. Sam noticed a commotion just to the left of Cotton, and he pulled the shotgun to his shoulder. Suddenly, a small bundle of white and brown fur scurried across the snow. It was a rabbit, but Cotton hadn't even flinched. Sam looked over toward Chiney and smiled approvingly.

"He's a bird dog, nothing else," Chiney said with the pride a mother has when she's told her child has earned straight A's. "Doesn't pay nothing else no mind at all."

"Someone did a heck of a job training him," replied Sam.

"That's just it. He's never been trained. It's just all in him."

Cotton completed an entire circle around the pile, stopping a few more times to test the air.

"Well, nothing there I guess. Let's go to the next one."

Chiney walked over to Cotton and placed his hand in front of Cotton's nose. He began walking toward the next pile, the dog a pace behind. When he was about thirty yards away, Chiney again smacked his hand on Cotton's rump, and the dog was off, zeroing in on the next spot. Cotton made a couple of adjustments, then, when he was about fifteen yards from the pile, he froze into a point. His motionless body almost disappeared into the snowy background.

"Stay here 'til I can get over to the left of the pile," Chiney whispered, "then move up about thirty feet."

Chiney slowly circled around the tree pile until he was

diagonal to Cotton and stationed a safe thirty yards away from the pile, then slowly waved to the men. Sam and Birddog eased up about fifty feet, leaving them about forty feet from the pile. Sam could feel his heart begin to pound, his adrenalin beginning to pump. There is no sensation that can compare to the moments before you're about to shoot your first bird of the day.

Why have I denied myself this pleasure for the last year? the businessman thought to himself.

Almost as if he had been signaled that all was ready, Cotton instinctively eased out of his point and slowly began approaching a portion of the pile, his tail beginning to wave in a slow, hypnotic rhythm, almost like that of a metronome. About that time, two birds came running out of the end toward Chiney. Chiney screamed, waving his arms wildly and forced the two birds off the ground and into flight.

Birddog squeezed off two rapid-fire shots with the pump, both missing, before Sam's first shot. Immediately following Sam's first shot, a flurry of feathers interrupted the bird's ascension which turned into a feather-filled free-fall to the ground. A half-second later, the second barrel of Chiney's old Winchester blasted, and the second bird met the same fate. By this time Chiney was running over to the two men.

"Did you see that? Did you see that?" Chiney was screaming.

"I sure did," Birddog said in amazement. "That second bird had to be forty yards. I didn't even want to waste a shot, and you brought him down."

"This Winchester might be old, Chiney," Sam said with a self-effacing laugh, "but it's dead on. It shoots a good pattern, too."

"Yeah, I have the shells loaded special. But still yet that's some fanciful shooting."

"Yeah, it's gotta be that gun, Sam," Birddog said with a mock explanatory tone. "Here, let me use the double barrel and you use the pump."

"Are you sure?" Sam asked. He knew this was a guise, that with its multiple shells, the pump was more effective than the double barrel.

"Sure, I'm sure. Bet you can't get three on a shot, though."

By that time Cotton had retrieved the first bird. His mouth

clamped over the head, not disturbing any of the body. He brought the limp clump of meat and feathers to Chiney.

"Good job, ole boy. Good job." He took Cotton by the collar, leading him over to Sam.

"Here you go, Cotton. Give the bird to Sam."

Cotton obeyed, dropping the bird at Sam's feet. Sam knelt to pat the dog and Cotton began licking him.

"Good boy. Good boy." Sam said as he placed his hand on Cotton's rump. The dog took off in a trot to retrieve the second bird, zeroing in after several direction adjustments.

Could there be a more beautiful bird in the world than a ring-necked pheasant? Sam thought to himself.

He ran his fingers over the brown chest feathers, examining them, so coarse, the feathers at the neck that looked like corrugated shingles, each feather tipped with either white or black. He studied the feathers going from almost a rust at the base of the neck, to an almost tan at the body, transitioning into a chocolate at the tail. He marveled at the tail, a full twelve inches long, so aristocratic, like the plume in the hat of a member of the royal family, and the neck, a distinct white ring separating the base of the neck from the body. He studied the various coral shades, some blue, some green, some purple, depending upon how the sun struck the feathers. At the end of the thick neck reigned a majestic, proud head, as black as a moonless midnight, with a deep red mask around the eyes.

Yes, this was a beautiful bird, Sam thought to himself, almost regretting having killed such a beautiful creation. Sam's scrutiny was interrupted when he noticed Cotton had dropped the second bird at his feet.

"Chiney, looks like Cotton's found himself a new pal," Birddog said.

"Well, I'll be hornswoggled, he's never gone to anyone else before, without me telling him to," Chiney said, rubbing his chin, then added in feigned anguish, "Cotton, you old two-timer. You done gone and broke my heart."

This time Sam grabbed the dog and hugged him, as Cotton licked his neck.

Chiney picked up the two birds and placed them into the

burlap sack he had brought along. The three men and the dog began walking to the third location.

"Sam," Birddog said, "if we jump two or more, I'll go for the first, you take the others."

"Got'cha"

Once again Cotton found nothing but B'rer Rabbit at the third briar patch, so they moved to the next pile. At the fourth, Chiney directed Cotton toward the pile while he once again set up to block the pheasants if they decided to run instead of fly. Three birds were jumped. Birddog downed the lead bird, and Sam bagged the two that trailed. Again Cotton brought all three birds back to Sam and dropped them at his feet.

The fifth pile resulted in no birds, or even any other scurrying animals, so the men decided to call it a day and headed back toward the truck.

"Guys, I can't think you enough," Sam said. "I don't' know the last time I've had so much fun."

"Well, Sam, we've enjoyed it, too," Birddog said in his soft voice, slapping his new friend on the back. "You seem to be a really nice fellow. So what are you going to do with your birds?"

"Well, I think I'll take one to Bud, in exchange for a most excellent barbeque sandwich," Sam said, turning to wink at Chiney. "I thought I might take one back to Myrt, have her fix them up, if she can."

"Are you kiddin'," Chiney said. "There's nothing Myrt can't fix. Have you had her biscuits and gravy yet?"

"No," Sam said, "Maybe I can have some tomorrow."

"Well, you're in for a treat," Chiney said, then got very serious, "but let me warn you, you have to be careful with her biscuits."

"Oh, okay," Sam said, his forehead wrinkled in a puzzling look. "What's the matter with them? Don't they taste good?"

"Oh yeah, they taste great, but they are so light…" Birddog spoke up, but then waited for effect, "…that you have to hold them down with one hand, and pour the gravy on with the other, or they'll just float away." Birddog and Chiney both bent over in laughter. Apparently the two men had teamed up with this story on other unsuspecting victims.

By this time the men had reached the truck, where Chiney

lifted Cotton's front paws up and onto the pick-up bed tailgate. The dog walked to the front of the bed and slipped into the box.

"Hey, I'll go get the gate," Birddog said.

Chiney got in, and Sam slid over next to the gear shift. They pulled through the gate Birddog had just swung opened. The professor then locked it back and started back to the truck.

"Well," Bird-dog said as he slid into the pickup, "I think the snow's gonna be gone by Christmas."

"Hey, by the way, wonder if Suzie Young's still doing okay?" Chiney said.

"You know," Birddog said, "I haven't heard since she got home."

"Her dad and mom came into Bud's when I was there this morning," Sam said, feeling proud he could share some local news. "They said she's doing good, but had a little headache today."

"Dad?" Birddog questioned. "Couldn't have been her dad. He got killed five years ago in a truck accident."

"Oh really?" Sam said. "What happened?"

"Well, he drove for the Mill," Bird-dog began explaining. "He and another man, Chuck Akers, were hauling cloth down Fancy Gap Mountain. They lost the brakes on the tractor-trailer. They met a station wagon carrying a whole family. Rather than take a chance on hitting the car, they took the rig over the mountain. Killed both of them."

"Yeah, Karen Young hasn't dated a man since that time," Chiney said, "though lotta men have asked."

"Well, she looked pretty chummy with the guy that was with her," Sam said, trying hard not to sound like a gossip.

"That would be good," Birddog said. "She's a beautiful woman who's gone through a lot. It would be great for her to find somebody to take care of her and Suzie."

"Yeah, Suzie deserves a dad," Chiney said, nodding his head up and down. "She is such an angel."

"So," Sam said, turning his head to both of the guys setting on either side of him, "what's the story of her getting hurt?"

"Well, this town's always been a right peaceful, loving town, never much trouble, to speak of," Chiney said, then hesitated, almost seeming as if the words were starting to bring him pain, "but about a month ago, we had a election for mayor that ended in a tie, and it really split the town apart. Everybody was afussin' and afightin'."

"Yeah, and then the Mill shut down right out of the blue, right here at Christmas." Birddog said, "so it was looking like a mighty bleak time."

"Well, that Suzie, she's just about everybody's darling in this town," Chiney said as he picked up the story. "She was going to climb up on the Mill to put up a banner that said, 'Peace on Earth, and in Fries too.'"

"Yeah," Sam said, "I saw that banner, but I couldn't read what it said, or what it meant."

"Well, one of our local trouble makers, Spunkie Akers, was trying to scare her into taking it down, by throwing rocks." Chiney said, his voice taking on a high pitch as he continued. "He hit her, and knocked her off the third floor of the Mill."

For the first time since Sam had met Chiney, he sensed a tone other than genuine gentleness. He detected an edge that would make him believe that if Chiney had his hands on this Spunkie Akers right now, he'd use one of the shotguns on him.

"The town thought for a day we might lose her, but then she came to." Birddog said quietly, "I can't imagine this town without Suzie."

"Yeah, she even prints our weekly newspaper," Chiney said, in an obvious attempt to restore his usual joviality. "She calls it the Fries Wildcat Spirit Weekly."

"So how old is she, eighteen or nineteen?"

Both men looked over at each other and laughed.

"No, she's only twelve, or maybe thirteen."

"You're kidding?" Sam said in surprise. "Girls that age are usually still playing with their dolls."

"Well, you've never seen a girl like this one, Sam." Chiney said, the sparkle back in his eyes, "If it's true that the good Lord sends his Angels to earth, she is certainly one of them."

"Hey, I just remembered," Birddog said looking over at Chiney, "Karen told me once that she really loved pheasant. Why don't you and Sam take her one of the birds?"

"That would be a right neighborly thing to do," Chiney said. "Would that be okay with you, Sam? Want to ride up with me to their house?"

"Yes," Sam said with a chuckle, "I think I'd like to meet this child prodigy who's a mixture of Joan of Arc and William Randolph Hearst."

18

Fifteen minutes later, the old pickup truck was entering town. There were only a few cars on the street. Chiney pulled over in front of the bank to let Birddog go to his car.

"Well, Gentleman," Birddog said in his best virtuoso voice, "it has truly been an aggrandizement of my existence to have had the bestowing of your extolled personage on such a peon as I."

"Ah, but my dear friend," Chiney said with a wink, "it is my burden to bear, to brighten your day."

Smiling and shaking his head, Birddog reached into the sack and removed one of the birds. He then waved goodbye to the two men and started to his car.

"Hey, Chiney," Sam said, "can you give me a second to run one of these birds down to Bud?"

"Sure, no problem," Chiney said, "I'll wait for you here."

Sam reached in the truck bed, opened the burlap sack, and removed a bird. Just as his hand appeared over the edge of the bed, Cotton began a low yelping, pressing his face to the wire mesh on the dog-box door.

"Hey, boy," Sam said to the dog, as he stuck his hand to the cage, letting the dog lick his hand, "you're everything they said you are. You're one heck of a bird dog."

Sam then started down the street, strolling with the pleasant thought that he was going to be able to repay Bud's kindness. He walked into the drug store smiling. Bud turned around at the sound of the bell announcing a customer was entering the store.

"Well, here's your bird," Sam announced.

"And a good looking bird it is," Bud said, as he handed a large paper bag over the counter to Sam. "How did you guys do?"

"We got five between us," Sam said, concealing the fact that four of the kills were his.

"Five? Wow, that was a good day!"

"It would have been a great day if we hadn't even seen a bird." Sam said with sincerity. "I'd forgotten how great it was to be out with a gun and dog."

"Speaking of dogs," Bud said as he chewed on the cigar butt, "what did you think of ole Cotton?"

"That, my friend, is a real bird dog. The best I've ever seen."

"Yeah, ole Chiney has been offered a fortune for him, but he won't sell him."

"Well, we've got to run. We're going to run one of the birds up to the Young's."

"Now, they'll appreciate that. Give my love to Suzie."

Sam walked back down the street toward the pickup. It was five o'clock and the bank was just closing. Phyllis and Mr. Phillips were locking the door as Sam walked by.

"Hi Sam from Arkansas," Phyllis said, her eyes sparkling even more in the sunlight than they had under the bank lights.

Sam did some quick math in his head as he began walking beside the young girl.

"Hi Phyllis," Sam said. "Do you and your husband like pheasant?"

"Oh, yes. My husband loves them, but seldom gets to hunt. Why?"

By this time the two had reached the truck. Phyllis bent over and waved at Chiney, who received the salutation from the beautiful woman and blew her a kiss. Sam decided although he would have loved to have had Myrt cook a bird for him, the thought of giving it to Phyllis left an even better taste in his mouth. He reached into the burlap sack and pulled out a bird and handed it to her.

"Well, we had pretty good luck today, so why don't you take this one home and fix it for him?"

"Seriously? Oh he would love to have it," she said, then put her arms around his neck and hugged him, giving him a slight kiss on the cheek. "I think I'll save it for our Christmas dinner."

The driver side door opened on the pickup, and Chiney stuck his head around the cab.

"Hey, what's this?" He said in mock anger. "I get a hug and kiss from Phyllis once every five years, you've been in town for one day, and you've already gotten one?"

Phyllis laughed, ran around the cab, and gave Chiney a hug and kiss on the cheek.

"Merry Christmas, Chiney," Phyllis said with a giggle. "That should last you for five more years."

She ran across the street and got into her car.

Sam climbed into the old pickup and looked over at Chiney. Both of them were glowing like school boys who had just gotten their first kiss in the cloak room.

"That Phyllis is one sweet girl," Chiney said with a roguish smile. "Sure makes me wish I was 10 years younger."

"Why? So she could be like your daughter instead of your granddaughter?" Sam said with a laugh.

Chiney started up the truck. Even though he had sat in the truck for over fifteen minutes, and the temperature had begun to drop into the low forties, he would never waste gas by letting the truck idle. As a matter of fact, he never even used gas when he drove down a steep mountain. He would always turn off his motor and drift down until his vehicle had all but stopped. The story goes that one day he was coming down the hill into town. He drove beneath the trestle, still drifting with the motor turned off. When he got to the STOP sign at the three-way intersection, he looked both ways, saw nothing coming, and drifted right through it and turned left onto Main Street. As the truck slowed to a halt, he coasted into the nearest parking space. By the time Chiney got out of the truck, Chief Smith was waiting for him.

"Chiney, I think you just run through a STOP sign back there," Bruce said in his agonizingly slow drawl.

"Oh, no Bruce, I didn't run through it. I drifted through it," Chiney said with his big toothy grin, sure he would joke his way out of a ticket.

Without saying a word, Chief Smith took Chiney by the elbow, escorted him down the street, crossed over, and walked to the front of the sign. Bruce reached up with his finger, pointing out the letters.

"Chiney, I think this sign says S, T, O, P. It don't say anywhere

D, R, I, F, T." Chiney began stopping at the sign.

The drive through town continued, with the old coal-hauler pointing out different landmarks along the way.

"Now right there is where Charlie lives."

"Right over there is where Bud lives."

"That's Bruce's house right there."

"Now there's the school, all twelve grades," he said pointing to the right, then turning to point to the left, "and there is the Baptist Church I go to and next to it the Methodist Church."

He then made a left turn and started up the terraced streets. Instead of turning off onto Third Street though, to complete the tour, he drove all the way up to the highest level, Top Street. Sam noticed that almost all the homes looked pretty much the same as if they had all been built from the same floor plan. Some were painted slightly different colors, some with shutters or small porches added. When he got to the end of Top Street, he pulled over to a wide place in the road and cut off his motor.

"Fellow can get a good view of the river, Mill and town from here," he said. "Specially in the wintertime with no leaves on the trees."

Sam looked down on the town spread out about a hundred feet below him. He could see the hydroelectric dam that was built seventy years ago to furnish the power for the mill and the town. He could see large chunks of ice catapulting off the dam like he had seen from the Boarding House window. He was surprised to see how large the mill complex was. He had only been seeing the front of the factory and the main office from Main Street. The entire mill was three times larger than he had thought. He could also see down into the town, and noticed where a building had appeared to have been removed.

"What kind of a building was there?" Sam asked, pointing a finger. "There, above the street, across from the bank."

"That's where the train depot sat," Chiney answered with a sigh. "The railroad stopped running mite neer eight years ago, then last year, they tore down the old depot. That really broke our hearts."

"Well, guess we'd better head down to the Young's' before it gets too late," Chiney said as he released the emergency brake, and pushed in the clutch. The truck began slowly drifting down the sloped street, made the sweeping turn, and, as if there were magical hands pushing it, coasted to the front of the house where it slowed to a stop without Chiney even having to use his brakes.

Even though identical in shape and size to the others, there was something different about this home. It had a fresh coat of paint and pretty lace curtains hung at the windows. Flower boxes filled the empty space between the sidewalks and the front of the house. The two men got out and walked to the door, where Chiney knocked three times.

The door opened, and Sam recognized the pretty young blonde that had come into the drugstore earlier that day.

"Hello, Miss Karen," Chiney said as he took off his hunting cap and held it like a fig leaf in front of him. "I do hope that Suzie is doing well."

"Well, hello, Chiney, you good ole soul you," Karen said. "She is doing just fine. Would you like to say hi?"

"Yes, ma'am. I'd like that mighty fine."

The two men entered the room. Sam recognized the man he had seen Karen with earlier in the day sitting on the floor with Suzie. A Scrabble board was laid out on the coffee table alongside a big bowl of popcorn and three glasses filled with Kool-Aid.

"Chiney! Hi!" Suzie said with a squeal of delight as she jumped up to hug him.

"My gracious, you are a treat for sore eyes, Suzie," he said as he lifted her off the ground in a bear-hug. "Young lady, you surely did throw a scare into us."

"I'll try not to do it again," Suzie said with a grin.

"Miss Karen, Suzie, I'd like for you to meet my friend, Sam," Chiney said after setting Suzie back down to the floor. "He got hisself stuck in the snow over on the interstate and banged up his car a tad, and I brought him home until they can get the car fixed."

"Hello, Sam. It's great to meet you. Any friend of Chiney's is a friend of ours," Karen said, offering her hand, then she turned in the direction of the coffee table, "And this is my good friend, John Helmsman. He has really been heaven-sent while Suzie was in the hospital."

John stood up, greeting the men with a big smile and a firm

handshake.

"Miss Karen," Sam said as he pulled a bird from the burlap sack, "we brung you a big old fat pheasant, if you'd like it."

"Like it? You know I'd like it. I love pheasant," she said, taking the bird. She then turned to John. "Have you ever had pheasant, John?"

"No, I haven't," he said, and then he added with a chuckle. "Always wanted to try one, though. Started to get one in a New York restaurant, but I wasn't about to spend $15 for it, not even if it was under glass."

"Well, you are in for a treat then," she said, and then turned back to the two men. "Thank you so much for the bird. So did you men have a good hunt?"

"We sure did," Chiney answered. "And don't thank me. Thank Sam. He's a sure dead-shot. Shot four times, got four pheasants, and they were all double kills, too."

Sam blushed somewhat, but enjoyed the compliment, especially since it had to do with hunting.

"Well, maybe Sam would like to join us tomorrow night to enjoy this big boy," Karen said.

"Oh, I'd hate to intrude on your dinner."

"Oh, no, sir. We'd love to have you."

"Well, if you're sure it's not going to be an imposition," Sam said with a smile, "then, yeah, I'd love that."

"But I do insist that you take both birds," he said as he handed the other pheasant to her, then turning to the young girl. "And oh, and by the way Suzie, I understand you are quite an asset to this town."

"Oh, I don't know about that," she said with a blush. "I just love Fries, and like to do whatever I can."

"I was told I could come to the committee meeting tomorrow. I understand you are on the committee."

"Yes, sir. I sure hope you can help us come up with some ideas. I'd hate to see the children not have a Christmas."

Sam smiled. He was beginning to see why the rest of the town was so enamored of Suzie. She was still a child herself, yet she was worried about what she could do to make sure the other children had a good Christmas.

"Well, Miss Karen, we'll go now," Chiney said, then hugged the young girl to his side. "You take care now, Suzie Sunshine."

"I will, Chiney. I hope you have a very Merry Christmas."

The two men got back into the truck and started down the steep road to Main Street.

"You're right. She is a sweetheart," Sam said.

Chiney didn't answer; instead was silent until they had almost reached the Boarding House. Sam was surprised at the silence, and was concerned that something had upset him. He was almost ready to inquire, when Chiney spoke up.

"So Sam, what do you think of ole Cotton?"

"Chiney, I own some good dogs," Sam said, taking on a very serious tone. "I have hunted with some national champions. That dog of yours is as good as I've ever seen. It's amazing, to be almost blind and deaf. He's a good one, a mighty good one."

Chiney was quiet for a few more minutes. The truck was turning onto Main Street at Bud's Corner Drug.

"Think you'd like to have him?" Chiney said slowly.

"You mean you'd sell him to me?" Sam asked, trying to decide if the man was serious, or was about to let him know it was all a joke.

"Sell him? Lord, gosh no! I'd never sell him. That'd be like selling one of your kids."

"Well, what do you mean then?" Sam couldn't believe what he was hearing.

"Sam, I've hunted with dozens of men, might near a hundred I'd say. Cotton has never warmed up to anyone like he did you today, the way he brought the birds to you. There's something special about you that dog really likes."

"Well, maybe it's just because I'm someone, you know, different."

"No. No. It's much more than that. I think Ole Cotton's telling me something."

"Chiney, I'd love to have that dog," Sam said, finding it difficult to express what to say. "You think about it for the next two days. Then, let me know if you still want to do it. If you change your mind, or even will let me pay you, I'll certainly understand."

"Well, okay." Chiney said. Sam could see Chiney's firm face, illuminated by the street lights as the man made a U-turn at the three-way intersection, "but I don't think I'll be changing my mind."

Chiney pulled up in front of the old inn.

"Thanks for the hunt," Sam said. "Best fun I've had in a long spell."

"Enjoyed it mighty fine myself, Sam."

Sam got out and started around the corner of the truck when he heard Cotton jump up in the box and began a playful bark. Sam walked up to the box, reached through the mesh wire, and petted the white dog. Cotton licked his fingers.

"Good night, old buddy," Sam said to his new four-legged friend.

Back at the Young's' house, the three were finishing the Scrabble game.

"I can't believe you beat me at Scrabble," John said in mock disbelief, "on a triple bonus word like q-u-e t-z-a-l." John spelled it out, not being able to pronounce it.

"It's pronounced quet zel," Suzie said with a giggle, bobbing up and down gleefully from her kneeling position. "It's a beautiful bird from Mexico. I saw it in National Geographic. That's who I'm going to write for when I grow up. Want to look it up in the dictionary? I'll bet you a nickel I'm right."

"If you don't want to lose your money, I wouldn't bet if I was you," Karen said. "That girl has a photographic memory. I bet she could even tell you what month she saw the article in."

"Well, I've already had my male ego significantly bruised. Don't guess I want to have my wallet bruised too," John said, crossing his arms and offering a pouty face to Suzie.

He turned to Karen and wrapped his hands around her fingers, totally enveloping them. He wanted to do so much more but didn't know if he should.

"Thank you both for such a wonderful evening," he said. "I honestly don't know the last time I enjoyed an evening so much."

Suzie came running in from the back room and jumped up onto a chair near the couple. Giggling, she held a piece of mistletoe over the two.

"Well, I guess we can't break customs," Karen said as she tip-toed so she was looking into his warm brown eyes. He smiled down at her, and the two, very awkwardly, kissed.

"Can I, umm, come up tomorrow?" he asked, the sweet taste of her lips still on his.

"Now, you know you don't have to ask," Karen said.

"What would be a good time?"

"Well, maybe after Suzie gets back from her Christmas Committee meeting. It's at 10 a.m."

"Oh, okay. I'll come up about 9:45 and pick Suzie up and drive her downtown."

"I'll see you then," Karen said, as she gave him another quick kiss, not quite as awkward this time.

"Goodnight, Suzie. See you tomorrow."

"See ya, John," Suzie said, and then added with a giggle. "If you'll play Scrabble with me again, I'll promise not to be such an autodidact."

John looked at Karen; both raised their eyebrows, and just shook their heads.

John had so many thoughts rushing through his mind as he drove back to the Armbristers. Tonight was the best night he could remember for a long time. For the first time since he was a child, he was going to bed without a worry, and excited about waking up to a bright tomorrow.

When Jason Campbell got to Lisa's house from the IGA that evening he was tired and sore. He had been called in early at eight a.m. to shovel snow from the sidewalk in front of the store, and then had worked until 4:30. Lisa and Jeremy had not gotten in from work yet, so Jason made a sandwich. He had been thinking about how to get the candy, nuts and oranges back to Fries. He dialed from memory his old friend Mike Clemons' phone number.

"Hello," a familiar pleasant voice answered.

"Hi, Mrs. Clemons. This is Jason Campbell. How are you?"

"Well, hello Jason, I'm good. How are you? Where have you been? We haven't seen you in ages."

"Oh, just busy with school. I'm in Pulaski during Christmas

break working. Is Mike around?"

"He sure is. Just a moment."

"Have a Merry Christmas, Mrs. Clemons."

"You too, Jason. Please come see us over the holidays."

Jason had always liked Mrs. Clemons a lot. He thought she liked him, too. Mike had once told him his mom had said that he was the only boy with which she trusted him to run around. Jason had taken this trust to heart, and had tried to stay out of any mischief while he and Mike were out doing what teenage boys so often do.

"Hey, college boy, how are ya?"

"I'm great, Mike. What you been up to?"

"Oh, just trying to get the basketball team to win a game, but they won't listen to me," he said with a laugh.

Mike Clemons had been Jason's best friend since Jason arrived at Fries High School as a tenth grader and went out for football. Mike had always been sickly; he was born as a "blue baby" and was not supposed to have lived to be a teen-ager. Mike loved sports, but could not play and had restricted himself to being manager of the various teams. But he put his whole heart into the job, making sure he took perfect care of the equipment and the athletes. During a football injury, Mike always beat Doc Marinius out onto the field, and would have the mouth piece out of the player's mouth, and the helmet unstrapped by the time Doc got there.

He had befriended Jason from the start. Jason had no brothers, only sisters, and Mike had no brothers, only one sister, so the two had become like male siblings. Like brothers, they argued, and Jason could always depend upon Mike to tell him like it was. That first year, when Jason seldom got to play football, Mike was there to lift him up when he was down. Then during his junior year, when Mike felt Jason was dragging his butt, Mike was there to kick it. Then his senior year, when Jason became a star and was about to get an ego to match it, Mike was there to let the air out of his balloon and bring him down to earth.

And on that final play of the last game, Mike was there to go to the hospital with him and spend the next 36 hours at his bedside. Yes, Mike had always been there for him.

"Whatcha gonna be doing Wednesday morning?" Jason asked.

"Hmm, nothing much I can think of. Why?"

"Well, I'm working at the IGA in Pulaski, and my boss has given me candy canes, nuts and oranges for the Christmas party. Think you could come down about ten in the morning and help me pack two-hundred bags, then take them back to Fries?"

"Well, yeah, sure. I guess I could do that. Might be fun, since you haven't had time to come see me. Now that you're a big fancy college boy."

"Well, I still like to mingle with the common people," Jason said teasingly. "Oh, and if you could, phone Herbie and let him know that I'll be sending this to the party. See ya Wednesday morning."

"See ya."

John was getting back to his old sleep patterns when he woke up Tuesday morning at his usual time of six a.m. He thought about jogging, but there was still just enough ice and slush to make it a little dangerous, so he did some stretching and calisthenics in the bedroom. He managed to do a 45-minute workout that made him feel a little less guilty about not having worked out over the last four days. Cynthia was still asleep, so he thought if he wasn't there, perhaps she would sleep later.

He drifted the Buick out of the driveway, started the motor, and then drove down into town, stopping in front of the Washington Inn. He had heard what great breakfasts the cook made here. It had been awhile since he had eaten good, homemade biscuits and gravy, and salty country ham. As usual in his profession, he walked in and looked around, studying the people in the room. There was only a middle-aged man.

"Hi, what for you?" Myrt asked, looking through the window between the kitchen and the counter.

"How about biscuits and gravy, two eggs over easy, country ham, and coffee, black?" John said.

"Coming up. Just grab yourself a table. Go ahead and pour yourself a cup of coffee from the pot there," Myrt said, as John heard the sound of egg shells cracking, followed by a plop and a sizzling that told him the eggs were being fried.

John turned around, and saw the only other customer smiling at him.

"Hi, remember me? Sam. Chiney and I brought the pheasant up last night."

"Yeah, sure. How are you this morning?"

"I'm good. Come have a seat and join me."

Normally John would have preferred to enjoy his breakfast by himself while studying notes or preparing a report. John's paradigm had gone through a definite metamorphosis recently though, and he actually enjoyed the thought of eating his morning meal while sharing communication with a stranger.

"So what do you do, John?"

John thought, then realized that he no longer needed a cover.

"I work as a security consultant and as a private investigator. I was called up by the Washington Mills group when they were getting some threats after the plant closing."

"Oh. So that's how you know Suzie, the little girl."

"Yes. I was there when she fell. I was inside. If I had been a little faster getting downstairs, I might have stopped Spunkie Akers from hitting her. I later drove Karen, her mom, to the hospital."

"I understand it was a little touch and go for awhile?"

"Yes. It really had us concerned. So what do you do, Sam?"

"Well, I run a few retail stores down south. I was on my way up north to look into some distributors when I slid into the median."

"Here's your breakfast," the little gray-haired cook/waitress said. "I brought you some fresh strawberry preserves and another biscuit, too. Let me know if you need anything else."

John looked down at the plate. Two large, full, fluffy biscuits were drowned in gravy that was practically running off the plate. Two huge golden orbs looked at him, each with a perfect white background, not a single burned spot or ragged edge. To the side lay a generous piece of fried country ham.

"Ah, Myrt, you are an artist. I've never seen such perfect eggs. And the biscuits look so light."

"Yeah," Sam said with a chuckle, a little louder than normal, "you have to hold Myrt's biscuits down when you pour your gravy on them, because if you don't, they're so light, they'll just float off into the air."

"You've been talking to that Chiney and Birddog too much," she called from the kitchen sink where she was washing pots and skillets.

John looked at the plate, and an old memory was brought back to him. It was a memory of visiting his grandma and grandpa on their tobacco farm in Elkin. He called to Myrt in the back.

"Myrt, only one thing could make this plate more perfect. Do you think you could...?"

"Yes, I will bring you a slice of tomato to go with it." She answered, finishing his question, as she started back into the dining room.

"Ah, thank you so much."

"I don't guess you're as much of a city-slicker as I thought you were," the cook said with a laugh.

John and Sam enjoyed their chat together, each not sharing too much information about their jobs, instead, comparing notes about the uniqueness of Fries. After what seemed like an hour, John realized it was almost 8:40. He excused himself to go pick up Suzie.

"Yes, tell Suzie I'll see her at the meeting."

John arrived in front of the house at 8:50 to find Suzie waiting at the door. In her hand was the black leather portfolio, complete with legal pad, note cards, and a Parker ball-point ink pen that John had bought her when he was in Winston-Salem. She quickly ran and jumped into his car, and smiled as she showed him she had brought the gift. At two minutes before nine, John pulled up in front of the door leading upstairs to the Town Council Chambers.

"Alright Suzie, you go on up." John said. "I'll go down to the Corner Drug. When you finish, come on down and get me."

"Okay. Thanks, John."

Suzie bounded up the steps to the council chambers. She was feeling much better now, with most of her strength back, and could have easily made the walk up and down the 300 or so steps. The truth was, she enjoyed spending time with John. It reminded her of the rides she used to take with her dad. She entered the chambers, and looked around. There sat the co-mayors, looking over the agenda.

As soon as Herbie saw her, he jumped up and went running to her.

"Hi Suzie, you're looking more like yourself every time I see you," the youth leader said as he hugged her.

Over the next few minutes, the three pastors showed up. Pastor Stanley and Hamm were in suits, but Pastor Young was in coveralls and a big plaid work coat, for he had been busy putting up the sparse town decorations. The pastors were soon followed by a few spectators.

Herbie, feeling more comfortable at such a small meeting, had agreed to lead.

"Well," Herbie said as he turned to the three pastors sitting at the table, "how did the Sunday services go?

"Best Christmas Service attendance we've had in years," all three pastors agreed.

"I do regret that we had to cancel the Monday night movie though," Mr. Armbrister said. "We just weren't sure about the snow going away in time, so we had to make a decision. Maybe it was nice for people to just have a night to themselves though."

"So let's move on to the rest of the activities then," Herbie said, "Suzie and I have worked together and have planned what we want to do with the caroling tonight. Did everyone get the messages about the times, and get it to their youth?"

The pastors assured him they had, and the youth would be waiting in front of the school at the appointed time.

"So I guess that brings us to how we can have as good of a Christmas party on Wednesday night as possible, with the limitations we have." Herbie said. "I guess the big expense will be the food. Any idea how much the food should cost?"

"Well, we figure about $1200." Jonathan said. "That includes the $800 for the 1500 pieces of chicken and ten trays of slaw from Kenny's, which they are giving to us at half-priced. The rest is for buying the food that will be prepared by the women. We are also getting a lot of food donated, like green beans and corn by people that live outside of town."

"How much money do we have?" Herbie asked looking at the

co-mayor.

"Well, actually we have almost $1500. Let's see, looks like $1458 to be exact. We've had some very generous donations from lots of people that don't live here anymore. As a matter of fact, after the Christmas play at the hospital Sunday night, we had several doctors and parents give us money—almost $300."

"Well, the food costs take up almost all of the donations, so we will have to get very creative deciding what to do about gifts." Herbie said, trying to conceal a sigh. "Does anybody have any ideas?"

"Maybe everyone could bring a used gift, something that their child no longer likes, but another child might enjoy," Pastor Hamn suggested. "This also would teach the joys of giving."

The committee nodded their heads in agreement.

"Now, we have received a few things donated. It's our understanding that there are about 120 boys and about 80 girls under fourteen. Let's see now," Herbie said as he began reading off from the list. "Terry Stoneman, you know, he played football for the Roanoke Buckskins, well, he is sending 50 miniature plastic Redskins footballs. Eddie Goodson is sending some baseballs from the Giants organization, and Chuck Manuel is sending some from the Twins club. Oh, and they also are sending some Topps baseball cards. Then Gayle Lafoon, who graduated a few years ago, works for a printing company, and is sending four-hundred comic books and eighty paper doll cutout books. Yeah, I even heard from Jason Campbell. He's working in Pulaski at some big grocery store during Christmas break from Tech. Apparently he got the owner to give enough candy canes, nuts, and oranges to all the kids."

"Well, it would still be great if we could buy some kind of a gift for the kids," Pastor Lyons said, "but I guess it's too late now, plus you can't get too much for $300. Besides, we don't ever know what they want for Christmas."

Suzie had not contributed to the discussion, but this portion of the conversation caught her ear.

"Oh, I think I know how to find out what they want," she said.

"Really? How?" Pastor Lyons asked.

"I'll be right back in five minutes." Suzie said as she jumped up from her seat and dashed out the door.

The rest of the committee had no other choice but to lean back in their chairs and begin talking among themselves. In a little more than five minutes, Suzie came running into the meeting. With her was Cecil Porter from the Post Office carrying a large canvas bag. Suzie proudly lifted it and emptied the contents on the table. Printed on the outside of each of the envelopes, in large print letters was the same name, Santa Claus.

"I remembered Momma always brought my letters to Santa and handed them to Mr. Porter, so I figured other parents did the same. Sure enough, he saves them all until after Christmas. Except," she said as she turned to Pastor Young, "I don't see any letters from the black children."

"No, child," the black Pastor answered with a big smile, his teeth like the white keys of a new piano, "they bring me the letters, and I take care of them. I still have them at my house."

"Well, it's good to have them," Herbie said, "but what good will it do? We don't have the time, or the money to buy what they have asked for."

Sam had been listening intently to the conversations. He was a shrewd businessman, who never made snap decisions. His determinations usually came after deliberate, incisive analysis in which he considered every possible scenario, weighing the positive gain against the negative loss. In ten minutes he had made a decision, though, of which he had never been more sure of in his life. Sam stood up and slowly raised his hand.

Herbie looked at him, not sure who the stranger was.

"Yes. May we help you?" the co-mayor asked.

"My name is Sam," the businessman said as he stood up. "Most of you don't know me. I slid into the ditch over on the interstate, and Chiney Alderman was good enough to bring me here until they get my car fixed. I, well, I have really grown fond of your town, and when I was young, I had to go without Christmas one year. I'd hate for any child to have to do that."

"Yes, sir, so what are you saying?"

"Well, I think I might have some contacts that could help us. Each child would get at least one, maybe two nice gifts."

The committee members looked at each other with expressions of disbelief.

"But, Sam," Jonathan spoke up, "we're talking about two-hundred kids. That would cost thousands of dollars, probably closer to $10,000."

"Yes, I know." Sam said with an assuring smile. "These are pretty good friends. I think they just might do it for me. I'll need to go over the letters, make a list."

"Let's do it as soon as this meeting is over," Suzie said, her enthusiasm making her bounce in her seat, as she so often did when extremely excited. "I'll help. And, Uncle Buster, would you go get your letters, and come help us?"

Herbie sat dumbfounded, unsure of what to do next. Here was a total stranger, agreeing to provide the Christmas gifts for two-hundred kids he had never met. The man looked stable, and apparently was a friend of Suzie's. But he was found in snowdrift. Why would he be doing this? *But it's not as if we have people standing in line to make us a better offer,* Herbie suddenly thought to himself.

"I say we wish Mr....Sam, the best of luck, and hope that his friends will come through for us." Jonathan Armbrister said. The other members quickly agreed.

"Well, umm," Herbie said, struggling to regain some semblance of composure, "we...we never decided who'd play Santa in the parade, and at the party. Any ideas who to get for Santa?"

The committee members looked back and forth among themselves. One by one they slowly turned their attention to the same individual.

"Well," Jonathan Armbrister said, "it appears we wouldn't be having this Christmas if it wasn't for the Santa sitting here in the room. Sam, are you planning on coming to the party?"

"Well, yes," Sam answered hesitantly, "I thought I might come if you'd have me, but, well, I've never played Santa before. I'd have no idea what to do."

"If you ask me, you've got all the qualifications we need," Pastor Lyons said with a deep uproarious laugh.

By now, the Christmas Spirit that was so long arriving in Fries had centered over the businessman from Arkansas, and had just dumped its entire festive essence over his head.

"Well, yes, I think I would enjoy playing Santa Claus," Sam

said, to the applause of the entire room.

"Okay, it's settled then," Herbie said, "and we'll get Bruce to drive you in his yellow Model-A."

"You can come up to my house around six p.m.," Jonathan added. "Then Bruce will be there to pick you up before 6:30."

A buzz of excitement began filling the room.

"Does anyone else have anything to add?" Herbie asked.

A middle-aged man stood up in the back and raised his hand. Herbie recognized the coal hauler, Horace Hawks.

"Yes, Horace, what is it?"

"Well," Horace said, then hesitated, totally unaccustomed to speaking to more people than the number that usually sits around his dinner table, "after seeing what this gentleman has offered, I'm almost ashamed to offer, but well, I wanted to do something, too. I have some letters I hoped you could give out at the party. I'd like to give away a hundred pounds of coal to each family."

"Oh, Horace" Pastor Hamm said in his retiring voice, "that is nothing to be ashamed of. That is very generous of you. You have made sure the families can stay warm this winter."

"Well, is there anything else?" Herbie asked, almost embarrassed that they could expect anything else. Then he saw another man, Clarence Wilson, stand up.

"Yes, Clarence."

"Well," he said in his long drawl, "as most of you know, I cut pine tips off my trees and sell them to the company down there in Mt. Airy that makes the garland. Well, I had some left over. Me and my boys, we made up about 500 feet of garland. It's out in the back of the truck. I thought the town might want to hang it up. It'd sure make the streets right pretty, with the lights you already have up."

"That would be wonderful. Buster, any chance you could get that hung today?" Herbie asked.

"Yes, sir, if the fire department will help me with that new fancy ladder truck, we should have it up in a couple of hours. And I think I'll also have just enough lights left over to decorate the big spruce tree that always set in front of the depot."

"Buster," Jonathan said as he turned to look at the mountain of a man who had the pure heart of a child, "we all know that with the Mill closed, you're not getting paid for doing these things. We surely do appreciate it."

"Well," Buster said, beaming with pride that the Mill Superintendent had singled him out, "my poppy always told me, 'Idle hands are the devil's workshop, but serving hands are the Lord's delight,' and I do so enjoy delighting my Lord."

"Well, I sure feel better than I did before this meeting started," Herbie said with a smile wide enough to seemingly slip a six-inch ruler into. "By George, I think we're gonna have ourselves a humdinger of a Christmas after all. This meeting is adjourned."

"Mind if I walk with you to get the letters, Uncle Buster?" Suzie said to the big black man as they stepped out onto the sidewalk.

"Sure child, you know how I cherish your company," he said as he took the girl's hand.

Suzie always liked to make a fist with her hand when Buster reached for it, and then feel how he would gently wrap his hand around hers, making hers totally disappear.

"How about you Sam? Want to go with us?" the girl asked.

"Sure, if I won't be a bother."

"No bother at all," Buster said. "The missus will enjoy meeting you. She had some kinfolk from down in Arkansas."

So the three went down the steps, and started down Main Street toward what was now just called, "The Hollow" or by some "Young's Hollow." Myrt, sitting on the front porch, waved as the trio passed the Boarding House. They then crossed the road at the only busy intersection in town at what is commonly called the "Turnaround," because everyone always used it to make a U-turn to head back onto Main Street. They then began walking single file on the side of the road to pass under the railroad trestle.

"Living this close to the tracks, I don't guess you miss the trains running all hours of the day, do you?" Sam asked Buster as they were walking under the big wooden overpass.

"Well, I kinda do miss it, Sam," Buster replied, slowly nodding his head reflectively, "especially the old steam engines. During the day, anywhere I might be working in town cutting grass, they whistled me a song that said, *Buster loves the Lord, Buster loves the Lord, Buster loves the Lord,* and well, at nighttime, I never paid them no mind. I just slept right through them."

"Uncle Buster sleeps so well because he works so hard," Suzie said, looking up at the ebony titan walking beside her. "He outworks any three boys who work with him."

Buster smiled his big toothy grin at her, turned loose of her hand and curled his arm up into a ninety-degree angle at the elbow. Suzie knew just what to do and immediately jumped up and wrapped her arms around his huge forearm that appeared as big as her neck. He then began swinging her back and forth.

"Miss Suzie," Buster said with his deep belly laugh, "I do think you got fat from that hospital food. Your Uncle Buster's not going to be able to do this much longer."

The three crossed Route 94, in front of the New River Motors service station, and started down the hill into "Young's Hollow". The pavement had ended, and the road had turned to scratch gravel. Along the left side of the street was a row of very small, plain, but neat, houses. They were all freshly-painted in the same colors. Each looked like there might be a total of two or three small rooms.

"The houses are very well-kept, Buster." Sam said, hoping he didn't sound condescending.

"That's because in addition to being the pastor, Uncle Buster's the unofficial mayor of Young's Hollow," the girl said, looking at Buster with pride. "He saves leftover paint from the Mill, and then makes all the families have a painting party every couple of years. And there, all the way at the end, is Uncle Buster's church. He has the best choir in the county."

"Now Suzie," Buster said, "if you don't stop bragging on old Buster, I'm gonna have to put a wider door on the church just to get my head through."

Buster started up the steps to one of the houses, stopping to carefully wipe his feet. Suzie and Sam repeated his action.

"Hello, Sugar Baby. I'm home," he called to his wife, "and guess who I've got with me."

Ma Young walked in from the kitchen, wearing a big flowered apron, with splotches of flour on her hands and face.

"Well, praise be the Lord, it's my angel, Suzie," the woman said, as she wiped her hands on a dish towel so she could hug the girl. "It's so good to see you child. Don't you throw a scare into us like that agin."

"And this is a visitor to our town," Suzie said as she wrapped her arms around the woman to give her a hug. "Sam slid into the ditch over on the interstate, and Chiney brought him to Fries. Sam's gonna help us with the Christmas celebration."

"Well, Sam," Ma Young said, extending her hand, "that is mighty kind of you, being an out-of-towner and all."

"Your community just seems to have a way of making even an out-of-towner feel welcomed," the businessman told her with a grin.

Buster walked over and sat down at an old, badly worn desk. Short pieces of two by fours had been used to replace two of the broken legs on the desk. It was apparent that it had probably been discarded from the Mill offices, to find new life in Buster's home. He used a key to unlock a drawer, and then began to collect envelopes scrawled with juvenile handwriting.

"Here they are," Buster said, "twelve letters from all the little ones. Nacine had told me she was too old for Santa Claus, but I know what she was wanting and can add that to the list."

"Uncle Buster, can we do our list here, on your kitchen table?"

"That would be just fine. Let me get us some paper and pencils."

"Well, if you are going to be setting at the table," Mrs. Young said with a duplicitous grin, "do you think you could help me get rid of these peanut butter cookies before they go to waste?"

"Oh, yes ma'am," Suzie said, her eyes approaching the size of the cookies. "We sure could."

So for the next forty-five minutes, with Sam and Buster calling out the names, Suzie prepared an alphabetical listing of the Christmas wishes of 119 boys, and 78 girls. The three of them were able to dispose of a platter of fourteen peanut butter cookies, four cups of coffee and two glasses of fresh cow's milk. Afterwards Buster left to walk Suzie back to Main Street. Just before Sam reached the Boarding House, Suzie turned to Buster.

"Uncle Buster. Don't you like pheasant?

"Oh yes child. I love that bird. Why?"

"Great!" She said. "Sam gave us two, and Momma and I are

fixing them tonight. Why don't you and Ma Young come up? Sam, and mom's new friend, John will be there."

"Now child, are you sure that would be okay with your momma? You'd better be asking her first."

"Now, Uncle Buster," Suzie said with an affected chastising, "you know we always have an extra plate for you. And besides, you could stop and pick up Sam at the Hotel. He will need a ride."

"Well, okay then," he said, "if you're sure it is alright. I don't think the Missus will make it though. Once she starts her baking, it goes on 'til midnight. Is there anything I can bring?"

"Since you did ask," the girl said as she licked her lips, "any chance of Ma. Young making one of her chocolate pies?"

"I'm sure she'd be more than happy to bake one for you."

"Okay, so we'll see you guys about five," she said, as Sam started into the Boarding House. Buster turned to go back home and place an order for one of his wife's famous chocolate pies, and Suzie continued down the street to the Corner Drug.

19

As soon as John had dropped Suzie off at the Council Chambers, he started walking down toward the east end of Main Street. It was another lovely day. The sun was bright with temperature already in the forties. The snow was almost gone; only a few dirty piles remained stacked on the north side of the street. He walked into the cafe. Bud smiled and nodded. John returned the greeting and looked around and saw all but one of the tables was empty. The men at that table turned to see who had entered, and John immediately recognized Chiney from the night before.

"Hello, Chiney," the young man said as he started over to the table, "I'm John Helmsman. We met last night. How are you today?"

"Oh, John, it's a cruel world, a cruel world," the man said as he shook his head sadly, then he looked up smiling and said, "but the ladies are lovely. But then again, I don't have to tell you that do I?"

"No you certainly don't," John agreed.

"Come on over and join us," Chiney said, and then stood and looked toward the counter, "Bud, think you can rustle up another cup, and refills all the way around?"

John pulled an extra chair up and sat down at the table. Sitting with Chiney were two other gentleman, one slightly younger than John, the other maybe twelve years older.

"John, these are my buddies Birddog and Wade," Chiney said pointing to the two men. "Birddog is a professor at the local college, over at Wytheville, and Wade here," pointing to the younger man, "he's the president of the college."

"President?" John asked, "You must be much older than you look."

"No, I'm thirty," the president said, "but it's a community college, Wytheville Community. So what do you do, John?"

"Well, I'm a security consultant," John said, glad he no longer had to deceive the new friends he was making in this town. "I do investigative work, security work, and sometimes I even teach some law enforcement classes."

"So what got you into this work?" Wade said, as he sneaked a glance over at Birddog.

"I was in the army, Special Forces. I served two terms in Nam. I really liked it and probably would've made a career, but I took some shrapnel and got discharged."

"Did you go to college?" Wade asked, trying to sound interested instead of inquisitive.

"Yes. I went to Wake Forest. I graduated with a degree in political science."

"Wake? Good school, or at least our local lawyer tells us so," Birddog said, then pointing toward Wade, "We're both Hokies."

"We've had some good games with you guys. I got to be good friends with Paul Long while he was at Wake two years ago."

"Ah, you mean Benedict Arnold Long, leaving the Hokies to play for Wake," Birddog said, as he and Wade began to chuckle.

"Yeah, he thought a couple of times about paying me to come to Blacksburg with him to act as his body guard."

"So, umm," Wade said, between sips of coffee, "how do you like teaching classes?"

"I kinda like it. Most of the students are older men, many of them ex-military on the GI bill, so I relate to them well."

"Ever think you'd like to do it full time?" Wade asked candidly.

"Well, I don't know. Why?" John said as he looked at them quizzically. The discussion had become less a casual conversation, and now resembled an interrogation.

"Well John," Wade said as he leaned over toward the young man, "it just so happens we are thinking about starting a two-year criminal justice program at Wytheville, and we're looking for someone, like you, to organize it and run it. Being a small department, you'd need to teach classes a lot for the first couple of years, but then it would be mostly administrative."

John's brain began spinning in an attempt to ingest the

information that was being fed to him. He had been looking for the answers to some questions, but was it possible solutions would be handed to him over coffee in a café?

"What do you think?" Wade asked, as he leaned back. The ball had been passed to John and was clearly in his court now. Should he pass it off, or shoot the game-winner?

"Well, I have to admit, if you had asked me last week, I would have said *no thanks*," John said, obviously deep in thought, but a smile was beginning to invade his contemplative visage, "but, well, opportunities have, umm, presented themselves this week that have made your offer very interesting."

"Yes, and would that opportunity's name be Karen Young by any chance?" Chiney asked with a wink.

"Karen Young?" Birddog said. "So this is the new beau eh?"

"Well, I don't know about beau," John said with a schoolboyish grin, "but, well, yeah, she does have *my* head spinning."

"Well, she is one fine lady, one of the finest this town has ever known," Wade said, "and that Suzie, she's a perfect child. A man would be lucky to a start a family with those two. There's not a single guy in this town that won't be envious of you."

"Yes, I would agree." John said, nodding his head. "Well, could I have a few days to think about your offer?"

"Sure," Wade said, "we won't be doing anything official until after the New Year. We'll give you until then."

The conversation then turned casually masculine. Would the AFL or the NFL win the championship game, and how pro football would be after the merger? How strong the Texas Longhorns had been in the NCAA that year, and if VPI would ever play for a National Championship, or be able to play competitively with schools like Texas? How Chuck Manuel did his first year in the pros with the Twins, and if they thought Eddie Goodson would be called up to the big league next year with the Giants?

The bell on the door rang and all four men turned to see Suzie walk into the diner.

"Hi, Mr. Jennings, Dr. Gilley. Hi Chiney. Merry Christmas to all of you."

All the men took turns getting a hug from the little blonde bundle of joy, and returned the wishes.

"What do you have there in your hand, Suzie?" Wade asked.

"It's a journalist notebook; John bought it for me," Suzie said, beaming as she looked at John. She opened it up so they could see what it held, especially the new Parker ink pen. "He said all the journalists in Winston-Salem were using these."

"Well, you should have one then," Chiney said, "because you're better than any of those ink slingers they have down in Winston-Salem."

"Yeah, especially the ones that graduated from Wake," Birddog said as he good-naturedly poked John in the side."

"Do you want something to eat before we go?" John asked.

"Bud sure makes good barbeque and french fries," she said, arching her eyebrows until her forehead wrinkled into an upside down smile.

"Okay, we'll both have that," John said, then turned toward the counter, "Bud, two orders of barbeque and french fries, and, how about a strawberry milkshake?"

Bud nodded as he continued chewing on his cigar.

"But if Mom has lunch ready when we get home," Suzie said with a premonitory wink, "you know we'll have to pretend to be hungry."

When they saw the food was brought to them, John led Suzie over to another table. Even though the diner was nearly empty, he strangely chose a table in the far corner, isolated from the rest of the dining area.

"So how did your meeting go?" John asked as he prepared to dip his fries into the ketchup.

"Oh, John, I am so excited! I think we are really going to have a great Christmas," she said in a low voice, so excited she nearly spilled her milkshake. "Sam, the guy we met last night, must have some very important friends, because he has promised to provide a nice toy for each kid, all the kids, in town."

"Are you serious? There must be a hundred."

"About two-hundred, but he says that's no problem. And John, so many people have given money, people that haven't lived here for years. It makes me feel so good, to have the Christmas spirit back in the town."

John was silent, thinking about how to approach a subject he had had on his mind for the last few days.

"Suzie, your mom hasn't dated anyone since, since your dad...passed away, has she?

Suzie smiled at him, knowing where this was headed. She thought about teasing him, but instead thought she would be honest. She held her head down, sliding her straw up and down in the milkshake, listening to the squeaky sound it made.

"No, sir. She hasn't dated anyone. She's not even looked at another man," Suzie said, then looking up at John, her eyes sparkling happily, she added, "at least, not until this week."

"Your mom is a wonderful woman, a very wonderful woman." John said, finally breathing again. "Any man would be lucky to have her, and you."

"Thank you, she is the best. As for me, if I'm anything good, it is only because of her. She has sacrificed a whole lot for me."

"Suzie, umm, would you have a problem with a man in your mom's life?"

Suzie looked at him. Her face changed before his eyes. No longer was she a thirteen-year-old giggly teenager, but now she took on the countenance of a young insightful woman."

"John, it would make me so happy for the right man to come into my mom's life. I'll be away in college in four more years, and will probably never come back to live in Fries. I don't want her to be alone."

"Well, I'm not sure I'm the right man. I'm...I'm just so different from the men from this area. But I do know that I would be the best to her I know how."

"My dad was different, too. He was only a truck driver, but he was so smart. He read all the time. And he had big plans."

"Do you, umm, is there any chance that...that your mom..." John just couldn't bring himself to ask the question. Suzie helped him.

"John, I have not seen my mom as happy, or laugh as much since Daddy died, as she has the last four days. My mom likes you very much," Suzie said, and then standing up, she leaned across the table, kissing him on his cheek and added, "I do, too."

John felt as if his entire body had illuminated. A warm glow radiated over him, and he felt the most amazing, but indescribable sensation swelling up in his chest.

"Well, the feeling is mutual, Suzie Q.," he said as he reached over and playfully pinched her cheeks. "Come on, let's head home."

After the meeting, Sam had walked back to the Boarding House.

"Myrt, is there a quiet, private place I could use the phones? I'll find out the charges, and leave them for you."

"Sure, Sam. No one will be using the office today. Just go in and make yourself comfortable," Myrt said as she unlocked the office door and turned on the light.

Sam sat down at the old, green state surplus desk and opened up the Christmas list. He reached into his wallet, and pulled out a piece of paper on which were written several names and phone numbers. Moving his finger down the list, he found the one he was looking for and dialed the number.

"Gottstein Toys. Stan speaking. May I help you?"

"Stan. Sam here. Happy Hanukah."

"Hey, Sam. Merry Christmas. You still going to be here tomorrow to talk some business, aren't you?"

"No, Stan. I've had car problems. I'm down in Virginia. Don't think I'll be able to make it."

"I'm sorry to hear that, Sam. I really hoped we could come to an agreement before the New Year."

"Well, Stan, I'd love to give you the order, but, well, I'm just not sure about your inventory and your delivery ability." Sam said, knowing he was baiting the toy supplier.

"Sam, I've told you that I can furnish you whatever toys you need, whenever you need them."

"Okay, tell you what. I have a list here, mostly bicycles, dolls, kitchen play sets, pedal cars. I need about two hundred toys in all. If you can prepare these, label them with the names I give you, put them on a truck in reverse alphabetical order, you know, with the A's closest to the back of the truck, and have them to a little town called Fries, that's spelled F-R-I-E-S, just off I-81, about an hour south of Roanoke, well, if you'll have them here by tomorrow night, no later than seven o'clock, then you'll have my business."

Stan was silent again for a few seconds.

"Does that include your new stores?"

"Yes. That includes my new stores."

"Sam. You've got a deal!" Stan screamed with excitement.

"Any chance you still have one of those semi-trailers available that had Santa's sled on the side?"

"Sure do. I'll send it."

"Okay. Put your secretary on. I'm going to give her the order. I'm also going to give some directions and some instructions to the truck-drivers.

"Sam, it's going to be a pleasure doing business with you."

"Just don't let me down Stan. A whole town is depending on this."

"I won't, Sam. I assure you I won't."

After giving the information to the secretary, Sam hung up, looked up a new number in his address book and dialed it.

"Hello. Haynes' Clothing. Teresa speaking."

"Hi, Teresa. This is Sam. Is Robert in?"

"Oh, yes sir. One moment please."

After a few seconds, the phone was answered.

"Hi, Sam, how are you? I thought you would have been here by now for our meeting."

"Yeah Robert, sorry but I had car problems. I'm still in Virginia."

Robert was silent for a few minutes. Sam let him ponder the matter. The clothing manufacturer began speaking again.

"Sam, I know I was a little higher than the other suppliers, but I thought at least you'd meet with me. You know my quality is better, and I'm more dependable on my shipping. I have my own trucks you know. I'm not dependent upon someone else."

"Well, Robert, I do think you have good clothing, but you were almost 10% higher."

"Well, I could cut maybe 4% off."

"Robert, I've never really been convinced that my average customer would be receptive to your clothing. You know, most of my young shoppers are very rural southern kids."

"Sam, you know we also have an excellent line of rural clothing, dresses, shirts, jeans. I guarantee you, once your customers try our merchandise, they'll not want anything else. And I promise that the day will come when those kids will want to start wearing the more urban styles."

"Well, maybe so, but do you think you can meet short deadlines? You know I'm expecting to double, or triple, my stores within the next five years. That's going to be a lot of clothes. I'll be your biggest customer by far."

"I can get you what you want, within any time-line you request. We have the capacity to easily triple production."

"Well, there's just one other consideration. You may think it's a big deal, but for me, it could be a deal buster."

"Name it, we'll work on it."

"Well, I know that you're currently using a northern textile mill. The people in the south have a problem with that. I know that you're having problems with the factory. If I can find a mill to furnish you cloth at the same or even lower prices, in Virginia, would you purchase all your cloth from them?"

The other line went strangely quiet. Sam would have thought that he had lost the connection, except for some background noises. The businessman's every instinct was to say something, but he knew by heart the old salesman's creed: *He who speaks first, loses.* Sam remained quiet. Finally he heard Robert speak on the other end of the line.

"Okay. Let me get this straight. If I purchase my cloth from a factory in Virginia, I can have the majority of your clothing purchases?"

"Robert, if you meet the conditions we've discussed, cut your prices by 5% and you can prove to me you can handle quick orders, yes, then you can have as much of my orders as you can handle."

"And just how do I do that, Sam?"

"You take an order I have for 120 pairs of jeans and shirts, and 80 dresses, and you have them to a little town in Virginia by seven p.m. tomorrow, and you promo this order. If the kids like the clothes as much as you say, the business is yours."

"Sam, that's a pretty expensive promo, that's...that's $2000 worth of clothes."

"Yes Robert. And that's about what your first *week's* profit will be once you get my business.'

"So if I say yes, is that it? Can we close the deal?"

"That's the offer, Robert. You could double or triple your existing sales by saying yes."

"Sam. You've got yourself a deal!"

"Okay, great. Put Teresa back on the phone to take the order. I'm also going to give her someone's phone number. You can phone him in an hour to work out the negotiations for the cloth."

"Great! Thanks for the order Sam. You've made my Christmas. I'm going to look forward to working with you."

"No Robert," Sam said. "It's made my Christmas. Merry Christmas. Now take my advice; go home after you call, and spend the holidays with your family. Don't come back until next week. We'll talk then."

After hanging up the phone, Sam then looked under the A's in the local phone directory lying on the desk, and then phoned a third person.

"Hello. Jonathan Armbrister speaking."

"Jonathan, this is Sam. How are you today?"

"Oh, Sam, I'm good. How are you? Just working on the Christmas parties. Are your friends going to come through for us?"

"Yes. I think they are, Jonathan, and in more ways than one. Within the next hour, you're going to be getting a phone call from a Robert Haynes. He's got an offer for you. It's no joke. I think you'll find the phone call very rewarding."

"Alright. I'll look forward to it. See you tomorrow."

"Yes, have a good day. Bye."

Just then Sam heard a familiar voice outside in the lobby. Soon there was a knock on the door, and Chiney stuck his head inside, waiting to see if Sam was on the phone.

"Hey, Chiney. How are you today?"

"I'm fair to middlin' Sam, considering what a cruel old world it is. I just got a call from Blair's garage. Your car's ready, want to go pick it up? I'll run you down."

"Yes. Sure you don't mind."

So Sam and Chiney retraced their route back to Ft. Chiswell to retrieve his car. Sam enjoyed the ride, getting to see the

269

countryside without its blanket of snow or riding white-knuckled in the cab of a coal truck. Sam was pleasantly surprised to find out that Claude had only charged $95 for the tow and repair.

Meanwhile, Suzie and John had arrived at the house on Third Street. Suzie practically jumped out of the car before it had stopped moving. She was very excited to tell her mother about the miraculous events that had occurred during the committee meeting, and about the work that had been accomplished.

"You two were sure gone a long time," Karen said as they walked through the door. "I have a feeling someone had a barbeque down at Bud's."

John and Suzie looked at each other and grinned.

"Oops. Busted." Suzie said.

John looked at his watch; it was 1:15.

"What time did you want to have dinner?"

"Well, I thought we'd eat about five. Suzie and the young people will be going caroling tonight."

"I need to run over to Galax to pick up some things," John said. "Is there anything you need while I'm there?"

"Well. Maybe some soft drinks, and napkins, if you don't mind picking them up," Karen said. She then added with a teasing chuckle, "and maybe some more popcorn. I think Suzie might want to beat you in Scrabble again tomorrow."

"Now Mother," Suzie said in a snooty, high-falutin' voice. "That was a most gaucherie thing to say, however accurate, for it is not John's fault he must face the chagrin of losing face to a confrere of the adolescent age."

"I think I might buy me a dictionary while I'm over there," John said as he walked out the door, shaking his head. "I still think she's making those words up. See you girls later."

He had started to put his jacket on when Karen came over to help. He could see she was hiding something behind her back. After his coat was on, she extended her hand, holding the sprig of mistletoe over his head, and then tiptoed, giving him a quick little kiss on the lips. She then ran into the kitchen.

While he was gone, the Young ladies were busy preparing dinner and baking cookies for the neighbors. While Karen was

JERRY L. HAYNES

elbow-deep in the dough bowl making biscuits, Suzie was rolling out cookie dough. At thirteen, Suzie was already an accomplished cook, thanks to her mom's lessons and Mrs. Rhudy's home economics classes at the high school. The young girl's favorite dish was potato salad, and she was asked to bring it to all the church dinners.

"Mom. Would it be okay if we made an extra dozen cookies?"

"Sure. What were you planning on doing with them?" Karen asked as she finished rolling the dough out on the cutting board, and began washing the flour off her hands.

"Well, I thought I'd call Cousin Richard and see if he'd take them up to the jail, to give to Spunkie."

Karen felt a flush of anger sweep over her, but then Christian compassion overcame maternal passion. *How wonderful it would be if adults could learn to forgive and forget as easily as children do*, she thought to herself.

"I think that would be very nice Suzie and why don't you make up one of your cards to go with them."

"Okay, I think I will. Thanks Mom."

"Thank you, Suzie." Karen said, and then added when her daughter gave her a puzzled look. "For reminding me how Christians are supposed act."

Karen then bent over the oven rack and began basting the two pheasants which were approaching a golden brown. Karen liked to cook her pheasant, let it cool before she sliced it, and then serve it with a hot raspberry sauce. She found herself hoping that John would like it this way. Well, and also Sam.

"Oh, Mom. I just remembered. I asked Uncle Buster and Ma Young to join us for dinner, but Ma Young can't come."

"That's fine; you know I always love to have Buster. We haven't had him for a meal since the end of summer when they were still cutting the grass. I understand he really gave a sweet prayer about you at the church service in the gymnasium."

"Momma, Uncle Buster is one of the nicest people I've ever known. Why did people ever make him and his people stay down in the Hollow away from everyone else, and call them that n-word?"

"Well, Suzie," Karen said, trying to decide how to explain

racism to a thirteen-year-old who had never known it first-hand, "it's not that they meant to be mean, or ugly, but well, people that are in the majority sometimes let their ignorance cloud their decisions. They are afraid of the things they don't understand. So black people, who were outnumbered, were isolated from whites. It's what they called 'segregation.' So let it be a lesson to you when you grow up and become a voter that you will make decisions for the right reasons."

"You know Momma, they say all things happen for a good reason. Maybe my accident was for the good. It seemed to make the people stop fighting."

"Yes, I've heard many people say the same thing." Karen said. "Some of them have started calling you 'Saint Suzie.'"

"Momma, I wish you hadn't told me that," Suzie said, her voice showing traces of fright.

"Oh. Why do you say that, Suzie?" her mom asked with a puzzled look.

"Because," Suzie said, her lower lip in an exaggerated trembling, but then a big smile erupted with a silly giggle, "Now I'm going to be afraid to go to any bonfires this fall."

Karen grabbed her daughter and squeezed her tightly.

"Suzie, you are such a nut! Didn't anyone ever tell you that a pun is the lowest form of humor?"

Suzie then became strangely quiet. She stood there, forming her cookies, and weighing her next words.

"Momma. Remember I told you about seeing Daddy. When I fell?"

"Yes, honey, I remember," Karen said. She had just finished basting the pheasant and had turned to the counter to begin making the raspberry sauce.

"Well, there was more. I didn't tell you because, well, it didn't make sense. I wasn't sure what he was saying after he told me I was going to be okay."

Karen set the dough she had rolled out down in front of Suzie, who then began cutting the biscuits. She enjoyed this job, using an old Silver-Cow evaporated milk can to cut out the perfectly round biscuits.

"After I saw him, I wanted so much to go to him." Suzie said, her voice almost inaudible. "I wanted to jump into his arms like I used to when he would get back from being gone for a few days. I wanted so much to feel him hug me and spin me around."

Karen clasped her hands to her mouth, and began to cry.

"I asked Daddy to come get me, and he said..." the young girl's voice began to crack. "He said, *Suzie, I can't take you with me. You have to stay here.* Then he began to walk away. I begged him to not leave, but he said..."

Suzie began to weep. Karen came over and took her daughter in her arms. Suzie took a couple of deep breaths, then between sobs, continued.

"...Daddy looked back at me and said, *Suzie, I have been with you the last five years, but I can leave now because you and your momma have somebody to take care of you, to watch over you. Somebody who will love you both like I did.*"

With that, Suzie began sobbing uncontrollably, her small body trembling as if she were having a seizure. Karen pulled her daughter to her tightly or the young girl would probably have collapsed to the floor. The mother just stood there, not able to speak, trying to take all this in.

Karen stood there for maybe two minutes, holding her daughter, pondering what she had just been told.

"Well, honey," the mother said, trying to make some logic of it all, "I've heard during times when you are unconscious so many things go through your mind, just like dreams. I'm sure it all seemed real, but..."

"No, Momma. No. It was real." Suzie said, looking up at her mother with pleading eyes, begging to be believed. "Believe me, it did happen."

Suzie wiped her eyes on her mom's apron, as she looked up at her.

"You do know that John loves you. Don't you Momma?"

"Oh, now how can you know that?" Karen said as she rocked her daughter back and forth soothingly.

"Because in the hospital room, and here in the house, whenever you would leave the room, or turn your back, and he didn't know I was watching, he would smile. Smile, just like Daddy used to smile at you Momma. The exact same way."

Karen dropped her arms from around her daughter and turned away so Suzie would not see the look of ultimate hope on her face.

"And something else, Momma, who is the only person that has ever called me 'Suzie-Q.', other than John?"

"Just,..., just your father," Karen said, her voice trembling. But her heart would not let her accept the possibility that she could have found love again.

"But, Suzie, John is from the city. He'd never move here, and I know you'd never want to move to Winston-Salem."

"Momma. You need to think about what is best for you. I'll be leaving for college soon. I'll probably not come back here, to live."

"But, but Suzie, I loved your daddy so much. I'm, I'm just not sure I could ever love anyone the way I loved him."

"But you don't have to love him the way you loved Daddy. It can be in a new, different way."

"Suzie Yvonne Young, I'm supposed to be giving you love advice," Karen said, kissing her daughter on the head, "not the other way around."

Karen then heard a car pull up outside, and she started toward the door, wiping the tears from her eyes and the flour from her face on her apron.

While driving back to Fries, John kept thinking, actually marveling, at how even the simplest things now seemed so pleasant to him. He had even enjoyed his afternoon of shopping, and was now excited to get back to Karen and Suzie.

He pulled the Lincoln up in front of the house. Before he could even open the car door, Karen appeared at the front door. John began getting some bags out of the back seat to carry them inside.

"Did you find everything?" Karen asked.

"Yeah, sure did. Finally. I had to go to several different stores though," he said.

"Yeah, it would be nice if you could find everything at one place."

"Hey, Suzie Q.," John said turning to the girl, "I noticed you didn't have a date book to schedule all your important meetings in, so I bought you this." He reached into a bag and handed Suzie a shiny leather Day-Planner with "1970" stenciled in gold leaf print on the front.

"Oh wow! This is great," she said as she reached up to give John a big hug.

"So if I gave your mom a nice gift, do you think she'd give me a hug?" John whispered to her as she hugged him.

"I bet she would," Suzie said with a wink.

"Now, John, you need to quit spoiling her this close to Christmas, or Santa won't bring her anything."

"Oh, okay. I'll wait and let Santa finish the gifts then." he said, and then added teasingly, "Well, with a couple of exceptions."

Both Young girls looked at him with a *What are you up to now?* stare.

"So, what can I do to help?" he asked, pretending not to see the looks being cast his way, as he set the bags of groceries down on the table.

"Well, would you want to peel some potatoes?"

"Peel potatoes? Peel potatoes? Are you kidding, I spent so much time on KP when I was in the army, I can peel spuds so thin you can read a newspaper through the skins."

Karen pulled a gallon boiling pot out from under the counter and handed it to him.

"Okay, then go out the back door, down the steps, and open the door to the cellar. Get a pot full of potatoes from the bin, and let's see how you do. If you do good enough, we might even promote you to slicing onions the next time."

When John got back upstairs with the potatoes, Karen had put a Christmas album on the record player and was singing "Silent Night" along with Loretta Lynn. John smiled to himself. Her voice was as pure and perfect as she was.

"Ah, a beautiful woman, a wonderful cook, and a lovely voice. Are there more surprises waiting for me?"

Karen laughed and smeared raspberry sauce on his cheek. She then kissed it away, blushed, and turned back to her sauce.

John sat down, feeling good about this evening, and began peeling the potatoes. He never thought he would actually enjoy peeling the bumpy spuds, but even this chore was making him happy, knowing he was here with her.

Before long, all three were singing along to the songs. Suzie could not remember the last time she had seen her mom so happy.

John was sure he had never been so happy. He looked around the simple kitchen with its worn linoleum floors. The walls were freshly painted a bright yellow. The house was probably at least fifty-years old, the appliances probably at least fifteen years old. This was much different from the house he grew up in. It just seemed so much more of a home, for some reason though even to him, a near stranger.

The three worked together, harmoniously, helping each other. Karen directed the preparation of the meal with the virtuoso of a maestro. At 4:45, Suzie began setting the table for five. Promptly at five o'clock, a vehicle stopped outside the house, and soon a knock was heard at the door. Suzie answered it, and invited the two men in.

"Hi, Sam." Suzie said, then turned and gave Pastor Young a hug. "Hi Uncle Buster."

"Maybe this is a good time for you to explain to these gentlemen why I'm your uncle." Buster said with a laugh.

"Well, you see," Suzie began explaining, "when I was about three, Pastor Young came by with his work crew cutting the grass. He was so nice to me so I asked him his name. He told me it was Buster Young. I went running into the house and told Momma that there was a big man outside who must be my uncle because we had the same name."

Karen laughed and picked up the story.

"I asked her who she was talking about, so she took me to the door and pointed and said, *it's him, it's Uncle Buster.* So I said, 'Now Suzie, he's not your uncle. For one thing, he's black and you're white.' Then Suzie said, *Well that's just because he works outside, and you always make me play inside.*"

Everyone laughed except Buster Young. He roared, like a Santa Claus ho-ho-hoing.

"Ever since then, he's been my Uncle Buster." Suzie said. "I even found out this week that Uncle Buster was one of the first people to hold me when I was born."

"And Suzie is my favorite niece." Buster said. "But I don't think I can hold you in one hand like I did that first time."

The two men then took off their coats and handed them to Suzie, who took them and laid them in the bedroom.

"My, my, my Miss Karen. Those birds do smell delicious." Buster said as he walked toward the kitchen.

"Well, you can thank Sam for that. He furnished the birds."

"Oh, you're a bird hunter, Sam?"

"Yes, I live for bird hunting, Buster. Monday was one of the best days I've had in years."

"Suzie," Sam said when the girl returned from the bedroom, "I saw some of your newspapers down at the inn. They were very good. You really have a wonderful way with words. Do you prepare them at home?"

"Yes, sir. Right here at the kitchen table. Momma lets me use her Underwood on the counter over there."

Sam looked at the typewriter. It had to be at least twenty-years old.

"So is this what you want to do? Write?"

"Yes, sir. I hope to get a scholarship and go to Harvard. It has one of the best journalism schools in the country. Then I want to work for *National Geographic,* or maybe be a war correspondent.

Sam looked at the young girl, barely a teenager. He had so many people come through his stores, in their twenties who had no idea what they wanted in life, and this young lady had her life planned.

"Well. Dinner is ready." Karen said. "Come on in."

Everyone sat down to the table. There were only four of the chrome and red vinyl chairs, so Karen sat in a wooden straight-back chair with a woven reed seat. John recognized the pattern on the plates and saucers. His grandmother had the same ones that had come free in boxes of Quaker Oats. He also recognized the glasses holding the ice tea as jelly containers.

John sat down next to Karen and soon felt her take his hand. Taking the hint, he then took the hand of Buster, who was sitting next to him.

"Pastor Young," Karen said, "will you bless our food please?"

"Heavenly Father, we thank You for the food that You provide us, in the air, on the land, and in the waters. We know that You will provide all that we need, if we will only ask. We ask that You bless this food to the nourishment of our bodies, and bless the hands that prepared it. Amen."

The five friends soon began a lively conversation while eating. It took some prodding, but John actually told some of his stories from Nam, the humorous ones, not the ones he tried to lock away. Like the great cook-outs they used to have. He also told about his experiences at Wake Forest, and why he decided to become a security consultant. Sam was very good at evading any questions about himself.

The rest of the evening, Suzie and Karen took turns telling stories about Buster. How the Mill bosses pulled strings to make sure their young boys got to work during the summers cutting grass for him, because he was such a role model. How he usually did the work of five of the boys. How strong he was, and even to Buster's embarrassment, the story of his lifting the Buick off of Ricky Moore when it fell on top of him.

"It was just one of the small Buicks," Buster said humbly.

John could tell the Youngs truly loved the jovial black man. Buster then began shifting the fun toward others.

"So, John," Buster said, "have you found our scenery to your liking here in Fries?"

"Yes, sir, I have," John said, picking up on the insinuation, and not to be outdone, answered slyly. "I've especially found the view from Third Street to my liking."

"Yes. I've cut grass all over this town," Buster said with a chortle, "and I do believe this is the loveliest sight in the whole town. Think you might be headed back this way again, in the near future?"

"Well, actually, to be honest," the young man said, turning toward Karen, "I'm not sure I'm going to be able to drag myself away from such beauty."

Karen looked at him, and a big smile swept over her face. Buster had asked the question, she had been afraid to ask.

"Now I think I *would* have paid $15 for that pheasant dinner," John said, alluding to the previous night's story about his New York City experience.

"Even if it wasn't under glass," Karen asked teasingly.

"Suzie," Buster said to Suzie after they had finished their main meal, "I think if you went outside and looked in my back seat, you will find something you and the others might like."

The girl jumped up, ran outside and came back screaming, "Chocolate pie."

"I'll pour some coffee," John said.

Everyone began eating their dessert, the adults drinking their coffee, Suzie drinking a glass of milk.

"Karen, I heard about your husband," Sam said sympathetically, "I'm really sorry. It must be so difficult raising a child as a single parent these days."

"Yes, but it would be much more difficult if Suzie wasn't such a good child."

"Yes, and Wilson was a fine man, too," Buster added.

"Yes, he was," Karen said, smiling as she rubbed the wedding band she wore on her right hand. "There will never be another Wilson Young."

John had walked to the coffee pot to refill cups. At the sound of these words, he felt as if someone had taken a butcher knife from the freezer and stuck it into his chest. The cold, shivering pain swept through his body, down into his arms, and he almost dropped the cup of coffee he was pouring. The words echoed through his head.

There will never be another Wilson Young.

About 7:50, a car stopped out front, and the driver blew a horn.

"That's Herbie," Suzie called out as she dashed toward the door, "I'm off for caroling. Goodnight, everybody. I'll be back about ten, Mom."

"No. Just stay at the church." John said. "We'll come down to pick you up."

The three combined churches were starting on Top Street and winding their way down to the Methodist Church, where all the carolers would have hot chocolate. The teens had made Christmas cards and were giving one to each household. Each card included an invitation to the Christmas Eve party.

At about 8:10, the carolers had arrived back in front of the Youngs' house. Sam, Buster, John, and Karen went out onto the sidewalk where they were serenaded with "Joy to the World." John looked over, and thought for a moment he saw tears on Sam's cheek, but if they were, they were quickly wiped away. Buster soon said he needed to get back, so he and Sam grabbed their coats. Buster gave Karen a big bear hug at the door.

"Miss Karen that was a most delightful dinner. Thank you so much."

"Oh, Buster, you know you're always welcome at out table. Thank Mrs. Young for the chocolate pie. As always, it was delicious. And tell her we're sorry she couldn't come with you."

"Thank you, Karen," Sam said, taking Karen's hand in his and squeezing it. "That was truly a delicious meal, and it was very thoughtful of you to invite me."

"We enjoyed your company, Sam." She replied, then added with a laugh, "and your bird."

The two men left, leaving Karen and John alone. For a few minutes, it was awkward. They had never shared such privacy. John sat down on the sofa and began to drink the last of his already cold coffee. That was okay though, because that's how he liked it. Karen walked over to the record player and turned on the Christmas record again.

She smiled and shyly walked toward the sofa, and sat down beside John, nestling her head on his shoulder until he took the hint, and lifted his arm and placed it around her, kissing her on the forehead.

They just sat for the next fifteen minutes, content to be beside each other. John thought how different it felt with Karen. He never wasted much time with dating, and when he did, it was usually with girls in their twenties, very often the stewardesses who trained for Piedmont down at Winston-Salem. Seldom had he ever been alone with a woman for this much time and had been content with only kissing her on the forehead.

After about thirty minutes, Karen moved her head from John's shoulder, and slightly turned upward to him. John looked down at her. Her smile, the warmth of her eyes, told him that she would welcome his kisses.

He lowered his lips to hers, as they experimented with the way their arms should wrap around each other. Her long blond ponytail tickled his forearm, while she rubbed her fingers through the back of his full, thick black hair. Almost orchestrated, their bodies turned, pivoting on John's hip, until they were lying on the sofa. Her short 5'2" frame easily fitted, but his 6'3" frame required that he bend his knees. His right arm beneath her neck, his left over her stomach with his hand wrapped around her right hip, he pulled her to him, their bodies meshing tightly, as they began to kiss, first softly, then more passionately.

John had found himself in this situation many times. He knew that this was the point of no return. That once a woman had gotten to this position, she had surrendered herself. Now his kisses, his caresses, his passion, had always from here forward never been rejected, or his advances denied. But he was finding this so totally different. He found their kisses and caresses, their bodies rotating to find the perfect position that maximized the surface areas of both making contact, was so different than he had ever felt before. Karen was being receptive, but John wasn't sure she was being inviting. This had never bothered him before, but tonight was different, oh so different. John had plans, permanent plans, and he did not intend to jeopardize them.

During the time, Karen also was feeling things so strangely, so wonderfully different, but also so very daunting. She hadn't felt so alive, so breathlessly alive, since she was a teenager, kissing Wilson for the first few times. She knew she was falling for this stranger fast, too darn fast. Even though she did not want to do anything she would regret tomorrow, she wasn't sure if she could stop herself. This man was very worldly, he seemed so sweet, but was this all he had been wanting? She felt herself stiffen, and then she felt John slip away.

Oh no, what will I do? I don't want to lose him. Should I pull him back, let him know I'm his, even if it's only for tonight.

She opened her eyes, not knowing what would be awaiting her. She saw him laying there, looking at her face.

"I'm sure I'm not the only man that's said you are the most beautiful woman he's ever seen, am I?

Karen looked up at him, his head resting on his hands, his elbow bent onto the couch.

"Well, it's been so long," Karen said with a slight smile, "I don't think I can ever remember any man telling me."

John just smiled at her, moving his eyes up and down her face.

"Well, you are," the man said softly, earnestly, "and I think I'd like to be the man to tell you that every day, for the rest of your life."

Karen's heart raced as she tried to decipher his words.

He kissed her softly on her forehead, then, as she closed her eyelids, he kissed each of her eyelids with soft, tender kisses. Not the kisses of a man looking for a one-night stand.

"Karen, I've never let myself get close to a woman before, but I've never known a woman like you before either. You're so, you're just so, perfect."

Karen looked at him quizzically, trying to decide if she was hearing these things.

"John. I do believe that you've known a lot of women before, a whole lot I'm sure. But I can't believe that I can come close to even comparing with some of them."

"No, Karen," he said as his eyes locked with hers. "They don't come close to you."

He looked at her skin, so clear, so perfect. Her eyes, bluer than the brightest coral he saw when diving in Aruba, and with more sparkles than a night-sky full of stars. Her lips were so soft, so deserving of being kissed again, and again. He had thought it before, but he knew it now. He was head over heels in love with this woman. But how to tell her, and did he dare?

He lifted his watch, and saw it was already 9:45.

"Guess we'd better go pick up Suzie," he said with an almost relieved grin.

"Yeah. If we were five minutes late, she'd start walking."

They helped each other with their coats, not to be courteous, but just to have an excuse to look at each other again. Karen rose up on her tiptoes, put her hand around John's head, and pulled him down to meet her. She gave him a long, loving kiss.

"Thank you John. Thank you for being such a perfect gentleman."

"That, my dear," he said with a chuckle, "might just be the first time I've ever been called that."

They walked hand in hand to the car. John opened the door and let her slide in before closing the door. This felt good and so natural. He was beginning to enjoy this feeling. They drove down to the church. By the time they got there, Suzie and several of the others were standing outside. Suzie told the others good-bye, then came to get in the car.

By the time John got them home, it was almost 10:30, so John walked them to the door and said he'd head back to Jonathan's house. Karen let Suzie go inside. Once she was out of site, Karen turned and gave John a good-bye hug and kiss.

"See you tomorrow for lunch?" she asked.

"Sure, I'll phone you in the morning."

"Okay. Pleasant dreams, sweetheart," she said, then giggled. It had been a long time since she had called someone other than Suzie by that name.

John turned back, with a pleading smile for one last kiss.

This was getting to be entirely too much like being teenagers, he thought to himself. Karen came into the house with an ecstatic glaze covering her eyes. Suzie was waiting for her, also with a big smile.

"Momma. I have a feeling you're falling in love."

"Now just what makes you say that?"

"Because you just don't seem to be able to stop smiling anymore."

"It's time for you to get to bed," Karen said, giving her daughter a playful smack on the rear.

"Momma, tonight, when you said what you did about Daddy, that there would never…"

"Yes, honey."

"Well, I think John heard you say that, and I think it hurt his feelings. He was in the kitchen, and acted very strange after you said it."

"Oh, well, I can't imagine why that would bother him, unless…" Karen said, but then stopped before finishing because she still couldn't believe that John could be interested in a permanent relationship. "Well, let's get to bed."

It was nearly an hour before Karen fell asleep. *Was it possible that John had an interest in marriage?* She just had so many thoughts demanding attention from her brain. She was so totally unprepared for the direction her life had taken. Socializing with the Armbristers, riding in parades in Corvettes, having a man that looked like Clark Gable telling her how beautiful she was. No, all this was going to take some getting used to.

Or would she wake up tomorrow, and realize it had just been a dream, or even worse, had she been misinterpreting John's intentions, and would he pack up and leave after Christmas? Oh, this was too much. She was getting a headache.

John also spent his five-minute ride back to Jonathan's trying to deduce what had happened in the last 48 hours, and what it meant to his life plan, a plan that until now had been so well-founded. He had always thought he would work hard until he was forty-five, save as much money as possible, then take the money from his father's estate, and move to the Caribbean, probably Aruba, and live the life of a wealthy retired bachelor.

But Fries was a long way from Aruba, in more ways than one. But for the life of him, he could not remember ever being happier in the Caribbean, or anywhere, than he had been the last three days here. He had grown up in a comfortable, but simple and conservative lifestyle, but his stint in the Rangers had changed all that. He came out of the service with ambition, a worldly view, and unfortunately, a little anger and hostility. He had his life mapped out, but now, he found himself at an unanticipated crossroads. A week ago he would never have considered a detour from his life's roadmap, but now, he was thinking of a detour into a very pleasant, slow-paced drive through the country.

He went to sleep that night and slept peacefully. Very peacefully, because he was sure of what he needed to do.

20

Jason pulled into the IGA parking lot at 9:45 on Christmas Eve morning. There sat his pal Mike in his dad's Chevrolet Impala S/S. The two friends got out, grabbed each other in a big bear hug, but then faked a couple of jabs to each other's head in case anyone should be watching.

"Thanks for coming, Mike."

"Well, I figured this was the only way the fancy college boy would spend time with his old buddy."

The two went into to the store and immediately walked to the back storage room. Jason pulled up a large box containing fifty pounds of red, white and green striped candy canes, a fifty pound box of oranges, and a twenty-five pound box of assorted nuts.

"Let me give you a hand," Mike said.

"No. No. That's it," Jason said, not wanting his friend to exhaust himself too quickly. "I just need to grab about five empty cereal boxes and some paper bags. Go ahead and sit down in that chair there."

Jason soon had everything needed organized around the two seats.

"Okay, you grab about ten of the candy canes and an orange, stick 'em in a paper poke, then pass to me," Jason said to his friend, "and I'll finish off with some nuts and stack them in the boxes."

"Did they teach you that in engineering classes, how to run an assembly line using cheap labor?"

"Hey, if it worked for Henry Ford..."

"Ford? You mean Fix Or Repair Daily."

"Oh, yes. I forgot I'm talking to Mr. Chevy guy."

"It's the only car to drive."

"Now don't tell me you wouldn't have traded that piece of

junk you drove down in, for that sweet Candy Apple Mustang I had."

"You've got to be kidding! That Chevy happens to have a 409 dropped in it," Mike said, letting out a mocking laugh. "Truth is, I was ashamed to even be seen in that little six-banger of yours. It didn't have enough power to pull a greased string out of a gnat's ass."

"That little six banger could shut down that Patton tank of yours any day of the week." Jason said, enjoying the bantering with his friend. He had missed it.

"You're dreaming now. My neighbor's riding mower has more power than your Mustang did. If it had any power, you wouldn't have blown it up when Katy Lynn dumped you back on the Fourth of July."

Jason winced, and Mike saw he had gone too far.

"Hey man," Mike said, slapping his friend on the shoulder, "sorry. That was a low blow."

"Oh. No sweat. I'm long over her."

"Really?"

"Oh yeah. With all those college chicks, you think I'd have time to miss her? I even have an older girl friend, a divorcee. She and her dad run a donut shop. She's about 28, and she's crazy over me. And she is one hot number. Come down one weekend and I'll take you to meet her."

"Well good then, so I guess it won't bother you when I tell you that she's wearing a diamond."

Jason swallowed hard. He wasn't surprised. He was sure they'd never get back together, but he really thought Katy Lynn would have waited longer than this to get engaged.

"Oh, really?" Jason said, trying to show total indifference. "Anyone I know?"

"Oh yeah. Her soldier boy. It seems he wanted to give it to her on Christmas morning, but she insisted on getting it before he went back to the base the first of the month. She wanted to show it to all of her girlfriends at school before the Christmas break."

"Well, good, I hope,…I hope she'll be happy. Be sure to tell her I said that."

"Okay. I'll tell her that when we get back to school. I'll tell her you'd call to wish her luck yourself but you're too busy with all your college girlfriends, and older women. Everbody knows how hot to trot those older women are."

"So how are your folks doing?" Jason asked, feeling the need to change the subject.

"Mom's doing great. She said to tell you hello. You sure have her fooled into thinking you're such a great guy and all. She's already told me that I need to do like you and go to college next year."

"Think you will?"

"Yeah, I'll probably go to Wytheville for a couple of years. Dad's not doing good, though."

"Really?"

"No. He's been having some bleeding problems. They've been running tests."

"Well, I hope everything goes okay. Mom had surgery yesterday, but I got a phone call last night and everything looked like it's okay."

"Oh, really? What was the matter?"

"They thought it might have been eye cancer, but apparently it wasn't the bad kind. They think she'll be alright now. The only thing is, she'll not be home for Christmas."

"Oh! That sucks. Why don't you come down to our house for a while Christmas day."

"I might do that, when we get back from the hospital. So, anything else new going on in town?"

"Naw, didn't have much of a football team and now we're not having much of a basketball season. It's sure been a let down from last year. I can't believe you never made it to any of the games."

"I was pretty busy at school, and…well, I wasn't sure I could take going back to the field again."

"Yeah, I kinda had a feeling that's what it was."

About sixty minutes later, all 200 bags had been filled. Jason looked at his friend. Even though the work had been rather easy, the exertion had left Mike's face a frightening blue.

"Mike, are you okay buddy?"

"Yeah, they just can't seem to get my medication right."

Jason began to think about all the things Mike had done for

him, and how little he had ever done for his friend.

"Mike. You're really a great friend. I don't know what I'd do without you."

"Hey. No sweat, pal," Mike said, and then gave his friend a sympathetic look, "I've always felt kinda sorry for you. You've never had much going for you."

Jason looked at this watch. He still had an hour before he needed to start to work.

"Well, that didn't take long," Jason said to his friend. "Let's take the bags out and put them in your car, then we can go next door to the snack counter. I'll show you one of those college girls who's been keeping me from thinking about...Eh? Now what was her name?"

Using two grocery carts, the boys were able to carry all five boxes, containing 200 bags of goodies for the boys and girls of Fries, to the Super-Sport. Two boxes went into the trunk, two into the back seat, and one in the front seat. They then walked next door to the snack bar.

"You'd better hold onto your socks," Jason said with a suggestive grin, "because this girl's going to knock them off."

They walked to a vacant booth and sat down. Within two minutes a short, but very curvy honey-blonde, with eyes the color of a clear summer sky, not quite blue, not quite gray, came up to the booth. She wore a short cotton navy blue mini-skirt, and a cotton blouse, with the top two buttons undone.

Jason scanned the menu fixedly, from milk shakes to french fries, as Mike eyed the waitress searchingly, from her pink-capped toe-nails in the open sandals, to the pink ribbon tying back her golden hair. The friend's jaw had dropped, and his eyes were the size of quarters. Jason had a sudden fear his friend might pass out from an accelerated heart beat.

"Good morning," the waitress said in a very professional voice with just a hint of seductiveness, "and what would you like today?"

"Hmm, I think I'd like an order of..." Jason said while studying the menu, and then looked up just as he pinched the girl on her waist, "Lynne!"

"Jason, you know I can't stand that," she said with a giggle as sweet and creamy as a bowl of Honey Nut Cheerios. She then plopped down beside him, scooting him over. Mike stole a downward glance, as the girl's mini skirt inched up her thighs to become a micro-mini.

"And just who's this good looking hunk you've got with you?" she asked, winking at Mike.

"Lynne, this is my best buddy, Mike, from Fries. He came up to help me pack the Christmas goodies for the kids back in Fries."

"Oh yeah. That really impressed my mom when you told us that at dinner last night." She said, and then added with a whisper. "Or were you too distracted to notice because I was rubbing your thigh with my foot."

"I must admit, that did get my attention."

"So, hi, Mike." Lynne said as she squeezed Mike's hand. "What kind of juicy tales can you tell me on your buddy here?"

By this time he had recovered enough to manage a "Hi Lynne, glad to meet you. And we don't have time for me to tell you all the things I know on this guy."

Then Mike began to regain his composure and started in on his usual ribbing at Jason's expense.

"So tell me, what do you see in this guy anyway?" As cute as you are, you could get a good-looking guy."

"Well, maybe I just will," she said as she jumped up and slid over to the other side. Mike could feel her bare lower legs pressed against his beneath his Bermuda shorts.

About that time, from the counter came an agitated female voice. "Lynne!"

"Oops!" She said, jumping up and raising her order pad to waist level. "And what would you gentleman like to order."

"Hmm." Jason said. "I'll take the barbeque, with slaw, French fries, and a large cherry Coke."

"Yeah. I'll take the same." Mike said, realizing he had forgotten to look at his menu.

"Coming right up," she said as she sashayed over to the counter.

"WOW!" Mike said excitedly. "You weren't kidding. She's a long shot from Katy. I haven't seen bo-sooms on a girl that big since we double dated with the Willingham twins down in

Greensboro summer before last."

"She is a cutie, isn't she? Her dad's a local doctor. You should see their house. It's as big as the Boarding House."

"So give me some details, man. How's your dates been?"

"Don't know yet. Friday night will be our first one. I didn't have a car until this week. Mom let me bring the Wildcat down."

"Oh, the Wildcat, eh? Umm, I bet there'll be a lot of Wildcat Spirit going on in that back seat Saturday night. How many touchdowns are you planning on scoring?"

"Now, Mike, you know I'm not that kinda guy. I just like her for her mind. She's a really intelligent girl."

"Well, if you don't become 'that kinda guy,' you're an idiot."

About that time, Lynne came by, and placed the orders down. In her best ditzy blonde impersonation she said, "Now which order goes where? I've forgotten."

She then slid in beside Jason where she promptly reached beneath the table, and using her four fingernails and thumb, pinched a major portion of his upper thigh.

"So, sweetie," she said massaging the spot she had just pinched, "will you be back to Pulaski by Christmas night?"

"No, I guess I'll still be in Fries."

"So I won't get to see you until Friday?" Lynne said, pushing her lips out into a pout, and then looking over at Mike with a seductive grin. "I might just have to give your Christmas present to someone else. I bet Mike would like it."

"I'll be down by eight, Christmas Night." Mike promised with a wink.

"Well, I'll guess I'll have to wait until Friday night then." She said, and then turned to make sure she wasn't being watched from the counter, and then gave Jason a big kiss on the lips.

"But I'll see you Christmas night, Mikey," she said teasingly.

"Well, guess I'd better get to work," Jason called to her as she turned to leave. "You can bring me the bill now."

"Don't be silly. You know I always put it on Daddy's tab." she said with an impish grin.

"Do you think she was serious?" Mike said as he and Jason stood up to leave, "because if she was, you can forget about coming to see me. I'm gonna be down here."

"Mike, my friend. Take my word for it. Your heart couldn't take a *Lynne*."

Jason walked his friend to the car. Jason wanted to tell his old pal so many things about what was going on in his life, the problems with school, his worries about his mom, but there never seemed to be time. It seemed each time he saw him, he was looking more ill. Jason just didn't know what he'd do if he ever lost Mike.

"See you Christmas day, around two," Jason said.

21

Karen did finally fall asleep, and woke up with an excited anticipation for Christmas Eve. Two weeks ago it seemed that all hope for a happy Christmas was gone. The anxiety grew even worse with Suzie's accident. But, as so often happens, when things seem at their absolute worse, God finds a way to bring blessings beyond anything a person could ever imagine. Karen decided she would not worry how long John would be in her life, she would just enjoy every moment that he was.

Within sight of Karen's house, but a three minute drive along the winding Fries streets, John was awakening. Unlike the uncertainty of the day before, John today felt a sense of purpose. His only anxiety would be if he had waited too long, and stores would be closed in Galax. *Why hadn't he made his decision yesterday, so he could have done his shopping while he was there and the stores were open?* He looked in the nightstand next to the bed and opened up the telephone directory. He was surprised. There were only five yellow pages of businesses in both Fries and Galax. *There must be fifteen pages of lawyers alone listed in the Winston-Salem directory,* he thought to himself. He looked under a few different categories and jotted down a few phone numbers and addresses. He remembered he had not made any plans with Karen today, and knew he should phone her.

John sat down to have breakfast with the Armbrister's. Cynthia had fixed oatmeal for them.

"Well, got a big day planned?" Jonathan asked.

"Yes. I think you could say that." John answered. "Thought I'd go to Galax for some last minute Christmas shopping."

"Hmm, another one of those men who waits until the last minute." Cynthia said with a chuckle, as she looked at her husband.

"I'll have you know I have had your present bought since last week." The husband retorted, then turning to grin at John. "And now I'm working on buying you a New Year's gift."

After breakfast, John phoned Karen.

"Hi, and how are you today?" John said.

"Good morning." Karen said with a sweet voice. "I'm good. Thought maybe you'd forgotten all about me."

"Umm, well. I think maybe I did, for about a half-hour last night while I was in a sound sleep and not dreaming about you."

"Coming up for lunch?"

"That's what I was calling about. I need to drive over to Galax for a few hours. I forgot to get a couple of things yesterday. I thought I'd bring us something back to eat. What would you guys want?"

"Wait. Let me ask Suzie." Karen said. John could hear the conversation transpiring in the background. "She said she'd loved to have two hotdogs with chili and slaw from Roses' snack counter. I'll pay you when you get back."

"Just take it off the tab for all my meals. I should be back about one o'clock."

"Okay. See you then, honey." Karen said, surprised at how easily the term of endearment flowed from her mouth.

John smiled to himself at hearing the word. It sounded so pure and genuine, not contrived as with his earlier girlfriends.

"Okay, sweetheart," he replied. For the first time in his life, he truly meant the word.

As John was driving through town, he saw Sam leaving the Boarding House. John pulled over and motioned for Sam to open the door.

"Hey, Sam. What're you doing?"

"Oh, hi, John. Just walking around, killing some time."

"Well, I'm headed over to Galax. I'm going to do some last minute shopping. Want to ride with me? Galax is an interesting little city."

"Yes. I would, thanks. I was thinking about doing some shopping also." Sam said as he slipped into the car.

For the next twenty minutes John gave Sam a windshield tour

of the area between the small town of Fries and the larger city of Galax. He pointed out the mansion known as Cliffside and told the story of the Baldwin-Felt's detective agency and the Coal Field Wars. He told about the shoot-out at the Hillsville courthouse. He pointed out the various furniture factories.

John had already made some calls, and knew exactly where he wanted to go. He pulled off Route 58 onto the Main Street of Galax, drove past Twin County Motor's Ford dealership, past the bank, and parked across from Bolen's Drug Store.

"Are there any office supply stores around here?" Sam asked.

"Umm, yeah, I think there's one on the next block down, on the left." Sam answered. "I think it's called Blue Ridge Office Supply. They look like they have most everything."

"That sounds like what I'm looking for," the business man said. "When do you want me to meet you back here at the car?"

"I'm going to be about an hour. When you finish, wait for me in Bolen's Drug Store. They have some great BLT's there."

"Sounds like a plan. I'll meet you there."

John crossed the street. Both of the stores he was looking for were open, and were adjacent to each other. He first went into Kylene's Boutique. After about thirty minutes he departed the store and entered the next store on his list, Lemon's Fine Jewelry.

Thirty minutes later, John crossed over the street and placed two large bags into the trunk, and slipped a smaller bag under the front driver's seat. He then walked to Bolen's Drug Store, where he found Sam, finishing off the last of a BLT. Beside him in the booth was a large bag with the name *Blue Ridge Office Supply* written on the front.

"Hey, you were right. This is a delicious sandwich." Sam said as he looked up at John.

"Did you get what you needed?" John asked.

"Yes, I sure did." Sam said with a very pleased expression. "How about you? Did you get your shopping finished?"

"Almost. Just a couple more stops, if you have time?"

"Oh, sure. I'm always glad to be able to check out retail marketing in other areas."

Ten minutes later John pulled off Route 58 into the Galax Plaza Shopping Center.

"I think this shopping center has only been open for a few years, and seems to do a good amount of business," John said, his keen intuition telling him that Sam had more than a casual interest. "Galax is a fairly modern city. This was one of the first shopping centers around. Galax has made its money in furniture manufacturing, and for years used a spur to share the railroad with Fries."

Sam looked with tremendous interest at the half dozen stores that were located at the site. His eyes became riveted on the large Roses store.

"I'm going into Roses for a couple more things and then grab some hotdogs for lunch," John said, then asked. "You like hotdogs? I'm sure Karen would love for you to join us."

"Yeah, I do. That's one of my basic food groups while traveling on the road, but I never get tired of them."

The two men got out of the car started toward the department store.

"I just need to pick up a phonograph and some records for Suzie in here. I have no idea what's good now though." John said, pulling a shopping cart from the rack.

"Want me to give you a hand?" Sam offered. "I know a little about them."

Sam stopped, and began studying the layout of the store. After a few moments, he started in a direction that sure enough, led them to the electronics. Sam looked around for a while, where he finally stopped in front of a group of players.

"This is what they call a Crosley Traveler," Sam said, sounding like a Salesman of the Month. "Teenage girls seem to like this because it's easy to pack up and take over to a girlfriend's house. It plays both the 45's and the L.P.'s. Now, this one is $29.95; that's not a bad price, maybe $2 higher than it should be, but if you want to spend another $15, this one also has an 8-track player. That's going to be the new and coming thing; kids are starting to buy 8-tracks. Before long, these records will be obsolete."

"Wow, Sam. You sound like you know what you're doing. You must have kids this age."

"Well, mine are older teens, but I like to stay up on what the hot sellers are now, and what will be even hotter tomorrow."

"Okay. Let me grab a couple of albums. Any idea what kids are listening to today?"

"Well, I know we sell a lot of Credence Clearwater Revival, the Beatles' 'Abbey Road,' and Fleetwood Mac."

"So you have several stores?"

"Yeah, a few," Sam answered, his modesty and desire to remain just one of the guys, prevented him from saying a few dozen.

John looked through the record rack and pulled out the three suggested albums. He then looked in the rack of 8-tracks and picked out a couple of the Golden Hits of the 60's, Volume 1 and Volume 2. He then walked to the clothing section.

"I was thinking about a sweater." John said, with a questioning look to his new shopping consultant. "What would you suggest?"

Sam looked at the sweaters hanging on the rack, studied the tags, felt the material, and stretched the sleeves.

"Well, this sweater is cheaper than the designer brand, but it's a better product. The higher priced one just has a better known name, which means they spend more on advertising. But the knit is better on this one. It'll last longer, and keep its color and shape better. It just goes to show that you can get good quality, at a lower price."

"Is there anything you don't know?" John asked, while shaking his head in admiration.

"Well, I make it my business to know these things." Sam answered.

John looked over the various colors and decided on a pale blue one, thinking it would look good with Karen's blonde hair and would match her eyes. He then noticed a bottle of Estee Lauder perfume in a gift pack, so he picked that up and placed it into his cart, and headed toward the front. He would have liked to have gotten more gifts, but didn't want Karen to think he was being excessive. Besides, hopefully, there would be other Christmases for him to spoil the Young girls.

"I'm going to head down to Krogers to pick up some drinks and other things. Want to go?" John asked Sam as he was having his purchases checked out.

"No. If it's alright, I'd like to stick around here. Will you mind coming back here to get me?"

"Oh no. That won't be a problem at all. I still have to come back to get the hotdogs." John said as he left to the front check-out register.

"If you'd like to have these complimentary wrapped" the check-out girl said, "you could leave them and they should be ready in about twenty minutes."

"Thank you. I think I'll do that. Have a Merry Christmas." He said with a pleasant smile.

"Yes, sir. Merry Christmas to you, too."

He only needed soft drinks and a gallon of milk, because he had drunk the last of the gallon the night before. It took him five minutes to find what he wanted in the grocery store, but thirty minutes to get through the long line of customers. For one of the few times in the last couple of weeks, he found his old trait of impatience overtaking him. He placed the bag from Krogers into the trunk of the Buick, and then went back into the Roses store. After about five minutes, he found Sam, wandering through the clothing aisles. John watched for a few moments as the businessman would flip a price tag over, then copy notes onto a notepad he held in his hand.

"Still needing to buy some more things?" John then asked.

"Oh. I just like to compare prices in any of the cities I'm in." Sam said with a chuckle, putting his notepad away. "Are you finished?"

"Yes. Ready to go as soon as I order up some hot dogs and pick up my gifts from the wrappers."

John placed his order for a eight hotdogs, all the way, and then went to pick up his packages. They had been beautifully wrapped, complete with curly ribbons, by a young red-head wearing a Galax Maroon Tide Cheerleader's sweater.

"Thank you. These look wonderful." John said, as he handed her a five dollar tip. "Merry Christmas."

"Thank you! Thank you very much. Oh, and yes. Merry Christmas to you, too."

John picked up the order of hot dogs, and the two men headed back to the car and toward Fries.

"Heck, it's already 1:15." John said as he looked at his watch.

"I promised Karen I'd be back by one. It just seems like it takes forever to pick up a few things, because you have to drive to a dozen different places. You'd think someone would build one giant store, where you could get everything you wanted in one place."

"Do you think people would go for that?" Sam said with a knowing smile. "They would be giving up the fun of going into town."

"The fun? You mean the fun of fighting for a parking space, then when you're five minutes late getting back, finding a parking ticket on your windshield? Or making trips back to the car from a half dozen stores?" John said in mock anguish.

"Well, if you think it would really work." Sam said, egging his new friend on.

"Yeah, Sam. I really do think it would work. Today's society looks for everything to be convenient, just like those new microwave ovens. Why take thirty minutes to cook something if you can get it done in five? Yeah, I think people would love to be able to go to one store and do all their shopping in thirty minutes instead of an hour and half."

"Well, would you ever invest in one of those? I mean, buy stock if it was offered?"

John thought about the money he had sitting in his trust, the fact that Suzie would need money for Harvard, but that he would still have money left over.

"Yes, Sam. I sure would, because I'm sure it would work. Don't you think it would be a shrewd investment?"

"Yes. I think I might put a few dollars in it, too."

The two men arrived at the Youngs' house and walked to the front door, their arms full of bags. John used his foot to knock on the door. Karen opened it.

"Gentleman," Karen said as she opened the door, "if y'all are some of those Christmas Eve traveling salesmen, we're not buying."

"Oh no ma'am. We're not salesman." John said, peeking over the bag. "We're two Wise Men, from the South, bearing gifts."

Karen just shook her head, then gave John a 'welcome-home kiss' as she opened the door.

"Did it take that many bags to put the hot dogs in?" she said.

"Well, I invited Sam, and he told me how much he loved hot dogs, so I had to get an extra dozen."

"Hey, I've got bags, too." Sam said, as he set the bags down on the sofa. "Don't I get a kiss too?"

"If those are hot dogs, you get a kiss from me." Suzie said as she came running in from the kitchen. She jumped up into Sam's arms, to give him a hug, and a kiss on the cheek.

"I hope it was alright for me to come along."

"Oh, well, it is Christmas," Karen said teasingly, "I guess we can spare a couple of hotdogs for a Wise Man from the South, so far away from home, without a family of his own."

Karen's words were sweet to Sam, but they really made him wince. It was the final conviction he needed to make him place some phone calls when he got back to the inn.

While Suzie and Karen started placing the hotdogs onto plates, John laid the packages under the tree. His presents, combined with the gifts that had mysteriously appeared since last night, surrounded the bottom of the tree. His eyes caught one package marked "To John, from Suzie."

The hotdogs, smothered with onions, mustard, chili and slaw, were soon devoured. Sam enjoyed them immensely, but felt a burning desire to hurry back to the inn to make his phone calls.

"Umm, those were fantastic, but I think now I need to walk this big lunch off," Sam said. "The steps out back go straight down to the hotel, don't they?"

"Yes, they do," Karen assured him.

"John, could you open the trunk for me please?" Sam asked. The two men began walking out to the car, but before they reached it, the businessman turned to John.

"That bag, that's in the back of your car from the Blue Ridge Office Supply store," Sam said quietly. "Will you bring it in to me tonight, down at the party?"

"Of course. I'd be glad to, Sam. I guess we'll see you tonight up at Jonathan Arbristers' before the parade starts."

"Yes, see you then," Sam said to John, then stuck his head back in the front door and said in a louder voice, "thanks again for the hotdogs."

In ten minutes Sam had reached the Boarding House. He enjoyed the walk, but appreciated the fact that it was down instead of up. He then thought about Karen and Suzie, having no car and walking everywhere in town. No wonder they were both so slim. Once reaching the hotel, Sam went searching for Myrt, finding her making beds on the second floor.

"Is it okay if I use the phone again for some long distance calls?"

"Of course, Sam. Make yourself at home. You know where it's at."

"Do you, by any chance, have the number for the Roanoke airport? That is the closest isn't it?"

"Yeah, it is. The phone number is written down on the front page of our phone book."

"Thanks, Myrt."

"Help yourself to a cup of coffee while you're on the phone."

"Yes. That'd be great. I'll help myself."

Sam returned to the first floor, poured his coffee, and went into the office. He took the phone directory from the drawer, found the handwritten listing and called the Roanoke Airport.

"Roanoke Regional Airport, Merry Christmas," a pleasant voice answered.

"Hello. Could you tell me if you have anyone that charters flights, and how I could contact them?"

"Well, yes sir. As a matter of fact, one of the charter pilots has just come in and is in the office here. Would you like to speak to him?"

"Yes, I would, thank you." Sam answered, and waited to hear the phone being picked up.

"Hello, this is Jeff Byrd. What can I do for you?" a youthful voice answered.

"Hi, Jeff. What would you charge for a flight to Fayetteville, Arkansas.

"Just a minute," there was a pause. Jeff then answered. "That would be $185. When were you hoping to leave?"

"Tonight, a little after midnight."

"Tonight? It's Christmas Eve. I'm sorry but I couldn't possibly fly you tonight. I have two boys waiting at home, and I still have to find a Johnny Unitas football for the oldest. All the Roanoke stores are out, and I'm going to probably have to drive to Greensboro, just to find one. If I can get there in time before the stores close."

"Tell you what, Jeff. You could go home right now, have a nice dinner with your wife and kids, put them to bed, come back, fly me to Arkansas and be back before your kids wake up. I'll pay you $300, *and* I'll throw in a Johnny Unitas football."

There was silence on the other end, as the pilot either pondered the very enticing offer, or was trying to deduce if the caller was for real.

"Really. Can you do that?" Jeff asked.

"Yes. I can do that. So is it a deal?"

"Well, yeah, sure. What's your name?"

"It's Sam. Be waiting for me at the front of the airport at 12:45."

"Okay. See you then, Sam."

Sam then hung up and phoned Chiney's number.

"Ho, ho, ho, this is a good old soul, and a Merry Christmas from the North Pole," answered Chiney in a rhyme.

"Chiney, this is Sam. Merry Christmas."

"Oh, same to you, my good friend."

"Chiney, you've done so much for me, but could you do a couple more things for me?

"Sure, old buddy. What is it?"

"Well, first of all, could you drive me down to Ft. Chiswell in your pick-up? I noticed you have a CB in it. I need to contact a couple of trucks I'm looking for, meet them, and escort them to Fries."

"Yeah, I think I can handle that. And what's the other thing?"

"Would you drive me down to Roanoke Airport tonight, after the party? We'll take my car. I have to be there by one o'clock."

"Well, sure, but why are you flying up to Pennsylvania if your car is ready?"

"Well, I'm not going to Pennsylvania. I'm flying home to Arkansas, for Christmas."

"Well, sure. I'd be glad to. I'll wait for you after the party. And I'm mighty glad to hear you're going home for Christmas."

"Thanks, Chiney. I can't thank you enough."

"No thanks needed, Sam. I've heard what you're doing for this town. I'm mighty proud to claim you as my friend."

Sam hung up, took a deep breath, and began smiling, as he dialed his next number.

"Hello," a woman's voice answered.

"Honey? Hi, this is Sam."

"Oh, hi Sam. I thought you were going to call tomorrow morning to tell the kids Merry Christmas. They're not here right now."

"That's no problem," he said with a joyous laugh. "Listen closely. I want you to phone Delton. Tell him I need him to run by the stores, and keep looking until he finds a Johnny Unitas football. Tell him also to throw in one of those Baltimore Colts helmets."

"Oh, okay, but what should he do with them?"

"Well, then he should drive with them to the airport about 3:00 in the morning, *and pick me up.*"

"Sam!" his wife said, her voice trembling. "You're coming home for Christmas?"

"Yes, I am!"

"But..., but what about your business trips? I thought you had to make them before New Years."

"Well, I've taken care of all that, or as much as I need to for now. I..." Sam hesitated as he felt his voice beginning to crack with emotion, "...I've decided that some things are more important than business, and Christmas is a time to be with those you love and care about."

"Sam, you didn't hurt your head when you hit that snow bank did you?" she said with a laugh.

"No, but, well, I've met some mighty nice people this week, some wonderful people. And, well, they've helped me change some of my thoughts about things. I can't wait to tell you about them. Oh, and guess what! I'm playing Santa Claus tonight. In a parade and for a Christmas party."

"Well, it sounds like you've made quite a hit. I can't wait to hear all about it."

"Oh, and don't tell the kids I'm coming. I want it to be a surprise in the morning."

At about 3:30 p.m., Chiney pulled up in his pick-up truck. Sam jumped in and greeted his new friend.

"So it's okay for me to use your CB?" Sam asked.

"Sure thing, go right ahead."

"Breaker, breaker, one five, breaker, one five," he said as he keyed into the mic. "How about that Santa's Sleigh coming down from Pennsylvania for old Fries town. Do you copy?"

Static. Static. Then, "Breaker, breaker one five, you've got Santa's Sleigh, loaded with lots of toys for boys and girls in the old Fries town."

"What's your twenty?"

"We be coming by old Roanoke town, what's your twenty?"

"We are headed to Fort Chiswell. When you get there, pull into Blair's service station, and we will escort you to Fries."

"Ten-four Santa. We'll find you there."

"Breaker, breaker one five, is this Santa?" Another voice asked. "This is Santa's sleigh heading down from the Big Apple, with a lot of swaddling clothes."

"Ten-four, this is Santa. What is your twenty?"

"We be almost to the Fort Chiswell exit. It's a blue van, with the company name on it. We'll see you there, Santa."

"Ten-four."

Sam smiled as Chiney looked over at him.

"Sam, you are one humdinger of an interesting fellow. I'm really glad I stopped to pick you up last Sunday."

"So am I, Chiney. So am I."

By five p.m., Sam and Chiney in the pick-up, a large tractor trailer with a mural of Santa's sleigh on the side, and a commercial van pulled in front of New River Garage at the town limits. The garage was closed, so Sam felt this would be a good place to leave the trucks until they pulled down to the gym at the appointed time.

"Hey, come on down to the inn. I bet I can get Myrt to warm up some food."

As they entered the dining area, Sam could hear the older woman cleaning up the kitchen. Sam walked in the back and noticed there was still some food on the old wood-burning cook stove.

"Myrt, I see you are busy. Would it be okay for me to fix up some plates for some hungry friends?"

"Sure Sam, take what ever you want. We usually offer a buffet for $3.25, so tell them to eat 'til their bellies pop."

"Well, Myrt, these are truck drivers." Sam said with a chuckle. "I'm not sure we should make that offer."

Sam prepared four plates. Chiney helped him carry them to the table where the men were talking, getting to know each other. Sam then poured four cups of coffee, and brought them to the table, along with the coffee pot.

Before long, it was 5:30. Sam gave his final instructions to the drivers, and then went to the older lady in the back.

"Myrt, I'll be checking out tonight, right after the party. Can you get my bill ready? This is what the phone calls came to."

Myrt sat down with a calculator, and soon brought out a bill.

"Are you sure this is right?" Sam looked at it and smiled. "I would have thought I had eaten this much."

"Nope, that's right. Rooms are $16/night, and then your meals. I've enjoyed having you Sam. I hope you'll come this way again."

"Well, if nothing happens, I may be coming back in the spring to do some more bird hunting with Chiney. I might even bring the wife then. I'll be mighty sure to stop in and say hello."

The total bill was $63.35, including his long distance calls. He pulled a $100 bill from his wallet, handed it to Myrt and said, "Keep the rest, Myrt, and have a Merry Christmas."

"Oh, Sam. This is too much, way too much."

"No, Myrt, you earned it. Have a good Christmas with it."

"Well, thank you Sam. I will now."

Sam then walked up the hill to Jonathan Armbrister's house, where his Santa's outfit would be waiting. He got there at 5:45.

After the late lunch at the Youngs' house, Karen, Suzie and John were relaxing. Suzie was lying on her stomach, her left arm crooked up at the elbow supporting her chin. She was closely scrutinizing the packages and dying to shake them. She reached toward a particular package that had the most beautiful wrapping and ribbons she had ever seen.

"No, you don't, young lady," her mother warned. "Not until tomorrow morning."

It was about five p.m., and John couldn't stand to wait any longer.

"Karen, don't torture that poor child. Let her open one present. As a matter of fact, both of you should open a package."

Without waiting for a protest, he jumped up and grabbed two identical packages. They were the ones Suzie had been admiring. The girl came running over to take hers as John carried the other one to Karen.

Suzie ripped off the beautiful purple foil wrapping paper with its gold ribbons, to find a box marked "Kylene's Boutique." Her eyes popped open wide. She had often walked by the store when in Galax, and had peered through the window at the beautiful gowns. She dreamed of the day she would go to the prom in one of the dresses with Jason Campbell by her side.

"Hey, slow down, Suzie Q.," John shouted with a chuckle. "Wait until your mom catches up before you open the box."

"I hate to open it. I've never seen such a beautiful wrapping." She said, her hands trembling, she slowly removed the ribbons, and carefully removed the foil without tearing it. Then Karen's eyes also widened. Kylene's Boutique. She had never even had the nerve to walk in to the fancy store, instead doing her shopping at Belk's, A & Z, or now, the new Roses.

John saw that Karen had caught up, and then smiled and said, "Okay, open your boxes."

Both Young girls now quickly obeyed, and together, gave a duet of "oh my's."

Both, then unable to speak, reached into the box and pulled out a shining, soft fur coat.

"Oh my, John. This is too much. We can't accept these." Karen said, praying he wouldn't take her serious.

"Now, Karen, don't get excited. They're not mink. They're called moutons. They're made from sheep."

"Well, they are still absolutely gorgeous. What do you think, Suzie?"

"Oh, Momma," the girl said as she rubbed the soft fur against her cheek, "it's the softest thing I've ever felt in my life."

"Well, it's gonna be cold out tonight in that convertible, and I didn't want my two girls to freeze."

Both ran over to John, each sitting down on a different leg, and gave him a big hug. Then Suzie gave him a kiss on the cheek, while Karen gave him a long kiss on the lips. John looked out of the corner of his eye at Suzie and was pleased to see her beaming at her mother's reaction.

Karen and Suzie slipped the coats on, and began prancing back and forth like runway models. Before long, it was time to leave. They all climbed into the Buick to drive to Jonathan's where they would get into the 'Vette for the parade. They arrived just as Sam was walking into the driveway.

"Hi, Sam. Ready to play Santa?"

"Sure am. A little nervous though."

Cynthia, holding up two red outfits, met them as they walked into the house.

"Oh, Suzie, guess what." Mrs. Armbrister said. "Along with the Santa's outfit, I found a Santa's elf outfit. With a little pinning, it should fit you perfectly. Want to wear it in the parade, and at the party, to help Sam?"

"Okay, as long as I can wear my fur coat over it," Suzie said as she held the coat forward to show Cynthia.

"Wow!! Looks like Santa's already visited the Youngs'," Cynthia said admiringly.

"Umm, Sam," Jonathan Armbrister said, "come to the front, and let me give you some final details about the parade route." When they got out of earshot of the others, Jonathan began speaking in a low voice.

"Sam, I just got off the phone with Robert Haynes. I don't know how in the world you did it, but we have everything worked out. This town will never be able to repay you for this. Never."

"Well, it was a business transaction, pure and simple," Sam said as he shook Armbrister's hand. "I demand top quality. After meeting people from this town, I know that is what I will get from this mill."

So Santa and his elf got dressed. A strange chugging noise, sounding almost like a washing machine, came from outside. It was Chief of Police Bruce Smith, driving his antique yellow convertible he fondly called "Sunflower."

22

It was almost parade time. As everyone left the house, they could hear the fire trucks and rescue squads sounding their sirens, and the percussion section of the Galax band as the members warmed up. They could see the earthen bank along Main Street lined with people. Most of these were people who lived out of town. They had parked in the lot where the old depot had once stood.

The townspeople were all gathered along Main Street, mostly on the porches of friends who lived along the thoroughfare. The people knew one of the few enjoyments they would have this holiday was the parade. The party would be the only other, so they were determined to enjoy every moment of the two.

So Santa, in his bright red outfit, climbed into the back seat of the yellow convertible, decorated with green garlands. Bruce pulled out of the drive-way, the engine chug, chug, chugging in its distinctive sound.

John slid back the top of the red Stingray, as Suzie waited excitedly to jump in. Her mouton coat covered the top of the green elf suit. He helped her in to the rear compartment.

"Okay now, be careful." John said, sounding evermore like a doting but concerned father. "Be sure to lean forward toward the front. Don't sit back on the trunk or you may fall out backwards." Then he added jokingly, "We don't want to crack that noggin a second time."

He helped Karen in, then ran around and dropped down into the car. Bruce had backed across the road to let John in front, but John stopped, his fingers on the key, to look at Karen. He wore a tender smile on his face, and a loving gleam sparkled in his dark eyes. She was so beautiful, in her hunter green ankle-length dress. Her long blonde hair was hanging long and full over the chocolate mouton.

"What are you looking at?" she asked with a grin.

"You're beautiful Karen, just so wonderfully, absolutely beautiful."

"You'd better get on your way," she said as she leaned over and kissed him, "before Bruce gives you a ticket for holding up the parade."

He obediently turned his attention around to Suzie.

"Holding on, Suzie Q.?"

"Yes sir!"

He turned the key, and the 400-horsepower exploded out of the 425-cubic-inch engine. The roar from the exhaust was almost deafening, as Suzie giggled and covered her ears. John eased into first and pulled out. He had to be careful not to "burn rubber", since the town cop was right behind him, and he didn't want to jolt Suzie and throw her off the rear. They edged into the curve to get their first look at Main Street.

"Momma, look at that!" Suzie screamed as she leaned forward, trying to make herself heard over the car's deep guttural rumbling, as she viewed the people sitting on the bank.

Once they finished the curve and started down the grade, they could see the sidewalk along Main Street was also lined with spectators, more people than Karen and Suzie could ever remember seeing at a Fries parade. Due to the late scheduling of the event, only one float was prepared, and it was just ahead of Suzie and the red Corvette. On it was the same cast that presented the Christmas play at the hospital. Instead of Suzie's reciting the scripture, a loud speaker was playing a tape recording of her voice. Standing as the Magi was the three pastors. Beneath them was a sign that read, "Wise Men Still Follow Him." Banners on each side of the float read, "Peace on Earth," and then beneath it, "The Combined Churches of Fries." On the rear of the trailer was the banner that read, "Peace on Earth, and in Fries too."

Ahead of the float was not only the Galax Band, led by their maroon clad majorettes wearing jingle bells, but also the Independence and Woodlawn bands. There were fire trucks from Galax and Hillsville, and rescue squad units from Cana, Ivanhoe, and Sylvatus with signs bearing messages such as "Have a Fire-

Safe Holiday," and "Don't Drink and Drive." Two Boy Scout and two Cub Scout troops were lined up just ahead. In front, to start the parade, was the American Legion Honor Guard, with Freddie Jennings, Chiney Alderman and John Shepherd marching in their uniforms and carrying their rifles. Just ahead of them was Pete Spraker, carrying the American Flag and counting cadence. John and Bruce eased behind the others. A rescue worker called ahead on his walkie-talkie, and the Honor Guard was told to begin marching. Within moments, the first band began playing as members passed the temporary reviewing stand, which was actually a flat bed hay truck with folding chairs on it. Seated were the Town Council and various other dignitaries.

The parade proceeded on at a snail's pace. The three deuces sitting under the hood of the Stingray growled at having to stay at a low 1500 RPM. Suzie, with her smile even bigger than usual, was waving rapidly, trying not to miss a single person in the crowd. Just ahead, several members of the various youth groups were throwing hard candy to the spectators.

Finally, to the delight of the younger children, came Sunflower, hauling its cargo consisting of a Fries legend and a stranger dressed in a red suit. Bruce was wearing his dress uniform, proud to be the bearer of Santa Claus. By the time Bruce had traveled a hundred yards; Santa Claus had lost his shyness, and was nearly rolling out backwards, with his HO, HO, HOs, and MERRY CHRISTMASSES.

Karen was also enjoying herself, having lost a little of her shyness, to wave at friends who were showing envy as green as an undecorated Christmas tree of her new friend, his car, and her fur. But then, all of them had to say to themselves that if anyone deserved this, it was Karen, and hoped she had found someone to share her life.

John didn't have time to enjoy the experience. He was too busy trying to find the right balance between first and second gears to maintain his speed without jarring Suzie from the back, and to keep the speed up enough to prevent the car from overheating. This car was made to fly like an eagle, not waddle like a duck. But he was happy. Last week he had no one serious in his life. No parents, grandparents or real girlfriend. But now, he hoped he was on the threshold of having a family.

For Suzie, the parade ended all too soon, at 6:50 p.m., in front of the high school gym. Santa and his fur coated elf went into the gym and into the back room to begin making plans as to how to handle the party. The bands and majorettes loaded on their buses and started home. The solitary float was pulled down to the ball park and left until after the party was over. The Boy Scouts broke ranks to meet their parents in their pre-assigned rendezvous areas. The Honor Guard got into a car and drove to the American Legion Hall where they changed into their civilian clothes.

John and Karen went inside to see what they could do to help set up for the party. When the couple got inside, volunteers, mostly Church youth who had rushed inside after the parade had finished, were putting up chairs that had been carried over from the two churches. Only 600 people could sit in the bleachers, so additional chairs were needed. Most of the children would be expected to sit on the floor.

Bruce stayed outside in case there was a traffic control problem, which was a definite possibility because Main and Railroad Streets had been turned into one-way streets to allow parking along the sides for the estimated two-hundred cars. Many people, knowing there would be a problem, had elected to walk.

Women from the three churches had sacrificed watching the parade in order to prepare the serving of food. Only fifteen minutes earlier, Kenny's had delivered thirty large trays of fried chicken, the steam and aroma already filling the room. Several trays of creamy slaw were placed among the trays of chicken. The rest of the tables held dozens of bowls of green beans, mashed potatoes, corn and stewed tomatoes, much of which had been donated by people who lived outside the town. A separate table held large trays of cobbler, with the plates, plastic ware, napkins, Kool-Aid, iced tea and fresh rolls.

John had not seen such a sight since some of the cookouts in 'Nam for the combined Special Forces. It was going to be nice, though, not worrying about keeping a gun at the ready while he ate, or having to throw a plate down and dive into a muddy fox hole. He remembered Sam and Suzie in the back room, so he and Karen put together plates for them.

By 7:20, the people began filing in. Wide-eyed children, followed by hesitant, somewhat reluctant parents still trying to decide if this was considered charity, began to drift into the court. Soon the relative silence of the food-preparers was broken by the sound of excited children.

At 7:45 Sam heard a noise outside. He looked out the steamed covered window, and there was the Santa's Sleigh Tractor Trailer, with the smaller van pulled over behind it. Wrapped in heavy coats were about fifteen Boy Scouts, anxious to earn their Community Service Merit Badge, ready to begin bringing the toys inside according to the name on the tag.

At 7:50 p.m., Jonathan opened the door slightly to give Sam and Suzie their final instructions.

"We will have about five minutes of welcoming comments and prayers. Then everyone will go through the line for their food. At about 8:30, Herbie will come up front, and we'll begin lining the kids up, and then we'll announce Santa. Suzie, you come on out with your list to help line the kids up so we can get finished hopefully in about three hours."

Thirty minutes later, Suzie saw Herbie start to the microphone.

"See you later, Santa," Suzie said as she walked out the door.

"Hey, kids," Herbie began speaking. "I believe I heard some hooves on the top of the gym, and we're going to be having Santa Clause soon." A hush went over the room; both the children and the adults had fallen silent.

"But Santa has a lot of deliveries tonight, so we need to help him out by getting in line and being very quiet. As soon as he calls your name, be ready to go up and get your presents. Okay? Now, I'm going to start calling the names, and when I do, run up to Suzie, and fall in line. Now listen closely for your name."

"Andy Anderson, Mike Andrews, Janie Barrett,..." Herbie started reading from the list. Outside, the Boy Scouts with their leaders, had for the last 45 minutes been removing the toys and clothing according to the name tags shown, and were ready to begin carrying the gifts in as soon as the names were called.

The kids jumped up as they heard their names, and quickly ran to Suzie. Some were faster than others, so Suzie had to re-align them, but surprisingly, in fifteen minutes, all the kids were in line.

Herbie nodded to Jonathan, and he walked over to the door, and opened it, gesturing to Sam. Then Jonathan walked to the exit door to let the Boy Scouts know to begin bringing in the gifts.

"Okay kids," Herbie instructed. "Now I want you all to cover your eyes, and begin saying 'We want Santa Clause, We want Santa Claus.'"

The gym erupted with a din of 200 children, not quite in unison, screaming "WE WANT SANTA CLAUS!"

On the fourth chant, there was a loud, *HO HO HO, HO HO HO, Merry Christmas! Merry Christmas!* and out came the man for whom the kids had been waiting. Santa set down in the large velvet chair that had been loaned by Pless Furniture.

"Oh, it is so good for Santa to be here with all you girls and boys." Sam said, holding his big pillow-stuffed belly. "So, my little Suzie elf, who is our first good little boy?"

"It's Andy Anderson, Santa." Suzie took the shy, five-year-old by the hand and brought him forward.

"Now let's see what Santa has for Andy," Sam said, looking at his list. "Here's a bag of goodies, and two comic books, and a real baseball card signed by Eddie Goodson. Now it seemed like there was something else you asked for from Santa."

"Yes Santa, but my daddy told me that you had lots of other boys that needed toys more than me, so this is all I wanted," Andy said, as he gave Sam a hug and started down off the man's lap. "Thank you Santa."

Sam began to choke up and wasn't sure he could continue. He looked down into the face of the young child who was so willing to give up his Christmas, because some other child needed it more.

"Well, Andy," Sam said, clearing his throat. "You were just too good of a boy this year for Santa to not bring you something else."

On cue, one of the Boy Scouts came pushing in a new red, 18-inch bike, with training wheels. Another Scout carried a bright red and blue striped cotton shirt and a pair of Levi jeans. Andy jumped off Santa's lap and ran to the bike, dropping to his knees, hugging the bike as he looked into the bleachers and called out, "Look Momma. Look Daddy. I got it! I got it! Santa did bring it." The tot screamed out so all in the gymnasium could hear. With that he ran back and gave Santa another hug. The Boy Scouts helped him roll his present to the wall, and left him there, still hugging his dreamy red metal with its rubber wheels.

So for the next three hours, Sam continued fulfilling the dreams of the children of Fries. Children who had been prepared not to get the gifts they had asked for, and were content to settle for whatever was given. By the time Santa got to the last child, Cora Young, his beard was soaked from the combination of wet, Kool-Aid kisses, and the tears of joy that had rolled down his cheeks.

"Well boys and girls, that's the end of Santa's list," Sam said. Then turning toward Suzie he continued, "but there is still a young lady who's the best little girl I have ever known. So now, Santa is ready to give a present to his favorite elf, Suzie Young."

Suzie was blushing as she walked back up to Sam, who then reached behind the recliner and pulled out a large box that had been left there, as instructed, by John.

"Suzie, Santa has heard about how the people of Fries depend upon your newspaper and how it takes you a long time to type on your old manual typewriter. I heard that once you were up all night. You must have been so busy, you didn't even have time to write Santa a letter this year, but Santa knows these things without being told."

Suzie pulled the box from the Blue Ridge Office bag. She did not know what to say. So many times she had looked at this exact electric typewriter in the Sears Catalog. She knew if she had asked, her mother would have sacrificed to have bought it, but Suzie would never have done this. She had contented herself with dreaming of the day she would get her job with *National Geographic* and they would furnish her with a typewriter just like this one.

"You really are Santa Claus," she whispered into his ear as she hugged him, "to know exactly what I have always wanted."

"Well, there might be one more thing you'll like," Sam whispered back as he returned her hug. "There's an envelope taped to the box that has my return address. Don't open it until you get back home. I have to leave right now to catch my plane to Arkansas. I want you to send me a copy of all of your newspapers, and I hope to be back in the spring. I'll come by to see you then. You are a very, very special girl, and I am so glad I met you."

With that Santa stood up, and with a choking voice, said "HO HO HO, MERRY CHRISTMAS, MERRY CHRISTMAS FRIES."

Chiney stood up, grabbed his coat, and followed Sam out the door. Sam rushed to the car, hesitating just long enough to thank the Scouts for the great job they had done. He tried to give each boy money, but was told this was their "good turn" for the day. They drove back to the Hotel in Sam's 65 Buick where Sam quickly changed, leaving the Santa outfit in the bedroom for Jonathan to pick up, grabbed his bags, and rushed out to Chiney waited in Sam's Buick. They then began their drive to Roanoke with only minutes to spare.

Back at the gym, there was a state of bewilderment over what had just happened. Who was that strange man with an accent playing Santa Claus? Where did these gifts and clothes come from? It had been reported that the Committee had gotten a few small gifts donated, but not bicycles, record players or kitchen play sets. The gym was overflowing with toys, and with deliriously ecstatic children.

"May I have you attention? May I have your attention please?" Jonathan Armbrister said in his eloquent voice. There were a couple of boos, but the catcallers were quickly glared down.

"I hope everyone enjoyed tonight's celebration," Jonathan continued. "It was truly a celebration of hope, of joy, of giving, and of love for one another. This concludes tonight's party, but I do hope we can carry this same spirit into the next year." He hesitated as he looked out over the joyous people. He then located Cynthia's eyes, and gave her a final questioning look. She flashed an elated smile, and nodded her head enthusiastically, giving him a tearful approval.

"As you leave tonight," Jonathan said, turning back to the townspeople, "Cynthia and I will be waiting at the door to give you our season's greetings, and for each of the families, we have a $50 dollar bonus and a gift certificate, from the Mill, to the Mick-or-Mack for a Christmas ham. Mr. Funk has generously offered to open the store for an hour after the party so you can pick up your hams. The umm, Mill, apologizes, for the confusion on this."

Excitement spread through out the gymnasium, as men began

slapping each other on the back. John looked at Cynthia, who was now crying joyous tears.

"The cruise would have been nice," the friend said to her.

"But this is nicer," was all Cynthia could say.

"Wait. Wait. Let me have your attention for one more thing please. Now, I do hope you have a good Christmas, but I do want to tell you not to over-eat, not to over-drink, and to not over-party."

The good naturedness of the employees turned sour, as they looked back at the Mill superintendent. *How dare he dictate what they did during their personal time?*

"Because I expect the day shift to report promptly at 7 a.m. Monday morning!" Jonathan said as a smile swept over his face.

Just as early morning fog fills the banks over the New River, silence filled the room as the adults tried to comprehend what they had just heard.

"All other shifts are to report at your regular times, also." The Cotton Mill superintendent said as he turned to walk to the door to meet his wife and hand out Christmas envelopes. Not a single person would complain the bonuses were three weeks late.

The gym then erupted in rapturous screaming and celebration. Jonathan and his wife were hugged tearfully as the families left the building, with many *God bless you's* mixed with *Merry Christmases*.

Mike was standing in the corner with his camera taking photos of some of the children holding up their bags of candy canes, nuts, and oranges. He was sorry his pal Jason wasn't able to come; he would have enjoyed the celebration. Just then he felt a tug on his sleeve. He turned to look down at a cute little blonde elf wearing a fur coat.

"Oh, hi, Suzie," he said.

"Hi, Mike. Merry Christmas."

"Merry Christmas to you, too."

"Umm, Mike. Is Jason Campbell going to come to your house tomorrow?"

"He said he hoped to after they got back from seeing his mom at the hospital. Why?" Mike asked teasingly, knowing the crush the young girl had on the ex-football star.

"Well, his mother told my mom that his favorite dessert was Boston cream pie. Will you call me when he gets to your house? I'd like to bring him one for Christmas."

23

In spite of the light snowfall, Chiney pulled in front of the Roanoke Municipal Airport at 1 o'clock.

"So will you be back this spring to get Ole Cotton? He's been pining for you. He wakes me up every morning crying *Sammmm, Sammm, I miss you Sammm.*"

"Yes, I'll be back in the spring." Sam said. "I'll call you in April and let you know exactly when."

"I'll be looking forward to it. You're a good old soul, Sam, and Fries appreciates what you have done."

"Well, Chiney, old buddy, thanks again to you. You'll never know all the things you and the rest of Fries have done for me." Sam said as he offered his hand and gave his new "old" friend a hearty shake. "I hope you'll do one more thing for me. Take the car by and leave it for Karen Young. I'm giving it to her."

Then just as Sam closed the door to rush into the airport, Chiney leaned over the seat and unrolled the window.

"You know Sam. I don't even know your last name."

Sam thought for a moment. For the last eighteen months, he had either been brown-nosing Wall Street gurus, or having ambitious suppliers buttering him up. Life had been delightfully different for the last four days. He had just been a good old boy, and he liked it.

"To my friends, Chiney, I'm just plain Sam," the businessman said, then turned and walked into the airport to meet the pilot that would fly him home to his family.

Jason Campbell pulled into the hard-packed dirt drive of his dad's and mom's house on Brush Creek at 9:25 p.m. The inventory had not taken as long as he had expected. Mr. Powers had told Jason that he was the fastest person he had ever worked with on inventory.

From the cars already parked out front, he could tell that Josie and Lisa were already there with their families. Jason always loved seeing his nephew and three nieces. He knew this would not be the joyous Christmas Eve it usually was. The house did look festive though. Colin was always excited to celebrate Christmas, and by the end of the first week in December, always had the house decorated. When he was home, it was Jason's responsibility to make the trip to the woods behind the house to cut pine tips. Colin would then take staples and nail the fifteen-inch-long pine boughs and the strands of the outdoor Christmas lights to the wooden framing of the large picture window on the front of the house facing the highway. He would outline the side porch leading into the kitchen the same way.

Colin would tie strings around the pine tips and light strands, and hang them by nails from the house trim behind the guttering. One year, he tried to save time by hanging the decorations from the actual guttering. A heavy ice storm came a couple of days before Christmas, layering the pine tips with half an inch of ice. In the middle of Christmas Eve night, everyone was awakened by a low moaning, screeching sound, followed by a crash. Everyone rushed to the outside expecting to see Santa's sleigh laying on its side in the front yard with Santa mortally injured, but instead, found the entire forty feet of guttering on the ground, the lights and pine tips still clipped to the metal.

Jason walked around to study the lights. He laughed to himself as he remembered the December day he had gone down to visit the Marshes. It must not have been Christmas Eve, because his sisters and their families were not at the house, just his dad and mom. When he was about half way home, about 300 yards from the house, a cold fear swept over him. This was the only point in the walk where he could see the front of the house, and it was on fire! Red, blue, yellow, and green flames leaping out! He began to run to warn his parents, still trapped in the house, perhaps asleep. Within minutes, the flames would be inside the house, if they weren't already.

He tripped over corn stalk stubs as he ran through the garden. Finally he was in the yard, and was rounding the corner of the house, running toward the front door. Then he got a full view of his "flames." They were the red, yellow, blue and green Christmas lights flashing on and off along the guttering, behind a wall of icicles, some up to two feet in length, which were hanging from the guttering like a row of stalactites.

Jason had sat down on the front porch to rest, so he would not have to explain to his parents, whom he found sitting calmly at the kitchen table, why he was so out of breath.

Jason felt something cool and exhilarating on his face, and looking up into the sky, saw that it was beginning to snow. He leaned his head back, letting the flakes land on his tongue. He had always heard that every snow flake was a different shape, and thought that this was probably just one more thing God did just so we'd always have something to look forward to. Just like every Christmas was different. This Christmas would be very different, but not in a good way.

But Christmas is a time for rejoicing, and spending time with family. Jason had all of his family, a dad, sisters, brothers-in-law, nephew and nieces, everyone except his mother, awaiting him. They owed it to her to enjoy this wonderful celebration of Christ's birth. Christmas was a time of miracles, and God had answered their prayers that the cancer would not be malignant. Jason turned from the front of the house, taking one last look at the decorations, and opened the back door.

As soon as he walked in, the nephew and nieces ran up to hug their Uncle Jason. They ranged in age from nine months to nine years. Each one had their own uniqueness. Josie's two; Roxanne and Jeff were special to Jason because they had lived at the Brush Creek house on two different occasions when they were both young, so Jason got to know them as their big brother. He remembered being terrified once because he was supposed to be watching Roxanne, who was then a toddler. He had gotten distracted when suddenly, he heard a crash in the living room, and the little girl began screaming. She had pulled a straight back wooden chair down onto her head, and she was bleeding. Jason, who was only ten at the time, was terrified that he had killed the little girl. He grabbed her and went running out to Josie, who was hanging clothes on the line.

"She's bleeding to death," Jason had screamed to his big sister.

Josie came running to him, grabbed the baby and looked at her head. Josie smiled, licked her finger and rubbed it over the little girl's head, removing the small spot of blood. By this time Roxanne had stopped crying.

"I think she's gonna live," Josie had said as she handed his niece back to him. "Just be more careful from now on."

Then the second time they came to stay, Jason could remember he was taking senior math in high school, and Jeff was in the first grade. Jason taught Jeff to say, *A is proper subset of B, if and only if, every member of A is a member of B, and B has more members than A.*

Jeff promptly went to school the next day and recited his new bit of wisdom to Mrs. Waddell, the first grade teacher. That evening when Jason got home from high school, he had a note waiting for him from Mrs. Waddell.

The note read:

Jason, I am so glad you are taking such an interest in your math at Fries. Good luck with your studies, but let's leave the first grade teaching to me.

Mrs. Waddell Now since living with his younger sister during the summer and the Christmas holiday, Jason had really gotten close to Lisa's two daughters, Stacie and Sherry. Sherry the oldest, was now in Elementary School, and was just beginning to bloom. Sherry had taken her Uncle Jason to school one day during Show and Tell, because he was going to be an engineer. Jason had been at the hospital when Stacie was born. The infant seemed to have a keen sense of knowledge when Jason was going out on a date because she would pick those times to pee on him, leaving a stain on his pants, just before it was time for him to leave.

Jason bent over on one knee to hug the kids.

"Hey guys, guess what!" Jason said with exaggerated excitement. "Go look out the front window. It's starting to snow a little, and I am positive I saw Santa's sleigh way back in the sky, probably around Pulaski. He'll be here in about five hours I bet."

The four ran quickly to the front picture window and immediately began seeing the light that must be Santa. Josie and Lisa sat around the kitchen table. They gave a half-hearted smile as they greeted their sibling. Jason was seven years younger than

Lisa, and ten years younger than Josie.

"Hi, little brother," they greeted him. He could tell they had been crying.

"Hi, guys. Y'all doing okay?"

"Yeah. We're doing okay."

"Where's all the men folk?"

"Well," Lisa said, "Jeremy and William have run up to Shepherd's to get a case of pop. Dad's in the living room just staring at the tree. He's really upset. Hasn't said hardly a word all evening. He didn't even want to go to the church service."

Jason went into the living room. The kids were excitedly watching a few flakes fall here and there. His dad looked up at him. It was obvious he had been crying.

"Hi Dad."

"Oh. Hi Jason. Glad you're here." The father said as he stood up to hug his son. "I was afraid the roads were going to get bad."

"You okay?" Jason asked.

"Yeah. Just a little down in the dumps," his father said as his chin began quivering and he began crying again.

I hope Dad and Mom live for a long time, but when they do go, I hope Dad goes first because he'd never be able to live without Mom, Jason thought to himself.

"Well Dad, let's just be thankful she's going to be alright. That will be a great Christmas present."

"Yeah, you're right. I am thankful. I don't know the last time I prayed so much."

"Come on," Jason said as he laid his arm around his dad's shoulder. Only during the last year had Jason grown taller, and it still seemed strange to now tower above his father by a good three inches. "Let's go in the kitchen and sit at the table with Lisa and Josie."

The father and son walked into the kitchen, leaving the kids searching the sky for the first glance of Santa's sleigh.

"Dad, try to not be so upset. Mom wouldn't want us to be." Josie said as she patted her father's hand. "We'll let the kids open presents in the morning, and then we'll drive down to the clinic about ten."

"No. No. I've already decided." The husband said, wiping his eyes with a paper towel. "I'm getting up at five in the morning, and driving down to the hospital. I want to be there when she opens her eyes. Y'all can drive down later."

The brother and sisters looked at each other. They knew they wouldn't be able to talk him out of it.

"Well, maybe we could open the gifts tonight." Jason suggested.

"What will we tell the kids?" Lisa questioned. "They expect Santa to bring the gifts. We can't just bring them in from the car."

"Well, we could let them go to bed. Then get them up about midnight, open gifts, then go back to bed." Josie suggested.

"No. We've always opened gifts on Christmas morning." Colin said forcefully. "You guys do it like we always do. Just tell the kids Poppy has gone to see Granny."

The phone ringing in the hallway interrupted the discussion at that point. Colin got up to answer it.

"Hello."

He heard an operator on the other end asking if he would accept the charges for a reverse call from Leah Campbell.

"Yes! I'll accept."

"It's your mom." He said, turning his head toward the kitchen with an anxious look.

"Hello, Colin. Is this you?" Leah said in an obviously agitated voice.

"Yes, Leah. What is it? What's wrong?"

"Colin! I've been trying to phone for over two hours, but these stupid lines have been busy, and I couldn't get through."

"What is it? What's wrong?" Colin's said, his voice showing his panic. Jason, Lisa, and Josie jumped up and ran to their dad.

"What's wrong? Is everything okay with mom?" They all began asking.

"No. Nothing's wrong, except you've got to get in the car, and get down here fast." Leah said. "The doctor came by at eight, said everything looked fine, and I could go home tonight. I'm afraid if I wait until tomorrow, they'll change their minds."

"Okay Leah. I'll be right down. Bye, honey. I love you," Colin said as he hung up and turned to the three, who by this time were crazy with fear.

"Daddy! What's happened? What's wrong with mom? Why are you going down tonight?" All three siblings were asking at once.

As quickly as a dark black cloud passes over the sun, turning a gloomy, cloudy day into a happy sunny one, the father's apprehensive look transitioned into an expression of exhilaration. Colin began to cry uncontrollably, as he grabbed the three. Finally he stopped crying long enough to take a breath.

"Jason. Grab your coat," the father said as he turned toward Jason. "We're going to Roanoke. Leah's coming home tonight."

As John, Suzie and Karen left the gymnasium; arm in arm, John looked up at the snowflakes falling from the sky and was thankful he had taken the time to put up the convertible top before he went into the party. Suzie squeezed into the back space of the 'Vette, anxious to get home to open the typewriter, and to read what was in the mysterious envelope. As soon as they pulled up in front of the house, Suzie began pushing against the back seat, urging her mom to open the door.

"For Pete's sake, Suzie," Karen said with a laugh, "let John get the car stopped before you jump out."

Once the two girls were out, John waited for them to go into the house, out of sight. He then, took a deep breath, reached beneath his seat, pulled out a small bag marked 'Lemon's Fine Jewelry' and stuck it into his coat pocket.

By the time John had walked in the front door, Suzie had pulled the typewriter from its box and was studying the manual.

"Momma! It's an IBM Selectric. That's the best that's made. All the big-time magazine companies use it. It even has different balls that I can use to write different types of print," Suzie said excitedly. She then saw the envelope taped to the top of the box. She pulled it off and tore the envelope open, and withdrew a sheet of paper. A yellow strip of paper fell from the folded letter to the floor. Suzie picked it up and looked at it. She turned to her mother with a puzzled, but dreamy look in her eyes.

"Momma, is this a check? Is it for real? Is Sam actually giving this to me?"

"Oh God! This can't be real." Karen said as she looked at what was obviously a check, her hand flew to her mouth as she handed it to John. He studied it.

Pay to the order of…Karen Young for Suzie Young, in the amount of…$25,000.

John just began to shake his head, trying to comprehend if this was genuine, or the result of a confused old man's wishing he could do some good. But then he remembered that the toys that had been given out that night were very real.

"Well," John said, still with some apprehension. "I don't *think* Sam would play a joke, and he's too good of a businessman to make a mistake like this."

Then John looked at the signature, and the name at the top of the check. His mind began to go into a memory recall mode as he searched his recollection. He then smiled as he remembered a recent *Life* Magazine article.

"Yes Suzie, I can assure you it's no mistake and it is for real." John said.

"What does the letter say?" Karen asked, noticing the sheet of paper still in Suzie's hand.

Suzie began reading the letter aloud.

Suzie,

I love our country, and the opportunities it offers us. But our freedom, our self-enterprise system is being threatened by liberal members of the press. I believe our country needs young people like you who will report the truth and be fair. I think you are a very special person. I have already talked to Mr. Phillips at the bank. I want you and your mother to take this down to him and purchase a three-year certificate of deposit. Study hard, make good grades, and in three years, use this to begin paying your tuition to any college you desire. I have checked, and this money will pay your expenses at the best universities in the nation.

And to you, Karen, you are a wonderful lady, who has bravely overcome a great loss. The other night when I walked down the steps to the hotel, I thought what it must be like for you and Suzie to have to walk everywhere. I have instructed Chiney that after he drops me off at the airport he's to bring my Buick back to you. I will mail you the title next week.

To you, John. I can tell that you are a good man, in need of a good woman. I think you have found one. I have a feeling when I come back in the spring to bird hunt, you'll still be in Fries. If you are, I want to tell you about a very good investment that will be available this summer. An investment in a company which will make it possible for shoppers across the nation to go to one super store to do all their shopping.

Thank all of you for showing me what Christmas is all about.

Your friend,

Sam

The three just stood looking at each other and then joined in a hug. They all wondered if tonight was a dream and that tomorrow they would wake up to find out it was Christmas, and Santa had not visited Fries.

"I know it's late, Mom," Suzie said, "but please let me stay up to try out my new typewriter."

"Well, okay. For a little while."

Karen and John walked to the kitchen door and, pushing the cotton curtains to the side, looked outside. The snow was now falling, or almost floating, outside. It was not going to be a heavy snow, but it would be enough to qualify as a White Christmas, which would be the perfect touch to an already unbelievable Yuletide. John wanted more though. He wanted it to go beyond unbelievable to inconceivable.

"Let's go out on the porch, Karen," John said in the softest tone Karen had heard him speak. He tried to remember if he ever felt this many butterflies before his missions in 'Nam.

Once on the porch, they looked down on the town below. The Christmas lights were glowing, leaving hazy halos through the falling snow.

"It looks like a dream, a winter wonderland dream, doesn't it." Karen said, as a slight shiver overtook her, either from the cold, or the moment. "Like one of those snow globes you buy at souvenir stores. You shake it, and the world becomes all dreamy."

Karen turned around, and looked up at him. She looked deep into his dark eyes. They seemed more alive than when she first met him, no longer distant. But he still had the same firm jaw. So strong. So determined. She had fought for five years to be strong for Suzie, but it was difficult, because it just wasn't in her nature.

Was it too much for her to think she could have a second true love? Was that being selfish? she thought to herself. She remembered how soon after shaking a globe, the "snow" would quickly settle to the bottom, leaving reality instead of a fantasyland.

"It's not a dream, is it, John? I pray it's not."

"If it is, Karen, I don't ever want to wake up," he said as he kissed her softly. He could tell she wanted to feel his kiss longer, but he had to speak now, while he still had the courage.

"Karen, the last ten days, they've been the best days of my life," he said, then took her trembling hands, although they were not yet cold, in his and brought them to his chest. She could feel his heart race against the back of her hand.

"I know that you loved Wilson very much. He was a wonderful man. I know I'm not as half as good of a man as he was. I've killed people, Karen. I've looked into the eyes of Viet Cong soldiers, and I've killed them. There's things I did in 'Nam that I could never tell you. And, if it wasn't for the rescue squad getting there last Saturday, I think I would have killed Spunkie Akers."

"Yes, I know, John. Richard told me. But he said that he had no doubt that Wilson would have reacted exactly as you did. You were just so scared about Suzie."

"I was never what you'd call a Christian, until last Sunday. And even now, I don't know what I'm expected to do. But I do know this, Karen. I've never wanted to be everything to anyone, as much as I want to be everything to you."

"Oh, John..." Karen said, wanting to say how much she loved him, but she felt weak. She fell against his chest, welcoming so much his strong arms around her, holding her, making her feel safe.

"Karen, I know you may need time to decide, but I don't. I'll understand if you're not ready, but...," he stopped talking long enough to reach into his coat pocket and pulled out a gray felt-covered box. He opened it and pulled from it a ring with a diamond that in the moonlight looked as big as one of the peas Karen had served with the pheasants earlier in the week. "But, Karen, I promise you that if you'll marry me, I'll love and worship you, and Suzie, for as long as I live."

Her hands trembling, she wrapped her fingers around John's hand, holding the ring.

"Oh, John. I do want to marry you so much, but, could you ever settle for this? Would we need to move to Winston-Salem?"

"No. We would stay here. I know Suzie likes it here. Then, in three years, we'll move anywhere you want to. It's up to you. I'll be happy anywhere you are."

"But, what about your job? I know you love what you do. You'll hate me one day for making you give it up."

"Who says I'm giving it up? I'm expanding. I've hired a new field consultant, and I'll run the office work from here."

Oh, do you think you'll be able to find someone qualified that easily?"

"I already have," John said, now feeling assured enough to laugh. "Apparently your cousin hasn't told you everything. My new field agent is…*Richard Carrico*."

"Richard? My cousin Richard?"

"Yes. I'll pay him $1200 more a year than he's making now. Plus, he gets to carry my German pistol. I think he'd be willing to work for free just to use it. And I'll be busy here, doing the paperwork, and…and with my new job," he said, his smile growing wider by the moment.

"What new job?" she asked, as she took her fist and began playfully beating his chest. "Just how many secrets have you kept from me this week?"

He lifted her chin and looked into her eyes. In the near darkness, they looked even more like sparkling stars.

"You're looking at the Department Head of the new Criminal Justice curriculum at Wytheville Community College."

"Are you kidding, John? How have you worked all this out, in just a few days?"

"That's it, Karen. That is why I know that this is supposed to happen. God must be making these things happen. All of this has just fallen into place. And, if you'll marry me, and since I'll be going to Wytheville during the day already, then I've taken the prerogative of a husband to talk to Jonathan."

"What have you talked to Jona…to Mr. Armbrister about?"

"That you may not be coming to work after January because you're starting to Wytheville Community College to become a teacher."

"Oh, John. I would love that, but we couldn't afford that, until we see how things work out."

"Karen, trust me, we can afford it. My father left me with more than $100,000, but I've never touched it. It's probably closer to $115,000 now because I never felt I had done, or had anything in my life worthy of it. Now I do, that is I will, if you'll marry me."

Karen hung her head. John's heart dropped. *All of her reasons, they were just excuses to avoid hurting his feelings. Truth was, she was happy with her life the way it was.* How egotistical it was of him to think that she needed him in her life.

"John, there's something else I have to tell you," Karen said, her heart ready to break. She had thought about not telling him, but knew their life had to be based on total honesty. "When I had Suzie, there were complications. They thought it best for me to not have any more children, so, well, they tied my tubes. I can't have anymore children, and I know that's not fair to you."

John thought about what she had said. He had to admit, he had thought about teaching a son how to play football, or to ride a bike. But when confronted with the option of not having her, he did not feel the necessity.

"Karen," he said, "I can't imagine ever having a child of our own that was more perfect than Suzie. Why would we even want to try?"

His words and the memory of Wilson's same words nearly fourteen years before, overwhelmed her. She knew then that God meant for the two of them to be together.

Karen lifted her head, the corners of her mouth turned up, catching tears as they flowed in a steady stream from her eyes. She bit her lips, unable to speak, and only lifted her left hand, offering her ring finger to him.

"Should..., should we go discuss it with Suzie?" he asked before sliding the ring on.

"No, we don't need to," Karen said softly. "She and her father have already given us their blessings."

John slid the ring on her finger. He took her in his arms and kissed her. He kissed her the way she had missed being kissed for the last five years.

She wiped the tears on her dress sleeve, took John's hand and walked inside to the dining room where Suzie sat typing.

"Momma! John!" The girl said as she heard the two come in the back door. "Come look how great the new type looks."

John and Karen looked down, and read, in large script type, the next headlines of the *Fries Wildcat Spirit Weekly*

YES, FRIES VIRGINIA, THERE IS A SAM-TA CLAUS

Karen and John read the beginning of the article. Suzie had used carefully crafted analogies to describe how a stranger had come into a town, and had left as a friend.

"This is very good, honey, but you still have a small portion of newspaper left," her mother said, in a rare critical voice. "I think you need to add a new section to your paper."

"Oh, okay. Like what momma," Suzie asked.

"Oh. I don't know. Perhaps something like..." Karen said, as she lifted her left hand to her chin in thoughtful consideration. "Engagement announcements?"

The flashing of the Christmas light then caught in the brilliant reflective stone on Karen's finger. Suzie jumped up and grabbed her mother, hugging her. She then turned to John, and running to him, jumped into his arms.

"Will you mind if I call you 'Daddy?'" She whispered into his ear.

John Helmsman, strong and composed, always in control, felt his reservoir of emotion that had been kept in check for years, rupture as tears of joy cascaded over his face. All he could think to say was,

"To hear you call me that, would be like heaven on earth, Suzie Q."